EMMA ROUND
AND THE
HOLY
ROWLINGS

The **HERETICS IN OCCUPIED EDEN** Trilogy

The **HERETICS COMPANION** Works:

Emma Round
And The
Holy Rowlings

HERETICS IN OCCUPIED EDEN
BOOK SEVEN

KENNETH ALAN MOE

STRANGE ANGEL PRESS
Phoenix, Arizona

Copyright © 2017
Kenneth Alan Moe

Cover, interior design and cover photos by Ethan Moe

Cover painting is "The Pilgrim at the Gate of Idleness" by Sir Edward Coley Burne-Jones

Cover photo was taken at Tlaquepaque in Sedona, AZ

First Printing

This is a work of fiction. The characters, conversations, organizations, and incidents in this book are products of the author's imagination. Any resemblance to real people, living or dead, is coincidental. Emma Watson's visit to Sedona and the dialog associated with it are fictitious, as is the letter ascribed to J. K. Rowling. Where actual people are quoted, the wording conforms to that of the sources cited. The Facebook comment by Dr. Carol Oster is real, adapted from an exchange with the author. The names of actual places are included, but the events described in connection with such places are fiction.

ISBN: 978-0692875254

Dedicated to the Harry Potter Generation

Once I had this beautiful book in my possession, I did nothing but study it night and day.
Nicolas Flamel

Hermetic Books have such involv'd Obscuritys that they may justly be compar'd to Riddles written in Cyphers.
Robert Boyle

You are an alchemist; make gold of that.
William Shakespeare

CONTENTS

I
THE GIFT OF FANTASY

*The gift of fantasy has meant more to me
than my talent for absorbing positive knowledge.*
Albert Einstein

*Myths are public dreams; dreams are private
myths.*
Joseph Campbell

CHAPTER ONE
THE INTERVIEW

KJZZ reporter Ferry Leitz sat up straight and in a carefully modulated voice said, "In the studio today is Emma Round, founder of the Alchemical Church of Harry Potter Prophecy in Sedona. They call themselves Holy Rowlings and use the Potter books as their bible. Welcome Emma."

"Thank you, Ferry. It's good to be here at my favorite radio station," Emma replied.

"Your young congregation has been in the news lately -a nice write-up in the Verde Valley Intelligencer that was picked up by USA Today and Huffington Post. Our listeners are eager to hear more about this novel religious phenomenon."

Emma groaned and started to comment on the pun but was cut off by Ms. Leitz.

"Before we get to that, however, tell us about the fascinating coincidences surrounding your name," the interviewer continued.

Emma nervously adjusted her glasses, running her fingers past the stems and pushing back her light brown hair. The question was entirely unexpected. Her piercing blue eyes focused on Ferry's lips. After clearing her throat, Emma said, "To begin with, Emma Watson and I were born on the same day, April 15, 1990."

"The actress who played the role of Hermione Granger in the *Harry Potter* films," Ferry interjected.

"Right," said Emma. "But I should confess up front that people in my spiritual community are generally quite critical of the *Harry Potter* films because of screenplay flaws and excessive special effects, but we all make exceptions for the actors, whom we admire."

"But of course you've seen the movies," Ferry responded.

"Oh certainly. Multiple times," Emma said. "We have periodic movie marathons, where we play a game while watching."

"And the game is?" Ferry asked.

"We shout out what actually happened in the books when our favorite screen play errors appear and we moan about what's been left out."

Ferry decided not to make a catty remark about this revelation and instead said, "Please tell us more about *Harry Potter* related coincidences in your life."

"When I was ten, and after having read the first four books in the *Harry Potter* series," Emma explained, "my mother told me they had considered naming me Hermione, after the character actresses Hermione Baddeley and Hermione Gingold. My mom loved both of them. She was especially fond of Hermione Gingold in the film *Bell, Book and Candle*, which was about a witch. But my dad thought my school peers would tease me for bearing such an unusual name, and as a result, I would come to hate my parents. By way of compromise, they came to agreement on the equally old fashioned and more literary name Emma, after Jane Austen's Emma Woodhouse."

"So you and Miss Watson share the same birthday and same first name," Ferry said. "Although the respective roles you have come to play amid the phenomena of *Harry Potter* are as distinctly different as your blue eyes to her brown."

Ignoring this, Emma said, "Of course, my mother *could have* given me Hermione for a *middle* name, which I pointed out to her. But instead she drew upon the author of the novel *Emma* for my middle name -Austen.

"The truth is that I would have proudly carried the name Hermione, and by the time I was in fourth grade, my classmates would have envied me, and I would have exulted in the foresight of my mother. At first, after she told me, I was disappointed that she had not had the courage to stand up to Dad and insist on naming me Hermione. But after the first *Harry Potter* movie was released, I decided that Emma was an equally significant name, especially since the actress fated to portray Hermione and I share that common birthday."

"What does the character Hermione mean to you?" Ferry asked.

"Well, I certainly identify with her," Emma responded. "I was a bit of a know-it-all in elementary and high school. My brothers called me bossy, and not without reason." She laughed deferentially. "I always made top grades. For those who understand the reference, I got straight Os on all my exams. On the other hand, I didn't pal around with any boys with tragic scars or who came from large, poor families."

"No Harry or Ron in your early life?" Ferry asked.

"That's right, but there are a few other coincidental associations between my life and the fictional world that Jo Rowling created," Emma said. "I was born in Phoenix, which isn't particularly coincidental, but at the time I was born, we lived in a house on Fawkes Circle, and Fawkes is the name of Dumbledore's pet phoenix bird."

"Did these coincidences lead you to believe you were destined to found a church based on the world of *Harry Potter*?" Ferry asked.

"I see them less as destiny and more as confirmation that I'm going in the right direction," Emma answered. "BHP, that is before I'd read *Harry Potter*, I wanted to be a heroic lady in armor rescuing a sensitive, wounded knight. AHP, I dreamed of being a brilliant witch with a wizard boyfriend who was an equal partner. Almost overnight I went from reversing the usual roles of knight and fair lady to intermingled equality."

"I don't see Hermione as particularly spiritual, but you have chosen a career that is all about spirituality," said Ferry.

"Well, I guess there's a bit of Harry in me, too," Emma responded. "More than a bit, actually. For all his efforts at getting in trouble, I think Harry has a deeper interest in things of the spirit than any of the other students in the series. Over all, I'm more Hermione than Harry, but I do wear glasses and have a distinctive scar."

Ferry scanned Emma's forehead, seeing nothing but a few freckles.

She did in fact have multiple scars, but she preferred not to talk about the faint one on her forehead that she routinely covered with makeup or about the deeper one on her leg. "No, it's not anywhere on my face," said Emma. "It's not visible to you."

"An inner scar?" Ferry responded. "It's a universal experience to have mental scars from childhood. Tell me about yours."

"No, it's a real scar," Emma explained. "You can't see it now because it's covered up by my blouse. It's just beneath my left breast. Would you like to see it?"

"What shape is it?" Ferry answered noncommittally.

"Round," said Emma. "Here, let me show you." She unbuttoned her blouse and pointed to a small white ring of tissue surrounded by tanned skin.

Ferry was momentarily surprised that Emma, who was not wearing a bra, would so casually open her blouse, but she had done her reportorial homework and quickly remembered the other church that Emma was involved with, which explained Emma's lack of tan lines.

"Yes, I see," Ferry said. "Since the radio audience can't see, however, I'll say that Emma's scar is about three quarters of an inch in diameter, roughly a circle. How did you get this, Emma?"

"When I was learning to walk, I took a tumble and landed on a round, sharp plastic block, and it cut into me pretty deeply. I've been told that my brother laughed when I fell, but started to cry when he saw I was bleeding. A trip to the emergency room fixed me up, but I've had this souvenir ever since, and it has grown with me." Emma buttoned her shirt.

"Shifting from Harry and scars back to Hermione, how would you rate Hermione's importance in the books?" Ferry asked.

"That's one of those open-ended questions you're famous for," Emma responded. "As an attempt to answer it, I would say that Hermione is one of the four essential characters in the novels."

"The others being…?"

"Harry, Professor Dumbledore, and Voldemort," Emma explained. "I won't rank them in importance, but Hermione was the second character Jo Rowling created, after Harry himself. Hermione is the brains of the outfit. Ron is important as Harry's best mate and partner in misadventures, but his role could just as well have been fulfilled with Neville or someone else. Without Hermione's combination of intellect, competence, and courage, most of the mysteries would not be solved and the problems would not be overcome. She's the first one of Harry's classmates brave enough to say Voldemort's name out loud, and the only one until Ginny does it after Dumbledore's death. And, of course, Hermione serves as Harry's conscience. When most of us hear a warning in our minds, it's in our mother's voice, but Harry hears Hermione when confronted by matters of conscience. Dumbledore may function as the writer's voice of experience and source of the wisdom of the ages, but Hermione is where Rowling's passion and sense of justice show through."

"Really?" Ferry said.

"Yes, in an interview in April 2010 at the White House Easter Egg Roll, where she gave a reading from *Sorcerer's Stone*, Jo revealed that in an earlier version of the novel, Hermione was Harry's next-door neighbor in Godric's Hollow, and her father was quickly on the scene on the night of October 31, 1981 when the Potter house was blown open by Voldemort. Mr. Granger saw Harry being taken from the rubble. Hermione remembered the story she had heard as a child when she first met Harry on the Hogwarts train.

"Rowling didn't say who rescued Harry in that earlier version or how that person got to the scene so quickly. Presumably those on the scene -at a minimum Hermione's father and mystery person X or perhaps Hagrid, Dumbledore, or Sirius Black- would have found the bodies of James, Lily, and Voldemort, as well as the living infant Harry.

"But regarding the plot revision, changing Hermione from next-door neighbor to Muggle-born daughter of dentists proved to be a very significant shift, because if Hermione had come from a Wizarding family, she couldn't occupy the role of Muggle-born Mudblood, which is a crucially important thematic element in the series. Tolerance is what the whole thing is about.

"Also, authors often put parts of themselves in their characters, and Jo has admitted that she modeled Hermione, at least a little, after herself. In the *Harry Potter* series, Hermione is the alter ego of the author, solving problems with as much skill and ingenuity as Rowling used to create them. If you want to know what the author thinks, look at Hermione's dialog.

"Rowling's commitment to social justice is reflected in Hermione's campaign for the welfare of elves and other creatures. Jo's first job out of college was research assistant for Amnesty International, and she was deeply affected by what she learned there about how totalitarian regimes abuse and torture people. That exposure shows through in her books, especially through Hermione. That's why Hermione consistently practices situational ethics. Despite her reputation for following the rules, when circumstances warrant it, Hermione does not hesitate to ignore them, even violating some serious laws for a higher cause.

"By the way, Hermione is also responsible for the lawyer taunt in **Deathly Hallows** that I believe reflects Rowling's experience with that profession, from going through a divorce to being subject to a frivolous lawsuit for copyright infringement and other legal issues related to publishing and buying property. When Scrimgeour asks Hermione if she intends to pursue a career in magical law, she says no because she wants to do something useful with her life."

Emma paused to evaluate whether the interviewer wanted her to continue or stop. She had much more to say on this subject, but guessed that Ferry might have more questions.

At that moment, Ferry was not looking at Emma, but gazing at her own fingernails. Always alert for the onset of dead air time, however, the momentary silence caused her to perk up, and without conviction she said, "Fascinating. You are obviously exceedingly well versed in **Harry Potter** lore. Do you imagine that you will ever meet Emma Watson in person?"

"That would be wonderful," said Emma. "I've certainly thought about it, but I'm not holding my breath."

"Tell us how you came to create a new religion using the **Harry Potter** books as your bible," Ferry said.

At last we're getting to it, Emma thought. The radio audience heard her take a deep breath but could not see the broad smile that spread across her face.

CHAPTER TWO
PARALLEL WORLDS

Growing up in a family of naturists, Emma was six before discovering that most people did not run around their homes naked whenever they felt like it. The clothing optional environment in her own home seemed so sensible that it had never occurred to her that it was not the norm in other households. She had wanted to invite a girlfriend for a sleepover, and her older brother Jared told her that if she did so, she would need to wear pajamas.

"What do you mean?" Emma asked. "Pajamas are for places where it's cold. Nobody wears pajamas in Phoenix."

"A lot you know," said Jared. "Just because we don't fuss about clothes in our house, doesn't mean other people feel the same way. The fact is, most people even in Phoenix wear clothes to bed."

"In bed? That's the silliest thing I've ever heard," Emma replied. "I mean, it's OK to stay dressed when company comes over, but not for *sleeping*. That'd feel like -I don't know- being tied to the bed or something."

Her younger brother Cameron had been listening quietly but now pulled his bent forefinger from his mouth and said, "I wore jammies when I was a baby."

Emma and Jared ignored their three year-old sibling.

"Sorry, Em, but it's the truth. Ask Mom or Dad. They'll back me up," Jared said with full confidence. "And not only that, but everyone else in the house would have to wear them too. Think about all the grumbling about that before inviting someone to stay overnight."

"But they wouldn't have to stay dressed in their own bedrooms," Emma argued.

"Yeah, but if Dad wanted to go to the kitchen or watch TV in the rec room, he'd have to get dressed to do it if your friend stayed over," Jared explained.

This bothered Emma in part because of the officious way nine-year-old Jared addressed her, but also because she was embarrassed not to have known such a mundane piece of information. To Emma, knowledge was authority. On that occasion, the invitation went undelivered, and by the next day, Emma had become incensed at the injustice of it all.

Eventually, she was invited to a sleepover at her girlfriend's house, and her mother bought her a pair of pajamas for the event. This struck Emma as an unfortunate waste of money, for she would probably outgrow them before having any further reason to wear them. As things turned out, Emma and her friend stayed up most of the night talking, so she had to endure only a few hours of trying to sleep in uncomfortable attire that bunched up around her limbs.

David Round liked to take his family on overnight camping trips. When Emma was eight, he organized an outing in the Superstition Mountains. Having grown up hearing stories about the Lost Dutchman's Gold Mine, Emma inveigled Jared to slip away from camp with her to search for it. She told her parents they were just going to look around the area and would be back in a few minutes.

A quarter mile from their camp, the youngsters came upon a cave that Emma decided was the entrance to an abandoned mine.

"This was so easy to find that it's very unlikely to be the Lost Dutchman's mine," Jared said.

"I know that!" Emma replied. "But it's still interesting. Let's check it out."

Jared was leery about going inside, but Emma pulled a flashlight from her backpack and stepped into the darkness. A few paces later, she slipped and tumbled down a shaft, screaming as she fell ten feet to a rocky shelf, and then dramatically increased the volume of her cries as she felt her right arm crack.

Knowing it was a stupid question, Jared called out, "Emma, are you OK?"

Her continued pain-induced wailing told him that his sister was injured. "Stay right there, and I'll go for help," he shouted. As Jared ran back to the camp, he berated himself for telling Emma to stay there. What choice does she have, dummo, he thought.

Jared led David, Hannah, and Cameron to the cave, where they could hear Emma yelling for Jared to do something.

David carefully entered the cave, ascertaining that Emma was not far below. Lying face down with his head over the edge of the shaft, he said, "Where are you hurt? Anything broken?"

"The flashlight is broken, Dad. I'm sorry," Emma whimpered.

"Damn the flashlight, Emma. I meant *you*!"

"My arm hurts. I hit it on a rock," she replied.

"Can you stand up?"

"Yes," she said. Wincing as she did so, Emma slowly got to her feet.

"I can't see much, but I'm going to put my arm down into the hole. Feel around and grab hold if you can."

Moving in the direction of his voice, Emma raised her left hand and felt along the side of the shaft but was unable to reach as high as her father's outstretched hand.

"Can't find you," she said. The pain had reached a level of intensity she had never before experienced, but she said nothing about that.

"OK, I'm going to send down some rope. When you find it, grab on with both hands, and use your feet against the side as I pull you up."

She located the rope without difficulty, but when she raised her right arm, an excruciating stab shot through it. "I can't use my right arm," she said, suppressing a whimper.

"Well, then hold on with your left with all your might," David instructed.

Emma grasped the rope with one hand and in response to her father's slow pull, pushed her way upward, finding crevice holds for her feet as she rose. Then her left hand quivered and went numb.

"Just a few more feet," David said. "Hold on, Emma!"

Half a minute later, while grasping his end of the rope with his right hand, he reached out with his left and grabbed the top of his daughter's backpack and with strength he did not know he possessed, pulled the top half of Emma over the edge. Then, letting go of the rope, he grabbed her belt and swung her legs up onto the shelf.

Emma gasped for air as she lay on the floor of the cave. Her right arm throbbed and burned, but when her eyes took in the sight of her parents, she released a feeble laugh. Hannah was straddling her husband's backside and had not yet climbed off.

"It's not funny," Hannah said. "I needed to anchor your dad so he didn't get pulled in with you."

The camping trip was cut short, as they drove directly to Desert Samaritan Hospital in Mesa, where a simple fracture was confirmed and Emma was fitted for a cast.

The broken limb mended in due course, and the scars on her arm were barely visible. She seemed prone to minor injuries from walking into swinging doors or slipping on wet driveways, but years would pass before Emma again saw the inside of an emergency room. Her life unfolded serenely, with casual nudity in her home and casual clothing at school. Nothing much challenged her or captured her imagination until fourth grade. That was when the school nurse tested her vision and sent her home with a note to her parents advising them to take her to an optometrist. Before the week was out, Emma appeared at school wearing glasses.

She assumed that other kids would tease her, but nobody bothered. The biggest surprise was that her handwriting improved dramatically, and she won the first of a series of awards for cursive penmanship.

This was also the year that her parents formally joined the naturist church they had been attending off and on for about a year. All five members of the Round family stood together in the pool next to the chancel for the total immersion baptismal rite officiated by the pastor, Kwan-yin Burns.

From Emma's perspective, however, the most significant development in fourth grade came over the winter holiday break when she began reading **Harry Potter**. She had known about the Potter phenomenon, of course. Classmates talked about the boy wizard with enthusiasm, and in September she had watched a segment of **60 Minutes** when Lesley Stahl interviewed Joanne Rowling.

The winsome author succeeded in whetting Emma's interest until she told Lesley Stahl that she approved of cracking the spines of books while reading. Emma did not like this at all, and she would have written Rowling off as a crackpot, but then she said that publishers had rejected her manuscript for the first book because it was 'far too long for children,' and this caught Emma's rebellious fancy. She took that editorial criticism as a personal challenge. Eventually she would succumb to the call of the young wizard, she knew, but the inertia of daily life held her back from carefully opening the first book. And then at Christmas, the means, motive, and opportunity came together in one place.

Emma laughed knowingly after reading the opening page of *Harry Potter and the Sorcerer's Stone*. She knew the Dursleys all too well, from her own neighborhood. Though her family had recently moved to Scottsdale, she retained a Phoenix native's bias toward the place, often referring to it as Snotsdale. In her mind she meant that epithet to apply only to North Scottsdale, anything north of McDonald Drive, where she in fact now lived. Old Town and South Scottsdale, however, retained their artistic and neighborly charms. In that moment of connection between Surrey and her city, she knew also that she was hooked by J. K. Rowling's first novel.

The sun-drenched world of saguaro and prickly pear cactuses where she lived bore no resemblance to the grassy plains of England or the mountains of Scotland. North Scottsdale and Little Whinging looked nothing alike. The artsy Old Town Scottsdale was shiny and new compared with Diagon Alley. Yet in the recesses of her young mind Emma recognized the Dickensian world created for the *Harry Potter* novels. Her memory played a magic trick upon her consciousness to convince her that she had been there; she had shopped in Diagon Alley; she had lived in a dorm at Hogwarts.

Jared, three years older, had been given hardbound Scholastic editions of the first three *Potter* books for Christmas but was in no hurry to read them, so Emma appropriated the first one and then devoured all three in a marathon session. She holed up in her bedroom, stopping only for calls of nature and to fix sandwiches and milk to consume in her room until she was finished reading. She savored the deliciousness of the literary excursion.

Then she returned the books to Jared. "You definitely need to read these before going back to school," she told him.

Jared took the books and examined them, fanning through pages looking for stains and creases. "Are you sure you read these? I know you've been hiding in your room, but were these just cover for doing something else?"

"What a weird thing to say," Emma responded. "Why would you say something like that?"

"Because they're in pristine condition," Jared said. "They look brand new. You can't tell that anyone has been reading them."

"Books are my friends," said Emma. "I treat them with care and respect. In this case, they belong to you, and I always try extra hard to be careful with other people's property."

"Yeah, that's true. I appreciate that about you," Jared said.

Emma couldn't let it go at that. "If you don't believe that I read all of them, ask me a question. Open one of them at random and ask me about what you find on that page."

"No, I believe you," said Jared. "But after I've read them, I may challenge you to a trivia contest."

"I can't wait," she said. "But after you've read them, I want to read them again."

"When is the next one coming out?" he asked.

"I don't know. Sometime next year, I think," she replied. "Probably not till the Christmas season. It's a long time to wait."

"Maybe I should wait until all the series is done, so I can read them without having to wait forever for the next one to come out," Jared said.

"Well, if you're going to do that, I'd like to borrow them back right now. I can get in another read before school starts," Emma said.

"No, I think I'll start today," Jared responded. "But to show how good a brother I am, I'll give you the first one as soon as I'm done with it, and you can read that again."

And this is how Emma read the first three **Harry Potter** novels twice over Christmas break. From then on, she knew that her life was going to be intertwined with the works of J. K. Rowling and consciously modeled her behavior, especially in school, on Hermione Granger.

The first trivia question Jared put to his sister was this: What song did Uncle Vernon hum as he boarded up the front door to stop Hogwarts letters from coming in?

Emma answered, "It's called 'Tiptoe Through the Tulips,' although it's probably a made-up title. I've never heard of it, anyway."

"I've never heard of it either," said Jared. "But it could be a real song. Let's ask Mom."

When Hannah assured them that this was indeed an actual song that had been quite popular in the 1920s and again in the 1960s, they were astounded. "It was an enormous hit by a falsetto singer named Tiny Tim when I was a little younger than you are now, Emma," Hannah added.

"Sing it for us," said Jared.

"Yeah, we want to know how it goes, so the next time we read that passage we can sing along in our heads," Emma said.

"I don't remember all the words, but I can hum it," said Hannah.

"Oh good. That's what Uncle Vernon did," said Jared.

Hannah hummed the song, eliciting a response from her children that it was just the kind of lame tune that Harry's uncle would like.

The fourth book, **Harry Potter and the Goblet of Fire**, was released half a year later, on the same day in North America as in Britain, July 8, 2000. Though it was considerably longer than any of the previous novels, by the next day Emma had devoured it. Then she had to wait three years for the next installment.

As that eon of waiting for the next book stretched on and on, Emma felt the need to connect with Harry's world in a new and meaningful way, so she wrote a letter to J. K. Rowling describing the inner feeling of existing in another world -a world she knew she belonged in- while reading the **Harry Potter** books. She added that she hoped she would be sorted into Gryffindor, but had to confess that she had strong Ravenclaw attributes, and she felt conflicted about that, because she really wanted to be a Gryffindor.

A month later, Emma came home late from school, having stayed after for spelling bee practice. She was weary and went straight to her bedroom to stow her backpack and lie down for a few minutes. A letter was propped up against the lamp on her bedside table. The elegant envelope attracted her immediate attention, and as soon as she saw the crested initials of the sender in the return address corner, all weariness evaporated and she released a piercing scream.

Jared, in the kitchen at that moment pouring the filling for a lemon meringue pie over the crust he had made from scratch, turned to his mom and said, "That was Emma. Something's wrong." As the pie dish was not yet full, and he was very particular about pouring his signature pie fillings, he urged his mother to find out what had happened, but Hannah laughed.

"I think you'll find that nothing is wrong and everything is perfectly wonderful as far as your sister is concerned," Hannah said. "I was expecting that sound. Wait here. She should be running toward us about…now!"

At that moment, Emma, red-faced and ecstatic, rushed into the kitchen and squealed, "J. K. Rowling answered my letter!"

"I didn't know you had written to her," Hannah said. "But I surmised you must have when I saw the return address on the letter."

"That is beyond cool," Jared said.

Cameron appeared in search of chocolate chip cookies and said, "What's beyond cool?"

"Emma just got a letter from J. K. Rowling," Jared said. "How cool is that?"

"Out of the blue?" Cameron asked.

"No, silly boy, in response to a letter I sent her," Emma said.

"Well, don't just stand there; read it to us," Hannah said.

Emma's hands shook and her voice choked up several times as she read:

Dear Emma,

Thank you for your kind letter. As a writer, I am always encouraged by the words of readers who have found a home in my alternative world. As to your conflict between Gryffindor and Ravenclaw, you are in good company. Hermione was in the same position. Take it from me, it is quite possible to have a Ravenclaw level intellect and be a true Gryffindor.

Best Wishes,

Jo Rowling

When she finished reading, Emma carefully refolded the letter along its original creases and set it on a clean counter away from the clutter of Jared's baking enterprise.

"Congratulations," Hannah said.

"Yeah, congrats," said Jared. "And for that, I'll dedicate my lemon pie to you. We'll have it for dessert tonight."

"Thanks, Jar," said Emma. "For a thirteen year-old, you make the best pies ever, even if you've never learned how to load the dishwasher properly. I guess they don't teach that on those TV cooking shows you're addicted to."

"How can I learn when you won't let me near the thing?" Jared responded.

"Well, you can watch me tonight and learn," Emma said. She grabbed a dishtowel and playfully snapped it at him.

Jared snatched it away from his sister and said, "And you still haven't learned how to whip a towel so it stings."

"I wasn't trying to hurt you," Emma said. "But I could if I wanted to."

"I picked the lemons from our backyard," Cameron piped in.

"And you are by far the best lemon picker in the family," Jared teased.

The next day, Emma had the letter matted and framed behind polarized glass and hung it on the wall above her bed.

CHAPTER THREE
SEPTEMBER 11

Tuesday, September 11, 2001 was especially traumatic for Emma's family. Her father had personal friends who perished in the fall of the twin towers of the World Trade Center. David had been five when President Kennedy had been assassinated and ten at the time of the murders of Martin Luther King, Jr. and Bobby Kennedy. These events had seared into his brain a combination of resignation and determination to wring while he could whatever profit and benefit were available in life, because it was all so tentative and subject to the whims of cruel fate. The fall of the twin towers and the planes crashing into the Pentagon and the field near Shanksville, Pennsylvania reinforced these feelings.

Subdued and anxious, he drove to his office, listening to news reports on KJZZ along the way. At work, he told his staff and agents that they could check in with clients and then go home. "Just listen to them and try to be reassuring, but be authentic. No canned spiels, and don't go after any new business today."

"Give us a little credit, David," said an agent. "We're not so stupid as to pitch any investments on a day like this."

"You're right. I'm sorry," said David. "I'm just shaken up right now."

Everyone had completed their calls and departed before noon, and David drove home. Emma and her brothers had been dismissed early from school, and when dad arrived home, Emma thought that she had never seen her father's face look so solemn and fearful.

Because of his anger, doubts, fears, and grief, David was reluctant to go to church the following Sunday. Yet he felt a mixture of reluctance

18

and relief when Hannah insisted that the whole family attend. Saturday evening, David received a phone call from their pastor, Kwan-yin Burns, asking him to offer a special remembrance during worship, because he knew some of the victims of the attack. This buoyed his spirits and dissipated his reluctance, and he gladly agreed.

Standing naked before the congregation the next morning, David spoke without notes. "I'll leave it to the pastor to make theological sense of the catastrophe last Tuesday. It was the worst day of my life. Like many of you, my grade school years were traumatized by repeated images of slain national leaders. I grieved for them, but I had not known those great men personally. I admired them from afar in the simple and naive way that children adore heroes.

"As I grew into adulthood, I thought nothing could be worse than those tragedies. But the events of September 11 have shaken me to my core in ways I have never experienced before. Two men I knew well, two men who invited me into their homes, whose wives and children I knew by name, two men with such integrity that they never fudged their golf scores even a little bit, two men who laughed with me over long lunches involving too much alcohol were blown from their perches high up in the World Trade Center by exploding aviation fuel.

"Copious tears of gratitude fell from my eyes as I watched the television coverage of the heroic first responders saving as many lives as possible. And I cried again not caring who might see me in such an unmanly state when I received word that Bob Washington and Aasif Khan, my colleagues in business and my dear friends, were not among the survivors. Bob, who savored good scotch and bad puns, and Aasif, who was partial to Vernors ginger ale or fresh-squeezed orange juice and was always pleased to be the designated driver, are dead at the hands of terrorists.

"So now, all I can do is exhort every one of you here, whether or not you knew personally anyone in those towers, or the Pentagon, or that Pennsylvania field, to resolve to remember that a multitude of good, decent, fine human beings perished that day. I swear, Bob and Aasif, that I will never forget you or the countless unnamed people who shared your awful fate." Eyes moist, he bowed his head and returned to his pew.

Emma had never been more proud of her father than this moment, and the applause that followed David's words felt sweet in her ears.

When the applause stopped, Kwan-yin rose to the pulpit and said, "Let us pray." The room was engulfed in a solemn hush as she bowed her head and confidently intoned, "God of Love, we are gathered before you in a state of grief, mourning the loss of people that most us never knew existed before now. We are haunted by images of death and destruction that fill our television screens. We are moved to tears by the bravery of rescue workers. Powerful feelings have coursed through our minds and bodies over these last few days: anger, fear, pity, depression, love, hate, despair, hope, sadness, determination, humility, pride, and courage.

"We confess, O God, that we need acutely to feel your presence in our lives right now. We ache for heavenly comfort and for peace on earth. Cradle us in the safety of your love and sing us a lullaby to sustain us during our time of grief. And then lead us out of our grief into a world with staggering needs. Strengthen us and grant us the tenacity, wisdom and courage to follow paths toward the greater good.

"We pray, of course, for all who have lost friends and loved ones in these attacks. We pray too for the survivors who have been brutalized and traumatized by the destruction. And we pray, as Jesus would, for the misguided souls who are so filled with hate that they would contemplate further acts of senseless devastation.

"God of Grace, we pray for the return of simple pleasures. In the midst of the hard work of recovery that we accept as a mission for our lives, grant us a return of laughter. Grant us deeper appreciation of simple meals shared with people we love. Grant us peaceful sleep and intervals of gentle joy.

"And let the people say amen."

The congregation offered a resounding amen.

The laughter that Kwan-yin prayed for returned for David Round on September 20th. David and Hannah were fans of The Daily Show with Jon Stewart, but the live program had not been broadcast following the terrorist attacks. That day, the show resumed, and David and Hannah shed more tears listening to Jon Stewart's monologue but also let slip their first glimmers of laughter.

Jon Stewart reflected on the nature of comedy and the human need for it in the midst of tragedy. David experienced a rage of agreement when the comedian said that any fool can blow up something, but then profuse tears fell when Jon Stewart extolled the heroic first responders. Along with countless people with their television sets tuned to Comedy

Central that night, Hannah and David felt their throats constrict with grief and pride when Jon said, "The view from my apartment was the World Trade Center and now it's gone. But you know what the view is now? The Statue of Liberty."

"It feels good to laugh," David said to Hannah when the program was over. "But I can't help being sobered by the thought that it's our children's generation who will be called on to deal with the military consequences of all this. The bloodshed has only just begun, and it will go on for years. And the casualties won't be people that we know but people Jared, Emma, and Cameron know."

"Oh God, I hope you're wrong," said Hannah.

"I do too," he said. "But I think the war will be fought by Millennials, led by senior officers who are hard-bitten and cynical Gen-Xers. Meanwhile, we Boomers will sit on the sidelines and fret. And the financial markets will be heading straight to hell, except for Defense Industry investments."

"You're quite the prophet of doom, today," Hannah said.

"I'm not having any fun at it, though," he replied.

Emma, for her part, sought to understand the 9/11 attacks through the lens of *Harry Potter*. She likened the religious zealots who obediently committed suicide in order to appease their ruthless leader Osama bin Laden to Death Eaters enslaved to the iniquitous designs of Voldemort. And she accepted as an article of faith that young people of her generation would be called upon one day to face this evil man and to prevail over him. In her mind, the events of September 11, 2001 made the next *Harry Potter* installment more important for the future of human society. The narrative that J. K. Rowling had spun out so far paralleled events in the real world. It was therefore critical, in Emma's judgment, that the world know as soon as possible how the tale of the Boy Who Lived would develop.

Answers about the fates of Harry Potter and Osama bin Laden remained years into the future, but an inkling that J. K. Rowling might be a true prophet nestled in Emma's mind. This notion was strengthened in November, when the U. S. invasion of Afghanistan, though widely supported, was still a fresh wound to the American psyche. Kwan-yin preached a sermon that for different reasons brought both Emma and David to tears.

"Everything has changed since September 11," the pastor said. "This is a cliché but true enough. One thing that has changed for all of us in this congregation is the role of the church. On September 10 and for a long time leading up to that day, it was fashionable for religious bodies to argue fine points of theology, expending vast energies on tiny semantic differences in creedal statements. Even our mostly peaceful NCC has engaged in these debates, although not with the rancor of older and larger denominations. In times of peace, we can enjoy the luxury of this kind of ecclesiastical quibbling, but not now. There will one day come a time when we can again engage in such small word games, but this is not the time.

"For the time being, we must get beyond church sponsored doctrinal disputes -except one. We must stand up and say no to the abusive claims that God is punishing America through the actions of terrorists. That's not a fine point of theology but a blasphemous bludgeon.

"What we need to focus on now is healing. Not peace, but healing. Whether we like it or not, we are living in what Ecclesiastes calls a time for war, and immediate calls for peace will not be heard. In the context of our present world situation, healing is as close to peace as we are likely to come. Members of this congregation have been praying and caring for people dealing with cancer, divorce, addictions, depression, and a host of other ills. Now we must add to those tasks caring for people touched by war in our homeland as well as its extension to Central Asia. In practical terms, this means everyone in this congregation. All of us have been wounded, and some among us or their family members will soon be directly and physically in harm's way.

"We must gently care for one another and for the suffering strangers we meet. We must remain mindful of victims of war the world over, including Afghan civilians who find themselves in the wrong place when bombs begin to fall and the inevitable refugees with nothing to eat and nowhere to hide.

"War has a way of testing our most cherished beliefs. Sometimes those beliefs do not survive the battle. And yet what rises in their place is usually stronger and more profound. War will break our hearts. Do not expect to get through this time of trial unwounded. So pray for two things -courage and healing.

"Beginning this afternoon, we will offer a service of healing in this sanctuary for any who wish to come or need to come. It will be informal and consist mainly of listening, prayer, and anointing. Unlike the morning service, clothing will be required, so that we may invite textile neighbors and strangers."

On the way home, Emma and Jared interpreted the sermon from the back seat of the van.

"The Death Eaters have struck and war has been forced upon us," said Emma.

"And we need a Dumbledore to lead us through it," said Jared. "But all we have is Gilderoy Lockhart continuing to read children's books while the world is under attack."

"Well, **Harry Potter** is supposedly a children's book," said Emma. "But I think those books can save us, give us hope and guidance."

"And yet we have to wait indefinitely for that guidance, because the words of the next **Harry Potter** novel have not yet been written," Jared countered.

"J. K. Rowling is the leader the world needs right now. She is the one who can bring healing," Emma said.

"Rowling for president!" Jared said.

"That's not what I meant," Emma said. "I am now certain that Harry will be tested in ways beyond our imagination, but I have faith that we will learn how to live better lives because of his trials."

Though she did not say this aloud, Emma also deeply believed that as the series unfolded, Harry Potter would be severely wounded and in the end possibly killed. This did not, however, diminish her devotion to Rowling's novels.

Jared began following a Comedy Central quiz show called Beat the Geeks, in which contestants matched their pop culture trivia knowledge against a team of fanatical experts. To make it fair, the questions asked of the geeks were significantly more difficult. From time to time, Emma watched the program with her older brother, hoping that Harry Potter related trivia might be used, but it never came up in the shows she watched. However, an urge developed in her to become a Harry Potter geek. And to do that, she would need to re-read all the books to date and make notes on plot lines, themes, and characters, and to research available biographical information about J. K. Rowling. In addition to her notes on the narratives, Emma also began collecting newspaper and magazine clippings and printing out Internet articles about her favorite subject.

<><><>

Around the dinner table one evening, Hannah expressed nostalgia for their old house in Phoenix.

"But you were excited about moving into a bigger place," David said.

"I know, I know," Hannah responded. "That doesn't mean I can't have fond memories of the old house."

"So do I, but this one is so much nicer, and far more prestigious," David responded. "With the address we have here, we're living right in the midst of potential clients. Being surrounded by wealthy transplants gives me a leg up for contacting potential investors. This address gives them confidence in the agency's success."

"Our previous home in northeast Phoenix was in a wealthy enclave," Hannah said. "It couldn't have been a detriment to your work. I just miss that house, that's all. It had a lot of character."

"Me too," said Emma. "That was the house I grew up in."

"Grew up?" Jared choked. "You were still in primary school when we moved here. You've really grown up here."

"You know what I mean," said Emma. "Sometimes I feel like a Muggle-born living in Malfoy Manor."

"How do you know it's a manor?" Jared asked.

"That's what Draco called it in ***Chamber of Secrets***." Emma replied. "And the Malfoys are filthy rich. Manor, mansion, or whatever, with the airs they put on it's got to be a prestigious palace."

"Poor Emma, a Muggle-born forced to live in a prestigious manor," Jared said with his best snide voice.

"It's not that exactly. This is a nice place, too. It's just that I still miss the old house," Emma said. "Is there anything wrong with that?"

"Nothing at all, Emma. It was a nice house, a decent residential address for owning a business," David admitted. "But this one has character too, and is better for contacts to grow my already successful business. It means more money for my family to enjoy the fruits of."

On this score, David and his middle child disagreed. More accurately, Emma did not care about improving already generous profit margins. The females, Hannah and Emma, missed and preferred the old house. The older males, David and Jared were partial to the new one, and Cameron was too young to remember much about the Phoenix abode, so he was fine with living in North Scottsdale.

The Round family now lived in a neighborhood of beautifully landscaped mansions that made the Durseley's suburban abode look like lower middle class bungalows. The seven-bedroom single story home covered 8000 square feet on the east side of a one acre plot. One of the bedrooms David used as a home office, and another was designated as a classroom for use by a governess. The home architecture seemed better suited to a villa overlooking the Mediterranean Sea rather than amidst expensive desert landscaping, but the surrounding homes were such a hodge-podge of architectural styles, that the Round villa looked indigenous in comparison.

After this nostalgic family conversation, Jared began referring to their home as Malfoy Manor, and Emma shot him a sour glance every time he did it.

CHAPTER FOUR
UNCLE HENRY'S MANSION

Emma's twin cousins, Annagreta and Jeffers Fife, spent a lot of time with the Rounds during the summer of 2002. Their parents, Henry and Mabb, were separated, and it was clear to all that the marriage was doomed. Thus family life for the twins was laden with anxiety as they shifted back and forth between the family home where Dad stayed and the apartment Mom had moved into.

Because Mabb and Hannah openly detested one another, Fife family invitations to the Round home in Phoenix had been few and years in the past. Since his sister and her family had moved to North Scottsdale, neither Henry nor his children had visited the new Round residence.

Given the circumstances, however, Hannah felt a strong urge to tend to the needs of her younger brother's children as they faced their upcoming senior year in high school as children of divorce. She therefore took it upon herself to provide a safe place for them to while away the leisure days of summer. "Come on over and enjoy our pool," Hannah told them in June. After that, she let them know that they were welcome to hang out whenever they wanted to. Hannah did not think Henry would mind if his daughter and son skinny-dippped along with her three children, although she did not bother to tell him that bathing suits were banned at the Round estate. As she told the twins when inviting them to swim nude, "Nobody's square at the Round house."

"Yeah, even your dining room table is round." Annagreta quipped. "You have your own little Camelot here, perfect for free-spirited knights and ladies."

"Yes, and we're known for dining without armor," Hannah responded.

26

It never occurred to Emma that her uncle was unaware of their naturist activities, although she did notice that initially Annagreta and Jeff had textile tans. As the summer progressed, her cousins' tan lines disappeared.

The following summer, however, when the divorce was final and the twins had adjusted to the situation, Emma was surprised to learn that Uncle Henry had bought property near Camp Verde that he turned into a naturist retreat and her cousins were spending the summer there rather than with their mother. The word from Hannah was that the U. S. invasion of Iraq had caused Henry such mental agitation that he had run away to hide in the woods to escape the incessant war news updates.

In the interim, Hannah had at last succeeded in finding an occupant for the bedroom set aside for a governess, and a new skinny-dipper joined the Round household.

"We're going up for a weekend to visit Henry's mysterious clothing-optional retreat," Hannah announced at the dinner table one evening.

"Do they have a pool?" Jared asked.

"No, but a creek runs through the property," Hannah explained.

"When are we going?" Emma asked. "I can't go if it's the Saturday **Order of the Phoenix** is released."

"Fret not," said Hannah. "We're going this Friday."

"Whew!" Emma said.

David steered the family minivan slowly down the dirt lane and parked in front of the garage. Jeff and Annagreta rushed from the porch to greet their cousins, aunt and uncle.

After efficiently hugging the twins, Hannah said, "Now that you've been properly greeted, you can help us with the food trays."

As he carried a platter of cheeses and cold cuts toward the porch, Jeff said, "Dad has put out an extra hamper that you all can use for your clothes."

Henry stepped outside and took his sister in a wide hug while reaching across to shake hands with his brother-in-law. He saw their three children laden with food and beverages and also a woman he didn't know who looked to be in her late twenties.

Letting go of Hannah and David, Henry reached out for the hand of the strange woman, noticing now that her skin glowed with a slight orange tint. "Henry Fife, younger sibling of Hannah Round," he said.

"Xandra MacUmberland," the woman said with a Scots accent as she grasped Henry's right hand. "Governess to the Round children."

"Impressive," said Henry. "I heard Hannah was in the market for a nanny, but governess exceeds all expectations."

"Mom dislikes the word nanny," said Jared with a slight sneer.

"For your information, young man," Hannah interjected, "the word nanny does not convey the breadth and intellectual responsibilities associated with Xandra's employment. Governess is far more suitable. And as you have already manifestly noted multiple times, you're far too old to require the services of a nanny."

"Whatever," said Jared. "And her passport says her name's really **Alexandra**."

"Xandra joined our family two months ago," offered David. "Jared, Emma, and Cameron have yet to discover the mind enriching and edifying dimensions of her duties."

"Do I detect a Midlothian lilt to your speech, Xandra?" asked Henry.

"Born there and three decades of life spent in the drizzling cold of Auld Reeky. I left it behind this spring for a rebirth in sunny Arizona," she explained. "And it's Xandra if you please. Alexandra's much too common. And don't you dare call me Sandy!"

"So you grew up in Edinburgh?" Henry continued.

"Aye, my parents own a flat in India Street. Very comfortable, but as I neared thirty I had to get away or be forever captive to my mother's growing frailty. And how do you come by this fair knowledge of Scotland?" she said.

"I have a good ear for dialects," said Henry. "And I've been on several tours of literary Britain, the Lake District and so on, and of course, Scotland. And with a name like Fife, it's not surprising that I'd know a wee bit about the land of my ancestors. I teach English at Prickly Pear High School in Phoenix."

"I majored in English literature at University…at Edinburgh," Xandra said with an engaging chuckle. "What do you like best in Edinburgh?"

Henry said, "Great school. I love the whole city, but the Merchiston neighborhood is my favorite area. And the Robert Louis Stevenson Museum tickles my imagination."

"They call Merchiston Writers' Row," Xandra said. "I'm sure you know that."

"Why don't we continue this conversation over food," said Annagreta. "The sooner you Rounds get your clothes off, the sooner we can retire to the meadow and break out the calories."

The garments of six people were quickly consigned to the hamper, which was now overflowing. Three Fifes, five Rounds, and Xandra MacUmberland carried blankets, food, drinks, and because evening was approaching, insect repellant out to the meadow, where they ate and chattered.

Silence prevailed for an interval of ingesting, and then seeking to change the subject, Henry said, "We were speaking earlier of Edinburgh and its literary acclaim." He looked at Emma. "Do any of you know how Auld Reeky's newest literary lion, J. K. Rowling, is coming along with the fifth **Harry Potter** installment?"

"Oh, I can't wait," said Emma. "It's called **The Order of the Phoenix**, and it's coming out a week from tomorrow, and I'll be in line when the bookstore opens at 12:01 a.m. If it's anything like the other books, I'll have it read before dinner that day."

Cameron took the knuckle of his left forefinger out of his mouth and said, "We've all read the first four, but Emma is **obsessed** with Harry; thinks he's a real person." As was his habit when not speaking or eating, Cameron put his knuckle back in his mouth and sucked on it. His teeth were slightly bucked from this life-long habit, but Hannah had defended Cameron's right to a security gesture, declaring that orthodontia would easily solve the problem when Cameron was ready to give up sucking his finger.

"Well, which book so far do you like best?" Henry asked Emma.

"I suppose the first one. But **Goblet of Fire** is awesome," Emma answered.

"Emma wants to go skinny dipping with Harry Potter," said Jared.

Blushing, Emma said, "So what? It's only a harmless fantasy. I know he's not real. But I don't suppose you ever fantasize about anything, do you Jared?"

Now it was Jared's turn to blush and he did not respond.

"The thing I **don't** like about **Goblet**," Emma continued, "is that Harry is so prudish about his body when Moaning Myrtle visits him in the Prefects' bathroom."

"Well, he's fourteen and insecure," explained Annagreta. "Young teens in general are not very confident about how their bodies look."

"I'm thirteen and I'm not insecure or prudish," said Emma. "I'm a year younger than Harry, the same age as Ginny Weasley. She's not bashful -well, except around Harry, but that's not about prudishness."

"Yes dear, but you've grown up with naturism," said Hannah.

"Wouldn't it be great fun to invite Harry Potter here to run around naked in the woods?" Emma continued. "Or any other character. Who do you fancy, Jeff?"

"I'd rather invite the Patil twins," he replied. "OK, everyone, fess up."

"Severus Snape," offered Jared with a provocative tone.

"Yuck!" exclaimed Emma. "You're just saying that to shock people."

"No I'm not. I appreciate Severus, that's all. He's a richly layered character."

"Well, I'd want to be with Hermione," said Cameron.

"When it comes to great conversation at a nudist picnic," said Annagreta, "there would be no better guest than Albus Dumbledore."

Xandra said, "I rather fancy a nude dip with Remus Lupin. It would be exciting to splash about naked with a werewolf, don't you think? One might get bitten in the buff and start howling at the moon."

No one could tell from her tone of voice whether Xandra was joking or sincere.

"Uncle Henry?" Emma asked.

"I'm torn between Annagreta's choice and Cameron's," he said. "Dumbledore or Hermione."

"That leaves only Mom and Dad for their preferences," Emma said. "But they haven't read any of the books."

"How can you be sure?" David said. "Maybe we have read them on the sly. Hannah and David and the secret reading mystery or something."

"I'd really be impressed if you had," Emma said. "Have you?"

"Unfortunately not," Hannah said. "But I may be forced to do so in self-defense. I've learned so much listening to you three talk in detail about sorting houses and such."

Xandra turned to Jared and said, "Do you really want Snape at your picnic? Fancy yourself a Slytherin, do you?"

"Do you have a problem with that, Governess?" Jared responded. "I fancy myself a Slytherin with a Ravenclaw intellect, and as such, I am interested in astutely observing and analyzing interesting people."

"Oh, let's get an old hat and do a sorting ceremony," said Emma.

"Another time," said Henry, as he swatted at some unrecognized tiny creature buzzing about his ear. "It's time to pass around the insect repellent."

As Hannah was spraying repellent on her daughter's back, Emma turned toward Xandra as an idea flashed in her mind. "Xandra, since you lived in Edinburgh, have you ever met J. K. Rowling?"

"Never met to talk to her," Xandra said. "I did catch sight of her in front of the Balmoral Hotel once, but she disappeared into it. I find it best to leave writers alone in public, because they tend to be such introverts and don't handle talking with strangers at all well. On the other hand, you being in correspondence with her puts you ahead of me among the literati."

"Nice try at buttering her up, Xandra," said Jared. "She wrote one letter and got a terse reply."

"I've read the letter over Emma's bed," said Xandra. "And it's clear that J. K. Rowling actually read Emma's letter and responded specifically to it. No matter how small a matter it may seem to you, Jared, at one point in her life, J. K. Rowling was aware of your sister's existence."

"Whatever," said Jared.

By the time the fifth **Harry Potter** book was published in 2003, Emma was a quarter of a year into the ranks of teenager, and standing a willowy five feet eight inches tall. Still wearing glasses, she had changed into new frames three times since her first pair, although her prescription had remained much the same. For her most recent birthday the previous April, her parents had given her prescription sunglasses.

On the eve of the release of **Harry Potter and the Order of the Phoenix**, Emma planted her svelte frame among a costumed crowd of children, teens, and twenty-somethings, along with a few middle aged and senior adults in mufti. Most of them -male and female alike- bore lightning bolt scars drawn with magic markers on their foreheads. The occasion was the midnight opening of the Scottsdale Barnes and Noble bookstore where she would get her pre-reserved copy of the book. Emma was not in costume, not wanting to risk having anything torn or stained in the jostling horde, placing her firmly in the minority of her age cohort.

She found herself casting judgment on a group of giddy girls in line who did not appreciate, she was quite sure, the subtleties and depth of the series. Nevertheless, she felt a surge of adrenaline when the countdown to midnight was shouted in unison as if it were New Year's Eve. Uncontrolled twitching coursed through her body as she inched her way toward the cash register with the two copies of the book she had reserved. One was for reading and the other to join her collection of mint editions of the first four books on a special shelf in her bedroom.

Hannah waited in the car, and as soon as Emma had clicked her seatbelt into place for the return home, she pulled out a flashlight and began reading. The fifth Harry Potter installment was nearly twice as long as book four, so getting through it would consume much more time than she had anticipated.

Emma stayed up all night reading with occasional breaks for catnaps. Everyone else in the house was asleep, so she had no one to groan to or rejoice with at various points along the narrative. Her spirits rose and fell along with Harry's high and low moments. At times, she felt angry at Harry's juvenile behavior. But then she remembered Jared behaving like that when he was fifteen. She decided that Rowling was presenting a more realistic Harry in this book, but she was not sure she liked that.

One aspect that she loved was the equity between male and female characters. The gender parity among the six students who went to the Ministry to rescue Sirius was a stroke of brilliance, she thought.

Hannah let her stay home from church Sunday morning so she could continue her quest to be the first among her friends and family to finish reading it. She closed the book early Sunday afternoon and carried it into Jared's room, where he happily opened it.

"When I'm done, we'll talk," he said.

"Be prepared for a long talk," Emma responded. "This book changes everything."

Later in summer 2003, Emma and her family returned to Uncle Henry's retreat, and on Sunday morning, they all piled into vehicles to attend worship at the Sedona NCC. Emma was introduced to the pastors, Cloud and Terp Morgan, at this service but had no idea that the couple would become vitally important to her in years ahead. Nevertheless, at this first encounter, the clergy pair impressed Emma with their appearance and substance. Cloud wore what he called John Lennon glasses, but what Emma thought of as Harry Potter glasses. Shoulder length graying hair framed his clean-shaven face in a Dumbledoresque fashion. Terp had the muscled legs of a liturgical dancer. What Emma liked best about Terp's appearance, however, was her silver hair and granny glasses.

Beatrix Northwich, divorced with two children, was the new love in Henry Fife's life. While she and Sarah and Thomas were visiting Henry at his naturist retreat, they also went to the naturist church in Sedona, just as Henry had done earlier with the Rounds.

Back home in Phoenix, Beatrix took her children to visit the naturist church there, where she chanced to meet the Round family. Beatrix was as taken with Cloud and Terp as Emma, and because of a conversation she had carried on with Terp, she had already corresponded with the Phoenix pastor, Kwan-yin Burns, with questions about the naturist denomination. While Beatrix and Hannah were engaged in conversation during the fellowship time after the service, Kwan-yin approached and invited Beatrix to her office for a discussion.

"What about Sarah and Thomas?" Beatrix asked.

"They're welcome to run about the place if they'd like. They'll be quite safe. There are games in the back yard," Kwan-yin assured her.

Having overheard this exchange and curious to learn more, Hannah said, "They can hang out with my clan. Emma would be happy to show them around. I'm sure she could tell them enlightening stories about Jeffers and Annagreta."

"Do you like Harry Potter?" Emma asked Sarah without preamble.

"Of course," said Sarah.

"What character do you most want to go skinny-dipping with?" Emma continued.

"Gee, I've never really thought about that," Sarah said with a note of surprise in her voice. She paused and then added, "I really like Ron Weasley, though."

"Oh good! We're compatible then," said Emma. "It's Harry himself for me. But I think the Burrow would make an ideal naturist retreat, don't you? And Ron threatened to go to the Yule Ball naked rather than wear the fancy robes his mom picked out for him, so I'm sure he'd be game for skinny-dipping with us."

Jared interjected, "As I recall, Molly told Harry to take a picture of Ron naked to have a good laugh."

Emma ignored her older brother and turned to the heretofore silent Thomas, saying, "And what about you?"

"I've only read the first two by myself. Sarah read *Azkaban* aloud to me," Thomas reported. "My favorite is Neville Longbottom. I think he's going to be important later on in the story -a real hero. Why else would the Sorting Hat put him in Gryffindor?"

"That's very astute -what's your name again?" responded Emma.

Sarah said, "He's Thomas. Not Tom or Tommy. He's always been Thomas."

"And how old are you, Thomas?" Emma asked.

"Nine," he said. "Ten next month."

"Well, Thomas, I'm very impressed with your insight about Neville, and I quite agree," Emma said.

Cameron removed his left forefinger from his mouth and said, "Emma's impressed with anyone who says nice things about the *Harry Potter* books. I'm Cameron. I'm ten, and I have good vibes about both of you, Thomas and Sarah." Earnestly he shook hands with each of them in turn and then tucked his finger back between his teeth.

"At the Natural Church in Sedona, the preachers did a sermon about the theology of *Harry Potter*," Sarah announced with an authoritarian vocal cadence. "It was simply awesome!"

"Oooh, and we missed it," moaned Emma. "Which preachers? The married couple, Cloud and Terp Morgan?"

"Yes," said Thomas. "They were very cool."

"Yeah, they are cool," agreed Jared. "I call them Clomo and Termo, and I only make up nicknames for people I respect."

Kwan-yin gently touched Beatrix' hand. "To my office then?" Before departing, she said to Emma, "I'll get you a copy of the *Harry Potter* sermon."

Emma thanked the pastor profusely, and then turned her attention to Sarah and Thomas. At thirteen, Emma was comfortable assuming the role of babysitter for the Northwich children, two and four years younger respectively. "Come along Sarah and Thomas, we'll get some lemonade and cookies and get a patio table outside."

As she led them outside, along with her brothers, Emma thought about the *Harry Potter* sermon. It made sense to do that, because there was plenty of spiritual meaning in the HP canon. She was anxious to read that sermon and wondered if Cloud and Terp had preached any other sermons exploring Rowling's novels.

Once settled around a picnic table under an awning, Emma took a bite of a giant chocolate chip cookie and then opened a discussion about *Harry Potter* characters. "Of course, speculating about what will happen to Harry and the others must be based on what has already been written. There are clues hidden everywhere."

"Sure," said Jared, "but it's just as much fun to speculate beyond the confines of the actual words on paper."

"They are two completely different tasks," said Emma. "Sarah and Thomas, as our guests, you can decide. Should we speculate about what happens in the next book or make up something out of pure fantasy?"

"You can pick, Emma," said Sarah.

"Thomas?" Emma asked.

"Yeah, whatever you want is OK," he replied.

"Then let's do both," Emma announced. "First, what do think will come of Harry and Cho Chang? Will she and Harry end up together, or will someone else end up with Harry?"

"No way Cho and Harry are a match," said Jared. "Rowling has been setting up Ginny to be with Harry from the first book."

"Not Hermione?" asked Emma.

"Nope," said Jared.

"OK, smart guy, provide evidence from the books," she responded.

Jared and Emma went back and forth, trading incidents and suspected foreshadowing. Eventually, Cameron said, "I'm bored, Let's switch to fantasy."

Jared had an idea.

When Beatrix arrived to retrieve her children, she found them listening intently as Jared and Emma expounded on an imagined naturist picnic at the Burrow with *Harry Potter* characters.

"Hermione has brought a beaker of Polyjuice Potion," Jared said. "She and Ginny get Harry, Ron, Neville, and Luna to go with them to the hayloft for a Polyjuice game."

"I can see where this is going," Emma cut in. "They're going to exchange hairs so they can transform into one another. Knowing you, of course, it would have to be hair from some *particular* anatomical area."

"Don't go there, Emma," Jared said slyly. "Naturally, they'd pluck strands from their **heads**. But the question is **who** does each one appropriately switch with? Mathematically, at least two of them would have to trade with an opposite sex person."

"I know who I'd want to swap bodies with," said Emma, "but I want to hear Jared's scenario first. Go on then, let's have it."

"Well as it happens, I have the perfect answer," Jared said. "Since he rescued her from the Chamber of Secrets, Harry should become Ginny and vice-versa. They've both been unpleasantly intimate with Voldemort, you see, but in different ways. They could gain insights into fighting him that way."

Emma frowned disapprovingly but remained silent.

"And," Jared continued, oblivious to Emma's facial gesture, "because they're always arguing or hurting the feelings of each other, Ron and Hermione should transform into the other's body. Each one needs to discover what it feels like to be in the other's skin. And Neville and Luna have both known the sting of being teased and ostracized. But Neville has been more proactive in challenging it, while Luna has better coping skills. Now that they've both become a little bit cool for having been at the Ministry with the other four, they could gain more insights by switching bodies with one another. I really hope there's more Polyjuicing in the coming books. It would be so totally cool if some of the characters switched bodies with their friends. What do you all think?"

"Sounds to me like you're into cross-dressing potions," Emma said snidely.

"Not at all, little sister. Just the opposite," Jared retorted. "Cross *undressing!*"

The conversation was briefly interrupted when Sarah and Thomas were escorted away by their mother, and then Emma said, "Though reluctant to encourage you, Jared, I have to admit your Polyjuice game is a great idea."

"Thank you, Em. I am deeply touched," said Jared while rising and then bowing theatrically.

"And I suspect you are right about the proposed pairings of the characters," she continued. "As much as I want Harry and Hermione to get together in the end, as you said, it's clear that from the first book Jo Rowling has set up Ginny to be Harry's ultimate partner."

"And that means that Hermione will end up with Ron," said Jared. "A dismal prospect if I ever considered one."

"Yeah, Ron would be a better match with Luna than Hermione," Emma said. "But that leaves Hermione all alone."

"There's always Draco," Jared said with a leer in his voice. "Hermione could end up living in Malfoy Manor for real."

"Eww gross!" Emma spat out. "Get serious!"

"How about Hermione and Luna, then?" Jared suggested. "They're both really smart, but in different ways."

"That wouldn't work," Emma declared. "Hermione thinks Luna's ideas are loony. She'd be better off with Ron than Luna."

"I disagree. It's better to be alone than with an intellectual inferior," said Jared.

"I suppose so," Emma conceded. Looking sad, she left the table and went for a solitary walk around the grounds.

On Saturday afternoon, February 14, 2004, Beatrix and Henry doffed their clothes to be married in a naturist ceremony at the Sedona Natural Christian Church.

Awaiting the couple as they stepped up to the chancel were naked paranymphs drawn from the blending of their families. Annagreta was maid of honor and Jeffers was best man. Sarah and Emma served as bridal attendants, along with Willow, the daughter of the Yavapai woman who served as caretaker of Henry's property. Thomas, Jared, and Cameron enjoyed their roles as ushers and groomsmen. Terp and Cloud co-officiated, and Emma was again impressed by the co-pastors and made a point of talking with them about *Harry Potter* during the reception.

CHAPTER FIVE
THE MAGIC OF INVISIBILITY

Uncle Henry and his new wife Beatrix, in the summer of 2004, had been introduced to the paranormal world of out-of-body exploration. Pastors Cloud and Terp Morgan had been leaving their bodies for decades, and they taught Henry and Beatrix how to do it. In turn, Beatrix and Henry taught their children, Annagreta, Jeff, Sarah, and Thomas. When the Round family came up for a weekend visit, Jeff and Annagreta taught their cousins, Jared, Emma, and Cameron to induce out-of-body experiences at will, and Henry taught his sister and brother-in-law.

Among the Rounds, Emma was most excited about this new skill, seeing floating as a form of magic directly linking her to the *Harry Potter* universe. She continued to evaluate every new thing she encountered against that world.

"Just imagine," she said to Cameron. "We now have our own perfect invisibility cloaks. It's a miracle, don't you think?"

"I suppose," her younger brother responded. "But to an 18th century person, TV and even radio would seem like a miracle. Leaving your physical body is just a matter of technique."

"Well I think this is brilliant!" she replied. "As far as I'm concerned, it's magic."

Throughout the remainder of the summer, Emma went on repeated floating expeditions by herself, sailing bodiless across Scottsdale and Phoenix, including multiple flyovers of Camelback Mountain, Pinnacle Peak, and Mummy Mountain.

<><><>

Emma started high school in August, though her choice of school created friction in the family. David wanted his daughter to go to a private prep school or at the very least to a highly rated charter.

Jared had been attending the Arizona School for the Arts since fall 2001. The public charter school for college prep and performing arts, founded in 1995, would have been a good choice for Emma, in David's view. But Jared had a punishing daily commute into Central Phoenix to reach the 3rd Street campus, and this was something that Emma did not want to go through. Jared rose before sunrise on school days and often got home late. The time commitment was worthwhile for Jared, who was focused on a career in theater acting and directing. Emma, however, had no interest in the performing arts and preferred an easier commute to school.

She wanted to enroll at Pinnacle High School on Mayo Boulevard in Phoenix. Hannah, who was a champion of public education, supported her daughter.

"But Pinnacle's not even in Scottsdale," David lamented.

"We live within the bounds of its district," Hannah countered. "And for the record, it is a wealthy district. Emma's education will not be shortchanged by lack of resources."

"That's good to know," said David.

"It's a scandal, actually," Hannah retorted. "Kids in low income areas should have the same educational resources as those in high income areas. Or more, to even the playing field."

"How did I end up marrying such a bleeding heart?" David said.

"Because you are one too – except for money," Hannah replied.

As usual, the females in the Round family prevailed, and Emma enrolled at Pinnacle High School. But David had the last word on the subject. "Lest I be accused of snobbery," he said to his daughter, "I call your attention to the fact that Harry Potter went to a private school." Emma conceded the point.

The Rounds joined the Fifes for a family gathering at Henry's place beginning New Year's Eve. After dinner on New Year's Day 2005, Thomas said, "Everybody here knows how to leave our bodies, and the cold doesn't affect our souls. Why don't we get out-of-body and go outside for a float?"

"Great idea," Emma said, and a quick consensus led to fifteen people finding spots on the floor to lie supine and pop out of their skin and venture out into the freezing weather.

They floated around the property in a pack, venturing past Fife land to follow the creek for a stretch. On their return, as they neared the house, Willow communicated the suggestion that they all move into one space, as she, Sarah, and Thomas had done once before in a moment of peril. Fifteen souls thereupon merged, creating a starburst of auras that glistened in rainbow colors and caused a unison chorus of telepathic oohs and aahs.

Emma said, "If this isn't magic, I don't know what is."

"It's a crescendo of massed souls," Cameron responded

"Wow, Cam. That's really deep. But I'm going for a more earthy response. That was bloody hell positively orgasmic!" said Jared.

Henry laughed at the enthusiasm of his niece and nephews. "As for magic, I would offer the wisdom of Arthur C. Clarke, who said, 'Any sufficiently advanced technology is indistinguishable from magic.'"

"What about orgasm?" Jared said.

"Advanced use of brain chemistry," Henry replied.

"The next time you're in a romantic mood, I'll remind you of that remark," Beatrix said.

"Gee, I always thought of chemistry as quite romantic," said Hannah with a chortle.

Emma had no difficulty finding fellow Potterites to hang out with at Pinnacle High. There seemed to be more girls than boys who self-identified as Potterheads, but those males who did so tended to be stauncher in their support for all things Harry. The boys who were either indifferent or dismissive of the world that J. K. Rowling had created leaned toward absorption in the realm of cartoon superheroes. Emma's friends understood themselves as part of an international generation that had grown up with Harry Potter, looking forward to each new book as they themselves matured and feeling more excited with every succeeding volume released into the world. Ever present was a sense of being part of something bigger than the individual. They had their own Potterese language, which they graciously shared with older adults who had also fallen under Rowling's spell, but to Emma's generation it was their native language, whereas when adults used it, it sounded like an acquired second language. Emma thought that her mom could never quite get the accent right.

On July 16, 2005, Emma again waited in line at Barnes and Noble for the midnight release of the sixth **Harry Potter** volume. During the ensuing twenty-four hour period, **Harry Potter and the Half-Blood Prince** sold more copies than the top-selling book of 2004, **The Da Vinci Code**, had sold in an entire year. Dan Brown's blockbuster had sold 4.3 million copies.

Shortly after Emma's 16th birthday, Susan Sinew, one of Emma's Potterhead friends at Pinnacle High invited her to a Friday night pajama party at her nearby home. "There'll just be a few people; my sister and a couple of neighborhood girls who go to Xavier. We'll make popcorn and stay up all night gossiping."

Emma said, "Sounds like fun. Are pajamas the fashion of the day? Or night in this case."

"We're not legalistic about that," said Susan. "You can wear whatever you like, what you normally wear to bed. A nightgown maybe? Boxers and a top?"

"Normally I wear nothing," said Emma. "So, I'll need to go shopping for pajamas."

"Oh don't bother with that," Susan said. "You can stay dressed until we get settled in for the night, and then you can sleep in bra and panties."

"I don't wear bras," Emma said. "I hope this isn't getting too complicated for what sounds like a great event."

"Well then, tee shirt and panties. That's close enough to pajamas," said Susan.

"That works," said Emma. "I've got a large collection of HP related tees. And maybe I can talk some of the other girls into experimenting with sleeping in the nude. It's really healthier than being wrapped up with cloth all night. Your skin needs to breathe. I'm a lifelong naturist, so I might evangelize about the benefits of the lifestyle."

"That would add a delicious temptation to our gossip," said Susan. "But if we actually did it and my mother found out, she'd freak."

"Is you mom a prude?" Emma asked.

"Yeah," said Susan. "But mostly she's just afraid I'll turn out lesbian like one of my cousins. I haven't come out to her, but I've made provocative comments, and she's afraid to flat out ask me."

"Naturism is not about sexual identity," said Emma. "It's about being a free human being."

"Yeah well, until I'm on my own, I won't be free to be who I truly am," said Susan. "I really admire my cousin, if you know what I mean."

Emma nodded in understanding.

"You can back out," Susan said. "Having to wear clothes is a decent excuse."

"Of course I won't back out. Why in the world would I do that?" Emma responded. "And if you like, someday I'll invite you over to my house for a swim."

"Thanks. But I can swim at my place," Susan replied.

"Without a bathing suit?" Emma asked.

"I see what you mean," Susan said. "Would my mom need to know?"

"Nope," said Emma.

Susan produced a broad smile.

"But it would probably be coed, with my brothers around," Emma added.

"Not a problem," said Susan. "No temptation or threat on that score."

At the sleepover, Emma learned from the Xavier girls that one of their teachers had given an extensive lecture on the evils of **Harry Potter**. "Most of the teachers are great, but there is this one who is right out of the Dark Ages," said one of them.

"There's always one at every school to spoil the educational experience," said Susan.

"For a Catholic school, you'd think we'd be taught as if it was the fifties or something," said the other. "But overall, we get a pretty rigorous college prep education."

"I hope one day the literature of J. K. Rowling will be included in every high school curriculum," said Emma. "It's vitally important for the emotional development of adolescent boys and girls."

"What has it done for you?" asked Susan's fourteen year-old sister Zane.

"Well, I have consciously developed Hermione as a role model and therefore have never questioned whether it was bad for a girl to be smart.

The idea of playing dumb or helpless to attract a boy seems ludicrous to me, and I credit Hermione for at least part of that," Emma explained.

"I would give credit to the feminist movement," said Susan. "But HP certainly reinforces the equality of the sexes. And I think you have more self-confidence than most sixteen year-old girls. Sometimes I think of you as Hermione with a BlackBerry instead of a wand."

"Wow! I take that as a real compliment," said a blushing Emma.

"I like that image," said Zane. "Hermione with a BlackBerry. Cool!"

As the slumber party extended into the middle of the night without any actual slumbering, Emma spoke about naturism and the naturist church she belonged to. "I don't suppose the Natural Christian Church has come up in any of your religion courses at Xavier," she said.

The Xavier students agreed simultaneously that it had not.

"I think we should get naked," said Zane.

"Mom would kill us," said Susan.

"She'd kill you, maybe," said Zane. "Because she suspects you might be queer. But she knows I like boys."

"No, she'd kill us both," said Susan gravely. "And she's as snoopy as Scotland Yard. So whatever we do, we better have our stories aligned."

In the end, they adopted a modified form of sleepwear, removing their panties and pajama bottoms, thus being nude from the hips down, but had a sheet ready to cover themselves if Mrs. Sinew should decide to investigate. But she did not, and the girls reported for a late Saturday morning breakfast fully dressed.

The next weekend, Susan and Zane came to Emma's house for an early evening swim. Jared, home from college for the weekend, and Cameron joined the three females in the water and then participated in **Harry Potter** related repartee as they dried off in lounge chairs.

"This has been great fun, but we'd better head home," said Susan as 9:00 approached.

Zane and Susan donned their panties, jeans, tee shirts, and sandals and stuffed their unused bathing suits into a tote bag.

"If I were you," said Emma, "I'd dip your suits into the pool, wring them out by hand, and take them home wet."

Susan gasped. "Absolutely. Thanks for having a devious mind, Emma."

As the summer unfolded, Susan and Zane walked the four

meandering blocks to the Round home once a week or so for skinny-dipping, always remembering to dip their suits in the pool before going home. On several occasions, Emma spoke in more depth about her family's membership in the Natural Christian Church.

"When you first mentioned it at the slumber party, I didn't believe there actually was a church where people go ***naked***," Susan said. "You are such an expert with fantasy literature, I thought you were just spinning a tale to shock the Xavier girls. Or maybe teasing me because I go to a conservative church."

"She's not," said Cameron. "The church is real."

"You're welcome to come along with us some Sunday morning," Emma said. "You, too, Zane."

"We can't," Susan explained. "We belong to the Community Church of Evangelical Blessing, and mom makes us go every Sunday unless we're physically sick. I tried telling her I was sick of the preaching once, but it would be an understatement to say that she did not accept that excuse."

"I've heard of them," said Cameron. "It's one of those mega-churches that brag about having a gazillion members or something."

"More like 5000," said Zane. "They make a big deal out of feeding the 5000 on the word of God."

"They're big into publicity. I call them the Community Church of Entertaining Bigotry," Susan said. "The church is officially opposed to LGBT people, to the point of refusing to acknowledge that such people exist. It's funny though, because the preachers spend a lot of time railing against sodomy and other abominations and the so-called gay lifestyle. So their denial of our existence is completely illogical."

"Well, our church is open to all people regardless of sexual identity," said Emma. "Several of our pastors here in Arizona are gay, and have been ordained for a long time. And we've been doing same-sex weddings for decades, even though they're not legal."

"I find that as hard to believe as that you go to church naked," said Susan.

"Once again, it's completely true," said Cameron. "Maybe if you told the pastor at your community church that you're gay, they would boot you out, because you don't really exist."

"That's not helpful," Zane responded. "Mom and Dad would boot her out of the house and refuse to help with college expenses."

"I'm going to tough it out till I start college, and hopefully I'll be far enough away to stop going to church," Susan said. "The only problem is that Mom wants me to go to a Christian college in Texas that has mandatory chapel attendance. She might compromise and let me go to Grand Canyon University, but then I'd have to commute to campus and keep going to the bigots' church on Sundays."

Emma didn't know what to say, so she nodded in sympathy. Eventually she mumbled, "I'm sorry."

"Yeah, it's no fun having religious Dursleys for parents," Susan said.

"Speaking of which, how do your parents feel about you reading **Harry Potter**?" Emma asked.

"They know about it and don't like it, but they tolerate it as long as I never mention the books in the house," Susan said.

"Susan and I talk about HP stuff when they're not around," added Zane. "But we can get in sly allusions in front of them, because they've never read the books. Like, one time I asked Susan to pass the mashed potatoes, and she said, 'What's the magic word?' And I gave her a huge thumbs up before saying please."

"Mom and Dad had no idea that we were acting out a **Harry Potter** scene," said Susan.

"And they think I have a friend at school named Olive," Zane said with sly inflection. "Sometimes I'll say something like, 'I **wander** what **Ollivander** family are doing this weekend.'"

"My dad watches Fox News exclusively, so I'll say something like, '**Phoenix** weather was mentioned again today on **Fawkes** News,' and they don't get that we're deliberately yanking their chains," Susan added.

"You guys are so bad," said Cameron. "I love it!"

"I wish there were some way we could get you to come to our church," Emma mused. "Then you'd be able to see what a truly open and progressive church is like."

"When I finally get to quit church, I'll be gone for good," Susan said. "I don't believe any of it, the doctrine, the creeds. I used to, but I don't anymore. When I make my break, I'll never go back to any Christian church, no matter how progressively they package their beliefs."

Emma bowed her head and said nothing.

"But if you ever hear of a Harry Potter church, let me know," Susan added.

Emma, Cameron, and Zane laughed heartily.

"If they do that, I'll be in line in front of you," Emma said to Susan.

At the start of her junior year, Emma came home from school with sports news. "They're starting a fencing club, and I want to join it," she told Hannah.

"That sounds dangerous," said Hannah. "You already have a track record of broken bones and such. Are you sure that's wise?"

"Broken bone - singular not plural," Emma responded.

"Knock on wood," said Hannah.

"I really want to do it, Mom. It'll help me become less of a klutz," Emma said. "Please? I brought home a permission slip."

"Complete with a liability waiver, I notice," said Hannah. "We'll confer with your father and see what he thinks."

At dinner, Emma raised the subject again.

David said, "Fencing is a prestigious sport. I give you credit for gravitating toward something with class."

"It's not the prestige that attracts her," said Hannah. "It's the closest thing to dueling with wands that she could find."

"Oh, yes, Mr. Potter and friends," David said. "What I want to know is how much the equipment will cost."

"It's all here in this information sheet," Emma said. She held her breath as David scanned the page, for the foil, mask, glove, and protective clothing were not cheap.

"Hmmm. Well, not as bad as I thought it would be," he said.

"It would be good for learning balance," Emma said. "And the coach said no one he's trained has ever broken a bone."

"That's good to know," said David. He looked at his wife. "What do you think? A good investment in Emma's physical fitness?"

"And self defense if it comes to that," Hannah replied.

Emma joined the fencing club, choosing the foil as her weapon. Her muscles ached from the long practice sessions, and she came home with circular bruises on her chest and abdomen more often than she liked.

Twice she sprained her ankles, once on each leg, and she badly bruised a kneecap, but these setbacks did not dissuade her from continuing with the sport. She was determined that the financial investment her parents had made in outfitting her would not be chalked up as a teenager's expensive passing fad.

At one practice session, as Emma waited in position for a bout to begin, another club member lobbed a stuffed fabric snake in front of her. "Talk to it Emma," she said. "Make it go after your opponent."

"Very funny," Emma said with disgust.

"Actually, it is funny," said her waiting opponent. "Except that any Potterhead would tell you that Hermione is not a parselmouth."

"Now *that's* funny," Emma said. With a flick of her foil, she lifted the toy animal and tossed it into the waiting arms of the practical joker.

As Emma returned to position, the snake lobber said, "*Touché*, Hermione!"

As a sophomore at Anasazi College in the fall of 2006, Jared began dating freshman Willow Black, whom he had liked since first meeting her at Uncle Henry's place. Willow and her mother Kiee lived in the caretaker's apartment there. Then over the Christmas break, Jared decided to come out to his family and friends. When he returned to school in January, he told Willow that he was gay.

Emma was surprised at Jared dating Willow but not surprised when he revealed his sexual orientation. Willow was not surprised either, and was quite happy to spend time with Jared as a friend, because she was more interested in Henry's son Jeff, although at the time, Jeff treated her like a little sister.

CHAPTER SIX
POTTER GEEK

Preceding the release of the seventh Harry Potter book in the summer of 2007, Emma Round was selected to join a tour of Potter experts to put on shows for Potterheads in bookstores throughout Arizona, demonstrating knowledge of every conceivable narrative detail in the series. They conducted trivia contests and awarded prizes for the best customer costumes.

The members of the tour billed themselves as the Order of the Potter Geeks. As Emma explained to a fan who questioned the nomenclature, "Geeks are advanced experts. Heads are fans in general. Only a small portion of Potterheads know enough to be considered Potter geeks."

"As part of the selection process, we had to take a tough trivia test," Charlotte Callum added.

"How tough? Give me an example of a question. I bet I can answer it," the fan responded.

"OK, who was the Minister for Magic before Cornelius Fudge took office?" Charlotte asked. "I was one of the few who got this one right."

The fan's face went blank. "Well that's really trivial. It's not important to the story," the fan said.

"But it is important to geeks," Emma said. "And for the record, I got it right too."

"Well, who was it?" the fan asked.

"Millicent Bagnold," replied Charlotte."

"And given the known chronology for Fudge, she must have been Minister during the time that Margaret Thatcher was Prime Minister of the UK," added Emma. "And considering Rowling's generous use of historical allusions and parallels, and knowing the dates of Thatcher's term in office, Bagnold was probably Minister for Magic on the night Voldemort killed Harry's parents."

"Wow! You guys really are geeks. I'd take my hat off to you if I was wearing one," the fan said.

"I'll give you another chance," Charlotte said. "What Christmas gift did the Dursleys give to Harry in **Chamber of Secrets** and why is it significant?"

"Are you just pulling out the most obscure bits you can find?" the fan said.

"This is a minor detail, but it may be important in the scheme of the narrative," Emma said. "Until we read the seventh book we won't know if it proves to be a foreshadowing."

"And what was it?" the fan said.

"It was a toothpick," Charlotte said. "And it was significant because of how it was delivered. What did Vernon Dursley hate coming in to his house?"

"Owls," said the fan. "I got one right."

"Which owl delivered Harry's toothpick?" Emma said.

"Oh, it must have been Hedwig," said the fan. "But that means that the Dursleys used magic, or at least a magical owl. Weird! Cool, but weird."

"Got there at last," said Charlotte.

Members of the squad were pressed to make predictions about what was to come. The most frequent question was whether Harry would live or die, followed by whether Snape would turn out to be good or bad. Emma's predictions proved correct on both counts.

At one venue after another, attendees posed arcane and difficult questions that had no canonical answers, such as: How did Hagrid get to the island, where Uncle Vernon had taken Harry to avoid all the Hogwarts letters, when he rescued Harry on his eleventh birthday? He said he flew, but surely he was too big for a broom, and his skill at magic was not advanced. And how did the Dursleys get off the island when Hagrid took their boat?

In *Goblet of Fire*, Mrs. Weasley got gold for him out of Harry's vault at Gringotts, which she told him after the fact. How did she get access?

Why would Barty Crouch, Jr. (posing as Madeye Moody) suggest to Harry in *Goblet of Fire* that Harry should consider becoming an Auror? Crouch had been caught by Aurors and would have no need to encourage Harry about the future, because he had already taken Harry into his confidence. And he was working a plan that would end Harry's life, so comments about Harry's future would be at best passive-aggressive taunting. Crouch as Moody also tells Hermione to consider becoming an Auror. Why, then, would Rowling choose to introduce the career of Auror to Harry and Hermione through Barty Crouch, Jr.?

Why couldn't Madame Pomfrey or one of the healers at St. Mungos correct Harry's eyesight? They can easily fix far worse conditions.

And what's the deal with Prefects? They are chosen in the fifth year and continue in that role for their remaining years. So does this mean there are Prefects in their fifth, sixth, and seventh years overlapping their tenures? Wouldn't they get in the way of each other?

According to *Goblet of Fire*, Voldemort lost his powers and his *body* when his curse backfired, though he remained alive in some spirit form. So, what happened to his body? Was it buried in the same cemetery as James and Lily? Or did it apparate into non-being? And what happened to Voldemort's wand? How did he get it back? There was plenty of speculation on the Web that Voldemort was blown to bits, so there was no body to dispose of.

Emma had a theory about Voldemort's wand. Since he had passed on the secret of the Potters' hiding place, Peter Pettigrew would have reason to hover around Godric's Hollow to see what would happen. Emma was sure that Pettigrew would have stolen in and grabbed the Dark Lord's wand from the rubble, and because it was a valuable artifact, hidden it in a safe place for future retrieval.

At nearly every show, someone would inquire about Harry's scar. Is Harry a Horcrux? Emma answered that she doubted that he was, because, she averred, making a Horcrux required purposeful intention.

Once in a while, someone would ask a question about Joanne Rowling rather than about her books. When that happened, the group usually turned to Charlotte, who was their biography expert. Charlotte had a favorite anecdote that she told again and again to the delight of the gathered Potterheads.

"In August last year, our favorite author was in New York on business," Charlotte would begin. "While there, she did a bit of work on the manuscript of what would become **Deathly Hallows**. For her return flight to London, she had with her the unbound manuscript, partly handwritten and with no backup copy of what she had put to paper while in New York. Our beloved TSA in New York stopped her at the security checkpoint and refused to let her carry it on the plane. Because of terrorist activity, officials in the UK had decreed that no hand luggage was allowed on flights to the UK, including books, newspapers, and eyeglass cases. The TSA advised her that those pages were thus prohibited, and she had to hand them over to be stowed in the hold.

"Now, would you want to hand such a precious item to strangers? Even if they promised to stow it with checked luggage? Well, J. K. Rowling took issue with their instructions and refused to part with the manuscript. Whether it was her strength of character or fame or probably both, the TSA relented and allowed her to keep the manuscript with her on the plane, but only after they had taken action to bind it securely so it could not be used as a weapon. That is, they wrapped it in rubber bands. Can you imagine the temptation that manuscript would have been for some poor baggage handler? Or how easily it could have been lost among all those suitcases? Thus the book we are all anxiously awaiting was preserved."

At this point in the account, Emma usually piped in with, "My theory is that the TSA officer in charge had children who were Potterheads and who would have been furious when the story of confiscating Harry Potter book 7 hit the news."

Emma enjoyed the thrill of searching for clues in the narratives and speculating about what they might portend for the yet to be published book. If she happened upon a plot development that struck a familiar chord or triggered an intuitive thought, she would spend hours pouring through previous volumes to find foreshadowing and nearly always found something.

Another member of the Harry Potter Geek Squad, Duncan Cooper, grew fond of Emma. Tall, klutzy, and shy, with a bushy mop of brown hair, Duncan would begin his sophomore year at ASU at summer's end. A week into July, he decided to risk altering their friendship.

"Hey Emma, the **Order of the Phoenix** movie opens on the eleventh," he said.

"Of course it does," she said. "Everybody knows that."

"Do you wanna go with me to see it?" he asked.

Emma paused to consider what he had said. "As in a date?"

"Yeah, as a date," he answered. "But if you'd rather...that is, if you're not allowed to date college men, we could go as friends."

"Yes, I'd love to go with you – as a date," she said.

This would be her first date with one person. To this time, Emma's peer socializing had been with groups of friends. Because she knew that her mother would have reservations about her going out with someone in college, even though Duncan was only two years older, she told her parents only that she was going with a friend from the Order of the Potter Geeks, not mentioning that it was a date.

During the scene where Harry and Cho Chang kiss, Duncan reached over and took hold of Emma's hand. She did not resist. After the show, while driving to a restaurant, Emma and Duncan dissected the film.

"There are parts of it that are very well done," she said. "But overall, it suffers from what it left out."

"Right," Duncan said. "Of all the movies so far, this one has the weakest screen play."

"Spot on," said Emma.

Their second date was to watch **Order of the Phoenix** a second time, searching for details and insights they overlooked the first time. As they left the theater parking lot, Duncan said, "I was thinking about **Half Blood Prince**."

"The movie?" Emma said. "Do you know when it's due out?"

"No, the book," he replied. "I was thinking about one of its recurring motifs. I'd be in favor of practicing some of it."

"What do you have in mind?" Emma asked.

"Snogging," he said.

Emma was pleased with this development and said, "Well, you'd better find a secluded place to park if we're going to snog. I want more than a peck on the lips like you gave me at my door last time."

Duncan had already thought of a place to park, and he quickly drove to it. Their kissing was exuberant and involved bodily caresses by both sets of hands as well, but Duncan made no attempt at anything that involved removal of clothing.

<><><>

At the Borders bookstore in Chandler, an avid fan challenged Emma to make a guess about the most unexpected death in the forthcoming *Deathly Hallows*.

"Considering that J K Rowling has made ample use of the foreshadowing technique, I suspect that Dobby will sacrifice his life for Harry," Emma responded.

"Oh, no way!" said the fan. "Absolutely not! That's not gonna happen! What could you possibly find to foreshadow that?"

"Well," said Emma, taking on Hermione's voice, "At the end of *Chamber of Secrets*, Harry asks Dobby not to try to save his life ever again. And Dobby just smiles but does not reply. No promise. That has to be significant."

The fan gasped and said, "Oh that's perverse. God I hope you're wrong."

"If I'm right, it's only because of how carefully J. K. Rowling planned out the entire series in advance," Emma explained. "From the very beginning, even before she had written the first book, she knew how it would end. Knowing that makes it easy for the author to plant clues along the way."

An elderly man with a white beard asked about the death of the headmaster. "Is Dumbledore really dead? If so, do you think he will be resurrected? Is he a Gandalf figure?"

"That's another big question," Emma said. "A lot of people don't believe that he is really dead and will reappear through some magical means. After all, his pet and his Patronus are symbols of resurrection -a phoenix. Personally, I don't think so. Making Dumbledore another Gandalf is too derivative. It's not Rowling's style. I think he is dead. But I suspect in death he will play a role in what is to unfold for Harry. His presence will be felt in *Deathly Hallows*."

As she discovered on July 21, when the conclusion to the epic was released, Emma was right regarding the demise of both Dobby and Dumbledore, satisfyingly so regarding the headmaster and unhappily about the elf. She was utterly wrong, however, in her guess that the last novel would reveal that Professors Dumbledore and McGonagall had been in a discreet relationship for many decades. This was simply something that Emma wished for, though it was unsupported by any clues or foreshadowing.

Emma did not wait in a line for the midnight opening of a big box bookstore to get a discounted copy, but arrived at 8:00 a.m. at the

Quirky Edges Book Shoppe in central Phoenix to retrieve two copies that her Aunt Sheba had set aside for her. Sheba was assistant manager of the independent store. Emma had to pay cover price, as the indie establishment could not sustain the loss-leading discounts of the big stores, but saving a few dollars on a book by J. K. Rowling was not important to her. Thus, Emma was rested from a good night's sleep when she began to read the story that would sell 11 million copies that first day of release, becoming the fastest selling book of all time.

Harry's embarrassed discomfort when six of his friends, by means of Polyjuice Potion, transfigured into the form of his body and then casually commented on aspects of his bare anatomy disappointed Emma. She thought that scene was perfect for Rowling to affirm the goodness of the human body, but the author had other ideas and knew the behavior of her character better than Emma did. Yet Emma did not remain perturbed for long, as she devoured the engrossing conclusion to the magical epic.

Emma's faith in **Harry Potter** was rewarded at the climax in chapter thirty-five, where she experienced sublime pleasure and gratification with the nature of Harry's ethereal nude scene. "J. K. Rowling got it right, of course," she crowed. "We shall enter the next life naked, the same way in which we entered this one."

The next day, Emma laughed out loud when her father wordlessly handed her the editorial page of the Arizona Republic. It featured a Steve Benson cartoon showing President Bush proclaiming, "I have read the final report from my top expert and I will be implementing his recommendations against the evil-doers." The president was holding up a book titled **Harry Potter**.

Though she expected the relationship outcome of Harry marrying Ginny and Ron marrying Hermione, the epilog to the seventh book left her unsatisfied. Knowing that there were Internet communities devoted to considering various relationships between members of the cast of characters in the **Harry Potter** universe, Emma searched the web for a suitable shipping site. Shipping had become the Millennial generation's group term for developing or promoting relationships among several of Rowling's characters.

Deep in her psyche, Emma continued to be a Hermione-Harry shipper, although when pressed, she grudgingly admitted that Harry and Ginny made a good match. Now she thought that Ron and Lavender belonged together, a shift from her earlier assertion that Ron and Luna were a good fit, but that had been after having read only five of the books. She declared, over and again that Ron and Hermione would end up divorced. She minimized the developing romance between Hermione and Ron, that was clearly evident from book four onward, relegating it to a necessary plot device regarding alchemy (the quarreling couple), but not a healthy relationship in real life, because they were not equal partners.

As to the Draco-Hermione shippers she encountered in this chat room, she felt disgusted, in her mind labeling them as sick, although out of a sense of courtesy she did not say so online.

After exploring a number of other shipping sites, Emma discovered that there were also Harry and Ron shippers, which though completely non-canonical, she tolerated because, she decided, gay men need their fantasies too. Another gay fantasy shipping subject was called MWPP: Moony, Wormtail, Padfoot & Prongs. That didn't bother her, but she objected strenuously to Snape and Harry shippers, because Snape was an adult and Harry a minor. That's criminal, she declared, and so is Snape-Hermione shipping. It's beyond sick.

The deeper she surfed into shipping groups on the Internet, the more things she found that disturbed her. The worst of these was a subgroup of incest shippers, fantasizing about sibling and parent-child sexual relationships.

A feminist blogger in the shipping group Emma used most often posted a rant that Emma found intriguing:

"None of the male characters are true equals of Hermione -certainly not Ron and intellectually not Harry. Perhaps some under-developed character from Ravenclaw might do for her, but, alas, there is no canonical support for this. I am thoroughly disgusted with the way Hermione settled for a lesser person. The weaknesses of the male characters are realistic, as are some of the females, but the series is in need of stronger female characters. Even Hermione needs to grow some eggs about deferring to boys. As much as I hate to say it, J. K. Rowling has not advanced the feminist cause."

This argument stayed with Emma, resonating within her psyche, though she did not feel angry about how the characters were portrayed and thought that Rowling was a positive force for feminism.

One day, while surfing the web for new sites dedicated to shipping, Emma saw an ad with a photo of Emma Watson claiming to be the best site for Hermione lovers. She clicked on it and immediately realized it was click-bait. Multiple images of Emma Watson as Hermione and Alan Rickman as Snape were displayed in photoshopped romantic and pornographic poses. She moved the cursor to the top right of the screen to leave the page and found it frozen.

"Effing hell!" she spat out. After a minute of repeated clicking on the X, a message popped up advising her that a malicious script was operating, and she moved the cursor to select the stop script option.

"That's it," she yelled at the screen. "I'm done with shipping!"

CHAPTER SEVEN
SYLVIA

Emma continued to date Duncan Cooper as the summer waned, and their petting increased in intensity, although falling short of consummation. Once they had returned to their respective schools, however, Duncan stopped calling her. At first, she was disappointed, but as senior year activities and homework began to pile up, she felt glad for the relational respite. And she had made a new HP friend, who took up most of her social time.

Cameron was now a freshman, but rather than follow Emma to Pinnacle, he came out a winner in the lottery for new students and enrolled at his older brother's alma mater, the Arizona School for the Arts, majoring in music performance. He had a knack for picking up different kinds of instruments, reed, brass, string, and percussion. His interest in musical instruments had blossomed at age ten, when his former governess, Xandra MacUmberland, started teasing him for sucking his finger. Every time Xandra saw Cameron stick his finger in his mouth, she did the same with a theatrical flair and sound effects, which nearly brought the boy to tears. Hannah instructed Xandra to stop the mocking behavior, but she continued to do it whenever Hannah was not around. After three days of this, Cameron decided he would deny Xandra the opportunity to tease him and ceased the habit.

To compensate for the loss of oral gratification with his forefinger, Cameron took up the clarinet and later the trumpet, surprisingly becoming a master at both. He developed a taste for big band swing and imagined himself the new Benny Goodman or Harry James.

<><><>

Sylvia Fast and her family had moved to Phoenix from Southern California, transferring their NCC membership to the Phoenix congregation. Like Emma, she was a senior in high school, though not at Pinnacle. What guaranteed that Sylvia and Emma would become dear friends was that both were devotees of all things Potter. Sylvia was Emma's peer when it came to knowledge of the canon.

After church on Sundays, Emma and Sylvia would find a shady spot under an orange tree and drill each other on HP trivia and delve into implications and theories. They soon become inseparable friends, sitting together in church rather than with their respective families.

One day their conversation explored coeducational housing. At the Hogwarts infirmary and also St. Mungo's Hospital, people of both sexes were treated and housed in the same room. But the dormitories at Hogwarts were strictly segregated by sex, with boys unable even to enter the girls' sleeping areas (although not vice-versa). Why would opposite sex adults be housed in the same ward at St. Mungo's and children allowed to visit them, while children at school were puritanically separated, except in the infirmary?

Emma maintained that Rowling was either inconsistent on this matter or she deliberately made the customs of the wizarding world inconsistent. "You can't make the distinction that adults and children are treated differently, because adults and children of both sexes are housed together in the Hogwarts infirmary at the same time."

"Yeah, and the prefects have a coed bathroom," said Sylvia. "For all their insistence on propriety with their badges on, I'll bet at least some of the prefects have skinny-dipping parties in that pool."

"Wish there was a way to ask Myrtle," said Emma.

On another day, they discussed experiencing memories in the Pensieve. "You know what really bugs me," Emma said. "How can the person whose memory it is, and concomitantly those observing the memory in the Pensieve, see him or herself in the memory?"

"I know," said Sylvia. "The person with the memory would only see what his or her eyes would see and not be able to observe her or himself as a whole third person."

"Weird," said Emma. She looked across at Sylvia and squinted her eyes, seeing a silvery white aura radiating around her friend that was tinged with yellow or gold; Emma couldn't decide which.

"Why are you looking at me that way?" Sylvia said.

"Just something in my eye," Emma replied, feeling guilty for having been caught spying. She repeatedly winked in an exaggerated fashion. "I was trying to wink it out. It's gone now."

"I see," Sylvia said, but she did not believe Emma had anything in her eye. Instead, she interpreted the squinting as a peculiar gesture of affection, which she did not want to second-guess.

A third topic of discussion, on another Sunday, was psychological speculation. Sylvia said, "Barty Crouch, Jr. and Tom Marvolo Riddle both killed their fathers and idealized their mothers. Voldemort may have been angry at his mother for dying, but he revered her pureblood status and lineage. Do you think Rowling is hinting these arch-villains have Oedipus complexes?"

"I think you're onto something," Emma said.

One Sunday afternoon, Emma mentioned that she had watched *Harry Potter and the Philosopher's Stone* the previous night.

Sylvia responded: "Gotcha on that one. Unless you went to England to see it, you watched *Sorcerer's Stone*. Either that or you meant to say that you read it."

"Actually, I did watch *Philosopher's Stone*," Emma explained. "The altered title with Sorcerer was released only in the US and of all places India. Everywhere else in the world the first HP movie was titled using Philosopher."

"Yes, and we live in the US," said Sylvia. "And the British DVD format isn't compatible with ours."

"You are quite right about the European format," Emma said. "It's called PAL, and I do not have a converter or adapter or whatever you need to make a PAL disc compatible with NTSC format. But, NTSC is used in North America, and I happen to own a DVD of the film version released in Canada."

"Oh wow! You have to let me watch it," said Sylvia eagerly. "Is it very different?"

"Not much. The differences are in four scenes where Philosopher's Stone is said rather than Sorcerer's. First there's the trio in the library when Hermione finds Nicholas Flamel in a book. There is also a visual of the word Philosopher's on the page. Then the trio at the door of Hagrid's cabin, and then in the forest when Harry responds to a question from Firenze, and finally the scene where the trio go to McGonagall trying to find Dumbledore, and they say it's about the Philosopher's Stone. Everywhere else they just say the Stone."

"Still, it's more authentic, isn't it?" Sylvia responded. "It's the true version."

"It is indeed," said Emma. "And I thought you would want to see it." She reached for her purse and pulled out the DVD, handing it to Sylvia.

"I'll take good care of this," said Sylvia solemnly.

"I don't doubt it," said Emma, releasing a triumphant smile.

Fan fiction had become a huge enterprise in response to the *Harry Potter* novels, and for a period of several months, Emma surfed the Internet and read as much of it as she could tolerate. But the net was inundated with this material, and most of it, she thought, was poorly written. And though she felt confident she could do it better, Emma made a conscious decision not to get involved producing it.

According to a Wikipedia article that Emma found, *Harry Potter* fan fiction was, at that time, the most searched-for subject of this genre. Harry Potter fan fiction writers met in Internet forums, aired podcasts, attended conventions, and made tours, as well as stayed in regular contact with one another online.

FanFiction.net had nearly 500,000 *Harry Potter* related stories on its site. FictionAlley.org had more than 80,000 Potter stories and 20,000 Potter art works. HarryPotterFanFiction.com was reported to generate the most hits of all the Potter fan fiction sites.

In late 2007, Rowling indicated she would not take legal action against fan fiction writers posting on the Internet. According to her attorneys, this was subject to the provisions that the writer make clear that Rowling had no role in producing the material, that the fan fiction was not sold, and that the material not contain any racism or pornography. But Rowling directed her attorneys to send cease and desist letters to web sites that posted fan fiction of an adult nature.

An important part of deciding not to write fan fiction was that Emma was beginning to see herself as a serious literary analyst and exegete of the *Harry Potter* canon. In this, she was influenced by *How Harry Cast His Spell* by college professor John Granger, who described in detail the literary alchemy undergirding Rowling's plots and identified the extensive Christian symbolism in the books. Online, Granger billed himself as the Hogwarts Professor.

Emma kept up with developments in the Harry Potter universe through Mugglenet and the Leaky Cauldron websites. Thus she closely followed the news that J.K. Rowling had testified in New York in a lawsuit against Steve Vander Ark, a fan who was in the process of publishing *The Harry Potter Lexicon*. As long as Vander Ark's work was maintained as an online encyclopedia compiled by the fan, Rowling had no problem with it. But when he sought to publish it for monetary gain while including massive use of direct quotations to describe characters, places, spells, and more, Rowling and Warner Brothers filed a lawsuit against RDR Books. A related factor in the decision to take action was that Rowling had repeatedly stated that she intended to publish an encyclopedic companion to the HP books.

The case was heard on April 14, 2008. Five months later, the court decision, based on the law of fair use of copyrighted material, favored Rowling. New York Federal District Court Judge Robert Patterson wrote that the *Lexicon* "appropriates too much of Rowling's creative work for its purposes as a reference guide." Approval was granted in December for a revised and abridged version of the lexicon, which was released in January 2009 as *The Lexicon: An Unauthorized Guide to Harry Potter Fiction*.

Much of the HP material Emma found online, including fan fiction, consisted of fantasizing about the romantic relationships of various characters. To Emma's distress, Draco Malfoy and Severus Snape seemed to be very popular characters, and a number of fans enjoyed writing speculations about relationships that these two males would have with Hermione and Ginny.

"I gave up the shipping sites, but I can't seem to get away from it in fanfic," she lamented to Cameron.

"What's going on?" he replied.

"There seems to be a *Grease* kind of theme going on in *Harry Potter* fandom, where the innocent girls are attracted to the bad guys," she said.

"Who's writing it, boys or girls?" he asked.

"Both," Emma said.

"Bummer," Cameron said.

<><><>

Emma and Sylvia attended a Harry Potter Meet-up at the Phoenix Convention Center, where cosplay proved to be the norm. While there they each bought Hermione wigs, Gryffindor ties, and black robes. Both young women already owned Hermione's wand, the most expensive 15-inch replica that came in an Ollivander-like collector's box from The Noble Collection catalog. Sylvia also bought a pair of Harry Potter glasses with window glass.

"Now my glasses almost match yours," she said to Emma.

"Except that mine are prescription," Emma said.

"Let me try them on," Sylvia said. "I want to see how bad your eyes really are."

Emma slipped them off and handed them to Sylvia.

"Wow!" Sylvia said when she had put on Emma's glasses. "Your vision is every bit as bad as Harry's must be."

At the vendor table of a local artist, Emma saw a mirror the size of one that would hang on a bedroom door. This one, however, featured a handmade oak frame engraved and stained with "***Erised stra ehru oyt ube cafru oyt on wohsi.***"

"Ooh, the Mirror of Erised," she said while poking Sylvia, who was busy looking at fan art at the table across the aisle.

Sylvia turned around and peered at the mirror. "It's beautiful. Are you going to buy it?"

"I've already spent too much," Emma said. "I brought all my accumulated birthday and Christmas money and want to keep some in reserve."

Sylvia spoke to the artist. "Did you make this yourself?"

"Yes," he said. "A labor of love."

"How much do you want for it?" Sylvia continued.

"Two hundred dollars," he replied.

"It's definitely worth that much," Sylvia said. "Emma, how much do you have left?"

"A hundred and fifty dollars," she whispered but loud enough that the artist could hear.

"Cash?" the artist asked.

"Yes," Emma answered.

"I can let you have it for that, tax included, if it's cash. Two hundred if credit card."

"Do it, Emma," Sylvia said.

"OK, but then I'm broke, and if we want anything to eat, you're paying," Emma said to Sylvia.

"Deal," Sylvia responded.

Rather than carry it around, Emma arranged to pick up the mirror before leaving the convention hall.

As they continued to stroll around, Emma saw a pre-teen dressed as Hermione carrying a cheap replica of Hermione's wand with a flashlight tip, and felt a glimmer of disdain. She started to make a snide comment to Sylvia before silently reproving herself for being a snob.

When Emma reached home, Cameron asked her what the Meet-up had been like.

"There was this huge room filled with display tables and sales booths where they sold homemade wands, artworks, books, posters, artifacts, and costumes," she said. "I was tempted to buy the whole lot, so to speak, but unlike Harry's vault of gold, my resources were limited. Even so, I spent all the money I had on me. There were social activities for people to make friends. That's not my thing, and Sylvia was with me, so we skipped that aspect. But they had seminars on all sorts of HP themes and subjects. We went to one on shipping and came away just as disgusted as before.

"Cons often have special guests, who lead a seminar or two and give interviews to the local press. Phoenix didn't have a big name there, but I saw posters advertising cons in L. A. and New York with guest stars Matthew Lewis, Melissa Anelli from Muggle Net, and Andrew Slack, founder of the Harry Potter Alliance. "

"I'd love to meet Matthew Lewis," said Cameron. "I've never heard of the other ones."

"I think meeting any of these people would be a dream come true," Emma replied.

"So, what else?" Cameron continued.

"A funny thing," she said. "I noticed that most of the cosplayers were dressed as supporting or minor characters. Lots of Snapes,

Bellatrixes, Dobbys, Dracos, Voldemorts, and a handful of old men as Dumbledore. Hardly anyone was dressed as Harry and few were Hermione or Ron."

"What do you think that means?" Cameron asked.

"Perhaps dressing as Harry or any person of the trinity is some kind of religious taboo or breach of some pious norm," she said. "Or maybe cosplayers by temperament associate themselves with the darker characters."

Alone in her room at bedtime, Emma placed the mirror against a wall and stood back from it so that she could see the reflection of her entire body. Seeing nothing unusual, she squinted her eyes, the way she did when trying to see someone's aura, wondering if she could be able to see her own.

Emma had never told anyone that she saw auras and did not remember when or how she first discovered this gift. Hannah called it Emma's scoffer face, assuming that her daughter was passing judgment or expressing skepticism when she did it, and Emma did nothing to dissuade her mother from her false impression.

Now, when Emma squinted into the Mirror of Erised, she was unable to see her own aura. Through some mental or visual trick, she saw her own naked body but with the face of Hermione and wearing Harry's glasses.

Startled, she opened her eyes wide and stared into the reflecting surface, but now saw only herself as she actually was.

"I am definitely not going to tell anybody about this," she announced to the room.

After J. K. Rowling revealed that she had always thought of Dumbledore as gay, Jared celebrated by forming a fan club for gays on the campus of Anasazi College. He named it Gays in Dumbledore's Army and created its motto: Do ask! Do Tell!

By now, Emma had accumulated a large collection of Potter material. She owned copies of the books for reading and for maintaining in pristine condition. Although she had both the Scholastic and Bloomsbury editions, she only re-read the Bloomsbury books, because they were in her mind authoritative. She also bought Latin translations of the first two books, even though she had never studied the language.

Harrius Potter et Philosophi Lapis and *Harrius Potter et Camera Secretorum* were prominently displayed in her Harry Potter bookshelf. Bloomsbury had published the translations by Peter Needham, and when Emma discovered this fact, she simply had to own them. This led her to search Amazon for other foreign language editions, and she found far more than she could possibly afford.

Emma had always been a fanatic about dog-eared pages, broken spines, and other ways of damaging books, but with Rowling's works, she was even more careful. She agreed with Madam Pince about the horror of writing in books, but in one respect she behaved recklessly around her treasured tomes. Defying the librarian, Emma occasionally ate chocolate while reading. She was mindful and tried carefully not to stain any pages. But once when she snapped off a chunk from a bar of dark chocolate, a few small flakes fell onto the title page of **Chamber of Secrets**. Tiny smudges remained after she blew them off, and she cursed herself for carelessness. Luckily, it was what she thought of as a working copy that she had read five or six times. Still, she could mentally hear Madame Pince wailing that she had despoiled, desecrated, and befouled the book.

CHAPTER EIGHT
AUNT SHEBA'S GARDEN

Sheba was Emma's favorite aunt. This was not a difficult position to achieve, as her Uncle Henry's first wife wanted nothing to do with the entire Round family, and though his second wife, Beatrix, was a lovely person, Emma had not known her long enough to develop a close relationship. But Emma maintained that if she had a dozen aunts, Sheba would still be her favorite. The special bond they shared deepened when Emma reached her teens.

Sheba had been involved with drugs, sex, and the hippie movement in the late sixties and early seventies. She used marijuana and occasionally LSD but preferred peyote to LSD, because, she asserted, it was natural. She avoided cocaine, deeming it a drug for snobs, and heroin, because she had seen several friends die of overdoses. As for speed, she repeatedly told fellow hippies that she wanted to be mellow not manic. As a mature adult, she would take an occasional toke to be sociable, but that was her limit.

Though essentially clean for three decades, Sheba was no less bohemian, which appealed greatly to her niece. Sheba was also a piscatarian. Emma was drawn to this healthy philosophy of eating, but didn't like fish, preferring to ingest protein by means of chicken or turkey.

Bathsheba Round was born in 1951, an only child for seven years, until her unplanned but clearly favored brother David appeared on the scene. Several times she started but never finished college and never married. In her sober thirties, using an inheritance, she bought a house on Flower Street, at the north end of Phoenix College and decided to live the rest of her life in the two-bedroom red brick ranch house with a tall redwood fence in the back yard.

The exterior of Sheba's home in the Campus Vista Historic District of Phoenix did not attract visual attention. Built during World War II, when the nearby campus of Phoenix College was only a few years old, it blended compatibly with neighboring homes. Nothing about the place, from an outdoors perspective, would hint at the flamboyant décor of its interior. Sheba filled the rooms with bright, colorful pieces of art, displayed upon rainbow painted walls and dark stained heavy oak tables from Mexico. Emma loved to visit and savor the earthy, primitive furnishings, which contrasted with the carefully high quality but understated Danish Modern décor of her parents' home. Spending time in Sheba's wild and fragrant garden was a special treat for Emma.

Sheba worked for modest pay as assistant manager for Quirky Edges Book Shoppe, an independent retailer in central Phoenix, but her income was supplemented by an annuity from the trust her late parents had established. They had reduced her cash inheritance in favor of an annuity, because they thought she would blow it all on drugs and gifts to friends. Instead, she used the cash to buy a house outright, with no mortgage.

Sheba often wondered what her parents would have thought of her financial prudence. Her mother died of ovarian cancer in 1983, and to compensate for his grief, her father overate and ballooned in weight. He died of a heart attack nine months later while having sex with his secretary, who was trying to console him with her physical charms.

David did not get an annuity but a significantly larger cash share, which he cannily invested. Sheba, however, preferred not having to pay rent or a mortgage and was quite content to live modestly. Unlike her brother, gaining material wealth was not important to her. After the hedonistic extroversion of the drug-filled years, Sheba was quite happy to live in relative solitude, feeling lucky to be a survivor. Perhaps her greatest pleasure was influencing her niece Emma to deepen her liberal outlook.

While Emma was in high school, Hannah was reluctant to let her to go places alone with Sheba, not trusting her sister-in-law to behave in age-appropriate ways around her daughter. Her real concern was not her sister-in-law but Sheba's friends, whom she imagined to be a band of dangerous druggies. Nevertheless, Hannah didn't mind Emma visiting Sheba's house or sunbathing nude in her garden every once in a while. They weren't likely to get into trouble merely sunbathing in the backyard, Hannah reasoned.

On one such occasion, on a warm Saturday afternoon in early October, three months after the seventh **Harry Potter** book had been published, Emma and Sheba lay naked on lawn chairs surrounded by trellised vines in Sheba's backyard garden. Unsurprisingly, the subject of J. K. Rowling's novels arose. Working in a bookstore, Sheba had, for what she called professional reasons, read the whole series.

"They're good, brilliant even," Sheba told Emma. "But except for periodic snogging, the students wander through Hogwarts laden with sexual tension and no release. Not even a hint about self-pleasuring. And you'd think the faculty would be slipping into one another's beds from time to time, but they all seem to be celibates. That part is boring."

"Well, the books are about magic, not about sex," Emma defended.

"I always thought sex was magical," Sheba said.

Emma laughed. "Sorry to say that I wouldn't know from personal experience."

"That's a blessing," Sheba said. "You probably don't think so right now, but I suspect it won't be too much longer before you discover that particular kind of magic. And I'm just being my usual provocative self. Still, in all honesty, I really wanted the Hogwarts students to attend a sex ed class and ask about magical birth control methods. Maybe a Slytherin girl getting knocked-up or a Hufflepuff with chlamydia would add spice."

"You're not serious," Emma responded.

"Maybe I am," said Sheba. "What I'd like to know is how many students ended up going to see Poppy Pomfrey in the hospital wing with STDs."

"Speaking of sex ed," Emma said, "I've wondered about all the courses at Hogwarts that seem to be missing. There is no mention in any of the books about courses on magical literature, which is odd because Joanne Rowling majored in classic literature at Exeter. Except for translating ancient Runes, nothing is said about courses in foreign languages or the languages of non-human magical beings, although some characters speak other languages, such as French, Mermish, Gobbledegook, and Troll."

"The unspoken assumption is that the students have already learned the basics of reading, writing, and math by the time they arrive at Hogwarts," said Sheba. "But one can also assume that these are integrated into the magical course work, because long essays are required, for example. And advanced math would be part of studying astronomy. Or maybe even Potions, which is the magical version of organic chemistry."

"But where did Dumbledore and Barty Crouch learn all the languages they speak? Clearly there are implied means for post-graduation education for specialized careers," said Emma. "But they are never spelled out. No universities of magic mentioned."

"If they were, the books would have to be considerably longer," said Sheba.

"You say that as if it were a bad thing," Emma replied. "I say the longer the better! I want more!"

"I know the feeling," said Sheba, "but in this case, I think the books are just about right. And for what it's worth, what I like best about the world of Harry Potter are the misfits."

"Misfits?" said Emma.

"Lots of them," said Sheba. "I resonate with misfits. I *appreciate* them."

"I'd never thought of the characters in that way," said Emma. "I just think of them as representing diversity. Tell me more."

"The best of the good guys all have problems, stigmas, or are not among the social elite of the wizarding world," Sheba said. "Many members of the Order of the Phoenix and the most ardent members of Dumbledore's Army are odd lots, outsiders, misfits, underdogs, half-breeds, or bumblers. Remus Lupin, Arthur and Molly Weasley, Hagrid, Mundungus Fletcher, Tonks, Sirius Black, Madeye Moody, Neville Longbottom, Luna Lovegood. Need I go on?"

"I see what you mean," Emma responded.

"Since you go to church regularly, surely you can see the parallel between the disciples of Dumbledore and the disciples of Jesus," Sheba continued.

"I must have missed that," Emma said.

"Take a look at the outcast band involved with Jesus," Sheba explained. "They came from the edges of society, an odd lot of unlettered fishermen, a tax collector, a Samaritan woman, a zealot, and so on. Blatant sinners for certain. They say that Mary Magdalene was a prostitute, but I don't believe that for a minute. Still, she challenged the gender norms of her society. Hold on a second."

Sheba rose from her lawn chair and dashed into the house, returning a minute later with a copy of **Goblet of Fire**. "I book-marked this passage, which I absolutely love. Listen to this. Hagrid is talking about Dumbledore. 'Dumbledore…trusts people, he does. Gives 'em second chances…tha's what sets him apar' from other heads, see. He'll accept anyone at Hogwarts, s'long as they've got talent. Knows people can turn out okay even if their families weren'…well…all tha' respectable. But some don' understand that.'"

"That part always makes me tear up," said Emma. "You're right. Dumbledore's ability to see the possibilities in people does relate to Jesus accepting tax collectors and sinners and his ability to see the goodness in people, such as the Samaritan woman at the well."

"And if that isn't enough to make the case, both Jesus and Dumbledore received a great deal of criticism because of their openness to people," Sheba said.

"Oh yeah," said Emma. "Like Jesus healing the leper and Dumbledore helping Remus Lupin!"

"Right," said Sheba. "From the first, I've thought of Remus as a leper symbol. You know, someone with a dreaded disease who's an outcast. Something people are afraid of, like HIV."

"He was infected by a werewolf and was shunned by society because of it, but Dumbledore accepted and defended him," said Emma.

"Not only that but let him serve openly in the Order," added Sheba.

Emma visited her aunt on a Saturday afternoon when Sheba was in one of her occasional clean-out-the-place moods. The living room was strewn with cardboard boxes of many shapes and sizes. Sheba answered the door with a box cutter in her right hand.

"Come on in and make yourself useful," Sheba said. She brushed hair out of her face with her left hand and used the box cutter as a pointer to a pile of cardboard pieces in the kitchen. "Those need to go in the recycling bin. And there will soon be more to follow."

"No prob," said Emma. Gathering an armload from the pile, she made her way from the kitchen to the back porch and through the screen door into the yard. She dropped the cardboard on the ground so she could open the bin, noticing as she did that it was already half full. After adding more material, she left the lid open in anticipation of her next load.

The pile in the kitchen that Emma had drawn from for her first trip to the recycling bin had grown from Sheba's cutting.

"Where did you get all these boxes?" Emma asked her aunt.

"Oh, they just accumulate over time," Sheba said. "I can't stand to throw away nice looking boxes, but eventually they take over the house, and I get in a nasty mood to cut them to pieces and offer them to the god of recycling."

A dull screeching that sounded like an animal in panic came from the backyard, and Emma went out to investigate. The lid was closed on the recycling bin, and the noise emanated from inside it. Emma stood to the side of the blue plastic container and warily lifted the lid. Whatever was inside, she expected, would be leaving by the front.

But the feral cat that had entered with enough energy to knock the lid closed did not exit according to Emma's expectations but rather hissed and jumped at Emma, scratching her shoulder and chin in the process before leaping onto the closed lid of the adjacent green garbage bin, continuing to the ground, and running away.

Sheba had followed Emma into the yard. "A neighborhood stray. Let me look at you. Hmmm. Not much damage here. You're barely bleeding." Sheba used her index finger to draw a circle around the claw marks on Emma's shoulder. "Well, maybe a bit more than barely right here."

"I was due for some more scars to add to my pitiful collection," said Emma.

"Let's go inside so I can clean these and squeeze on some disinfectant."

"What fun," said Emma, her voice laden with sarcasm.

Once cleaned and dressed, Emma's wounds proved to be minor.

"I'm sure these will disappear soon enough," Sheba assured Emma. "No new permanent scars from this misadventure with the cat in the bin."

"Does that cat have a name?" Emma asked.

"If so, I don't know it. But from now on, I'll call him Professor Binns."

Emma groaned. "Not Mad Eye?"

"No, that would be merely an allusion," Sheba responded. "Puns are of a higher order."

"Yeah, historic," said Emma.

<><><>

On another sunbathing occasion, Emma told Sheba about the American name for ***Harry Potter and the Philosopher's Stone***. "Arthur A. Levine edited the Harry Potter books for Scholastic. With the first book, Harry Potter and the Philosopher's Stone, he did major editing, eliminating many British words and substituting American idioms and vocabulary. The first two books in the series suffered the most from this heavy-handed retranslation into American English, thus oddly putting American expressions into the mouths of British school kids."

"If I'm reading English literature, I prefer British vocabulary and spelling," said Sheba.

"Levine also decided that Americans would not buy a book with the word philosopher in the title and thought sorcerer was a more intriguing word," Emma continued. "I think, because J. K. Rowling was a newly published author, she wasn't in a position to argue the point, and she came up with sorcerer as a substitute. It could have been even worse, I guess. ***Harry Potter and the Magical Rock*** or something. The problem is, the Philosopher's Stone in the title is associated with the ancient practice of alchemy, and the first book is specifically about alchemy. In fact, all the Harry Potter books are steeped in the tradition of literary alchemy, as used by the likes of Shakespeare and Dickens. So Levine trampled on an important marker of what the books were about, as well as underestimated the intelligence of the American audience."

"At least her British editor didn't have a philosophical problem with the title," Sheba quipped. "Do you know who that is?"

"Yes, Barry Cunningham. And I'm so grateful he was smart enough to pick up the book for publication," said Emma. "But I still have a couple of bones to pick with him. To begin with, he's a bit of a sexist."

"How so?" Sheba asked.

"He told her to use her initials as the author to disguise that she was female," Emma explained. "He thought boys wouldn't read the book if they knew a woman wrote it. That doesn't say much for his opinion of his own sex either."

"How quaint. In my day we would have called him a male chauvinist pig," Sheba responded. "Of course, that puts Rowling in the same literary deception boat as Pamela Lyndon Travers," Sheba said.

"Who's that?" Emma said.

"P. L. Travers. The woman who wrote all the ***Mary Poppins*** books," Sheba said.

"Oh yeah, I've heard of those," said Emma. "Before my time, though."

"Actually, they're quite witty," said Sheba. "Darker than the movie Disney made. If you're bored some afternoon, get a *Poppins* from the library. You'll be pleasantly surprised."

"Anyway," said Emma, returning to the subject of publishing *Philosopher's Stone*, "Joanne Rowling didn't have a middle name. Apparently some parents just assume their daughters don't need one because of using their maiden names when they marry. Bad assumption as far as I'm concerned. So Jo had to invent a middle name. She chose Kathleen after a paternal grandmother. That's how J. K. Rowling was born, or more accurately manufactured."

"Don't take it so personally," said Sheba. "A lot of good authors, women and men, have used pen names."

"I know, but in this day and age, you'd think they wouldn't have to anymore," said Emma. "Another thing is that he pared down the Sorting chapter, in the process eliminating all mention of Dean Thomas. This is a rare instance of the American edition being more authentic, because Scholastic kept Dean's sorting into Gryffindor."

"OK, while we're busy criticizing editors, let's have some fun," Sheba said. "Since Levine changed the name of the first book for the lowbrow American audience, let's make up American names for the rest of them."

"Cool!" Emma responded. "The American title of *Chamber of Secrets* should be *Harry Potter and the*...what?" She pondered for a moment before pronouncing, "*the None of Your Business Room*."

"Good one," said Sheba. "I was going to suggest *Harry Potter and the Place Where the Snake Hides*."

Emma laughed. "*Prisoner of Azkaban* is pretty straight forward. How can we simplify it? How about *Harry Potter and the Escaped Convict?*"

"*From some place no one ever heard of,*" Sheba added.

"Right," Emma responded. "For *Goblet of Fire* we might Americanize it to *Harry Potter and the Flaming*...no, too literary...*the Burning Wine Glass*."

"*My turn,*" said Sheba. "It was my idea, after all. I think *Order of the Phoenix* should be changed to *Harry Potter and the*...*Bird Club*. How's that?"

Emma giggled as she flipped a bird at her aunt, who returned the gesture. "I take that as positive affirmation," Sheba said. "You can take a stab at *Half Blood Prince*."

"I've got one," Emma replied. "*Harry Potter and the Mongrel Wizard*."

"Not simple enough for Americans," Sheba said. "You need something like *Harry Potter and the Fake Royal Guy*."

"Yeah, that's better," Emma admitted. "For *Deathly Hallows* I think maybe *Harry Potter and the Halloween Ghosts* would be more suitable for American readers."

"Well done!" Sheba shouted. "And this gives me an idea. Do you think there's a market for the Bloomsbury editions in the United States?"

"Absolutely!" said Emma. "I paid big bucks to Amazon.uk to have them shipped across the Pond."

As a result of this conversation, Sheba researched sources and ordered ten sets of the Bloomsbury *Harry Potter* books from a book wholesaler in Ottawa to sell at Quirky Edges. Emma volunteered to do a talk at the store about differences between the British and American editions and to call her Harry Potter friends and let them know about it.

"We won't be able to offer a discount," Sheba explained to Emma. "And what with the price on the covers in pounds, we'll probably end up charging a little more than list price to compensate for shipping costs."

"It won't matter to the people who want them," said Emma. "They'll pay a premium without batting eyelashes."

She was right. A dozen people, including Sylvia, gathered for her presentation, and all ten sets sold within fifteen minutes of her finishing it.

"We'd better order more," said a pleased Sheba to Emma. "The owner is really happy. Could you do another Harry Potter thing? I think I could get the owner to pay you something to do it. Of course, we'd need proper publicity."

"Sure," said Emma. "And I won't need to be paid for it. It's a labor of love."

"And I'll join in too," said Sylvia. "I'm sure we can pull off some really dazzling wordplay in costume."

<><><>

Emma's high school graduation gift, in the summer of 2008, was a trip to the United Kingdom, where she and Sheba toured various sites connected with the **Harry Potter** books and films. After arriving at Heathrow Airport, they took a taxi into London to their hotel in Bloomsbury. On the agenda were visits to King's Cross Station, Paddington Station, Charing Cross Road, and Tottenham Court Road. They wandered on foot through the Bloomsbury area and visited the British Museum.

Happening upon a shop for used and rare books a block from the museum, Emma told the clerk she was searching for items related to Harry Potter.

He eyed her thoughtfully for a moment before saying, "You don't strike me as the typical Potter fan. How serious are you?"

"She's quite serious," Sheba said. "A budding scholar, in fact."

"Well then, I have something that might interest you. Follow me please, miss." He led Emma and Sheba to a locked glass-front cabinet, pulled a key from his pocket, and pushed it into the lock.

"Whatever you have must be expensive if you keep it in there," Emma said nervously. "I may be a scholar, but I'm on a limited budget."

"Not to worry," he said. "Not to worry at all. We well know the life of the impecunious scholar. Not everything locked is monetarily costly, but dear in other ways."

The clerk withdrew a thick paperbound book and placed it in Emma's hands. Its title was **Culpeper's Complete Herbal** by Nicholas Culpeper.

Gazing at the cover, Emma said, "This must have something to do with either Herbology or Potions."

Pleased to see her make the connection so quickly, the clerk said, "Correct. Both, in fact. This is a reprint of the 1900 revision of Culpeper's original work of 1653. He was an English botanist, herbalist, physician, and astrologer. He was a brilliant man and known for holding less than appreciative opinions of other physicians, as well as priests and lawyers."

"Then this must be what J. K. Rowling used to research potions ingredients and such," Emma said.

"Indeed," the clerk said. "In the cabinet we also have rare editions of this fine work, but not within the range of a student's budget."

"How much is this reprint?" Emma asked.

"Ah, the straight-forward American. Wouldn't you like to leaf through it or heft it in your hands or breathe in the aroma of the pages first before descending to the bottom line?" the clerk said.

"I'll do all those things if I can afford it," Emma replied. "But I don't want to fall in love with a book I can't afford."

"Very wise," the clerk said solemnly. "This particular edition is…oh, I'll round it off at £20."

Emma immediately began paging through the book and quietly speaking aloud words that caught her attention. "Wormwood. Asphodel."

"She'll take it," Sheba said. "In fact, let's make it a gift to my favorite Potter scholar. I'll pay for it."

Emma looked up and said, "Thank you, Sheba. This is so cool."

"That's the latest academic slang," Sheba said to the clerk. "Everything in the realm of higher education these days is either so cool or way rad or I don't know what."

The clerk turned to Emma and said, "I expect great things from you, young lady. Wonderful and great things."

While in London, Emma and Sheba spent a pleasurable hour searching for the entrance to Diagon Alley, which from the Muggle world is reached through the Leaky Cauldron tavern on Charing Cross Road. Only witches and wizards can see the Leaky Cauldron situated between a bookshop and a record shop. Charing Cross Road runs up from St. Martin-in-the Fields Church across from Trafalgar Square to Oxford Street and is renowned for bookshops, new, second-hand, and antiquarian. A book lover like Joanne Rowling would naturally gravitate to Charing Cross Road when in London. Emma and Sheba looked for the presence of a bookshop and an adjoining record shop so they could at least pretend to see the door to the Leaky Cauldron, but without success.

And then they traveled by train and coach to Northumberland to see Alnwick Castle, which had been used for Hogwarts in the films.

Next they journeyed to Edinburgh to visit coffee shops where J. K. Rowling had hand-written much of the ***Philosopher's Stone.*** Sheba photographed Emma standing beneath a plaque on Nicolson Street identifying the site of the now closed Nicolson's Café, where the staff had allowed Rowling to nurse one cup of coffee for hours while she wrote. The plaque advised that Rowling had produced the early chapters of her first book at this place.

The Elephant House a short distance away also displayed a sign in the front window advertising itself as the birthplace of Harry Potter. Sheba dutifully photographed Emma next to this sign also. The signs Emma enjoyed the most, however, were the ones that advised, "J. K. Rowling never wrote here."

Departing from Edinburgh Airport, they flew to Toronto, and then on to Phoenix. Suddenly waking from an uncomfortable nap on the plane, Sheba turned to Emma and said, "My mind was flitting though strange territory just now. I was wondering why J. K. Rowling has such a fondness for names that end in *ey* and especially *ley*."

"I noticed that too," said Emma. "From the top of my head I remember Chudley, Dudley, Dursley, Finch-Fletchley, Kingsley, Weasley, and Yaxley."

"Without the *l* there are Creevey, Hokey, Pomfrey, and Trelawney," Sheba added.

When she got home, Emma went through her notes and found her list of characters. Counting through it, she discovered that Rowling had ended the names of 28 characters with *ey*, 16 of them *ley*. Gilderoy, Malfoy, and Troy were the only names ending in *oy* that she could find, and only Murray ending in *ay*.

CHAPTER NINE
THE HERMIONE TWINS

As soon as Emma returned from the UK, she called Sylvia to fill her in on all the details.

"I'm feeling restless," Sylvia said. "Why don't you come over, and then we can go somewhere. We can talk in the car on the way."

"Where do you want to go?" Emma asked.

"I don't know. Anywhere," Sylvia replied.

"Well, we could go to my aunt's bookstore, the Quirky Edges Book Shoppe," Emma suggested. "It's a fun place to poke around for unexpected treasures."

"Perfect!" Sylvia said. "Let's go in costume. We can be Hermione twins."

"I have a better idea," said Emma. "Let's cross-dress. Cross-character-dress, that is. We can be both Harry and Hermione."

"Even more fun, but how will we pull that off?" Sylvia responded.

"You have HP glasses, so we could put lightning bolt scars on our foreheads with eye liner to represent Harry, and we could wear Hermione wigs and carry her wand."

"Cool! And we could wear white blouses with Gryffindor ties and jeans and trainers," Sylvia said.

Sheba saw the pair of them as they strutted into the shop bearing wide grins.

"Well, well, well," said Sheba. "Are you two trying to make a statement of some kind?"

"Just having fun," said Emma. "Sheba, you remember Sylvia from my Bloomsbury edition talk, right?"

"Of course, and I remember that the pair of you haven't done that dazzling presentation you promised. We have the British volumes in stock now."

"Well, I was sort of busy traveling around the U. K. with you, Auntie," Emma said smartly.

"Now you have even more ammunition for a new talk," said Sheba. "But we should schedule a time for you two to do your literary thing. How about next Saturday?"

"Can't," Emma said. "We're going to a trivia contest then and need to study hard for it. No time to put together something for your shop."

"Yeah, we would want to do it up right for you," said Sylvia.

"For what we're paying you, I can't argue with your calendar," Sheba said. "How about the Saturday after that?"

Emma and Sylvia looked at one another for concurrence and then in unison said, "Sure. That works."

"In the meantime, do you have any new HP treasures in stock?" Emma asked her aunt.

"Nothing new, I'm afraid," Sheba said. "But after your plunder in the UK, I would have thought your budget was busted."

"It is," said Emma. "But Sylvia's isn't."

"Head over to the fantasy section. There might be one or two items that Sylvia would be interested in," said Sheba.

Poring through the shelves of fantasy literature was a red-haired Potterhead of high school age. When he saw the twin Harry-Hermiones approaching, he stood up and with accusation in his voice said, "What are you up to?"

"Having fun," Sylvia said. "Anything wrong with that?"

"I don't think it's right to cosplay more than one character at a time, that's all," he said.

"Not right or not fair?" Emma said.

"Both, I guess," he said. "And I'm not sure girls should pretend to be boy characters. I'd never dress up as Ginny, even though she's my favorite character."

"What about the seven Harry Potters?" Emma said.

"That's beside the point," the boy said.

"You are so Hufflepuff," said Sylvia. "Lighten up! We're making a social statement."

"Hufflepuffs are the salt of the earth," he said.

"True enough," said Emma. "But try to absorb a little of Dumbledore's ethos of toleration and acceptance, and you'll make Helga Hufflepuff proud."

"That is so Gryffindor," he said. "Gryffindors are good at breaking the rules in the name of social justice."

"I take that as a compliment," said Sylvia. "Thanks, Ginger."

"I've been called that before, and it doesn't bother me," he retorted.

"But you know, it must be against the rules for a ginger to have a thing for Ginny Weasley," Emma said.

"Kinky at the very least," said Sylvia.

Sheba walked over to see what was going on. "Everything alright?"

"It's fine," the young man said. "There's nothing new here since the last time I was in."

"I hope my niece and her friend weren't pestering you," Sheba said.

"Nope. They're just a couple of Hermos having fun," he said. As he departed, he turned and said, "Bye, Hermos."

"Bye, Ginger," the twins said in unison.

Emma and Sylvia had prepared well for the Harry Potter costume and trivia party on Saturday evening in Paradise Valley. Both dressed as Hermione (without the Harry additions) and took on the trivia challenge as the Hermione Twins. By luck of the draw, they would go last.

With only two teams remaining, the most any of the others had been able to answer was six questions in succession before missing one. The penultimate team, billed as the Trio, Two Guys and a Gal, had answered six correctly and were ready for the seventh.

"Excluding Harry Potter for technical reasons, how many specifically named Hogwarts students died while they were still enrolled at school? And what are their names?" the host said.

"I want to say four," said the gal. She looked at her male teammates who nodded. "Four," she reaffirmed.

"Correct; and their names?" said the host.

They conferred in whispers, and then the gal said, "Cedric Diggory, Vincent Crabbe, and Colin Creevey for certain. We're drawing a blank on the fourth at the moment. This is not our answer, but it might be Lavender Brown, except that the text says she was wounded but still alive. She might have died and the readers don't know it. There were plenty of unnamed dead at the battle of Hogwarts."

"I need an answer," said the host.

One of the guys whispered in the gal's ear, and she looked up and said, "Regulus Black."

"Is that your final answer?" the host asked.

"Yes," said the gal.

Emma looked at Sylvia and mouthed, "Moaning Myrtle."

Sylvia grinned.

"I'm sorry, Regulus Black is not correct," the host announced. "It is possible that he may have still been in school at the time of his death, but the indicators are that he had already left Hogwarts when he visited the cave with Kreacher, and there is no textual evidence to back up his being a student when he died. She turned to the assembly. "Anyone?"

A chorus of "Moaning Myrtle" filled the room.

All three of the Trio did face palms.

Emma and Sylvia would need seven correct to win.

Emma looked at Sylvia and grinned.

"OK," said the host, "we turn now to the Hermione Twins."

Emma and Sylvia shifted in their seats, ready for the challenge.

"We'll start with an easy one. Name the first train station mentioned in the series," the host said.

In unison, Emma and Sylvia shouted, "Paddington!"

"I wasn't done with the question," the host said. "Please wait until I look at you for a response. And a more subdued response would be appreciated."

"Oops, sorry," said Sylvia.

"To continue," the host said irritably, "name the book and the city of said station."

"Book one, *Philosopher's Stone*," said Emma.

"London," said Sylvia.

"Correct," said the host. "Staying with the subject of places, here is question number two. In addition to many fictitious places, Rowling has mentioned more than one hundred actual place names throughout the seven books. Only two, however, are cited in each of the seven books. Name them."

Sylvia looked at Emma and smiled. Emma nodded. "The first is the same as I answered in the previous question. London," Sylvia said in a sober voice.

"And the second is also related to the previous question," Emma said. "King's Cross Station."

"Correct! Now onto question three. Pensieve is an apt name for a device in which to see memories re-enacted, making association with the word pensive, meaning meditative, reflective, or contemplative. But it is also an anagram for a famous fantasy family. Name the family and the author who created them," the host said.

"Too easy," Sylvia responded without consulting her partner. "Emma and I were talking about this on the way here. The family name of the children in C. S. Lewis' **Narnia** novels is Pevensie, the letters of which rearrange to spell Pensieve."

"Correct! But the questions get harder as we go along, so don't get too smug," the host declared. "Counting Harry's scar, Voldemort created seven Horcruxes. Each was destroyed by the act of a different person. Name each Horcrux, who destroyed it, by what means, and which house the destroying person belonged to while in school."

Emma and Sylvia conversed quietly for a moment before Emma began their answer. "Harry, a Gryffindor, stabbed a basilisk fang into Tom Riddle's diary. That's one."

Sylvia said, "Dumbledore, who was a Gryffindor while in school, used the sword of Gryffindor to crack open the Slytherin ring. That's two."

"Ron, a Gryffindor, used the sword of Gryffindor on the Slytherin locket. That's three," Emma said.

Sylvia continued their response. "Hermione, a Gryffindor, used a basilisk fang to destroy the Hufflepuff cup. Four."

Vincent Crabbe, a Slytherin, created the fiendfyre that caused the destruction of the Ravenclaw diadem," said Emma. "That's five of them."

"And Neville, a true Gryffindor, used the sword of Gryffindor to kill Nagini." Sylvia said with a note of pride in her voice. "That's the sixth and last of the *intentional* Horcruxes." She turned to Emma and said, "You have the honor of naming the seventh."

Emma smiled with confidence. "And Voldemort, Slytherin of Slytherins, committed partial suicide by casting a killing curse which slew the Horcrux in Harry's scar."

"Well done," the host declared. "Here's your fifth question. With one exception, the names of students in the sorting ceremony are fictitious. Who is the real person, in which novel does this person appear, what house was this person sorted into, and why did J. K. Rowling do this?"

Sylvia took this one. "In *Goblet of Fire*, Natalie McDonald was sorted into Gryffindor. Natalie was a nine-year-old Canadian *Harry Potter* fan who was suffering from leukemia in the summer of 1999. She wrote a letter to J. K. Rowling, which reached the author after Natalie had died. Rowling communicated with Natalie's mother and decided to memorialize Natalie by including her name in the sorting."

"That's five correct," said the host. "One more right answer and you're tied for the lead. Here is your question. Because of the time-turner episode in *Prisoner of Azkaban*, where Harry and Hermione go back in time to rescue Sirius and Buckbeak, the day lasts 27 hours, making it literally longer than any other day in the series. This is also one of those rare times when Rowling specified the day of the month. What was the date that the time turner events occurred on, day, month, and year, and what is the historic significance of that date? Also, name the title and author of a famous book connected with this date."

"I'll take the first part, and you can do the second," Emma said to her partner. "This longest day was June 6, 1994, which happened to be the fiftieth anniversary of the Allied D-Day invasion of Normandy in World War II."

"It was commemorated in Cornelius Ryan's famous book, *The Longest Day*," said Sylvia. "Incidentally, the action on this particular day in *Prisoner of Azkaban* extends for 103 pages, the second largest number of pages in the series devoted to describing the events of a single day. The largest number of pages devoted to a 24-hour period extends from dawn on May 1, 1998 to sunrise the following morning. Rowling devotes 227 pages to the day that begins at Shell Cottage and ends with Voldemort's demise."

"Correct, but too much information," said the host. "I was planning to ask about the most number of pages devoted to a single day."

"Really? I'm sorry," said Sylvia.

"Not really," said the host. "I just like to puncture know-it-alls. Anyway, the Hermione twins are now tied for the lead. If you get the next question right, you win. Are you ready?"

Though the experience was more fun than serious, Emma's body tensed and her hands went cold. Her competitive instincts took control, and she focused on the challenge ahead. Sylvia experienced the same sensations as Emma. "We're ready," they said simultaneously.

The host gave a sly smile. "J. K. Rowling makes multiple references to the Wellington boots left outside on the lawn at the Burrow. These boots were named for the Duke of Wellington. What was the Duke's real name, and how does this represent a visual pun?"

Sylvia looked at Emma and whispered, "Do you know this one?"

Emma nodded and spoke aloud to the group. "The Duke of Wellington was Arthur Wellesley. Thus the boots make a nice pun on Arthur Weasley."

"Congratulations," said the host. "The trivia crown goes to the Hermione twins, Emma and Sylvia."

For the next hour, Emma and Sylvia basked in the praise of fellow Potter geeks. Friends pressed glasses of mead on Emma, but she declined, saying, "No thanks. I'm the designated driver. I'll stick with non-alcoholic butterbeer."

Sylvia imbibed what Emma declined, and both were in high spirits when they said their farewells and climbed into Emma's car.

"That was so much fun," Sylvia said. "I can't wait for the next party."

"They'll be gunning for us, though. We need more study. They'll be searching for incredibly obscure details," Emma said.

"Studying with you, Emma, is so much fun," Sylvia said. "Let's get started tomorrow."

Emma nodded in response.

"Of course, now that we're champs, it would be fun to ask the questions instead," Sylvia said. "I think we could come up with some mind-boggling trivia."

"I'd love to ask the one we talked about in church last Sunday," Emma said.

"You mean, who was the Hogwarts teacher who showed up in class without a stitch of clothing on?" Sylvia responded.

"Yeah," said Emma with a chuckle. "Or we might phrase it, what Hogwarts faculty member practiced naturism?"

"I can just see them mentally scrolling through images of naked professors," Slyvia said with a tipsy giggle.

"How long do you think it would take someone to think of Firenze?" Emma said.

"Centaurs certainly don't wear robes, do they?" Sylvia noted.

To drop Sylvia off at her home, Emma drove north on Tatum Boulevard, stopping at the red light at Shea Boulevard. As the car idled, Emma grinned broadly, visualizing a parade of naked professors and relishing the thrill of winning the contest. When the light changed to green, she responded automatically, moving ahead in her lane without taking note of surrounding traffic. When the car reached the middle of the intersection, a drunk driver on Shea cruised through the red light and T-boned Emma's car, propelling it into the empty westbound lanes ahead. The car spun and slammed against the curb but did not roll over.

CHAPTER TEN
THE TWIN WANDS

Sylvia, in the passenger seat, was killed instantly, and Emma was pummeled by the air bag and smashed her left leg against the door, causing the femur to snap. She also sustained three broken ribs and facial lacerations.

The driver of the other car, a 22 year-old white male, survived. When the ambulance arrived, Emma was transported to John C. Lincoln Hospital in Sunnyslope.

By the next morning, the effects of the pain medication had diminished and Emma regained consciousness. For a moment, she had no idea where she was or why her left leg was in traction, and then two things became evident simultaneously. One was acute pain in her chest, and the other was remembrance of the deafening sound of her car being struck and the feeling of being violently thrown against the car door while being simultaneously smothered by a giant pillow.

A familiar voice intruded into her thoughts. "She's awake. Emma, are you awake?" Her father's face appeared over hers. "How are you doing, Emma? We're all here." The faces of her mother, Jared, Cameron, and Sheba swam into view.

"Somebody hit us," Emma said. "How is Sylvia? I'm sorry the car is wrecked, Dad."

"Don't worry about the car," David said. "It's covered by insurance, and I've already engaged an attorney to handle the matter."

"I hope it's not one of those guys who advertise on TV," Emma replied.

"No, our attorney is so expensive he doesn't need to advertise," said David.

Then Emma realized he had not said anything about Sylvia, and cold dread spread through her body, numbing the physical pain while inducing the mental kind. "Is Sylvia dead?" she whispered.

Hannah took Emma's hand and said, "I'm so sorry, dear. They tell us it was instant. She did not suffer."

For some minutes Emma could not speak, as tears flowed freely into her pillow. Then she asked, "What about the other car?"

"He was drunk," said David. "A young man. He was treated and released, but he's in custody now."

"You have fractured ribs and a femoral shaft fracture," Hannah explained. "They're going to operate to nail it closed."

"Ouch!" said Emma.

That evening, after dutifully consuming most of her bland dinner, except the gelatin salad, which she instructed Cameron to flush down the toilet, Emma asked her mother to bring her the seven **Harry Potter** books. "The Bloomsbury editions," she specified. "I need to read them in the original English."

"Which ones are the Bloomsbury editions?" Hannah said.

"Jared or Cameron can show you. They're on the top shelf in my bedroom bookcase."

"How about if I bring just the first one?" Hannah said. "You need to rest. All seven would take too much time. You can read the others when you get home. You'll have plenty of free time then."

"Please, Mom, humor me," Emma said. "I'll breeze through the first three books in a day or so. I don't feel like watching TV. It's important to me."

"How many times have you read them already? Wouldn't you prefer something new and fresh?" Hannah said. "Why do you want to read something where you know what will happen next?"

"Every time I re-read the **Harry Potter** books, **while** I'm reading, it feels like going home," Emma said.

"OK, dear. You'll have them tomorrow morning," Hannah said. "But I still don't understand why it's so important. You've practically memorized them already."

"I've got to study for the next trivia party," Emma said. "I've got to win it for Sylvia."

Instinctually, Hannah wanted to challenge her daughter, to tell her in clear terms that she did **not** need to study. She needed to rest, and when she wasn't doing that, she needed to reflect on the death of her friend in order to come to terms with it. She wanted to tell her daughter to get started on the stages of grief instead of retreating into a fantasy world. But an inner voice of wisdom told her to keep silent, and she obeyed this voice.

Then Emma gasped.

"What's the matter?" Cameron asked.

"My wand. Where's my wand?" Emma said. "It was in the car."

"Your father and Jared went to the junkyard to get the papers and personal possessions out of it," Hannah said. "I'm sure, if it's there, they retrieved it."

"Call him right now!" Emma said. "And where's my phone? And purse?"

"I have them. Your wallet is safe," Hannah replied. "Nothing to worry about."

"Call Dad now or give me my phone and I'll do it," Emma insisted.

Hannah gave a deep sigh and called her husband. After a brief conversation, she thanked him and turned to Emma. "They found two identical wands. One is broken. Jared told your father that the broken one must have been Sylvia's, because they found it under the passenger seat."

Emma exhaled in relief.

"The puzzling part is that your father was going to throw the broken one in the trash, but Jared stopped him. Jared said that you would definitely want to keep the pieces," Hannah continued.

"Thank God for Jared. Jared is absolutely right," said Emma.

"Well, I don't understand," said Hannah, "but apparently it has something to do with the arcane world of Mr. Potter. Do you want to return the broken thing to Sylvia's parents?"

"Selfishly, I want to keep it as a remembrance of my Hermione twin," said Emma.

"Well, I don't think they would mind," said Hannah. "Very likely, they would not even think to ask for it."

"If they do, I'll give it to them," Emma said. "But they called Sylvia's love for **Harry Potter** an obsession. They tolerated it but were hoping she would grow out of it. I would be very surprised if they would even think about it."

Hannah reached into a tote bag and extracted Emma's phone. "You may as well have this," she said as she set it down on the bedside table.

"Thanks, Mom. But I'm going to turn it off for a while,' Emma said.

Emma started reading **Harry Potter and the Philosopher's Stone** the next morning. Following successful surgery to repair the fracture a day later, she intended to begin delving into **Chamber of Secrets** that evening, but she had not counted on the effects of pain medication and long periods of deep slumber. Two days passed without Emma reading a single word.

Then she was ready to disappear into printed pages. During the course of her hospitalization and subsequent transfer to a rehabilitation facility, Emma would read through the entire collection, accompanied by periodic stops for cathartic crying when encountering passages about the deaths of treasured characters.

In the middle of the night, when sleep eluded her, she reflected on sudden death and the fragility of life. Survival guilt and a sense of responsibility for the accident intruded into her mind. If only she had waited a second or two before proceeding into the intersection, she told herself, Sylvia would be alive. The self-taunting was relentless. Why did I need to accelerate as soon as the light changed? I'm always doing that. I'm just a jackrabbit behind the wheel. Why wasn't I paying attention to the road instead of basking in the glory of winning a stupid trivia contest? Why did I insist on driving that night? Sylvia could have taken her car. The she'd be alive and I'd be dead. No, we would have gone a different route if she had to take me home and we'd both be alive.

When Jared came to visit the next day, she put up a good front, joking about now having a real scar on her face, just like Harry. In the end, it proved to be a faint one easily covered with makeup. Over the next few days, Emma received visits from her cousins, Annagreta and Jeffers as well as Uncle Henry and Aunt Beatrix. Her friend Willow and Beatrix' children Sarah and Thomas came to see her when she reached the rehabilitation center. The surprise came when her former governess, Xandra, dropped by one afternoon.

While still at the rehabilitation center, Emma finished the seventh book, and as she drifted to sleep shortly after closing it, scenes from **Deathly Hallows** flew across her consciousness. Suddenly her eyes opened and fatigue left her, as a particular detail from late in the narrative demanded her attention. The chronology was askew. She grabbed the book and turned to the chapter where Harry reads Snape's memories in the Pensieve. One shows Snape conversing with Dumbledore's portrait in the headmaster's office about a plan to move Harry from the Dursley house before his birthday.

"But that can't be right," Emma said aloud and then shifted to unvoiced conversation. "The move happened before Snape became headmaster and before the Ministry had fallen, when Snape was still in hiding. How could Snape get into the headmaster's office to talk to Dumbledore's portrait about a plan to protect Harry?"

Emma decided that she would have to ask some knowledgeable Harry Potter aficionado about this, and quickly if she were to get any sleep. Who did she know that she could contact about this?

Among her Facebook friends were many Harry Potter fans from all over the world. She could message one of them at any time night or day, even though it would mean she had to wait for an answer. Her mind quickly settled on Carol Oster, a Chicago area psychologist with a hobby of crafting wands, and more importantly, who enjoyed charting the narrative arcs of various characters. Neville Longbottom and Severus Snape were among Carol's favorites.

Emma reached for her phone and called up her Facebook page. It took a few minutes to compose the question suitably before sending it. "Now I can sleep," she told herself. "And when I wake up in the morning, an answer or at least a clever guess will be waiting for me."

When she awoke, Emma had not forgotten the message she had sent the night before. Eager to check Facebook, she carried her phone to the bathroom and checked the site as she sat on the toilet. A reply was waiting.

Carol had written, "My theory about that has always been that Dumbledore had set up a fail-safe for Snape...from the end of Harry's 5th year, if not in the first war...that allowed Snape to floo or portkey directly to Dumbledore's office in the event of an emergency (such as being on the verge of death). You'll recall that Dumbledore's office sealed itself against Umbridge. I imagine the castle had ways of letting in those who legitimately needed in...who the castle itself might have declared allegiance to, or who had demonstrated their allegiance to the castle/school and her headmaster."

"Yesss!" Emma proclaimed from the throne. Her business on the toilet was completed except for the paperwork, but she remained seated there so that she could reply right away. "Oh thank you, thank you, thank you, Carol. I had assumed that it was an author's chronology error, but I like your theory better. It resonates perfectly with the ethos of the place and the way Dumbledore thought."

By the time she had returned to the chair by her bed, Emma had received a reply from Carol. "Mission accomplished."

By the end of rehab therapy, Emma had progressed from crutches to a cane. The facility provided her with a sturdy one to take home, but Emma had already visited the Noble Collection website to order a replica of Mad Eye Moody's staff that she planned to use in its stead.

The only strenuous exercise she was allowed was swimming, which suited her well. Once home from rehab, Emma used the strongest glue she could find to attempt mending Sylvia's wand. The result left the piece slightly crooked, but it held well enough to satisfy Emma. If she waved it around, however, Emma was certain that it would break again. Rather than risk that, Emma bought a glass display case similar to Snow White's glass coffin though much smaller and reverently displayed the repaired wand inside it.

When the Noble Collection walking stick arrived, Emma decided that it was too nice to risk breaking, and so only carried it around the house in a ceremonial fashion, for calls to dinner and such. The cane from the rehabilitation facility was put to more active use.

Sylvia's body had been cremated, and the Phoenix NCC waited until Emma was out of rehab to hold a memorial service. Kwan-Yin Burns officiated. Sylvia's parents made a point of telling Emma that the accident was in no way her fault, even partially. They blamed the drunk driver and no one else.

Emma wanted to correct their use of the word accident, but out of respect kept silent. But she did correct her mother when Hannah used that word. "It was not an accident. It was a crime!"

The event changed Emma's outlook and made her fatalistic and despairing that the death of Sylvia had no meaning. At first, she also felt leery of driving, but within a week of getting home, at her mother's insistence, she took the car out for a few errands. However, Emma avoided going through the intersection of Tatum and Shea. She also refused to say the name of the man who killed Sylvia and injured her, only referring to him as "the 22 year-old white male."

One afternoon, Emma was a passenger with her mom driving, when Hannah turned onto Tatum from Bell Road.

"Don't go there, Mom," Emma said with a tremor in her voice.

"Don't be silly," said Hannah. "You've been on this road a million times."

"I'm not being silly. I'm serious. Turn off at Thunderbird. That's a better route anyway," Emma said.

Hannah continued south on Tatum, saying nothing.

"Mom! Listen to me! Don't go through that intersection! Please!"

"Oh, all right," Hannah said with a heavy sigh. "I'll detour at Thunderbird. But I think you need to get beyond this fear and confront the scene of the accident."

"I've told you before, Mom. Don't call it an accident. It was a crime. It is a murder scene. Can't you understand that?"

"Even more reason to confront the scene of the crime," said Hannah.

"Later, Mom. I'm not ready to do that just yet," Emma said.

"I thought you were a Gryffindor," Hannah said.

This caused Emma to burst into tears, and Hannah quickly apologized.

"Don't lay a guilt trip on me, Mom. I'm not *afraid* to go there," Emma sputtered. "It's not about fear but respect. And I know I'll be stabbed with regret just passing through that intersection."

"Well, you know the acc…crime was not intentional," said Hannah. "It was essentially random."

"Is that supposed to make me feel better?" Emma said. "Sylvia was only a victim of bad timing and recklessness?"

"I didn't mean it that way," said Hannah.

Something flashed in Emma's brain. "However twisted, perverse, and vile the motivation, there was a reason for the murders of Harry Potter's parents. The killings were calculated and intentional. You're right, Mom.

Sylvia's death was not intentional, and that does make a difference. It was terrible timing that could happen to anyone. But the twenty-two year-old white male was incredibly reckless and deserves to face the full consequences of his behavior."

"I agree completely," Hannah said as she made a right turn onto Thunderbird.

"I've been blaming myself, at least a little, for what happened," Emma said. "The bad timing was as much my fault as the other driver. But I just now let go of that feeling."

"I'm so glad," said Hannah. "And you did get a very nice cane out of the deal."

"That's not funny, Mom," said Emma.

"No, I guess it's not. I was just trying to lighten the subject," Hannah replied.

"You did not succeed," Emma said. "And I'm still struggling with the reality that the murder of my best friend has no meaning."

"It does have meaning," Hannah said. "Or it will one day."

"Can you decode that?" Emma asked.

"Its meaning will depend on what you make of it, how you respond to it, and what you do with your life," Hannah said.

Emma said nothing but inwardly accepted the challenge.

II
A HOLY CURIOSITY

Never lose a holy curiosity.
　　　Albert Einstein

*Symbolic language is the one foreign language that
each of us must learn.*
　　　Erich Fromm

CHAPTER ELEVEN
LITERARY TECHNIQUES

Emma visited Aunt Sheba the weekend before starting college. After spending Saturday indoors talking and listening to music, Sheba said she wanted to go for a Sunday morning ride to the East Valley.

"Any particular place?" Emma asked.

"Perhaps," said Sheba.

Eastbound on the Superstition Freeway, the car crossed into Mesa and Sheba soon turned off onto Alma School Road, continuing southward. After passing Baseline Road, Sheba said, "Keep your eyes out for a church with a rainbow sign. It'll be on the right."

"Are we going to church?" Emma said with a voice that registered surprise.

"I thought it would be nice," Sheba responded.

"I didn't know you ever went to church," said Emma. "You never come to our naturist church."

"No, I'm not much into organized religion," Sheba said. "But I've heard about this place and wanted to check it out."

"There's the sign," Emma said. "A big rainbow on the left side and the blue and white symbol of the American Calvinist Church on the right. That seems odd. Calvinists celebrating?"

"I see it," Sheba said and turned right just past it and then right again into the parking lot of Celebrating Creation Church. "Apparently they've evolved."

"What's the deal with this one?" Emma asked.

"A friend told me about it. It's open and affirming of LGBTQ people," said Sheba.

"Hence the rainbow on their sign," said Emma. "Aren't there lots of churches that are open and affirming?"

"A growing number," said Sheba. "But my friend said I should check out this place because it is authentic. I'm told they welcome everyone, even the socially outcast straight white males."

"Will they assume we are partners?" Emma asked.

Sheba laughed. "My guess is they'll assume you are my granddaughter."

"More likely your daughter," said Emma. "You don't look that old."

"Oh thank you, dear one," said Sheba. "Grab your cane and let's find out."

After signing the guest register, Emma and Sheba were given name tags and bulletins. The greeter said, "That's an unusual name. Were you named after the Queen of Sheba?"

"No, my actual name is Bathsheba, but people have been calling me Sheba since I was a child. I was named after the naked woman King David lusted after," Sheba responded.

"Well, alright then!" the greeter said.

"I've been asked so many times, I'm afraid you got my standard answer," Sheba said with a smile.

"Standard or not, I'm glad I asked," the greeter said, returning the smile. "You may sit anywhere you like."

As soon as they had settled into chairs on the left side of the sanctuary, the pastor, Kathleen Ford, approached and greeted them. Since they were early, there was time to chat and Emma found herself telling the pastor that she was a member of the Phoenix NCC. To Emma's surprise Kathleen not only knew about the denomination but knew an NCC pastor.

"Terp Morgan up in Sedona is a good friend of mine," Kathleen said. "We keep in touch through liturgical dance circles, but she used to be a colleague in the ACC."

"Terp Morgan was a Calvinist?" Emma said with a slightly disbelieving tone.

"Yes. She left the ACC in the 1980s," Kathleen said. "For good reason. I was confronted with similar circumstances but didn't have anywhere else to go, so I stayed and fought a long siege with the regressives. We now have full inclusion in the ACC."

"Terp and her husband have preached about the theology of *Harry Potter*," Emma said. "I'm really into HP."

"My husband's a bit of a *Harry Potter* geek," Kathleen said. "I'll ask Terp to send me her Potter sermons for him to enjoy. In the meantime, I'd better get ready for church."

After the service began, the visitors were soon back on their feet passing the peace and receiving hearty welcomes from all manner of strangers. Following a prayer for reconciliation, Emma watched as a slender old man with wispy gray hair pulled back into a ponytail stood and moved to a place by the wall where a boom box had been placed on a tall stool. She thought he looked like a refugee from hippiedom that Sheba might have known in the sixties.

She turned to her aunt and whispered, "Do you know that dude?"

"No, but he looks like I could have," Sheba whispered back.

"Yeah, I thought so," Emma responded quietly.

Kathleen summoned all the children to come forward and sit on the edge of the chancel facing the congregation. She then strode to the back of the sanctuary and slipped off her shoes and removed her preaching robe. Beneath the robe she wore a flowing, translucent purple gown over a white leotard.

The old hippie pressed a button on the boom box, and the opening strains of Barbra Streisand's cover of "Children Will Listen" from *Into the Woods* filled the room. Kathleen glided to a spot in front of the wide-eyed young people and began to dance to the song, using her hands and arms and her whole body to tell the story warning adults to be careful of what they say. Emma and Sheba alike were mesmerized by the pastor's movements. As the service unfolded, they were equally rapt at the profound words of Kathleen's sermon.

As the service drew to a close, the congregation was invited to form a circle to pray for joys and concerns. A middle-aged woman with frizzy hair standing next to a young man who reminded Emma of a slender Neville Longbottom, asked for traveling mercies and blessings for her son, who was leaving for Sedona the next day to start at Anasazi College. She placed her arm around his shoulders, and he blushed as the congregation responded, "Amen!"

Feeling comfortable among these welcoming strangers, and moved by this request, Sheba raised a hand, and when given the microphone said, "I would ask the same traveling mercies and blessings for my niece Emma here, who is also leaving for Anasazi tomorrow."

Emma also blushed at the chorus of laughing amens that followed Sheba's words.

The pastor pronounced the benediction, ending with, "…and the God who made each and every one of us and called us good. Let the people say amen." Emma was so struck by the inclusive sentiment that she choked up, but when the congregation responded with the loudest yet amen, tears washed down her cheeks.

As the circle broke up, the Anasazi bound young man moved directly to Emma and said, "Hi. I'm Rob Luke. It looks like we're going to be fellow students."

"Emma Round," she said, moving her cane to her left hand taking his outstretched hand.

His eyes followed the movement of the cane, but he did not ask about the reason she used it. "There are snacks in the kitchen. You could sit here and I'll bring you something, or you could come see for yourself."

"I'd like to see for myself," she said and followed Rob to the table laden with healthy as well as sweet and high calorie edibles.

Sheba was deeply engaged in conversation with Kathleen, so Emma decided abandoning her for conversation with Rob was acceptable behavior. Rob steered Emma to a card table and then rushed back to the kitchen to get glasses of lemonade for both of them.

As soon as he sat down across from her he said, "I noticed your Deathly Hallows pin right away."

Emma looked down at the symbol pinned to her blouse. "Are you one of us?"

"Born and raised member of the Harry Potter generation," he said proudly.

"Then we have lots to talk about, Rob," Emma responded. "First a question about orientation." She paused to consider how she had phrased the statement and clarified it. "Not *that* kind of orientation. About the books. The question is Scholastic or Bloomsbury?"

"Very astute," said Rob. "A very telling question. My answer is Bloomsbury without any doubt at all."

Emma grinned. "Then there's a pair of us, at least. Do you know anybody at Anasazi?"

"Not a soul," he said.

"Well you do now," she said. "You know me, and I'll introduce you to my friend Willow. She's a junior. And my older brother Jared is a senior. I'll have to tell Jared about this church. He's gay. Of course, my church is fully inclusive, but it's not a mainline denomination."

Rob blushed again but Emma did not notice.

On the drive home, Sheba said, "I thought you'd be interested to know that the hippie dude doing roadie work for Kathleen is not someone I once knew. His name is Alan Ford, and he's the pastor's husband."

"How cool!" Emma said, and then in a delayed reaction she added, "Oh…he's the *Potter* geek. Damn! I wish I'd talked to him."

"Maybe you'll have the chance some day," Sheba said.

Emma enthusiastically supported Barack Obama in the 2008 presidential election. This put her in good company among her family, as her siblings and cousins, and her mother, aunts and uncle did also. Only her father supported John McCain, which led to an uncomfortable argument at home the night before she left for college.

"John McCain is an Arizonan," David said to her while ostensibly helping her to pack. "Surely you can see the value in supporting a favorite son."

"He wasn't born or raised here," Emma said. "He's a carpetbagger who latched onto a local heiress, but he's not really one of us."

"That's harsh," David said. "Lots of people have come from other places to find a home here, including the undocumented folks you so ably champion. Would you deny them the right to become Arizonans and represent us to the rest of the world?"

"You're right, Dad," Emma said. "McCain is an Arizonan now. And he's a war hero who deserves our deepest respect."

Amazed that he appeared to have prevailed in a discussion with his brainy daughter, David said, "So will you now consider voting for him for president?"

"Absolutely not!" Emma said. "His economic policies suck, he's in bed with right wing social causes, and his judgment in choosing a running mate is seriously deficient. Honestly, Dad, can you imagine Sarah Palin a heartbeat away from an old man with health issues? Other than that, he's a nice guy."

David now felt deflated.

"But I'm not voting against John McCain," Emma continued. "I'm voting for Senator Obama."

"I can't blame you for that," David said. "But I'm sticking with the local man."

When she started at Anasazi College in September 2008, Emma still used a cane but abandoned it within a few weeks. The architecture of the liberal arts institution had a healing effect on her. She especially appreciated the way the buildings blended naturally with the range of red toned rocks of the Sedona area. The school had been started as an educational experiment, with students encouraged to explore their interests through independent studies, but now it had evolved from experimental to a fully mature alternative educational experience.

Emma and Jared had gone to different high schools, but now they were attending the same college, and this, too, felt comforting to her. Her Fife cousins had graduated from Anasazi, and her friend Willow was here, so her enrollment felt like furthering a family tradition.

Anasazi had an intramural fencing team, and Emma wanted to join it, but she wasn't yet ready for that level of physical stress. The sport required a level of muscle control beyond her current confidence. Still, she needed some kind of aerobic activity. Her muscles were aching to move. Until she found a competitive sport to engage in, she did stretches and moderate muscle building exercises.

Once settled in to class and campus routine, Emma began attending the Sedona NCC on Sundays, and because she would be living most of the time in Sedona for years to come and longed to be a member of something as herself and not simply as an extension of her family, she decided to transfer her membership there from the Phoenix NCC congregation. An added plus was that she was able to converse regularly with pastors Cloud and Terp about Harry Potter.

She told Terp about meeting Kathleen Ford, and Terp's response was, "I wish I could recruit Kathleen to serve an NCC congregation, but she has done miraculous work as pastor of Celebrating Creation."

"I was really impressed with the CCC," Emma said. "Did Kathleen ever ask for your HP sermons?"

"Yes, and I sent them as email attachments," said Terp. "Alan is quite a fan."

Emma also found a fun and stress free physical activity to engage in. The church had a young adult group that divided into teams to play naked water balloon dodge ball. They adapted an element of paintball into the game by adding various shades of water-soluble dye to the balloons. No one paid much attention to the score, and by the end of a typical game, everyone was covered with rainbows of bright colors and laughing about it. Emma regained confidence in the strength of her left leg this way.

The game also provided the occasion for her first conversation with Sol Davar, who in addition to being a member of the naturist church was a sophomore at the college. Sol was working to organize a campus Quidditch team, and after Emma effectively splattered his chest with a bursting balloon filled with a garish green dye, he complimented her on her aim and tried to recruit her for Quidditch.

"I'll keep it in mind," she told him, very pleased to be asked. "But at this point, I'm hoping to get back to fencing."

Emma's dormitory roommate, April Augustus, was also a Harry Potter fan, which initially boded well for their compatibility. Yet as the weeks fell away, their friendship remained tepid. April had read and liked all the books, but only once, and she was more interested in the celebrity status of the movie cast than plot lines and narrative details. Also, April had never taken an online survey to see what house she should be sorted into and seemed indifferent to the process. She had never wondered what house she would belong to if she were at Hogwarts, which Emma found perplexing.

The difference between the two of them became clearer to Emma one afternoon while she was re-reading **Order of the Phoenix** and noticed ironic wordplay that she had previously missed. "Oh, this is so effing cool!" she said excitedly to April, who was reading a celebrity magazine.

"What's that?" April said distractedly.

"On page 452, the trio and Ginny are in the ward with Gilderoy Lockhart, and the healer tells them that with remedial potions he might improve. Lower case p. Then on page 459, Snape visits Harry to tell him he will be taking occlumency lessons but he is to tell anybody who asks that he's taking remedial Potions, with a capital P. Two different meanings of remedial. Isn't that incredibly cool?"

April looked up from the article about Benedict Cumberbatch she had been reading, and with a shrug said, "Yeah, I guess so."

Even then, the characteristic that prevented April and Emma from becoming closer was April's devotion to current clothing fashions and what constituted a properly stylish wardrobe. Emma was not completely indifferent to the fashion world, and easily accepted April's interest in it as just doing her thing. Because she enjoyed dressing up in costumes, Emma felt she had no reason to be critical of April. However, she disdained the entire enterprise of continually changing fashions in apparel, which she thought of as not only unnecessary but also a waste of money.

April is a nice person, Emma told herself repeatedly. We should be better friends. Yet at another level, what she needed from April was to be a new Sylvia, and that would never happen.

In November, Hannah called to tell Emma that the man who had killed Sylvia had been convicted of manslaughter, reckless driving and other charges and sentenced to five years in prison. Emma was relieved and sad.

After she came home for Christmas, Emma went out for a drive, with Hannah riding along in the passenger seat, to that tragic intersection, the scene of the crime. The light was red as she approached, and so she brought the car to a complete stop. When it changed to green, she paused to the count of three and said a prayer of thanks for Sylvia's life as she then proceeded through it.

During Emma's absence at school, a Noble Collection catalogue had come in the mail addressed to Emma, and Hannah had latched onto it as a good source for Christmas presents for her daughter. With Cameron's assistance concerning what Emma already had and might want, Hannah ordered a treasure trove for Emma: A Time-Turner with working miniature hourglass, a Wizards Chess set, a Gryffindor sword letter opener, Hermione's Yule Ball earrings, and Minerva McGonagall's wand.

Cameron explained that Emma already had Harry's, Hermione's, and Dumbledore's.

Emma was thrilled at Hannah's gesture and privately told Cameron what other Noble Collection items she wanted for her birthday, namely Neville's wand and a Deathly Hallows pendant necklace. "And by the way," she added, "in case they get bored with the catalog, Amazon has a diecast replica of the Ford Anglia from *Chamber*. I'd probably buy it for myself, except it costs about a hundred and fifty bucks. Dad wouldn't blink at spending that amount, but he might not think a model car was worth that much. Just a hint."

Cameron said, "Don't worry. I know how to slip in something like that. And you can pay me back by telling them how much I lust after a deluxe CD set of all the recordings of Harry James. That runs about as much as your Anglia."

"And more justified for the price as an important contribution to music history," said Emma. "Consider it done."

When she returned to campus after the Christmas break, Emma tried out for the fencing team. Though she was rusty, the coach took her broken leg recovery process into account and accepted her for the B team. Emma took the opportunity to work hard to improve her technique. The practices wore her out, but she kept at it. And yet, every once in a while after an especially difficult work out, she wondered if she had made a mistake in not going out for Quidditch instead.

Uncle Henry, as an adjunct professor, taught creative writing courses at Anasazi, and for the new term, he offered a course on writing techniques. He told Emma that he was using J. K. Rowling as a model and invited her to sit in on some of the lectures. Since everyone who signed up for the class had read all seven *Harry Potter* novels, he used these books as a source of examples.

"J. K. Rowling is a master of certain techniques that enrich the narrative and keep the reader reading," he began. "Let's start with foreshadowing. Who can tell me what it is?"

Since she was only sitting in and not registered for the course, Emma felt she should be quiet, but after a pause when no one spoke, she raised her hand.

"Yes, Emma. What say you?" Henry said.

"Foreshadowing is a detail introduced into a story that sets up, hints at, or is a clue to something important that will happen later."

"Full marks," said Henry. "Now remember, the foreshadowing detail may point to something that may not happen until much later in the book, or in Rowling's case, in a subsequent book. But it may also relate to what will happen soon."

Another student raised his hand, and Henry recognized him.

"Can music be used for foreshadowing?" he asked.

"It would have to be in an audio book, I suppose," said Henry.

"No, I was thinking of a movie, like when the music changes to something dramatic, and you know that something's about to happen," the student clarified.

"A good insight," said Henry. "I would invite all of you, when reading novels, to attach musical cues in your minds to details you suspect may be hints about what's coming. That will make it easier to remember them. The thing is, however, that we miss most foreshadowing the first time through a book. It's only on the second or third reading that things jump out at us. When *writing* a book, the author should plot out narrative items that would benefit from foreshadowing and then find places to add the hints.

"Here are some examples of how carefully J. K. Rowling used this technique. The first foreshadowing in the series is Hagrid delivering infant Harry to the Dursleys on Sirius Black's flying motorcycle. Scattered references to it appear in the series, but the full significance of this detail will not be known until book seven when Hagrid takes Harry away from the Dursley house for the last time on this same motorcycle.

"In *Chamber of Secrets*, the first paragraph of chapter 8, we find a rare instance of a scene without Harry. That in itself is an indicator of something important. In this case it is foreshadowing a climactic detail of this book. Here Rowling tells the reader that Ginny Weasley is looking pale and is bullied by Percy into taking a Pepperup Potion. At the critical point in the story we find out why she's been looking pale. She's been possessed by Voldemort.

"A more obscure foreshadowing detail in *Chamber of Secrets* occurs in the scene where Harry has been hauled into Filch's office and Nearly Headless Nick creates a diversion by having Peeves drop a vanishing cabinet on the floor above Filch's office. That damaged cabinet will play a critical role in book six.

"A foreshadowing occurs in **Goblet of Fire** when Fleur, speaking about the honor of being chosen a champion by the goblet, says, 'Zis is a chance many would die for!' As you all know, one of the champions, Cedric Diggory, does die.

"Incidentally, Potter scholar John Granger says that the near death and resurrection scenes in the first six books act as foreshadowings of the explicit death and resurrection scene in the **Deathly Hallows**. He is, in my judgment, spot on.

"**Deathly Hallows** is the book where all the theological hints and allusions come together in a definitive way. The book is prefaced by quotes from Aeschylus and William Penn. The Aeschylus quote is from a Greek play, **The Libation Bearers**, which is about a young man, Orestes, with a scar on his forehead who seeks revenge for the murder of his father. Does that seem familiar? Aeschylus wrote of the curse and torment of death and of the cure for it, ending with, 'Bless the children, give them triumph now.' This is certainly a foreshadowing of what is to come in this book.

"The William Penn quote also deals with death, including an allusion to 1 Corinthians 13 about a divine glass and seeing face-to-face. Penn concludes with, 'This is the comfort of friends, that though they may be said to die, yet their friendship and society are, in the best sense, ever present, because immortal.' This is clearly a foreshadowing that deaths of friends also lie ahead for the reader.

"Rowling sets up an interesting contrast with these two quotes, for before he took up writing plays, Aeschylus was a soldier in the Battle of Marathon, and William Penn was a Quaker pacifist.

"Sometimes Rowling includes a bit of dialog that seems like foreshadowing but never materializes later in the series. In **Order of the Phoenix** when Ron quips that they have as much chance of winning the Quidditch Cup as his father has of becoming Minister for Magic, I suspected, the first time I read it, that this foreshadowed Arthur Weasley's future. I guessed that Arthur would indeed be elected to that high post in the seventh book. Alas, this proved not to be a foreshadowing of Arthur's ultimate place in the Ministry of Magic but a set-up for Ron to be the hero who helped win the Quidditch Cup for Gryffindor. But there is another Minister for Magic foreshadowing in **Hallows** with a different outcome. Who can tell me what it is?"

Silence prevailed. Then a student beside Emma said, "She can tell you. Ask her."

"Oh all right," said Emma with resignation. "It's when Lee Jordan is interviewing Kingsley Shacklebolt on Potterwatch, and Lee asks about the 'Wizards first' philosophy. Kingsley lays out the trajectory of such thinking. The idea of Wizards first evolves to Purebloods first, which leads to Death Eaters first. That's where Rowling uses Kingsley's voice to express her deepest feelings. He says, 'We're all human, aren't we? Every human life is worth the same, and worth saving.'"

"How is that a foreshadowing?" said the student who suggested that Emma answer Henry's question.

"Because," said Henry, "as Emma well knows, Lee responds to Kingsley's words by saying that he has Lee's vote for Minister for Magic if they get through the current crisis."

"And at the end of the book, Kingsley does become Minister for Magic," Emma said.

"I knew that," the student said.

"Moving right along," said Henry, "upon learning that Snape will be teaching Defense Against the Dark Arts in **Half-Blood Prince**, Harry suggests that Snape would be gone by the end of the school year because the job is jinxed, noting that Professor Quirrell was killed because of it. In an uncharacteristically mean way, Harry says that he is keeping his fingers crossed for the same fate for Professor Snape. As the narrative developed, Snape was gone by the end of the year, and there was indeed another death but not the one Harry hoped for. Snape ran off because he killed Dumbledore.

"Switching to another subject, the point of view in the novels is third person limited omniscience, which is a fancy way of saying that with a few significant exceptions, the reader knows only what Harry knows. The reader is only privy to what happens in scenes where Harry is present or aware of the situation. Which means that if Harry is mistaken about what he sees, hears, infers, or believes, the reader will also be in the dark. This opens the door for a technique called narrative misdirection, which Rowling uses very well. She is a master at throwing the reader off the scent."

Another student raised her hand and was recognized. "Is that fair to the reader? We shouldn't deliberately deceive the reader, should we?"

"Well," said Henry, "this writing technique is what brings plot twists and surprise endings, which I submit make the ultimate reading experience all the more pleasurable."

"I see your point," the student said.

"Now," Henry continued, "an example of narrative misdirection comes in **Philosopher's Stone** when Hagrid tells Harry that there wasn't a single witch or wizard who went bad who wasn't in Slytherin. Hagrid was wrong, of course, and if he'd thought about it, he would have realized he was wrong, but even in recognizing his error he still would have been wrong about the non-Slytherin who went bad.

"Confused? The reader is supposed to be misled along with Harry. Naturally, Harry believed Hagrid's incomplete statement about wizards going bad. This sets the stage for the multiple plot twists in **Prisoner of Azkaban**, first when Harry learns that Azkaban escapee Sirius Black, a Gryffindor not a Slytherin, betrayed his parents to Voldemort, and then later that it wasn't Sirius but Peter Pettigrew, another Gryffindor, who went bad.

"The place to look for narrative misdirection is in dialogue. It is not the author telling the reader directly but the characters who provide the misleading information.

"Rowling makes good use of third person limited omniscience, where the reader only knows what Harry knows, but she has made a few necessary exceptions. Can you think of any?"

Emma raised her hand and was recognized. "The first chapter of the first book. Harry was an infant and not aware of what Dumbledore was up to. It would be a pretty slim chapter if we only knew what Harry saw."

Henry laughed jovially. "Of course! What else?"

No one responded, so Emma again spoke, "I think maybe the opening chapter of book four, where Voldemort is living in the Riddle house. Rowling describes what's happening there and the killing of a Muggle."

"Yes," said Henry, "but can you think of why this was necessary for the narrative?"

"Well, Harry actually sees some of the events of this chapter in a dream, which we discover later is more mental telepathy than a real dream. So in a way, it is a blend of plain old third person omniscience and limited omniscience. This is needed for the author to establish the mental connection between Voldemort and Harry, while maintaining narrative suspense and not giving everything away too soon."

"I'm impressed, Emma," said Henry. "You're quite the Rowling scholar."

Emma blushed.

Henry resumed his lecture. "The first and second chapters of book six, involving the Muggle Prime Minister and Snape's house in Spinner's End, and the first chapter of book seven, with Voldemort and company encamped at Malfoy Manor are the remaining exceptions to Rowling's primary point of view. All other chapters in the series include Harry's limited perspective on or awareness of events, leaving the reader to guess what's coming next along with Harry. Of course, for the reader that's part of the fun.

"Here's an easy question," he continued. "What genre does *Harry Potter* fall into?"

All the students raised their hands, and Henry invited them to respond in unison, but the result was not vocal agreement. Some said fantasy, while others said young adult.

"Correct to both," the professor said, "but works of fiction can represent multiple genres simultaneously. Bloomsbury acknowledged that the books were not only for adolescents but also adults by publishing different covers for the two markets. I submit that *Harry Potter* is also a post-modern novel. Post-modern works deal with the present era and with issues and conflicts of Western culture. In this case the issues are intolerance, terrorism, and the problems of being different in a conventional society. These themes are present from the beginning, but the last three books in the series clearly reveal the post-modern dimensions of Harry Potter. And there is a historical reason for this.

"Rowling had felt rushed by her publishers to produce the manuscript of *Goblet of Fire* in order to meet the expectation for a new book each year. But after that, she was in a position to call the shots and took the time she wanted with *Phoenix*. And in the interval while she was writing *Phoenix*, a number of events occurred that had profound societal effects in Britain as well as the US. 9/11 and the allied attack on Afghanistan happened while she was writing *Phoenix*, as did the weapons of mass destruction hysteria and the build-up to invading Iraq. The actual invasion of Iraq took place two months before it was published.

"These events influenced development and plot details in the last three **Harry Potter** books, linking them more profoundly to the present historical era. This is particularly so with the sixth book, **Half-Blood Prince**, which was published in 2005, when both the US and UK were bogged down in the Iraq War. The seventh book was published in July 2007."

"So, in a way," said Emma, "you could say Rowling started using models and images from World War II and the Cold War but was neck deep in the War on Terror by the time she finished."

"Yes, I think so," said Henry.

CHAPTER TWELVE
SINGING SPELLS

At the request of Cloud Morgan, Emma created and taught a class for the Sedona NCC called the Theology of Harry Potter.

As she began the first class, a member preempted her opening comment by blurting out, "My neighbor won't let her children read **Harry Potter** because of the evil spells and witchcraft. She's just worried about what she's heard but hasn't actually read the books. Do you have any words of wisdom that I can pass on to her?"

"Yeah, I know people who say that the books are diabolical," said a middle-aged man.

"Not diabolical," said his wife, "satanic."

"Same difference," said the husband.

Emma set aside her notes and said, "This is something I intended to get into later, but if there is this much energy around the subject, I may as well start with it. The most important thing for you to know is that the magic used in **Harry Potter** is **incantational** and not **invocational**. Invocational magic, the bad kind, involves calling on external spirits to produce an effect, like calling on a demon, an evil spirit, or a being from hell. In church, an invocation is used to invoke the presence of God, but this is not magic, and hopefully it's not meant to summon God to zap somebody, burn down a building, or anything like that."

"By being from hell, do you mean Satan?" asked a woman.

"In the Bible, Satan is a title, not a name, but yes, invoking the Satan to act in some malicious way would be an example of evil magic," Emma replied.

"What about praying to Zeus or Thor or one of those gods?" said a young man.

"Are you simply praying to them, expressing your concerns and desires, or are you seeking them to do your dirty work for you?" Emma responded.

"You got me on that," he said.

"I've heard preachers call on God to smite homosexuals and slay enemies," said an elderly man.

"Someone saying that while claiming to be Christian," Emma said, "is guilty of blasphemy. Invoking God for evil purposes."

"Amen," came a chorus from the class.

Emma resumed her explanation. "Incantational, the good kind of magic, consists of using ritual formula words to produce a desired effect. This is the kind of magic used by C. S. Lewis in his Christian novels. Since Lewis is a darling of evangelicals, I'd argue that if the magic in his books is acceptable to Christians, then the magic in Rowling's books must be also.

"Although it was already evident from the beginning of the series, Rowling made it explicit that the magic in her books is incantational when she introduced the Patronus charm in *Prisoner of Azkaban*. She has Remus Lupin say the Patronus is conjured by means of an incantation. And that incantation is? *Expecto patronum*. Which is Latin for I hope for or anticipate a protector or defender."

"Would you spell those words, please?" a young man asked.

Emma did so and added, "Here's the way I remember their distinctions. Incantation is related to the Latin *cantare*, which means to sing. Invocation is related to the Latin *vocare*, which means to summon or call. To remember the difference, think of the characters in *Harry Potter* **singing** their enchanting spells, using the magic of music. Even the bad guys casting bad spells do not invoke the devil. May they choke before they invoke. Thus, fearfully religious people concerned about the effect of magic in these books can relax and enjoy the story.

"Incidentally, the only place in the entire series where Rowling shows something akin to invocational magic is the graveyard scene in *Goblet of Fire*. In the ritual to create an adult body for Voldemort, Wormtail addresses himself, Voldemort's dead father, and Harry Potter, in a sense invoking their identities. He is not invoking evil spirits as in true invocational magic, but even in this close approach to it, invocational magic is shown as completely evil."

Another hand shot up, and before Emma could recognize her, the woman started speaking. "I've got it all figured out. The whole of Christian theology is condensed in book seven when Harry and Hermione visit Godric's Hollow on Christmas Eve. It's about Harry re-enacting the birth of Jesus. They have traveled to his ancestral home village, like Joseph and Mary. And then Harry is bitten by Nagini, who represents the serpent in Eden, and who thus infects Harry with original sin. But Harry, like Jesus, escapes the clutches of Satan in the form of Voldemort and is carried through the air and reborn as Christmas Day dawns and is then healed of original sin by Hermione representing the Holy Spirit. It's all there in one place. What do you think?"

"Very imaginative," Emma said. "I'm not as bold in my thinking as you are. I wouldn't be inclined to push the symbols quite that far."

"Well, how far would you push them?" the woman asked.

"Clearly, Harry becomes a Christ figure near the end of the book, but I don't see snakes in general or even Nagini in particular as symbols of evil or temptation and certainly not original sin. That's just my view, and I would encourage you to develop your theory more fully," Emma responded.

"How come snakes aren't evil?" the woman continued. "It's the symbol of Slytherin."

"The snake at the zoo in book one was friendly toward Harry and was a victim of captivity. The dead snakes in the Gaunt's yard were also victims of Morphin's cruelty. And Nagini was not inherently evil. The evil in Nagini was planted there by Voldemort. And though ethically challenged, the students of Slytherin House were not, with a few exceptions, evil. And in the end the reputation of the house is redeemed," Emma said.

The woman nodded her head thoughtfully, and though not convinced by Emma's answer said nothing.

Thinking that a joke might ease the tension, Emma said, "Incidentally, Dov Bruce Krulwich, author of **Harry Potter and Torah**, which was published in Israel, suggested that the first parselmouth in history was Eve, because she talked to a snake."

A smattering of chuckles broke forth.

"So now, if there are no more questions or comments, I thought I'd begin with alchemy," Emma said, glancing at her notes. "In an interview with Anne Simpson for the Glasgow Herald in December 1998, J. K. Rowling said that she had never wanted to be a witch, but rather an alchemist. 'To invent this Wizarding world, I've learned a ridiculous amount about alchemy…in order to set the parameters and establish the stories' internal logic.' Following up on this major clue about the meaning of the series, like Rowling I've done my own search for information about alchemy, but I want to acknowledge a debt to *Harry Potter* scholar John Granger for writing extensively about this arcane subject.

"Most people think about alchemy as the ancient quest to turn lead into gold. It was really an endeavor in search of spiritual gold, metaphorically to turn the alchemist's heart from lead to gold, to purify the soul. The metals used in alchemy symbolize the interconnectedness of all matter and energy and the essential unity in all creation. John Granger said the goal of literary alchemy is to change the hearts of readers from lead to gold.

"Literary alchemy has a long tradition in English letters. Shakespeare used it as a model for his plays. The best example is *Romeo and Juliet*. *The Tempest* and *The Merchant of Venice* are also built on alchemical plot frameworks. The plot has three stages in an alchemical novel, the black stage, the white stage, and the red stage.

"The black stage is dissolution, where things fall apart. The white stage is the washing or refining or enlightening of the hero and other main characters. The red stage is the reunion, reconciling, or resurrection of the characters. The reddening of this stage often comes through marking the white, refined characters with blood -in Christian symbolism the blood of Christ. In *Romeo and Juliet* it is Juliet's blood by Romeo's dagger. The goal of this literary framework is to use a story to bring about a resolution of opposites through personal transformation.

"Here's a simple mnemonic to help remember the color sequence, the old riddle: What's black and white and read all over?"

A chorus from the class shouted, "A newspaper."

"Exactly," said Emma. "Literary alchemy, in narrative order, is black and white and red all over.

"The practice of alchemy can be traced back as far as the third millennium BCE in Egypt and the 2nd millennium BCE in India. Historically, there have been different practices of alchemy for different religions. There are Arabic (Islamic) alchemy, Chinese (Taoist) alchemy, Jewish (Kabala) alchemy, and Christian alchemy. The English literary alchemy tradition has been modeled on Christian alchemy since the 12th century CE.

"According to John Granger's analysis, each of the seven **Harry Potter** books contains all three alchemical elements, black, white, and red, and the last three books form a complete alchemical process, with book five being mostly black, book six being mostly white, and book seven being mostly red. We'll look at some of these details more closely as we examine specific books in the next three weeks.

"Granger has also identified particular characters with literary alchemy by association with names or physical descriptions. For example, white characters are Albus (Latin for white) Dumbledore, who is himself an alchemist, Luna (silvery moon) Lovegood, and Lily Potter. The black characters are Sirius Black and all his relations in the House of Black. The red characters are Rubeus (Latin for red) Hagrid, Rufus (red) Scrimgeour, and all the redheaded Weasleys.

"Incidentally, the alchemical process uses two substances, sulfur and mercury, that symbolically represent the polarities of masculine and feminine. Together they are called the quarreling couple. Can you think of two characters who might represent sulfur and mercury and who would fit the description of quarreling couple?"

Several people shouted in unison, "Ron and Hermione!"

"Yes," said Emma. "I for one have never been comfortable with the pairing of Ron and Hermione. I so much wanted Hermione to end up with Harry. But the literary structure of the novels requires Ron and Hermione to be together. The symbolism inherent here makes these two necessary agents for Harry to complete his task."

"Yeah," said the elderly man. "I still don't buy the romance between those two, Ron and Hermione. It feels contrived and not authentic."

"My heart tells me that the real life equivalents of Ron and Hermione would end up divorced, but literarily, they are indeed contrived but nevertheless authentic," Emma replied. "Rowling intentionally created them, the redheaded, impulsive Ron Weasley and the quick-witted Hermione Granger, whose initials HG, by the way, are the periodic table symbol for mercury. And her first name is the feminine form of Hermes, the Greek equivalent of Mercury. And here's one more alchemical allusion: Redheaded Percy Weasley's owl is named Hermes."

Emma was buzzing with excitement from the class and wanted to keep talking about it with someone knowledgeable. Her cold, adrenaline saturated hands shook as she called up the number for Uncle Henry.

"What's up Emma?" he said in responding to his ring tone.

"Hi Henry. I just finished my first theology of **Harry Potter** class at the church, and I'm so stoked. I just wanted to tell someone."

"Why don't you come over for lunch," he responded. "I'd love to debrief you."

"That would be great!" she said. "I'll be there in three quarters of an hour."

She was still at the church and not yet dressed for the return to her dorm that she had previously expected. But it would be simpler to drive directly to the Fife place rather than return to campus. When she reached her car in the parking lot, as was her habit, she opened the trunk to retrieve her clothes for the journey across the Verde Valley. Nothing was there.

"Effing hell!" she said, now remembering that she had undressed in the church office because she was running late and needed to touch base with Zara Morgan about the classroom she would be using. She could trudge back into the building and get her clothes, or she could take a chance and drive the 30 miles naked. All she really needed was her purse and her class notes, which she had with her.

Knowing that she could borrow shorts and a top from Beatrix for the return trip, she elected for the latter course. On the back seat of her car was a towel she used to cover the steering wheel in summer months when the sun made it too hot to hold onto. She draped that over her breasts and lap and drove away. Within a mile, the towel had slipped down from her chest, but rather than pulling it up, she motored on.

When she pulled onto Route 260, she saw in her rearview mirror that a Highway Patrol car was now behind her, which caused her to think about the best strategy to avoid being stopped. Driving too slowly was as likely to cause suspicion as driving too fast. Either would guarantee flashing red lights. She therefore focused attention on driving between two miles per hour below and two above the speed limit, while keeping alert for posted changes.

She also tried to reposition the towel across her breasts, but it fell off, and she didn't want the car to swerve in the lane while struggling with the towel, so she let it go. An image of naked Harry Potter in the heavenly King's Cross Station came to her. Harry had only to wish for a robe and he was dressed in one. Emma wished for a robe, but as she expected, no such apparel appeared.

Upon reaching the intersection with I-17, the police vehicle entered the freeway, and Emma breathed a deep sigh as she continued eastbound on Route 260. When the turn off onto the dirt road representing the final stretch to Henry's house loomed ahead, she relaxed and tossed the towel into the back seat.

A few seconds after she had turned onto the unpaved road, however, a dark green pickup truck also turned and was soon only two car-lengths behind her. Whoever was driving the truck wore a black cowboy hat, but Emma was too concerned about the way ahead to spend much time staring into her rearview mirror for a better look.

Though driving closely behind Emma's car, the driver did not seem interested in passing her, even when Emma slowed and pulled to the right at a wide place. Now she was frightened but not panicked. She kept a prudent pace for the conditions of the road. At the three quarters mark of the two-mile course, the pickup turned left onto a smaller dirt road, and without thinking, Emma rolled down her window and waved at the driver of the departing vehicle, who waved back.

Emma's first comment when Henry greeted her on the porch was, "Do you have a neighbor who drives a big green pickup truck and wears a black hat?"

"Did he take the turnoff about a half mile back?" Henry responded.

"Yeah," Emma said.

"Probably one of the Smiths. They're good guys who like to dress in black."

"Like Snape?" Emma quipped. "His truck was Slytherin green."

"Oh much nicer than that," Henry said.

CHAPTER THIRTEEN
MATTERS OF INGESTION

Over lunch with Henry and Beatrix, the conversation quickly turned to literary alchemy.

"I always enjoy a good alchemical pun," Henry said.

"I didn't know such a category existed," Beatrix said.

"It probably doesn't," Henry replied. "And this may be stretching too far for an obscure allusion, but in *Order of the Phoenix*, when Harry and the Weasleys visit St. Mungo's, we learn that the entrance into the place, where for some odd reason magical healers wear lime-green robes, is through the display window of a department store called Purge and Dowse Ltd."

"If there's a pun coming, I don't see it," said Emma.

"Wait for it," Henry answered. "Purge means to clean something out, such as one's stomach and abdominal system or to purify from one's sins, and dowse means to locate water by means of a divining rod. Purging is related to the first, black stage in the alchemical process and washing in water is related to the second, white stage. Both processes are related to the practice of physical healing. To complete the series, Arthur Weasley's wound is subject to continuous bleeding, which adds the third, red stage to the St. Mungo's episode."

"That's it?" asked Emma.

"I said it may be stretching too far for a pun, but I think J. K. Rowling chose those names to make a humorous comment about alchemy."

Beatrix and Emma concurred that he had indeed reached too far for a lame pun.

"I've identified a bunch of alchemical references in *Goblet of Fire*," Emma said. "Tell me if you concur. The fiery tests, the flaming goblet itself and the fire-breathing dragons may perhaps be allusions to Malachi 3:1-3, which says that God's messenger is like a refiner's fire and that the people will be refined like gold and silver."

"That makes sense," Beatrix noted. "Malachi is Hebrew for my messenger."

"This refining imagery also relates to the alchemical process," Emma continued. "Harry was certainly tested by fire in this book, and he also went through all three stages of alchemy: the black stage where he was torn down emotionally, the white stage where he was washed in the lake and enlightened by his noble action, and the red stage where he was bloodied in the maze and involuntarily shed his blood for the rebirth of his opposite, Voldemort. In these three stages, Harry was tested and discovered pure courage, and most significantly, gained new knowledge that he would use to good ends in the future. Also consistent with literary alchemy, after going through the black stage where things fall apart, the white stage of cleansing and enlightening, and the red stage of painful reconciliation, Harry is a different, more fully integrated person than he was at the beginning."

"Excellent," said Henry. "Rowling really did her homework in constructing her novels. But she is even more clever than the average reader may suspect. The sequence of colors in the cauldron of liquid that produces a new body for Voldemort does not follow the Christian alchemical formula used for Harry. After adding the powdered bone of Voldemort's father, the potion turns poisonous blue. After adding the flesh of his servant, it turns burning red. After adding Harry's blood it turns white. Even if poisonous blue is taken to represent black, the sequence is still out of order and thus defective. It does not produce an integrated, refined soul but one that has had all the goodness and humanity washed out of it. Once again, Voldy gets it wrong."

"I hadn't thought of that. Thanks, Henry. I'll tell that to my class next week," Emma said.

"You told me once that you and Sheba had invented some humorous American titles for the series," Henry said. "I have a more serious one to suggest. Rowling sets up a contrasting parallel with two very significant vessels in *Goblet of Fire*. The book could have been titled *Harry Potter and the Vessels of Good and Evil*. The first vessel, the goblet is a roughly hewn wooden cup that produces fire that does not consume it, not unlike the burning bush that Moses encountered in the desert.

"The vessel used for Voldemort's rebirth is a large metal cauldron full of boiling liquid. The goblet chooses heroes who are essentially good and certainly brave. The cauldron produces the shell of a body for an evil villain. Both vessels are instruments that put Harry's life in peril, and Harry survives the effects of both.

"In one case, Harry enjoys the help and support of fellow students and people of the Wizarding community, with both good and bad motivations, as he faces the Triwizard challenges. In the other case, Harry is aided and supported by a great cloud of witnesses, those who have died and gone on to the mysterious realm of life after death."

"More fodder for my class," said Emma. "It pays to have an English professor in the family."

"Book seven is the richest, in my estimation," Henry continued. "To establish that **Deathly Hallows** is the book representing the third, red, stage of alchemical literature, the first words about Harry, in chapter two after the opening chapter about Voldemort, are that he was bleeding. A lot more blood will be described as the book unfolds. Another indicator of the final alchemical stage is the description of the color of Harry's Polyjuice Potion, which is a 'clear, bright gold,' the color of the successful alchemist's soul."

Emma borrowed shorts and a blouse for the drive back to school, but she didn't put them on until she reached the asphalt road. The next day, she called Zara to say that she would collect her own apparel the following Sunday.

In the spring term, Emma suffered a setback. A group of women in her dorm, restless to put on some kind of social event, proposed a Harry Potter trivia contest. Once launched into planning it, however, they descended into bickering over details, most significantly, which team Emma should be on.

One suggested that participants be put in teams of three, except Emma, who should be by herself. "Handicapping Emma is the only way to make things fair," she said.

Another event planner proposed that Emma should compose the questions for the teams to answer but was contradicted by another who said, "No, Emma's questions would be too hard. And that's what we have the male students for, writing the trivia questions. That's how we're going to get guys involved."

"Let's test Emma to see if her questions would be too hard," April said to the assembled event planners. "Emma, give us an example of the kind of trivia questions you might come up with."

"Off the top of my head?" Emma responded. "I'd need to go through my notes and look for apt items."

"No you wouldn't," April said. "Give us something you don't need notes for."

Emma thought for a moment and then said, "OK, here's something that's not easy but not very hard either. Sort of middle range difficulty. The two longest chapters in the entire series are tied at 31 pages each. The two shortest chapters are also tied at eight pages each. Name the chapters and the books they are in."

"You call that not very hard?" one of the planners asked indignantly. "That's cruelly obscure and meaningless."

"I think it's kind of interesting," April said in defense of her roommate.

"Well then, answer the damn question," said the disgruntled planner.

"No idea at all," said April. "Emma?"

"Any self respecting Potter geek would know this," Emma explained. "It's the kind of question you need to sort the genuine geeks from the mere Potterheads."

"I won't believe you know the answer to your question unless you tell us right now without running off to check your notes," said the other planner.

Emma sighed deeply, and with a disgusted look on her face said, "*Goblet of Fire* chapter 31 'The Third Task' and *Deathly Hallows* chapter 23 'Malfoy Manor' are the longest chapters. *Prisoner of Azkaban* chapter 20 'The Dementor's Kiss' and Goblet of Fire chapter 32 'Flesh, Blood, and Bone' are the shortest. Both of the shortest chapters depict what may be the darkest and most disturbing images in the whole series, namely, Harry about to have his soul sucked out by a Dementor and Voldemort's resurrection into a new body in a boiling cauldron. In Goblet of Fire, the chapter tied for longest immediately precedes the chapter tied for the shortest. Any questions?"

"Yeah, we'll need to get the guys involved," said April.

One evening, in the midst of this bickering, Emma suffered a flashback to the crash that killed Sylvia. Without knowing why, she began to shriek and rage at her fellow students, at first railing against their small mindedness, and then shouting, "I wish I had never read a line of **Harry Potter**! Then everyone would leave me alone! Just everyone leave me effing alone!" Looking about the room for something to pick up and throw, she spotted a pile of magazines on an end table. Descending on the spot, she grabbed a handful of them and began to rip them to pieces and scatter them. The spines were too strong for her unfocused efforts, so she hurled them at the gaping women.

Without looking at anyone, Emma stormed out, but her roommate stayed with the gathering and explained, "Don't sweat it. Emma is playing all tragic because a friend of hers was killed in a car accident. She wants to be Harry after Sirius died."

In the hallway, Emma paused to consider going back and apologizing for her outburst, but when she heard what April said, rage re-ignited within her, and she continued down the hall.

Once in her dorm room and shaking with fury, Emma searched through April's closet for a bottle of Champagne that she had seen in the past. It cost her two broken fingernails to get the cork out, but once she did, Emma quickly drank most of the bottle. For the first time in her life, she was drunk, sickeningly so, and did not like the way it felt. A frightening image of driving her car in this state looped through her mind. Desperate to clear her head and stop the spinning, she decided to medicate her condition by eating two large bars of Fair Trade dark chocolate. That's what one does to recover from Dementors, she told herself. The result for Emma was to collapse onto her bed and promptly vomit all over herself.

April appeared a few minutes later, and after quickly surveying the scene, called security to take Emma to the Campus Health Center. Once Emma had been undressed and installed in a bed there, a nurse cleaned her up. After a decent interval, April appeared at the Health Center. As soon as Emma saw her roommate, she said, "Don't worry. I'll reimburse you for the booze."

"Don't bother," said April. "You can't replace an heirloom. My brother gave that to me for my eighteenth birthday. It was a secret birthday present that I was saving for a special occasion."

"I'm sorry," said Emma.

"Well, your stunt wasn't special, but it was memorable, I'll give you that," said April.

Jared visited later that night. "April told me what happened," he said.

"Don't tell Mom," Emma pleaded.

"Not a chance of that," her brother responded. "She would not handle it well. She might think you like medical attention."

"Well I don't," Emma replied.

I'm just glad your baptism of booze wasn't more serious," he said and bent down to kiss her forehead.

Though her head ached, she managed to smile.

When Emma returned to her dorm the next day, she found that April had already laundered her sheets and blankets. Emma thanked her and offered her money for the Champagne, but April categorically refused. "It was a cheap brand, anyway."

For a subsequent Harry Potter Sunday school class, Emma began with an interview that J. K. Rowling had given to MTV in October following the publication of book seven. "Rowling said that Hogwarts is a multifaith school. Incidentally, those of us who study all things Potter seriously, refer to oral statements such as this as post-canon authorial commentary. It's authoritative because it came from the author, but it can't be found in any of the books. Two days later in an interview with the Leaky Cauldron, Rowling expanded on her earlier remark, saying that the whole series represents 'a prolonged argument for tolerance, a prolonged plea for an end to bigotry.' A major theme throughout all seven books is inclusion. Voldemort and the Death Eaters, and sadly most Slytherins are obsessed with purity, while Dumbledore champions and models full inclusion of all kinds.

"At the end of the last book, elves, gnomes, centaurs, a half-giant, and a rag tag band of witches and wizards all come out to challenge Voldemort even after being told that Harry is dead. They came together as a community despite differences in culture and beliefs and even in species. The portraits in the Headmaster's office of those who have gone before also provide guidance and important help during the course of the saga. This provides an allusion to Hebrews 12:1 about the great cloud of witnesses surrounding us.

"Before delving any more deeply into the rich theological implications of *Harry Potter*, a general description is in order. A few of you have told me that you haven't read any of the books and a few more have read only a few. You're here out of curiosity, and I hope what you learn here will send you scrambling to the bookstore or library to read the whole series. So here is an overview of the books' structure and publishing history.

"J. K. Rowling has produced a series of seven novels forming a single unified narrative. In an interview on *60 Minutes*, the author herself described it as one huge novel divided into seven for the convenience of her readers. The Scholastic hard cover editions used as reference for an American readership total 4100 pages. The first three novels are relatively short and the last four are longer. The midpoint for the entire narrative is page 150 of the fifth book, *Order of the Phoenix*. The Wizengamot has just cleared Harry for performing a Patronus charm in front of a Muggle, which he did to repel two Dementors. So you don't reach the halfway point until a hundred and fifty pages into the fifth book.

"The Wizengamot, for those of you who don't know, is a judicial court of 70 members similar in number to the Sanhedrin in first century Jerusalem. Dementors are hideous beings that suck the soul out of a person, a fate worse than death for those who believe the soul does not die when the body does.

"At or near the beginning of each book, Harry is staying at the suburban home of his aunt and uncle, the Dursleys, who represent the worst of middle class Britons. They reside at Number 4 Privet Drive, Little Whinging. At some point in each book, Harry reaches Hogwarts School of Witchcraft and Wizardry, although his adventures preceding arrival at the school take up an increasing part of the narrative as the years unfold. In the first six books, he returns to the Dursleys at the end of the narrative. In book seven, he does not reach Hogwarts until the school year is nearly over, and he does not return to the Dursley house at all. As Harry ages from 11 to 17, the story matures, becoming more complex and layered, with characters, good guys and bad guys, showing both gifts and flaws.

"The seven *Harry Potter* novels consist of nearly 1,100,000 words. The first book in the series, *Harry Potter and the Philosopher's Stone*, is a mere 77,000 words. When you've finished reading this first of seven books, you've only read 7% of the story. It was published in the United Kingdom in June 1997 and in the United States the following year with the altered title *Harry Potter and the Sorcerer's Stone*.

"The second book, **Harry Potter and the Chamber of Secrets** was released in Britain in 1998 and the third, **Harry Potter and the Prisoner of Azkaban** in 1999. Numbers two and three were both published in the United States in 1999. Thereafter, the books had become so popular that publication dates were synchronized worldwide.

"The fourth book, **Harry Potter and the Goblet of Fire**, hit the stores in 2000. Then the long wait for the fifth book began. **Harry Potter and the Order of the Phoenix** was not published until 2003. Number six, **Harry Potter and the Half-Blood Prince**, was published in 2005, and the seventh, **Harry Potter and the Deathly Hallows**, reached the public in July 2007."

Emma noticed a few nodding heads and glazed eyes among the class members. "OK, everyone stand and stretch," she instructed. "And if you're so inclined, take a minute to trade shoulder and neck massages with the person next to you." When pleasant sighs filled the room, she had them sit and resumed her lecture.

"Befitting books for pre and young teens, the first three volumes are relatively slender, while the remaining four are of epic length, suitable for older and more experienced readers. **Order of the Phoenix**, the longest in the series is over 257,000 words, more than three times longer than the first book. Speaking of slender books, the series has been published in Braille, which is anything but slender. The seven books run to 59 volumes in Braille. Piled flat on one another, the Braille editions stand more than seven feet high.

"The main plot action takes place over a seven-year period from the spring of 1991 to the spring of 1998. The first chapter of book one, serving as a prolog, opens on November 1, 1981, All Saints Day. The previous evening, Voldemort had murdered Harry's parents and tried to kill him. Then at midnight, at the cusp between All Saints Day and All Souls Day, Hagrid delivers fifteen-month old Harry to Dumbledore, who is waiting in front of the Dursley house. Little orphan Harry will be entrusted to the care of his maternal aunt and her husband. The tension between saintliness and soulfulness symbolized by this particular convergence of the church calendar will persist throughout the whole series. The seven-year saga begins in chapter two with a fast-forward to 1991.

"Remembrances and scenes from the Pensieve depict action back to the 1920s, 1930s, and 1940s for some characters and the 1960s and 1970s for others. A book within the book provides information about Dumbledore dating back to the 1890s, and the epilog in book seven is set in the future in the year 2017. The series incorporates and overlays multiple genres within its carefully crafted narrative. Examples of satire, social commentary, romance, courtly quest, murder mystery, pilgrimage, alchemy, fantasy, paranormal, ancient legend, manners, and religious allegory literary forms are present in the series."

Emma took a deep breath when this class was over. She felt that it had gone more smoothly than her previous efforts and looked forward with renewed enthusiasm to preparing more lessons.

In addition to daily logging in to Facebook to send birthday greetings to her friends, Emma developed a morning ritual of checking in with various Harry Potter related sites. Among her Internet bookmarks were The Leaky Cauldron, Muggle Net, Accio Quote, and John Granger's Hogwarts Professor.

Jared moved to Los Angeles after graduating from Anasazi College in the spring of 2009 to study at the Stella Adler Academy of Acting. He and Rob Luke had been dating, and Rob was heartbroken about Jared leaving, and he turned to Emma for solace and a listening post for his sorrow.

While attending acting classes, Jared got small nonrecurring parts in various television shows, including *The Big Bang Theory* and *How I Met Your Mother*. Emma was excited the first time she spotted her older brother in an episode of *Big Bang Theory*, even though he did not have a single line.

After Emma's screaming breakdown, the relationship with her roommate April had remained warily cordial the rest of the term, but a deep bond never developed. At the end of the year, April went home to San Diego and transferred to San Diego State University for the next school year.

Home for the summer, Emma spent most of her time with Sheba. She had lost contact with her high school friends and didn't feel much like socializing with peers anyway.

Sheba decided Emma needed a project to pull her back from the edge of depression. Music had always done that for her, so it might do the trick for her niece.

"I'm happy to listen to you exclaim about Harry Potter stuff," Sheba said to Emma. "But you need to reciprocate by listening to me rave about music."

"Of course," said Emma. "I'm interested in music history, too."

"The greatest decade for music in all of human history was the sixties," Sheba said with an authoritative tone. "If we're talking about a ten-year span not confined to a specific decade, I'd say 1964 to 1973."

"Well, I'd definitely have to go to a time before I was born for the greatest music decade," Emma responded, "so it might as well be the sixties, but for oldies I'm partial to the eighties. I learned a lot of those songs from Mom."

They spent hours listening to the discs that Sheba played on her stereo system.

"Now this one is perhaps my favorite album of all time," said Sheba as she carefully removed a record from its sleeve and placed it on the turntable. "Maybe because I identify so much with Grace Slick."

"Surrealistic Pillow," Emma read as she picked up the sleeve. "Jefferson Airplane. Didn't they become Starship?"

"Quite an evolution," said Sheba. "But this is their roots."

Sheba made Emma listen to the album three times without saying a word.

"Now you can talk," said Sheba. "What do you think?"

"I quite liked "White Rabbit," Emma said. "That's the best cut on the album."

Surprised, Sheba said, "Why that particular song?"

"Because of its associations with fantasy literature," Emma explained. "*Alice in Wonderland* has influenced many subsequent fantasy works. There are elements of it in *Harry Potter*, especially *Chamber of Secrets*."

"I should have known you'd find a way to link rock music with your Mr. Potter," Sheba said with a sigh.

"That's how my mind works," Emma said. "I can find some association with just about anything that connects with *Harry Potter*."

Reflecting about her aunt's attachment to Surrealistic Pillow, Emma asked Sheba about her drug use during the psychedelic decade, and Sheba admitted that there were many occasions when she could have died. "I am so grateful to be alive that I've stayed clean, apart from an occasional hit of weed, which is actually a lot better for you than alcohol." Sheba shunned alcohol.

Emma told her aunt about her episode with champagne and how that had curbed any interest she might have otherwise had in alcoholic beverages.

"Doing hard drugs, including alcohol, is like casting a Patronus that turns into a Dementor or a cheering charm that becomes a Boggart," Sheba added in a preaching tone.

As the summer proceeded, Sheba exposed Emma to albums by the Eagles, Donovan, and the Lovin' Spoonful. And she was not at all surprised that Emma's peculiar fascination led her to choose "Witchy Woman" as her favorite Eagles cut, "Season of the Witch" as the best from Donovan's *Sunshine Superman* album, and "Do You Believe in Magic" as the top hit from the Lovin' Spoonful.

Emma rummaged through some of Sheba's older albums that she had not brought out to play for her, and from these she discovered "Love Potion No. 9" covered by the British group the Searchers, which Emma found delightful. Also appealing to her essentially romantic spirit was the Drifters recording "This Magic Moment."

Indulging Emma's love of fantasy literature, aunt and niece went together to see the musical *Wicked* at Gammage Auditorium on the campus of Arizona State. Emma looked forward to the play, because she had read the book it was based on, *Wicked: The Life and Times of the Wicked Witch of the West* by Gregory Maguire. She thought the book was a great story marred by poor writing. She and Sheba agreed that in this rare case, the play was better than the novel. All the way home, the song "For Good" repeated in Emma's head. The next day, Emma bought the Original Cast Broadway album.

While taking classes at the Stella Adler Academy, Jared attracted a new friend. Fellow acting student Anna Magic seemed to home in on him from the first time they did scenes together, insisting that he accompany her to a health food restaurant after class.

Anna was a year younger than Jared, with svelte frame, flowing dark hair, green eyes, and an extroverted personality. "I think you and I are going to be thick friends," she told him as they munched on spinach and mushroom salads.

"Because?" Jared responded.

"Because you're gay and I'm not," she replied. "That means we can tell each other anything without worrying about judgment or sexual tension."

"That makes a good premise for a soap opera," said Jared. "Can a Kinsey six male find true love with a Kinsey zero female in a world dripping with bigotry and sexual tension?"

Anna laughed heartily. "You can write the screenplay, but what we really have will be much more fun than whatever obstacle laden plot you can come up with."

As things developed, Anna proved to be right about the ensuing relationship.

Over lunch one afternoon, Jared told Anna about growing up in a naturist family and having a Harry Potter geek for a sister. "I'm actually quite proud of Emma," he continued. "She's smart as a whip and so thoroughly sincere about her Potter enthusiasm."

"As well you might be," said Anna. "I, too, grew up with the Boy Who Lived, and was totally immersed in that narrative for many years."

"So did I," Jared added.

"I wouldn't admit this in class, because of a certain level of artistic disdain among drama intellectuals, but it was the **Harry Potter** movies that sparked my interest in acting," Anna said.

"Aesthetic snobbery mainly comes from those who aren't getting the good roles," Jared said. "So, who among the **Potter** cast most inspired you?"

"Of the male persuasion, I would have to admit to being stirred by Richard Harris and Alan Rickman. On the female side, I gravitated toward Emma Thompson, Maggie Smith, and Helena Bonham Carter."

"Not the child actors?" Jared said.

"Their acting matured spectacularly over the sequence of films," Anna said. "But I focused on the adult cast for inspiration. They were all so natural with seamless performances."

Jared entertained Anna with tales of the childhood **Harry Potter** fantasy games that he had played with his siblings, Polyjuice parties, skinny-dipping with characters from the books, and more, adding embellishments to improve the anecdotes.

<><><>

More than anyone else, in her sophomore year, Emma hung out with Willow, who was now a senior. Over lunch in the campus center on a sunny and clear September day, Emma said, "You haven't mentioned the Native American Church lately. Are you still a member?"

"Yeah," said Willow. "I don't go very often anymore, but I'm still a member."

"I'd like to go there sometime, that is if white people are allowed. I wouldn't want to be a distraction," Emma said.

"Sure, you'd be allowed, assuming you'd be as respectful as I know you would be," said Willow. "They may not give you peyote, though, unless they know you're not just a drug tourist."

"You could assure them that I'm not that," said Emma. "I don't do drugs at all, and I'm genuinely interested in all kinds of spirituality."

"I have a better idea," Willow said. "The main reason I don't go there much is that I prefer private meditation. I use Henry's sweat lodge for that. Why don't we go there and have our own service. I've got buttons for tea at home."

"Great idea. When?" said Emma.

"How about Friday afternoon? You can ride along with me and stay the weekend," Willow said. "We can come back Monday morning."

"That would give us time to do some out-of-body floating, too," said Emma.

With their Friday afternoon classes over, they met in the school parking lot at 3:15. Emma tossed her backpack next to Willow's in the bed of the pickup and climbed into the cab.

"Are you ready for an adventure?" Willow said as she turned the key in the ignition.

"Absolutely!" said Emma. The memory of her adventure driving naked from the church to Henry's place rose to consciousness, and she told Willow about it.

"What fun!" said Willow. "Let's do that."

From her position behind the wheel, she began to wriggle out of her shorts, and Emma followed in the dance of undressing. When both women were nude, Willow shifted into gear and steered her truck out onto the main road.

As they swerved through a traffic circle, the driver of a van going the opposite direction looked over at Willow and Emma and seemed to perceive nakedness, but he quickly turned his attention back to the road and thought that it must have been a momentary illusion. By this time, Willow's truck was well down the road.

Emma saw the man's glance, however, and slumped down in her seat. "We don't have to advertise," she said. "We're not exhibitionists."

"No, the fun is just knowing that we're naked inside the cab," Willow concurred.

"How do you like your truck?" Emma asked conversationally.

"Tonks serves me well," said Willow. "She's Henry's old truck. He gave her to me when I started college. Because I commute, he said I needed something reliable."

"Yeah, I recognized it," said Emma. "Who named her Tonks?"

"I did, as soon as the title was in my name," Willow said.

"Is Tonks one of your favorite characters?" Emma asked. "Is that why you named your truck after her?"

"Partly," said Willow. "I like her a lot, but as a kid one of my favorite playthings was a Tonka Toy truck. And I just like the sound of it. So the name's a three-fer."

"And when you toot the horn, she's a honky Tonks," said Emma. "That makes it a foursome." Her head, shoulders, and torso swayed as she imitated Mick Jagger singing "Honky Tonk Woman."

Willow groaned then laughed. She sat sufficiently low in her seat and Emma had scrunched down enough that for the rest of the trip their naked bodies did not attract any further attention from occupants in other vehicles on the road.

Henry and Beatrix were pleased to see that Emma had come home with Willow.

"Your usual sleeping quarters are available," Beatrix told her.

"We'll probably be out all night tonight," said Willow. "I'm making tea for Emma and we're going to the lodge for meditating."

"I wondered when you'd get around to that, Emma," Henry said.

"If you care to debrief over breakfast, we'll be eager to hear," Beatrix added.

Once they settled comfortably on thick towels spread of the dirt floor of the sweat lodge, Willow said, "We'll just meditate in silence for a while and then sip tea. Like I explained before, don't let its bitterness distract you. Try not to gag if you can help it."

Thus mentally prepared, when the time came to drink, Emma relaxed as the acrid brew flowed into her mouth and down her throat. Willow passed quickly into a dream state, and judging from the expression on her face, Emma assumed she had found a pleasant place inside her mind. Emma's brain pulsed for a few seconds, and then she flinched, as she perceived herself lying naked and without her glasses in King's Cross Station. She saw herself sit up but unlike Harry did not experience any desire for a robe.

"If I'm in King's Cross," she mouthed silently, "then I'll be able to talk to Sylvia." No sooner had she said this, than an also naked Sylvia appeared. She did not look quite the same, but Emma knew who this was. The merging features of Sylvia and Albus Dumbledore explained the difference in appearance. The face was Sylvia, the hair was Dumbledore, and the secondary sex characteristics were both.

Expecting Sylvia to speak of the crash that had killed her, Emma was surprised to hear her old friend's voice say, "Do you wish to go back or go on?"

"I have to make a choice, don't I?" Emma said. "If I go on, can I go with you?"

"You can go on as Harry or go back as Hermione," said Sylvia.

"That's not an answer," Emma said.

"Not one that you want, but it is an answer," Sylvia said.

"Can I go back and still be both?" Emma asked.

"If you go back, I dare say, you can do whatever you most desire," Sylvia answered.

The next thing Emma remembered was waking with a chill in the middle of the night. She roused herself and summoned the muscular effort to climb outside and find a spot to pee. Back inside, Emma took one of the light blankets that Willow had brought along and wrapped herself in it and then promptly fell asleep.

The Saturday morning debriefing happened over large bowls of oatmeal.

"None of this makes sense rationally," she said to the assembled Willow, Beatrix, and Henry.

"Why do you expect rationality?" Beatrix asked.

"I don't know," said Emma. "My real concern is not making sense of it but interpreting it."

"And?" Henry asked.

Emma felt exasperated. "Well, I do not have a death wish, but my asking if I could go on with Sylvia seems to imply that."

"Perhaps survivor's guilt," said Beatrix.

"Yeah, I've definitely felt that," Emma said.

"I think the only thing you need to focus on is the last part," said Willow. "It's loaded with affirmation. I would interpret that as equivalent to follow your bliss."

Henry and Beatrix concurred with Willow.

Following late morning naps, Emma and Willow floated from their bodies and went exploring.

"Let's go out to the paved road," Willow said telepathically.

"Cool!" Emma responded.

Once at the road leading to Camp Verde, the two college women amused themselves by floating through the engines of moving vehicles, telepathically laughing from the sheer joy of doing so without harm. Coming upon a pickup truck parked in a shady spot off the highway, they swooped into the cab and through the bodies of the teenage occupants who were passionately kissing.

Both lovers felt momentary but intense elation. Willow and Emma hovered just outside the window to judge the reaction.

The couple broke apart and one said, "You are a powerful kisser. I've never felt anything like that before."

"I was going to say the same thing," said the other.

"Mission accomplished," said Emma. "Let's head home."

Henry and Beatrix enjoyed hearing the floating tale over dinner.

CHAPTER FOURTEEN
THE SEVEN AFFIRMATIONS

In the spring term of her junior year, Emma signed up for a course in Comparative Religions taught by Dr. Magda Lena Zwingvin. Doctor Zwingvin, a short woman with the body of a former gymnast who has gained the weight of maturity, was an ordained minister in the Bohemian Episcopal Spirit of Memory Society. Though her English was impeccable, faint traces of an unidentifiable Eastern European accent appeared when she was lecturing on a subject she felt passionate about.

For the final exam, Magda assigned a paper in which students were to create a new church or religion. Students were allowed to build a reformed version of an existing religious body or create a completely new one, but they were required to show ecclesiastical distinctives, major doctrines, and a governing organization.

The choice was easy for Emma. She had developed and taught a course in the theology of *Harry Potter* for the Sedona naturist church and had just finished another of her marathon re-readings of the Potter canon, so the idea for the Holy Rowlings flowed effortlessly from her mind.

This is Emma's paper:

The Alchemical Church of Harry Potter Prophecy
(The Holy Rowlings)

Theologian Harvey Cox from Harvard Divinity School wrote in *The Secular City*: "Our technological fantasies become facts overnight. Why not our spiritual fantasies?" My spiritual fantasies have been formed from an intimacy with the works of J. K. Rowling. Therefore, I propose a church religion based on the canon of *Harry Potter*. These novels are loaded with

135

mythological symbolism and spiritual wisdom that readers are drawn to and absorb deeply. Christian symbols and those of other faiths permeate the narrative in every book, becoming more frequent as the story progresses. Book Seven even has direct quotes from the New Testament. Rowling has put all this together in a way that can be readily accepted not only by Christians but also those of many other faith traditions as well as secularists.

For a Time magazine "Person of the Year Runner-up" article in December 2007, J. K. Rowling said, "I did not set out to convert anyone to Christianity. I wasn't trying to do what C. S. Lewis did. It is perfectly possible to live a very moral life without a belief in God, and I think it's perfectly possible to live a life peppered with ill-doing and believe in God." Later that year, she commented, "I'm opposed to fundamentalism in any form, and that includes my own religion."

In **Harry Potter and the Order of the Phoenix** [635 & 777], Rowling described in a curious way the Department of Mysteries room where all the prophecies were kept. In one of Harry's dreams it is "a dimly lit room as high and wide as a church." This is an apt description of a sanctuary, especially a cathedral sanctuary. Then, when Harry and five other members of Dumbledore's Army actually entered the place, Rowling described it as: "high as a church and full of nothing but towering shelves covered in small, dusty, glass orbs...The room was very cold." What immediately comes to mind is the common criticism of many church sanctuaries that they are metaphorically dusty with cold congregations.

Could this be a subtle comment about traditional religion? Are many sanctuaries the cold repositories of dusty prophecies? Why else would Rowling twice describe the Department of Mysteries with church language? This could be understood as a call for a church that is not cold and dusty.

By way of contrast, in **The Deathly Hallows**, Rowling described a scene on Christmas Eve where Harry and Hermione heard villagers singing carols amidst the warmth of a pub, and Harry considered taking refuge there. Singing hymns in a bar expresses religious faith but is not an image of traditional religion.

Let us, therefore, use these books as the source for a warm and affirming humanist religion. A Harry Potter Church would offer emotional health and intellectual satisfaction because from the beginning there would be no chance of literal interpretation or fundamentalist rigidity. The doctrines or creedal statements would acknowledge that the source is fiction within which great truth abides.

Worship services would be led by a Hallowed Philosopher, who would preach sermons based on the Harry Potter canon, administer the rituals of the church, teach, and provide pastoral care. Church polity would be congregational, with a board of advisors to make decisions about financial matters and the day-to-day functioning of the church, but the Hallowed Philosopher would have full and exclusive authority for the maintenance of worship, choice of canonical lessons, and sermon content.

The Seven Holy Rowling Affirmations:

+Belief in God is characteristic but not required.

+Membership is not exclusive. One may be a member of another church simultaneously.

+The church is for people who love metaphor and myth and wish to explore them.

+Everyone is welcome at worship, but only those who have read the seven novels of the canon can be voting members. (There will be no written test given for membership, but members will be expected to offer opinions about arcane details of the narratives.)

+The biblical canon consists of the seven *Harry Potter* novels plus the three companion books (*Tales of Beadle the Bard*, *Fantastic Beasts and Where to Find Them*, and *Quidditch Through the Ages*). The canon is open, so that additional work published by J. K. Rowling in the future may be added to it.

+Quotes from J. K. Rowling given in interviews and speeches (such as her Harvard commencement address in 2008) are called Mishnah. Certain works by other writers analyzing, interpreting, or critiquing the Harry Potter canon are called Talmud.

+Joanne Kathleen Rowling is a truly inspired artist and in that sense holy but is fully human and not in any way divine or a deity.

Dr. Zwingvin used red ink to write a large O+ on Emma's paper. In parentheses she wrote (A+ for Muggle consumption). The professor liked Emma's proposal so much that she suggested that Emma do an Independent Study in the fall term of her senior year to develop the concept more fully. Emma was thrilled with the idea.

Over the summer break, Emma read through the canon yet again, taking more notes this time than she had for her theology class at the NCC, now with an eye toward ecclesiastical applications. She mulled over the possibilities for on order of worship and the language of ritual, eventually fine-tuning the flow of an entire service. Before classes resumed, Emma contacted a few fellow students and asked them to become an experimental congregation to listen to the sermons that she would write and deliver. Her first recruits were Cameron, Rob Luke, and two female Potterheads who lived in her dormitory, plus Professor Zwingvin, who advised and evaluated Emma's work as the term progressed.

She was assigned a classroom with a podium that was primarily used for speech and public speaking classes and for debates, and the speech teacher often sat in to coach Emma's homiletical approaches and delivery. The room was comfortable, with excellent acoustics, but to Emma it did not evoke transcendent feelings. It was, in her mind, a place for non-fiction prose rather than metaphysical poetry.

Speaking in front of Magda and the group of student peers brought back memories and the associated feelings of being on the traveling geek squad. Before preaching, Emma's hands and feet would get cold, and she flirted with doubts about the sermon that she had been so confident about while rehearsing. Once into the rhythm of her delivery, however, she soon warmed up and found a comfortable groove for orating. She discovered that she could feel when her artificial congregation was listening intently or mentally wandering. When it was the latter, she intuitively changed her pitch or tempo to regain their attention.

After a few sermons, Magda commented, "I notice that you do not exegete specific passages or texts, but preach thematically. Is that intentional?"

"It is," said Emma. "It's harder to focus on specific passages in the absence of uniform chapters and verses like the Bible. I thought about using chapter and page number designations, but that seemed clumsy. So, for the present, I plan to explore the canon more generally."

This is Emma's first sermon:

"Heterodox but Not Demonic"

Before we can freely delve into the spirituality of **Harry Potter**, there is a nasty issue we need to address and dispose of. This is an effort to do that. Fervent protests abound about the purported demonic influences of the

Harry Potter novels. In print, on television, in sermons, and on the Web, conservative Christian critics of J.K. Rowling's work have unleashed torrents of negative analysis about why reading Harry Potter is bad for children. Many of the published criticisms express suspicion that the books represent a conspiracy to undermine traditional Christianity or project motivations upon the author that she intends to bring the younger generation under the sway of witchcraft or the occult. Some of this material radiates an aura of paranoia, and a number of Harry Potter protesters have threatened violence.

In a July 2007 interview, Rowling compared the levels of Christian criticism that her books have received in the United Kingdom and the United States. "I had one letter from a vicar in England -this is the difference- saying would I please not put Christmas trees at Hogwarts as it was clearly a pagan society. Meanwhile, I'm having death threats when I'm on tour in America."

Carol Matrisciana, author of **Gods of the New Age**, characterized the **Harry Potter** series as a "true representation of witchcraft, and the black arts, and black magic. And yet we have people say this is merely fantasy and harmless reading for our children."

Before becoming Pope Benedict XVI, Joseph Ratzinger wrote a letter to a German woman saying the **Harry Potter** books "are subtle seductions that are barely noticeable, and precisely because of that have a deep effect and corrupt the Christian faith in souls even before it could properly grow."

Father Gabriele Amorth the Roman Catholic Exorcist of Rome added this: "Behind Harry Potter hides the signature of the king of darkness, the devil…magic is always a turn to the devil."

In a piece for the newsletter of the Society of Saint Pius X in Canada, Patricia MacLean wrote, "The **Harry Potter** books are about more than fantasy. We could equate them to a sort of marketing plan developed to sell the occult."

The **Harry Potter** books have been at the top of the American Library Association's list of most challenged books for a decade. Religious fundamentalists have launched strong efforts to ban them from schools and public libraries. In October 2006, a woman named Laura Mallory spoke to a representative of the Gwinnett County, Georgia Board of Education, calling Harry Potter evil and an attempt to indoctrinate children into the religion of witchcraft. Mallory, a mother of four, was involved with a fundamentalist church and had served previously as a missionary.

Mallory further stated that Rowling's works foster the kind of culture where school shootings happen. Between 2005 and 2007, Mrs. Mallory received worldwide attention for her crusade against the dangerously demonic **Harry Potter** books.

In May 2007, her suit against the county Board of Education, in which she sought the removal of Rowling's books from county schools, was tried in the Gwinnett County Superior Court. She lost the case. The following month, in a June 10th interview with the **Atlanta Journal**, Mallory said, "The mass media today knows [**sic**] all too well that 'sorcery sells,' and the market is none other than…? You guessed it - our children."

In his television broadcast on July 9, 2007, fundamentalist preacher John Hagee said, "As millions of people anticipate the release of the latest **Harry Potter** book and film, we're reminded once again of Satan's ongoing attempt to deceive and destroy. The whole purpose of the Potter books is to desensitize readers and introduce them to the occult. A U. S. consumer research survey reports that over half of all children between the ages of six and seventeen have read at least one Harry Potter book. The books and films teach moral relativism and numb the minds of children to profanity and off color humor. Many of you believe it's just harmless fantasy, but it's fantasy laced with witchcraft and demonology."

In response, mainline and progressive Christians have rushed to defend Rowling from what they see as ungrounded and unfair attacks. Christians with moderate to liberal stripes have rightly responded that the **Harry Potter** series is loaded with clearly Christian symbols and biblical allusions. They have also noted that the magic employed in Harry Potter is the same incantational kind used by C. S. Lewis, a favorite of evangelical Christians. The bad kind, invocational magic, does not appear in Harry Potter.

Many supporters of the religious values put forth in **Harry Potter** have made fine analyses of the seven books, pointing out the numerous references and associations with the Christian religion easily found in them. They identify the plot elements in Harry Potter that parallel Gospel accounts in the Bible and note Rowling's self-identification as a practicing Christian.

Children's literature author Judy Blume wrote an editorial for the **New York Times** in 1999 in defense of J. K. Rowling. Concerning criticism of *Harry Potter* from the religious right, Blume wrote, "I'm not exactly unfamiliar with this line of thinking, having had various books of mine banned from schools over the last 20 years. In my books it's reality that's seen as corrupting. With Harry Potter, the perceived danger is fantasy...According to certain adults, these stories teach witchcraft, sorcery and Satanism...My grandson was bewildered when I tried to explain why some adults don't want their children reading about Harry Potter. 'But that doesn't make any sense!' he said."

Blume's editorial continued, "My husband and I like to reminisce about how, when we were 9, we read straight through L. Frank Baum's Oz series, books filled with wizards and witches. And you know what those subversive tales taught us? That we loved to read! In those days I used to dream of flying. I may have been small and powerless in real life, but in my imagination I was able to soar. At the rate we're going, I can imagine next year's headline: '*Goodnight Moon* Banned for Encouraging Children to Communicate With Furniture.'"

As for promoting witchcraft, Starhawk, author, activist, and witch in the Wicca (Pagan) tradition commented: "The *Harry Potter* books have little or nothing to do with our theology, but most of us read them avidly and enjoy them immensely."

The Right Reverend David Lacy, then Moderator of the Church of Scotland, selected *Harry Potter and the Half-Blood Prince* as his book of the year for 2005. Lacy said to the *Scottish Herald*, "I can hear the sharp intake of breath from some of my Christian brothers and sisters who believe that these books are dangerous and anti- Christian. Sorry, I don't agree...I'm glad that youngsters are still being told stories about the victory of good over evil...My upbringing was gloriously Christian...And I was told all the standard fairy stories; I saw them enacted in pantomimes and films. I never thought they were real. But I knew they hold a truth. So does Harry Potter. And it's fun."

American *Harry Potter* scholar John Granger attributes the immense popularity of Rowling's work to, "the transcendent meaning of the books, and more specifically, their Christian content."

The many efforts to correct the false claims of the religious right are all to the good and very helpful. For the most part, however, *Harry Potter* defenders stop short of showing the progressive model of Christianity that undergirds Rowling's fantasy narrative. A further step needs to be taken. For as much as Rowling has imbued her fantasy saga with genuine Christian themes and imagery, the Christian theology arising from Harry Potter is not traditionally orthodox. The dots need to be connected to reveal a new picture of Christianity as drawn by Joanne Rowling.

Much has been written about the Catholicism and Medievalism underlying the fantasy works of J. R. R. Tolkien and C. S. Lewis. Rowling has produced Christian fantasy literature with a very different epistemological foundation from that of Lewis and Tolkien. Careful study of the seven *Harry Potter* novels reveals an unsystematic yet consistent theology not bound by the creeds of denominational churches or the needs of religious institutions. The religious vision in Harry Potter is not about going to church or even creating 21st century alternative Christian communities but about simply acting in faith to do the right thing.

The lesson that progressive Christians taught the world in the 20th century is that it is possible to be an authentic and even devout Christian without feeling compelled to defend and protect the doctrines of the faith, whatever they be. In the 21st century, Holy Rowlings see this kind of faith not as an exception but normative. We recognize the inherent freedom for believers to cling to any tenets they wish, as long as they don't force those beliefs on others. Claims of exclusive truth ring hollow in our ears.

Religious fundamentalism is clearly suspect to students of Harry Potter. We see similarities in the psychological dynamics of radical fundamentalists, be they Christians, Jews, Muslims, or Hindus. Religious fundamentalism is inherently violent, physically, intellectually, and emotionally.

In answer to those who fear that Rowling's work is full of New Age ideas, in 2000, Rowling said that New Age stuff leaves her cold. She has also stated that she never wanted to be a witch but was more interested in being an alchemist, which has direct Christian associations.

This stands in stark contrast to the darling of the right wing Tea Party movement, Christine O'Donnell, who told Bill Maher on his *Politically Incorrect* talk show that she had dabbled in witchcraft and hung around with people who practiced it. Not fantasy witches and wizards but the real thing. A decade later when she was running for the Senate, she tried to walk it back with her famous ad in which she said, "I'm not a witch." Well, neither is J. K. Rowling, and she has never dabbled in it either.

The charge that Rowling is indoctrinating readers into the religion of witchcraft completely falls apart when placed against the framework of Christmas and Easter holidays that Rowling makes a point of mentioning in every book. A clearly Christian Christmas Eve church service is noted in the seventh book. No Wicca or Pagan worship or rituals or services of any other non-Christian religions appear in the series. There is no New Age worship in the series. Dumbledore's funeral and Bill and Fleur's weddings are depicted as generic civil services.

Rowling's work may be heterodox, but it is in no way a reflection of demonic influences.

By midterm, Emma decided she did not like the words sermon or preaching, so she changed the service nomenclature to offering reflections. She considered using the word meditation for a while but came to the conclusion that a meditation was more free flowing than her carefully reasoned and crafted efforts.

More students were invited to sit in on the services as word spread around campus about what Emma was doing. Some weeks a dozen or more people listened to Emma speak about the values inherent in the **Harry Potter** epic.

In the course of the independent study, Emma recognized that though she had created an American church, the canon must be the Bloomsbury editions, because the Scholastic editions contain many word changes. Emma considered the early books almost a translation from English to Americanese. The problem with translating **Harry Potter** into other languages was the same as with the Bible, but Emma's elegant solution was to specify, for ecclesiastical purposes that all but the Bloomsbury canon were paraphrases.

"The differences in vocabulary between the canonical Bloomsbury and the edited Scholastic editions are bothersome and inauthentic," she told Rob Luke. "Doesn't it bother you that in **Chamber** the password for Dumbledore's office is Sherbet Lemon, but the American editor had the gall to change this to Lemon Drop?" she lamented.

"I didn't know about that change," he said. "It seems pretty close to me."

"But if you went to England and asked for lemon drops in a grocery store they'd look at you like you were a lunatic," Emma protested. "It's just not accurate."

"OK, it's not accurate but I'm not fussed about it," Rob replied. "What are some of the other editorial changes?"

"Well, in the UK sweaters are called jumpers, and sneakers are called trainers. In later books these words are left intact, but not in the first American editions. I will allow that changes in spelling from the original to the American versions are acceptable –but definitely not vocabulary, because that distorts the richness of Rowling's language. In **Philosopher's Stone** the vehicle Hagrid uses to deliver Harry to Privet Drive is a motorbike. But Scholastic changed that to motorcycle.

"Hoover becomes vacuum in America, glove puppet becomes hand puppet, cine-camera becomes video camera, aeroplane becomes airplane, baker's becomes bakery, barman becomes bartender, local comprehensive becomes local public school, post becomes mail, notes become bills, pudding becomes dessert, jelly becomes Jell-O, holiday becomes vacation, maths become math, car park becomes parking garage, sweets become candy. I could go on and on. These American renderings sound silly coming from the author's pen and the mouths of British characters. Probably the worst example is a passage in the first book where Rowling uses the phrase 'pasties and cakes' and the American text reads 'pasties, cakes, and candy.' Where in hell did candy come from? There is absolutely no reason to add that extra word. It clarifies nothing. It's just editorial…oh I don't know…arrogance!

"To be fair, Scholastic eased up on their verbal assault in later books. In **Deathly Hallows** Hagrid takes Harry away from Privet Drive on that same motorbike, which the American edition left unchanged," Emma proclaimed.

"I admit that I've picked up on British idioms from reading the Bloomsbury editions," Rob said. "Of course a lot of that is in the later novels. I especially like calling deserving targets stupid gits. And I don't like pudding in the American sense, but I get tickled calling ice cream and pie pudding."

"My aunt told me about the British invasion of music in the sixties, thanks initially to the Beatles," Emma said. "Thanks to J. K. Rowling, we have a 21st century invasion of British slang."

Thinking about what constituted a canon led Emma to decide that she needed a theology of inspiration for the authorized versions, much as various Christian bodies held doctrines about the inspiration of the Bible. In keeping with the humanist ethos of her church and the historical reality of its human author, however, her theory needed to avoid claims of Godly authorship. Emma hit upon the notion that J. K. Rowling had been inspired to write the books by connecting her creative mind into the Universal Consciousness. In this sense, the series can be considered inspired. And certainly, she maintained, the books are inspirational.

When the term was over, the students who had participated in the project did not want to disband. As a result, Emma continued leading services in a classroom at the college and promised to search for a permanent off-campus location. Since she was a member of the NCC, her first stop in pursuit of a venue was to see Terp, who told her the chapel might be available on Saturday afternoons. Terp also promised Emma that if she needed to she could live temporarily at Angel Nest until longer-term arrangements could be worked out.

On Emma's 22nd birthday she signed up for Pottermore, which had debuted the day before. She encountered problems logging in and was not impressed with its content early on, but she stuck with it, and added Pottermore to her growing list of bookmarked regular sites to check each day. When the site was revised, she found it much more attractive.

The years in college seemed a blur of memory to Emma at the 2012 commencement when she was awarded a bachelor's degree. As a graduation gift from her parents, she enjoyed a second visit to the UK that summer, and this time, Cameron went with her.

Among their tourist stops was the Warner Brothers Studio outside London, which had been the Leavesden Film Studios before WB took it over and made it into a money-minting theme park and museum. They also ventured into the West Country in search of places that served as models for fictional Harry Potter sites. The fictional Little Whinging is situated in the English county of Surrey, southwest of London. Godric's Hollow is somewhere in the West Country, in Devon or Cornwall. Since Hagrid passed over Bristol when taking Harry to Little Whinging, Godric's Hollow is probably in the northern part of the West Country, near Exmoor and not far from the Bristol Channel. Ottery St. Catchpole and the Burrow are in Devon. There is a real Ottery St. Mary along the Otter River about ten miles east of Exeter, where J. K. Rowling went to college. Shell Cottage is in Cornwall. Malfoy Manor is in Wiltshire, north of London.

Hogsmead and Hogwarts are somewhere in Scotland, and from descriptive hints, probably in the Highlands. So Emma and Cameron took a series of trains northward to see film locations in Scotland, including a model of Hagrid's hut in the Highlands.

After returning from the UK, Emma confirmed arrangements with the Sedona NCC to use the chapel on Saturday afternoons.

Moving her things from her dormitory back to Scottsdale now felt like a foolish endeavor, as she packed up that and more to move back to Sedona, this time into a room with kitchen privileges in the rambling ranch home of a new widow. Magda Lena Zwingvin had made the arrangement on Emma's behalf, so living at Angel Nest would not be necessary.

Emily Hale Norton had been married to Professor of English Thomas Burns Norton, who spent his career at the University of Montana exploring the contributions of Native American languages to American English and writing poetry filled with native words. At retirement, he and his wife said farewell to Missoula and bought a home in Sedona, which upon his death felt empty and lonely to his widow. Magda and Emily Hale had met at a campus social gathering and had become close friends. It seemed a natural turn of events for the professor of religion to suggest to Emily Hale that she take in a lodger.

Emma felt intimidated at her first meeting with Emily Hale, as she was called, as if she were a Sally Ann or Betty Jo, although she bore no resemblance at all to anyone carrying such regionally girlish names. Emily Hale Norton was an imposing woman, tall, with the broad shoulders of a competitive swimmer, flat chest and slender at the hips. Her gray hair was wrapped in a neat bun, and there was a faint odor of Vicks VapoRub emanating from somewhere about her body. But it was her classic face that arrested Emma's attention. It was the wrinkled face of a Pre-Raphaelite model who had survived into her seventies.

After an initial period of respectful awe on Emma's part, she sensed that Emily Hale was approachable, and the two women developed a pleasant relationship. Emma had not known her grandparents on either side of her family, and the childless Emily Hale had never known what it was like to fill that role. Instead of reading or watching television, Emma began to spend evenings telling Emily Hale about the world of Harry Potter, of which the widow was completely ignorant.

In turn, Emma listened attentively as Emily Hale talked at length about her western adventure married to Tom Norton, champion and poet of Native America. There was much more Tom in her narrative than Emily Hale. On the mantle was a framed photograph of the professor standing in front of a lodge on the Crow Indian Reservation. Peering at his image, Emma saw an obese man, a little shorter than his wife, with a sweet face and a kindly hazel-eyed gaze. The picture had been taken at a time when his sandy locks were in need of a haircut, if neatness were to be achieved. Emma suspected, however, that neatness had not been a priority for the man.

Emma's first ecclesiastical task was to advertise in order to recruit members to her fledgling congregation. She cajoled businesses in town to post signs in their windows. She asked faculty members and students to promote the church. Within a few weeks, local townsfolk, friends of friends, a few faculty members and their relatives, along with a handful of Natural Christians began attending Emma's services.

The chapel looked and felt to Emma like a place of worship, because in fact it was designed to be exactly that. Emma discerned a spiritual aura to the place and experienced a comfortable sense of belonging there. "This feels more satisfying than the classroom at school, and the feel of the place gives me energy," she told Terp. "But even so, my hands still get cold before starting the service and stay that way all during the reflection, and even when I'm shaking hands afterward."

"Mine too," said Terp. "And I've been doing this for decades. It's a fact of leadership life that you'll have to get used to."

As a means of recruiting members, Emma offered a marathon showing of the eight **Harry Potter** movies in the chapel. Watching them again reminded her how truly dreadful they seemed to her at frustrating intervals where there was stupid and unnecessary divergence from the books. Especially detested were the action scenes such as Harry versus the dragon and the battle of Hogwarts. The breaking of the elder wand in the final film was painful to watch, and she felt a strong desire to do bodily injury to the screenwriter who produced that scene.

CHAPTER FIFTEEN
SORTING

As late summer turned into early fall, Emma realized that she needed more structure for her congregation and more order in the service of worship. She began the process of creating practices and customs that would in time evolve into traditions. Some of her ideas worked while others were abandoned after a short time of trial.

Emma had reservations about initiating a sorting process because it would tend to work against developing a sense of congregational unity. But she also knew that people of her generation expected choices and were drawn to things that reinforced their individual identities. She presented the idea that members would self-sort into houses to gauge the response and received general enthusiasm. A few people resisted, however, and so in addition to the four canonical houses, Emma introduced a new category she called Unsorted.

Thinking about her own inner conflict over whether she belonged in Gryffindor or Ravenclaw, she developed a new house that she called Gryffinclaw. Several Slytherins protested that they also were as smart as Ravenclaws and demanded an option called Slytherclaw.

At this point, a delegation of Hufflepuffs approached Emma with a plea that Emma stick with the canonical houses that J. K. Rowling had created, claiming that changing the rules to suit individuals was not fair.

"What about Unsorteds?" Emma asked.

They agreed that it was fair to allow people not to be sorted, but not fair to create new houses.

Seeing Gryffinclaw as a failed experiment leading to headaches from demands for further refinements, Emma quietly dropped the idea.

Conflict inevitably developed over allowing Unsorteds to be full members. Emma argued in favor, but Slytherin members thought that people who opted out of sorting should not be voting members. They were welcome in church, but not on an equal basis with the sorteds. The Slytherins were adamant that enforced sorting into canonical houses was necessary for membership recognition, because anyone who did not belong in a house was a Muggle and not to be trusted.

Responding to the conflict in a reflection, Emma argued that sorting was a fallible art not a science. "Dumbledore not only mused that the sorting ceremony may take place too soon but repeatedly emphasized that personal choices matter more than genealogy, more than what family one is born into. The Sorting Hat listens to students and considers their choices when assigning them to a house. In *Philosopher's Stone*, Harry says, 'Not Slytherin,' and the hat grants his wish. In *Deathly Hallows*, Harry tells his son Albus Severus, who is worrying about the sorting ceremony, that he has a choice. Again and again, Rowling advances the view that people are not predestined by fate, by God, by social class, or by genetics. We all have choices, for good or ill.

"Sorting in our tradition is analogous to baptismal naming and being known by name by God, or in our case, the community," she said. "And some Christians choose to remain unbaptized. It was a common practice in the early Christian Church for people to wait until they were on their deathbeds to be baptized. By extension, our members should be allowed to remain unsorted as long as they want.

"In *Philosopher's Stone*, Ron says that his rat Scabbers might have died and no one would know the difference. In *Prisoner of Azkaban* we learn that the rat Scabbers is actually the animagus Peter Pettigrew, whom everyone thought had died because they didn't know the difference, because he had staged his own death. For our purposes today, this raises the question of how did Peter Pettigrew, who is a coward, ever get sorted into Gryffindor? This is strong evidence that the Sorting Hat is not infallible, so let's allow for a little grace in the sorting process. One never fully knows where one ultimately belongs until tested by the ravages of life. And people can change."

Since Emma was clearly the leader of the congregation and more knowledgeable of all things Potter than any of the members, everyone else deferred to her wishes, and except for minor grumbling from a few disgruntled Slytherin members, the uproar about sorting and membership soon died out.

When Emma devised apt biblical citations and mottos for each of the houses, she expected some resistance, at least from those members who had turned away from traditional Christian denominations or who had been wounded by judgmental congregations. To her surprise, however, the members embraced them.

To Gryffindor she assigned Luke 21:9, "When you hear of wars and commotions, do not be terrified," along with the motto: Willing to march into hell for a heavenly cause.

For Hufflepuff the biblical text was Luke 6:31, "Do unto others as you would have them do unto you," accompanied by the motto: Play by the rules.

Ravenclaw received John 8:32, "Ye shall know the truth and the truth shall make you free," and the motto: *Ars gratia artis.* Art for art's sake.

The text Emma found for Slytherin was John 18:38, "What is truth?" The motto: All's fair in love and war.

In due course, a group of Unsorteds came to Emma, humbly requesting a verse and motto as well. After pondering possibilities for an hour, she returned with John 10:16, "Other sheep have I, which are not of this fold...but there shall be one fold and one shepherd." The motto came to her in an instant: What's in a name?

Members began inventing idioms and private language for use in church. Someone referred to Great Britain as the Holy Land when describing a visit there to see **Harry Potter** book and movie locations, and it caught on. J. K. Rowling became variously known as the Creator or the Great Mind, and also the Mother of the Seeker. In church slang, she became Jo Ro, Jake, and the Jokar.

In order to clarify the place of the author within the Holy Rowling ecclesiastical world, Emma reflected on the matter in a service. "Jesus intimately addressed God as papa, so on a lower plane, we should have no problem addressing the creator of our canon as Jo. She is to be venerated, admired, and respected but not worshipped. She is fully human containing only the same trace of divinity as any other human being. In Judeo-Christian thought, she, like every other human being, was made in the image of God."

The Sedona NCC had a labyrinth on the grounds. Emma asked permission for ACHPP members to use it for meditations and received a quick yes. To aid meditation, Emma devised a ritual that she called

Stations of the Hallows, by which members could reflect on various stages of Harry's journey throughout the Battle of Hogwarts. Cameron quipped that it should be called Stations of the Horcrux.

She also developed a communion service using chunks of dark chocolate and butterbeer and called it the Ritual of Revival.

When a couple from the congregation asked her to officiate at their wedding, Emma's first thought was whether she could do it legally. A call to Terp informed her that the wedding license required only the officiant's signature, and Terp was confident that it would not be questioned. The next issue was that this would be an inter-house wedding between a Hufflepuff and a Slytherin. What counsel could she give to them about their differences?

"Well, it's not an interfaith marriage, so lighten up," the Slytherin partner told her when she broached the subject with the couple.

"OK," Emma responded but quickly added, "This is my first wedding, and I think it needs something distinctive to show forth the Holy Rowling culture."

"How about concluding with us walking under an arch of wands, like military weddings do with swords?" the Hufflepuff suggested.

And so they did, and it became traditional thereafter.

The next addition to the growing body of Holy Rowling spiritual practice was offering a pastoral prayer during the service, which Emma called transcendent conversation. In parallel with Christian prayers ending in the name of the Trinity, she invented an ACHPP Trinity to conclude her transcendent conversations, consisting of Headmaster, Chosen One, and Brightest Witch.

The regular worshipers grew in number to fifty or so on any given Saturday, mostly Millennials and Generation Xers. But a cadre of seven dedicated members spanning a larger age spectrum coalesced around Emma, volunteering to carry the work of the church, including participating as readers in the worship service. Among them, this core group represented the four houses plus one Unsorted. Professor Zwingvin also attended from time to time but sat in the back and declined invitations to speak or be sorted.

The Gryffindors among Emma's cadre were Rob Luke, Sol Davar, and Dwight Cooke. Frieda Waring represented Hufflepuff, as did Jordan

Inge for Slytherin. Alexis Whidge had sorted into Ravenclaw, and for several months was the only participant to do so. Karl Adler chose to be Unsorted.

Emma met Rob Luke at Celebrating Creation Church in Mesa the day before they both started classes at Anasazi College. He was among the first participants in Emma's college project and became the first charter member when the church incorporated. After graduation, Rob had taken a job as assistant director of the newly created Anasazi Alumnae and Alumni Association (AAaAA), which required him to live in the Sedona area. He handled the day-to-day administrative chores while the director traveled the country visiting graduates and raising money.

Frieda Waring, a pleasingly pudgy divorced woman in her forties, was a Pomona Sprout cosplayer who spoke often about her son in the Army.

Jordan Inge, a 24 year-old raven-haired woman with a predilection toward makeup that drew attention to her strikingly beautiful face and black clothing that outlined the curves of her figure, was also a Snape fetishist.

Owlish-faced, pigeon-toed, and platinum blonde Alexis Whidge, was geekily smart and doted on Luna Lovegood.

School psychologist Karl Adler, 40, remained unsorted for professional reasons. As a hobby, and to decompress from stressful counseling of students who were victims of violence at home or at school, he crafted wands in his shop at the back of his house, insisting there was nothing Freudian about this. Karl found the Holy Rowlings to be a sublime personal experience as well as useful, because it helped him get closer to students. Interacting with troubled young people, he made frequent reference to characters and story lines from *Harry Potter*.

Solomon Davar was a sculptor and musician who graduated from Anasazi College a year ahead of Emma and had been living in the Bay area until recently returning to town. Just shy of six feet and slender, he had been seeker on the Anasazi Quidditch team. His major contribution to the church was performing music solos on guitar, mandolin, and dulcimer, all of which he had mastered.

The oldest member of the congregation was 65 year-old Dwight Cooke, a retired detective sergeant from the Phoenix Police department and a Viet Nam veteran, who had served as an MP in the Mekong Delta. He stopped getting haircuts when he retired but kept his face clean-shaven. Thick glasses and a limp from being shot in the leg during a homicide investigation led church members to call him Madeye.

Dwight habitually came to church an hour early, because he enjoyed watching Emma go about preparing for the service. He smiled to see her flit about the chapel, checking sound levels, making sure the chairs were arranged properly, placing her reflection and notes on the lectern, conferring with the music soloist for the day –usually Sol Davar. Dwight liked to think that if he had ever married and had children, he would have had a daughter like Emma, and a tiny part of his mind accepted the fantasy notion that she was his child.

As she was generally ready for the service half an hour early, Emma had time to chat with parishioners, including Dwight. "So, Dwight, how did you come to be a Harry Potter expert?" she asked him one day.

"Because of Stephen Colbert," he replied.

"I thought Colbert was a Tolkien fan," Emma said.

"He is," Dwight said. "I was watching The Colbert Report one night, and Stephen was once again showing off how much he knew about *Lord of the Rings*. I'd seen him do it before, but this time for some reason I admitted to myself that his mastery of the material was impressive, and it motivated me to work at knowing a literary subject that well. A deep desire to be an expert in something other than law enforcement rose up in me. But it wouldn't be LOTR. I'd read the series several times, but didn't feel any energy for delving any further into it."

"Because?" Emma said.

"I suppose because I don't resonate with stories of worlds dominated by royalty," he responded. "I don't find tales of kings and queens romantic. Also because in places the writing is turgid and the narrative gets bogged down. When I thought about what fantasy series I would most enjoy exploring deeply in order to become well versed, *Harry Potter* rose immediately to the top of the list. I'd read the books twice, and so I embarked on a marathon third reading, this time taking notes. It was a mind-blowing experience. There was so much more there than I had recognized the first two times through."

"I'm glad you did that," Emma said. "And I give thanks for Stephen Colbert for motivating you."

"Without that, it's unlikely that I would have found my way to the Holy Rowlings," Dwight said and with a deprecating laugh added, "So it's Colbert's fault that I'm here."

On another Saturday Emma asked Dwight, "Does it bother you when people call you Madeye?"

"Naw," he replied. "When I was little, I imagined myself as a gallant Knight of the Round Table, but I never looked the part. I was an old fart when I got hooked on **Harry Potter**, and I identified with Kingsley Shacklebolt, but I didn't look anything like him." He tugged at his ponytail and winked at Emma. "Thing is, I *do* look a bit like Alastair Moody, even though I don't personally identify with his character. But he has a good heart, so to answer your question in a round about way, it doesn't bother me a bit that people call me Madeye. I take it as a sign of affection."

"That's a healthy attitude," Emma said. "Considering your police background, I didn't know if you'd find the portrait of paranoid Madeye Moody objectionable. Stereotyping law enforcement officers and such."

"I've known a few paranoid officers in my years on the force," said Dwight, "and who lacked the essential goodness of Madeye. I don't take any of that personally. There are literally good cops and bad cops."

"No doubt," said Emma.

She turned to talk with someone else, but Emma had opened a passageway in Dwight's mind, and he touched her sleeve to say more. "I was an MP in Nam, and I saw POWs who were beat up, tortured, and mutilated in the field before they were given over to Military Police custody. It sickened me. The thing you need to know about war -or at least that war- is that the safest place POWs could be was in the custody of American MPs."

"I didn't know that, but it makes sense," said Emma.

"I know you have to get on with other things," Dwight added, "but there's one more thing on my mind while I have your attention. I believe in reincarnation. And the reason I do is I've always had a feeling that I was a sailor killed in WWII. I've had it since I was old enough to hear stories about my dad's war. I think I was on a ship in Pearl Harbor, and when the Japanese attacked, I was trapped inside an upside down ship. An air pocket allowed me to breathe, and I kept tapping on the hull, but no one rescued me. I was trapped alive until Christmas Eve, when I died.

That's why I have taphophobia, fear of being buried alive. As my pastor, you should know that I am very claustrophobic."

"Oh my," said Emma. "That must have made your work as a detective difficult at times."

"I was pretty good about avoiding confining places," Dwight said. "I don't like caves."

The following Saturday, Dwight was true to habit in arriving early, and this time he engaged Emma in literary speculation.

"I have a fan theory about *Catch-22* and *Order of the Phoenix*, he said. "It's about Educational Decree Twenty-Two."

"Tell me more," Emma replied.

"The very first of the Ministry of Magic's Educational Decrees revealed in *Order of the Phoenix* is number 22," Dwight explained. "Now, this could be a matter of coincidence, but it seems to me that by introducing the feature of Educational Decrees starting with number 22, Rowling is making a punning allusion to Joseph Heller's World War II satire *Catch-22*. There is something akin to a Catch-22 involved in the decree that gives the Ministry the power to appoint a Hogwarts faculty member when the position it's first used for, Defense Against the Dark Arts teacher, has been jinxed for years and Dumbledore has not had much to brag about in his appointments thus far. What makes it truly a Catch-22 is that the Ministry can't win either."

"Dwight, I think you're right," Emma said, evoking a broad grin from the retired detective.

Next, it was Karl who buttonholed Emma with a recommendation for study. "I want to suggest a book edited by Neil Mulholland that's been very helpful to me," he said.

She borrowed Karl's copy of *The Psychology of Harry Potter* and read it over the next two days. In doing so, she discovered that the Harry Potter books were now being used for treating psychological problems. Neil Mulholland, a practicing psychologist in Canada, edited the book that contained articles about the psychological dimensions of the Harry Potter books. In his own article, he described the application of what he called Harry Potter Therapy, in which he used images of characters from the series in guided exercises to help clients deal with stress, anxiety, and depression.

Mulholland also suggested that the *Harry Potter* novels could be put to good use for the treatment of PTSD. Talking about the traumatic events one has experienced is crucially important in getting control of post-traumatic stress, and situations in this series offer good means for sufferers to connect with traumatic memories.

Emma remembered how she had used Rowling's books to help deal with Sylvia's death and her own injuries, and decided that Mulholland's collection was a treasure that would inform her own attempts at pastoral care as she grew into her calling as a pastor.

Another article in the book was written by Melanie C. Green, who had received a PhD in psychology and literature. Green taught at the University of North Carolina and focused her work on the persuasive power of narratives. Professor Green found the **Harry Potter** series particularly useful in helping young people deal with peer pressure and bullying.

The following Saturday, Karl greeted Emma when she came into the chapel, barely beating out Dwight, who was hoping for face time with her. "What did you think of the book?" Karl asked Emma.

"Spot on," she replied. "Thanks for lending it to me. I resonated with quite a bit of it, having used the **Potter** narratives myself to deal with traumatic experiences."

"This calls for a more leisurely conversation, but not in such a public place," the school psychologist said. "Are you free after the service?"

"I could spare a little time," she said. "We could find a quiet corner of the chapel to talk."

Dwight had been hovering around the edges of the conversation and now entered it. "Mind if I join you? I have a barrel of trauma stories to throw into the mix."

"Not at all," said Karl. "In fact, you could add a personal dimension to the conversation that I know only from doing counseling, not being counseled. And I'd be happy to lend you the book now that Emma has finished it. I think you'd find it edifying."

"Yes, please, and thank you," said Dwight.

"I brought it today to return to Karl, so I'll just pass it on to you instead," Emma said. "And if we're going to be a trio this afternoon, maybe you two gallants would escort me into town. There's a new English teashop I've been curious about visiting. We could talk over tea."

And so they did.

Emma ordered a cup of Downton Estate blend of Earl Grey black tea with vanilla, and the two men followed her lead. While waiting for their beverages to be served, Emma asked Karl about his wand-making hobby. "Do you identify with Mr. Ollivander?"

"I suppose I do," Karl said. "Wands simply facilitate magic, and as a counselor, I facilitate mental health. And as an ancient history buff, I like that Ollivander's forebears have been making wands since 382 BC. If I had written the book, I would have said 382 BCE, but that's another matter."

"What was happening in Britain in the 4th century BCE?" Dwight asked. "Is the date significant? I read somewhere that Ollivander's family made wands for the Roman occupiers of Britain."

"The Romans didn't get there until the 1st century BCE," Emma said. "They could have produced wands for them, but they'd already been doing it for centuries by then. I've delved into that date, 382, and found nothing specific," Emma said.

"What attracts my interest," said Karl, "is that the Ollivander family began making wands in Celtic Britain during the Druid Age. Druids were the intellectual class among the Celts. Though it's not canonical, I feel certain that their original wand customers were Druids."

"I love that idea," said Emma.

When their tea arrived, Karl said, "I've found Madame Pomfrey very helpful in counseling troubled teenagers. There's a passage near the end of *Order of the Phoenix* that takes place in the Hogwarts infirmary. Our resident healer said that thoughts could leave deeper scarring than almost anything else. This is an interesting insight into the way we wound ourselves and mentally beat up on ourselves, showing the effects of dysfunctional thinking."

"Healing is an important theme in *Phoenix*," Dwight said.

"I hadn't thought of that," Emma said. "I've focused my attention on all the blood and trauma in the story, but all that violence is countered by the presence of healers and wise counselors."

"By the way," said Karl, "I have a speculation about J. K. Rowling's personal life that relates to *Order of the Phoenix*. In the last week of 2001, Joanne Rowling married Neil Murray, a medical doctor. At the time, she was writing *Order of the Phoenix*. That's why I don't think it's a stretch to construe an episode in *Phoenix* as a snide comment about the practice of medicine, traditional and alternative. While in St.

Mungo's, Arthur undergoes what his Trainee Healer calls complementary medicine and which Arthur calls 'old Muggle remedies.' In this case it is sutures, which fail miserably.

"Molly does not appreciate the experimental adventurousness of her husband, saying that it sounded like an attempt to sew his skin back together, adding, 'but even you, Arthur, wouldn't be that stupid.'"

"That reminds me of an episode in **Star Trek** when Bones described surgery that involved making an incision into the body as primitive," said Dwight. "My guess is that Rowling included the St. Mungo's episode not as a snarky putdown but as a tribute to her new husband, the doctor."

Emma had full use of the kitchen at Emily Hale Norton's home and initially prepared meals for herself, which she ate alone in her room. But Emily Hale soon tired of that arrangement and cajoled Emma to take her evening repast in the dining room with her. They alternated preparing the meals, each trying to surprise the other with some unusual fare.

"We need my brother Jared here," Emma said one evening. "He's the chef in the family."

"Then we shall invite him to prepare a grand meal for us," Emily Hale said.

"The next time he heads east from L. A. I'll see if he'd make a detour from Scottsdale to show off for us," Emma said.

"I've been meaning to ask you if there are any Native Americans in your Harry Potter church?" Emily Hale said.

"No members, but I have a friend, Willow Black, who is Yavapai, who attends once in a while," Emma replied. "And one of the pastors at the host church we nest with is Navajo-Lakota."

"Really?" Emily Hale said. "The nudist church has a Native American pastor?"

"One of them, yes," Emma said. "They have a large staff."

"I'd like to meet him," Emily Hale said.

"Her," Emma corrected. "Wakhan Begay. Her husband, Camelot Wickham, is Anglo-Maori."

"I'd like to meet both of them," said Emily Hale. "And your Yavapai friend too. Invite her to dinner some time. In fact, invite them all."

"I'll see what I can do about Willow. She's in a long-distance relationship with my cousin Jeff. After he got his JD from ASU, he took a job with an environmental law firm in Utah. Willow's working on a Master of Forestry degree at NAU. If she's not in Flag, she's off to Salt Lake City to spend time with Jeff, or he's down here, and they don't often spend their precious time coming to church. But why don't you come with me to church some Sunday and I'll introduce you to Wakhan and Camelot," Emma said.

"That wouldn't do at all," Emily Hale responded. "At my age, I'm not about to appear starkers in public."

"You wouldn't have to," said Emma. "They have a textile service in the chapel on Sundays. I'll let you know when Wakhan is preaching at that service, and you can meet her then."

"Textile?" Emily le asked.

"Clothed," Emma said. "Everyone wears clothes. It's metaphorical naturism."

"Oh, I love metaphors, metaphorical anything," said Emily Hale.

"Then you should come to a Holy Rowling service also. We're all about metaphors."

"You're quite the evangelist," Emily Hale said. "Let me know when Wakhan Begay will be preaching at the textile service."

Emma supported Barack Obama for reelection in 2012, while her father preferred Mitt Romney. Emma's mother and brothers also backed the Democrat, but over the years they had learned to ignore the political pronouncements of the Round patriarch. David's position was that a President Romney would not do any damage to the social issues he supported, such as gay rights and reproductive freedom of choice, and he pointed out to his family that President Obama had not done much for gays in his first term. David preferred Michael Bloomberg, who was his ideal Republican, but since that was not to be, Romney was acceptable.

Emma thought her dad was crazy to think that Mitt Romney would protect gay rights. In a particularly frustrating phone conversation, she called him naïve, which he denied. In her personal assessment, she believed that she had effectively refuted his feelings about the Republican candidate with three words: Supreme Court nominees. But David argued that he thought Mitt Romney was secretly progressive on social issues.

<><><>

The time when she had led the congregation in a classroom on the campus of Anasazi College now seemed long ago to Emma. In those days, she had called her reflections sermons. At the urging of members who had been with the congregation then, Emma agreed to repeat her inaugural offering about the purported demonic influences in **Harry Potter**.

"The new people need to hear it," Rob told her.

Not willing to simply re-read the piece, however, Emma spent several hours editing and fine-tuning it before delivering it as a reflection.

Afterward, Dwight approached her and said. "That was great. For some reason it reminded me of that old standard 'Witchcraft.' We should sing it in church some day."

"I never heard of it," Emma replied.

"Frank Sinatra recorded it in the fifties," Dwight said.

"Him I've heard of," said Emma. "What's the song about -other than witchcraft, obviously?" Emma asked.

"Basically it's about sexual attraction," Dwight confessed.

"And thus perfectly appropriate for a church service," Emma said snidely.

"Well, it's a good kind of witchcraft, not demonic," said Dwight. "It's sung not invoked. That's the good kind, right? But what I like best, that reminds me of our Hallowed Philosopher, is the line about no nicer witch than you. That's a compliment, not a come-on, by the way."

"Thanks. I'll google the lyrics, and if they're OK, you can sing it as a solo," Emma said.

"Sorry I suggested it," said Dwight. "I have a lousy singing voice."

"I don't know about your voice, but I do know that you're not sorry you mentioned it," Emma said with a twinkle in her voice.

Dwight smiled broadly in acknowledgment.

CHAPTER SIXTEEN
HALLOWED PHILOSOPHER

Emma asked five people from the congregation to serve as an advisory board, which she named Merlin's Board. Charter board members, one from each house plus an Unsorted, were Dwight Cooke, Frieda Waring, Alexis Whidge, Jordan Inge, and Karl Adler. The first issue they advised Emma about was setting a standard for voting membership. After discussing the matter for several hours, the criterion they devised was an affirmation before the congregation that one had read all seven books of the *Harry Potter* novels in any language or edition. And seeing the movies did not count. Completion of the three companion volumes that were part of the church canon were not needed for membership, they decided. No doctrinal assent was required, and anyone could attend services and participate in the activities of the church, but only those serious enough to have read all the books would be allowed to vote on matters brought before the congregation.

Few such matters existed at that early juncture, but the members of Merlin's Board expected that they would in due course.

Emma was satisfied with the membership literacy standard, but she could not resist noting that if Christian churches required people to have read the entire Bible before becoming members, they would have long since vanished from the land.

"I think that's true," said Alexis, "but in our context, the requirement is not at all onerous or unrealistic."

Some of the music for worship consisted of recordings played on a boom box, particularly music from the *Harry Potter* films. "Hedwig's Theme"

161

served as a prelude to the services. Occasionally, various members would volunteer to sing solos, accompanied instrumentally by Sol Davar. Even so, envisioning the possibility of a fuller musical program, including a choir, Emma asked Sol to be the volunteer music director.

"Does that mean I get to choose all the music for the services?" he responded.

Emma hesitated for a few seconds and then said, "Sure. You already choose what you want to play. Why not what the soloists contribute too? And see if you can get some of the soloists to work together as a choir."

"OK, I'll do it," he said. "Being director of something will look good on my resume when I'm hungry and forced to look for a real job."

"It will look good in your **Who's Who** write-up when you're a famous artist," Emma said.

"Thanks for the vote of confidence," he said. "And my first action with my newly granted authority will be to find some music for the whole congregation to sing."

"Like hymns?" Emma asked.

"Like that but suitable for our peculiar kind of group," he replied. "I'll search through old folk music collections looking for things to adapt."

Sol had joined the Sedona naturist church as a child and had known Emma as a fellow member since her freshman year in college, and as such, they had seen each other in the buff. Now, as music director, he had many occasions to confer with Emma in front of the fully clothed Holy Rowling congregation, few of whom knew of their connections with the NCC.

In the course of recruiting a soloist for an upcoming service, the member asked Sol if he knew any songs about lightning shaped scars.

"I seriously do not," Sol said. "Maybe you could write one. But I'd check with the Hallowed Philosopher first. She might have some thoughts on the subject since she has a childhood scar of her own."

"Wow! I've never noticed it before," the member said.

"It's under her left breast," Sol explained.

"And she told you about it?" the member asked.

"Well yes, but, of course, I've seen it many times," Sol responded, forgetting for the moment which congregation he was representing.

"Whoa! TMI, Sol," the member said.

Now recognizing his ecclesiastical context, Sol said, "No, no, it's not what you think. Emma and I are both members of the Sedona NCC. That's all. There's nothing intimate between us. We're just friends."

"Well, you look like more than friends when you work together on church stuff," the member said.

"Really?" Sol responded.

"Yeah, you do," said the member.

Frieda tried everything she could think of to kindle a romantic relationship with Dwight. Repeatedly, she professed deep admiration for his military service in a war zone and cheerily referred to him as a hero.

Dwight treated her in a friendly manner but ignored her fawning behavior. Eventually Frieda decided direct action was needed to get his attention. After a church service in December, she approached him with two glasses of eggnog, one of which she pushed into his hand, and said, "Let's toast to a warmer relationship in the new year."

He raised his glass and drank the contents in one gulp. "I feel warmth from everyone in this church, including you, Frieda. I'm all in favor of warm relationships, but I'm a disciple of old Plato when it comes to intimate ones."

"Oh bosh," she said. "I'll bet there's plenty of steam left in your boiler. I'd like to help you to recover it. You know I admire what you've done and stood for in life." She ran her hand along his sleeve.

"Be careful, Frieda," he said, not in a menacing way but firmly. "It's not good to fall in love with someone's past. It's never what you think it is. There are plenty of failed affairs that I'd just as soon not dredge up or think about."

Deciding to let the subject drop for resurrection at another more opportune time, she changed the subject. "Did I tell you about my son Rick? He just graduated from the Military Police School at Fort Leonard Wood, Missouri. He's following in your footsteps. So we have that in common. I hope you won't mind my chatting you up about how his military career unfolds. You're the only one here who knows about that first hand."

"Of course, Frieda. Army talk is great for Platonic friendships," he replied and put a gentle hand on her shoulder. "Please, let me know how he gets along and where he gets posted. I am genuinely interested in Rick's progress."

Two days later, Frieda phoned Dwight at home and said, "Rick's got orders to Afghanistan. He's being deployed to someplace called Camp Eggers that he says is in Kabul. That's a safe base, isn't it? As an MP, he'll just be guarding the fort so to speak, right?"

"I can't answer your questions, Frieda, because I simply don't know," Dwight replied. Then sensing that a comforting lie would be better for her peace of mind than the existential truth added, "But he's not in the Infantry, out on the front lines. He'll be as safe at that base as any place in the country. Safer, actually."

"Oh thank you Dwight," Frieda said. "Now I'll be able to sleep tonight."

Emma escorted Emily Hale to a textile service in the NCC chapel, after which she introduced her landlady to Wakhan and Camelot.

Emily Hale was eager to tell them about her late husband's scholarly work in Native American linguistics. Looking toward Camelot, she said, "Alas, he did not venture into Polynesian languages."

"There is no end to the study of those," said Camelot. "But I'm fascinated by the language and literature of my wife's ancestors."

"You'll have to show us some of your husband's poetry," Wakhan said.

"Then you two will have to come to my home for dinner," Emily Hale said. "Afterward, I'll burden you with more verse than you can handle."

They arranged a date for dinner two weeks hence. The following Saturday, Emma brought Emily Hale along to a Holy Rowling service, which by prior arrangement, Willow Black attended. Thus Emily Hale met and was enchanted by the young Yavapai woman. Willow, too, was invited to the dinner party, now consisting of two Native Americans, one Anglo-Maori, and two Caucasians.

On the drive back home, Emma asked her landlady if she enjoyed the service.

"Certainly. It was filled with grace and not dogmas," Emily Hale replied. "Of course, I'm fairly easy to please when it comes to religious services. I fancy myself a devotee of omnism."

"What's that?" Emma said.

"It's the belief that no single religion has a monopoly on the truth, and that some truths may be found in all religions. Generally, I have been able to identify some kernel of truth in every service I've attended," Emily Hale said.

"I might claim the same belief," Emma said, "but I would add a corollary that all the major world religions also hold onto a number of falsehoods, including some that are pernicious."

"I won't argue with that," Emily Hale said. "But I suspect that among the religious populations of the world, you and I, dear, are a distinct minority."

"Speaking of minorities, the participants for your upcoming dinner party consist of four naturists and one textile," Emma said. "You'll be way outnumbered, Emily Hale."

"Child, I have been outnumbered my entire life and lived to tell about it," Emily Hale said. "But I must say I am enjoying the novelty of being labeled a textile. That's a new subject for my diary."

"How long have you kept a diary?" Emma asked.

"Since a month before my wedding day," Emily Hale said.

"So, you have a record available to write an autobiography," Emma said. "You've had such an interesting life. People should know about it."

"You have no idea how *interesting*," Emily Hale replied. "There are days when I think people *should* know about it. But I have always been a private person and not inclined to tell all, as they say."

"What will happen to your diaries after you're gone?" Emma asked. "Do you have any extended family they would go to?"

"The older volumes are safely stored away, and I've left instructions in my will for them to be destroyed after my passing," Emily Hale said.

The thought of such precious repositories being shredded or burned struck Emma with a sharp pain. "Oh no, you mustn't do that," she said. "You should share your life with the world, or let someone else do it."

"If I were to bequeath my diaries to anyone, it would be you dear," Emily Hale said. "But I wouldn't want any of my words to come to public light until I had been gone for some years."

"I have no right to such a privilege, but I would be humbly honored to be your literary executor," Emma said.

"You are saying that without any knowledge of the perversity that may be contained in what I have written," Emily Hale said. "Your faith in the value of my life gives me pleasure, but I must say, you do not know what you are asking for."

"Now you have me thoroughly intrigued," said Emily.

"And I shall say no more about it," Emily Hale said in conclusion.

Cloud and Terp's daughter Zara had a five year-old son whom everyone called K. P. Zara had first read the **Harry Potter** books to her son when he was three, and now at five, he was in the process of reading them for himself. K. P. also loved listening to the audio compact disc recordings of the series voiced by Jim Dale for Scholastic and Stephen Fry for Bloomsbury and delighted in pointing out changes in word usage between the two recordings. Zara said that K. P. reminded her of her younger self when he did that.

In the fall, Zara and K. P. began attending the Saturday afternoon services of the Alchemical Church of Harry Potter Prophecy.

"I so much enjoyed sitting in on your Harry Potter theology classes at our church, that I couldn't resist checking out this congregation," Zara said to Emma.

"I'm flattered that you're here," Emma responded.

"Harry and I go way back," Zara said. "In college, I wrote a paper on the first **Harry Potter** volume and ultimately found the entire series delightful and spiritually rich. I'm not surprised that a religion has developed around J. K. Rowling's Harry Potter theology."

"I expected more negative attacks for developing a religion based on a fictional character," Emma said.

"Attacks may come," Zara said, "but Harry Potter makes a healthier choice of role model than many of those put forth by established churches purportedly based on the words of various so-called holy men. Churches organized around guilt and punishment are inherently unhealthy. Some religious traditions claiming to be centered on the love of Christ, for example, seem closer to worshiping Voldemort than Jesus."

After attending for a few weeks, Zara affirmed that she had read all the novels and became an official Holy Rowling, sorting herself into Ravenclaw.

In conversation with Emma, at the new member reception following the service, she said, "Merlin's Board is a great name. Better than the one I would have suggested: Wizengamot."

"I thought of that, too," said Emma, "but it evokes a larger body than we need here."

"I assume you know the origin of JKR's magical court," Zara said.

"Are you referring to the Sanhedrin?" Emma said.

"That connection is there," Zara said, "but I mean a linguistic and historically British connection. In Anglo-Saxon England, there was a body called the **Witangemot**. It was an assembly of church and lay counselors that provided judicial and other advice to the king. **Witan** is Old English for wise man and **gemot** is Old English for an assembly. Rowling adapted witan to resemble the first syllable of wizard to create the judicial court of the Wizarding World."

"That's useful to know. Thanks," Emma responded.

"Your reflections are so deep and engaging," Zara said. "You have a natural gift for digging out nuggets of meaning from the narratives. Have you had any training in exegesis?"

"No, but I'd like to take a course in it someday," Emma said.

"I'll be happy to tutor you privately," said Zara. "You're already doing it well intuitively, so it would be fun to expose you to some scholarly approaches to interpreting texts."

Emma smiled broadly and said, "Thank you, Zara. I gladly accept your offer."

At their first tutoring session, Zara and Emma were sidetracked into a conversation about anachronisms in films.

"I hate movie anachronisms," Zara said. "But I haven't caught any in the **Harry Potter** films."

"Well, I have," Emma said. "You know the scene in **Deathly Hallows Part 1** where Harry and Hermione are dancing?"

"Even though it was not in the book, I like that scene," Zara said. "It's endearing, although I can't understand any of the song lyrics. Is that the anachronism?"

"Yes," said Emma. "The song is 'O Children' by Nick Cave and the Bad Seeds, and it was released in 2004, but the action in the film takes place in 1997."

"I had no idea who sang the song or what it was about, but considered it atmospheric music," Zara said.

"It's a sad song, but the chorus goes 'O Children, Lift up your voice…rejoice, rejoice,'" Emma explained. "In that sense, it parallels the epigraph by Aeschylus at the beginning of **Hallows**: 'Bless the children, give them triumph now,' from the tragic play ***The Libation Bearers***."

"I'm impressed the movie producers would make such a literary connection," said Zara. "But I'm disappointed at the anachronism."

In the first year of its existence, K. P. was the youngest participant in the Holy Rowlings church, and as a result, not only Emma but many other members pampered him. The next youngest was in college. Other children and high school aged teens did not begin to appear on Saturday afternoons until well into 2013. In the meantime, Emma and Zara became close friends.

The day for the dinner party at Emily Hale's home arrived, and Emma prepared her homemade vegetarian enchiladas for the occasion.

"The tortillas are stuffed with black beans, tomatoes, onions, olives, avocados, and extra sharp cheddar cheese," she told the assembled guests.

"Plus Macayo's enchilada sauce that she had to send to Phoenix for," Emily Hale added.

"Actually, I picked up a supply on my last trip visiting my parents," Emma explained. "I wouldn't use any other kind."

Conversation during the meal was dominated by responses to Emily Hale's questions about naturism and how each of her guests had become engaged in the lifestyle. After cookie dough ice cream for dessert, they adjourned to the well-padded study.

Wakhan said, "We've all told our stories, Emily Hale, but our hostess remains the mystery woman. Before we get to your husband's poetry, please tell us something of your unique life."

"There's nothing much to tell," she said.

Emma gave Emily Hale a surprised look but did not contradict her.

"You all have had far more interesting lives, young as you are," Emily Hale continued. "What fun it must be to run around naked and throw propriety to the winds. I'm fascinated by the notion."

"With a statement like that, I think we should work on getting you to a naturist service," Camelot said.

"Yes, you should come to a clothes-free service," Willow said. "It's definitely a bucket list item."

"You could ease your way into it," Wakhan said. "You could start by going naked around your house. I'm sure Emma wouldn't mind."

"No, I'd join you," Emma said.

Emily Hale changed the subject. "You came here for poetry, so let us indulge ourselves in beautiful words." She handed a notebook to Wakhan. "Would you read aloud, please."

Wakhan read poetry for an hour, nimbly enunciating complex and lengthy words taken from various Native American tongues. The verses were replete with animal and plant names. Chipmunk, caribou, skunk, raccoon, cougar, chuckwalla, sockeye, muskrat, puma, and more creatures rose up from the texts. Avocado, peyote, pecan, chocolate, mesquite, cashew, saguaro, sequoia, squash, and potato flew from Wakhan's lips with clipped Navajo intonations that added zest to her language and Tom's compositions.

"I'm impressed with your Navajo accent," Willow said. "You don't speak that way normally."

"I have a good ear, and I've listened to those speech patterns all my life," Wakhan said.

"Your recitation was splendid!" said Emily Hale. "Absolutely splendid! What a feast! I am so blessed to hear you read my husband's words with such passion. And now Wakhan, you must have something to soothe your voice. And the rest of us as well." She turned to Emma and said, "Time for the surprise."

Emma went into the kitchen and returned a minute later with a tray laden with five frosted mugs. "Butterbeer!" she said.

"I wondered how long we could go without bringing Harry Potter into the picture," Willow said.

"You know me too well," said Emma.

"I am grateful to Emma for preparing the dinner and drinks, and all I had to do was sit back and enjoy," Emily Hale said. "I am so blessed to have Emma living in my home and blessed to have all of you here as guests. You've brought joy to my elder years."

"Well, we would still like to know more about you," said Wakhan. "Please tell us a little something. What are you interested in?"

"Perhaps in time, my dears, perhaps in time," Emily Hale said. "In fact, why don't we gather again next month, just the five of us. I'll cook next time, and I might even let slip a little of my past."

After the guests had departed, Emma said, "I'm glad you had fun. Given your positive view about naturism, would you mind if I went about the place naked on occasion. Going from my room to the bathroom and such."

"Not at all, Emma. You may wear as little or as much as you like, even at the dinner table," Emily Hale said. "But don't expect me to do likewise."

"Thanks," Emma said.

To Emma's surprise and satisfaction, the made-up congregation prospered, and near the end of 2012, she completed and submitted the paperwork to incorporate the Alchemical Church of Harry Potter Prophecy as an Arizona non-profit and registered Holy Rowlings as a trademark. Early the next year, she applied for and subsequently received IRS tax-exempt status for the church. She had thought that applying for IRS status was a whimsical quest, and it would not matter if it were denied. But once the papers were in the mail, she began to fret and came to realize that she cared deeply and was convinced that this was a serious endeavor. She worried that the IRS would turn down the request and thought about appealing. Would she need to get a lawyer? Would she need to sue the IRS? Had she done everything she could and should to make her case stronger? In the end, none of this worry was necessary.

Emma had joined the Sedona Natural Christian Church her first year in college by letter of transfer from the Phoenix NCC, and despite the time she invested in the ACHPP, continued to worship there on Sunday mornings. The naturist church had been allowing her to use its chapel on Saturday afternoons for Harry Potter services, asking only a modest honorarium to cover janitorial costs.

When it became clear that the Holy Rowlings were not fading but would continue to grow, Emma approached Cloud Morgan about a long-term lease for use of the chapel on Saturday afternoons.

"The only things it might interfere with are weddings," Cloud said. "But the chapel is used for textile weddings, and there aren't many of those. I think we can work around that."

"Thank you," Emma said. "It's so exciting that the Holy Rowlings are growing into something bigger than ourselves."

"What about your status?" Cloud asked.

"I'm Hallowed Philosopher," Emma replied.

"I know that, but have you been ordained? Are you official in a way that matches your IRS status?"

"Well, I just appointed myself HP," Emma stammered. "That's OK, isn't it? I don't like the word ordained. It sounds like making me into a saint or holy person."

"All ordination means is being setting aside for a particular purpose," Cloud said. "If holiness were a criterion, there would be damn few ordained clergy in any denomination. And it would be smart to have your board take some formal action to ordain you as HP and have the congregation install you into that position for this particular church."

"That makes it sound like there will be other Holy Rowling congregations," Emma said.

"Who knows?" Cloud said. "I like to be optimistic."

"Me too," said Emma.

"And by the way, once you are ordained, there's good news and bad news about taxes," Cloud added. "Which do you want to hear first?"

"The bad news," said Emma. "I like to get bad stuff out of the way so I can better enjoy the good news."

"Very wise," said Cloud. "The bad news is that the IRS considers ordained clergy to be self-employed for tax purposes. That means you would have to pay both your own and your employer's share of the social security contribution."

"That sounds expensive," said Emma.

"It is," said Cloud. "But that's where the good news comes into play. Ordained clergy can deduct their housing costs from their earned income. You would need to have your board designate a projected amount for any given year as Housing Allowance. Every dollar you spend for housing, including utilities and furnishings, can be deducted from your income, up to the pre-designated amount. So it's a good idea to estimate a little higher than what you expect to spend."

"And that counter-balances the extra Social Security payments, I assume," Emma said.

"It's not an exact wash," Cloud said.

"But it comes out somewhere in the middle," said Emma. "That's fair. I don't mind paying my fair share of taxes. I look on it as a civic responsibility."

Merlin's Board set a date for the service in which Emma would be ordained as Hallowed Philosopher and formally installed in that position on behalf of the Sedona congregation of the Alchemical Church of Harry Potter Prophecy. Emma designed the service, which included her kneeling while the members of Merlin's Board solemnly placed their hands on her head and shoulders.

To close the service, Emma wrote a benediction that she hoped would become a signature piece for her. Standing before the congregation in her bright white alb, Emma raised her arms wide and pronounced, "May your Patronus ever light the way before you, may your spells be always kind, and may your potions be filled with love. Amen."

As she had hoped, the congregation embraced her words, and the board members unanimously encouraged her to use that benediction to conclude every service. Since her compensation was modest, the board also designated all of it as Housing Allowance.

Learning that Emma belonged to the Sedona NCC concurrently with the Harry Potter church, Jordan Inge asked Emma if she had ever been to Burning Man.

"I've never heard of it," Emma responded.

"You need to know about this," Jordan said. "It's a temporary town built late every summer in the northwest portion of the Great Basin, a place in the Black Rock Desert in Nevada. They do all sorts of New Age and hippie things, and art projects and ecological demonstrations. They're really big into environmentalism. Their goal is to leave no trace of the place when they tear it down. People can run around naked if they want to, and a lot seem to want to."

"Have you ever been to it, Jordan?" Emma asked.

"No, but I really, really want to," Jordan said. "No one, so far, has been willing to go with me. Would you go with me?"

"I'll give it some thought," Emma replied with her noncommittal voice. "But if you really want to see what it feels like to run around naked, come with me to the NCC service tomorrow morning."

"Thanks anyway, but it's a bit too Christian for me," Jordan replied. "I'm OK with the no clothes part but I left the religion part behind a long time ago."

"The NCC is very progressive," Emma countered. "Lots of people who have been wounded by other churches find a home there."

"Not for me, sorry," Jordan said. "But I do have a suggestion regarding prayer in our church."

"Really? Please tell me," said Emma with genuine interest.

"I was thinking we should have our own version of the Lord's Prayer," Jordan explained. "You'd need to compose the whole thing, but I've got the start. Our Auror who art a wizard, Harry be thy name. What do you think?"

"Hmmm," she said. "I'll play around with it and see if anything comes to mind." She had no real intention of giving it any further thought and was sure she did not want to go where Jordan's start might lead. Partly this was because she thought Jordan only wanted to make fun of the religion she had left behind, but also something in Emma did not want to share authorship with anyone else, particularly a Slytherin.

"Anyway, please really think about going to Nevada with me," Jordan continued.

Alexis, overhearing the conversation, joined in. "If I ever went to Nevada, I would rather go to Area 51, so I could talk to some aliens."

This provided Emma an opportunity to change the subject. "Do you really think there are aliens there?"

"Absolutely," said Alexis. "They are held prisoner there but they're not dangerous. They must be kind and gentle, because of their advanced civilization."

"Oh, do they speak English?" Jordan asked with sarcastic inflection.

"Well doh!" Alexis said. "All the years they've been here, sure they do."

"If they are secret prisoners, what makes you think the authorities would let you speak with them," Emma asked.

"I'm just saying I'd like to go there. If I got in, I'm sure I could find a way to the Hall of Mysteries where they're kept," Alexis explained.

"I have no doubt that you could," said Emma.

"Yeah, I hope you get in there, because I'd like to know what prophecies the aliens are guarding," said Jordan.

"In the meantime, I've got a service to get ready for," said Emma. "See you ladies later."

Seated in her chair on the chancel with two minutes until the service would begin, Emma mulled her conversation with Jordan about jointly writing a prayer. Clearly she did not like the idea of sharing authorship with Jordan, whatever that may mean about their pastor-parishioner relationship. But the idea of co-creating with someone else did hold significant appeal. The image of Sol came into her mind, causing her to smile just as he rose to lead the congregation in song.

The second dinner party at Emily Hale's home featured a green vegetable quiche that the host prepared to perfection. Emma made treacle tart for dessert, although she took pleasure in calling it pudding.

Having adjourned to the study for conversation, Emily Hale opened by saying, "I want you all to know that ever since our last dinner together Emma has been parading around the house without a stitch and it hasn't bothered me a bit."

"Have you been even a tad tempted yourself?" Wakhan asked.

"On occasion in the evenings I appear in an old bathrobe," Emily Hale confessed. "That's the best I can do, I'm afraid."

"Would you mind if we disrobed?" Camelot asked.

"If you wish, it would not offend me," Emily Hale said.

Everyone but Emily Hale removed their clothes.

The talk proceeded normally from that point, apart from the fact that four of the five people present were naked.

"I made a Harry Potter connection in my sermon last Sunday," Wakhan said.

"Oh, and I missed the service," Willow said. "What was it?"

"Well, you know the part in **Deathly Hallows** where Harry, Hermione, and Ron are on the move and hungry, and Ron wants Hermione to get food by magic. Hermione explains to Ron that magic folk can't just make food from nothing. It can be summoned and its quantity increased if some is already there, but not created out of thin air."

"What did you do with that in the sermon?" Willow asked.

"It's a parallel with the gospel accounts of Jesus feeding the 5000," Wakhan explained. "They had some loaves and fishes to start with, and Jesus miraculously or magically multiplied the amount."

"Cool," said Willow.

As the evening drew to a close, Emily Hale said, "I cannot tell you how delightful it has been to be in the presence of such vital minds and to observe your beautiful bare bodies. You have brought such blessings into an old widow's life. You give me hope for the future of humankind."

"It's not too late to join us," Wakhan said.

"I only wish I could," Emily Hale said.

"I wish we knew more about you and your life," Willow said.

"Well, I am prepared to let out one little secret," Emily Hale said.

Everyone turned toward her in rapt attention.

"Dear Emma has been evangelizing me about the gospel of young Mr. Potter," she said. "I have not yet succumbed to a born again experience of the Boy Who Lived, but I can see how that could happen."

"Have you been reading the books?" Emma asked with surprise in her voice.

"I have," Emily Hale replied. "And have found them delightful."

"But that's about the present. I want to hear about your past," Willow said.

"That's as much as you'll get tonight. You'll have to come back for more," Emily Hale said.

Emma initiated a stewardship drive, seeking contributions to cover the costs of rent for the chapel, liturgical supplies, and a regular weekly honorarium for herself.

Responding to Emma's first reflection on stewardship, Jordan teased her, saying the church was merely a hobby for Emma. "You're able to do this because you are lucky enough to have a rich daddy. You don't have to do real work."

Hurt by the remark, Emma defended her sense of call. "I believe with all my heart that this is *real* work."

"Real work in a fantasy church," said Jordan. "But don't get me wrong. I envy you the luxury of doing this. I wish I were a BMW socialist, so I could follow my bliss like you."

Emma reached into mental thin air for a suitable verbal response and after an embarrassing pause said, "That's grossly unfair, Jordan. For your information, I drive a four year-old Lexus RX hybrid, and that's only because my dad insisted on a safe car after my getting T-boned by a drunk driver. The insurance company replaced my mom's car which was totaled, and I got a Lexus to take to college in the settlement."

"OK, OK, I didn't mean to pound a touchy place," said Jordan. "But I still think you're damned lucky to have wealthy parents."

Emma was stung by Jordan's words and brooded about them for weeks. Being Hallowed Philosopher felt like her true calling. Creating the church seemed, in retrospect, an inevitable development in her life. Whatever this may be, she told herself, it is **not** a rich girl's hobby.

The more she thought about it, however, the deeper Jordan's taunt penetrated her psyche. If you're serious about this, she chided herself, then really ramp up stewardship and take a meaningful salary. Cut the financial apron strings to Dad. It is one thing for him to subsidize me through college, but not now, she decided.

David had characterized Emma's pursuit of the Harry Potter church as on a level with other students taking a sabbatical gap year to travel abroad after graduation, and he was happy to finance it for his only daughter.

The only member that Emma felt fully open with in sharing her doubts and concerns was Zara. And so she told Zara, "I'm reluctant to ask members for larger contributions, even though the church needs more money if it is to survive long term. The thing is, I don't think it's ethical to press people for money."

"Clearly, you are not into the hard sell," said Zara.

"And I know I'm the most financially well-off person in the congregation," Emma continued. "All the other Millennials in the congregation are screwed financially. They're working for low pay with long hours and no pensions."

"And with unprecedented loads of student debt," Zara added. "So what are you going to do?"

Her ultimate response to Zara's question was to ask her dad to arrange a monthly allowance from her insurance settlement. She told him, "just something to live on until I get clearer about a career." He agreed to the request, and set up a direct deposit into her checking account. However, without telling her, he did not touch any of the money in her settlement. He had benefited from an inheritance to get his career started, he reasoned, and he could do no less for his only daughter. Besides this, he was pleased and amused at the idea of underwriting her experimental career, no matter how odd it may seem to outsiders.

"We have more money than we have things to spend it on," he told Hannah. "So why not share it with Emma?"

"Do you think she will get bored with it after a year or so and seek a proper career?" Hannah asked.

"I do," he replied, and then corrected himself. "I certainly hope so."

As the months passed, Emma was dismayed to find the church descending deeper into financial trouble and repeatedly used her own money to subsidize the ministry. Worried about drawing down her insurance settlement, she called her dad to ask how much was left.

"Why do you want to know?" he asked.

"I just want to know where I stand," she said. "I don't want to use it all up, but I still need the stipend to live on."

"You have nothing to worry about, because all of it is still there, due to the gain from my investing it," he said.

"That's reassuring," she replied. "Thanks, Dad. I owe you a lot."

He agreed but did not say so. "Sleep well, Kiddo," he said.

What David left unexplained was that Emma's settlement had grown by 50%, and none of it had been used to subsidize her, but about this, Emma was completely unaware.

CHAPTER SEVENTEEN
CLOUD AND TERP

Emma's phone awakened her early Monday morning. Looking at the face, she saw that the call was from Cloud Morgan. "Hi Dr. Morgan," she said cheerfully.

"Hi Emma. I hope I didn't wake you."

"No, I was already up," she lied.

"Could you stop by my office sometime this afternoon?" he asked. "We'd like to discuss the church…the Harry Potter church."

"Sure. What time?" she responded. "I'm open all afternoon."

"See you at 1:30, then," he said.

When she arrived, she found Terp also present in her husband's office. Emma was directed to sit in one of the rocking chairs. "This is all very mysterious," Emma said.

"Not for long," said Terp.

"First thing on the agenda," said Cloud, "is that since you are fellow clergy with Terp and me, please address us personally by our first names. We know you speak of us that way among other people, and most parishioners call us by our first names anyway. And we also know about your brother's Clomo and Termo invention. Quite flattering, actually. So, no more of this Dr. Morgan business, OK?"

"OK, Cloud," she said. "Not a problem."

"Second, I read your reflection on Snape from last Saturday, and I'd like to discuss it with you," he continued.

"Me too," said Terp.

"Is that why I've been summoned here? To defend my views on Snape?" Emma asked with a note of astonishment in her voice. "I took a lot of flak from giving that reflection. I knew it would generate heat but felt I needed to be honest. We have a few Slytherins in the church. Numerically, they're the smallest house in the congregation, but usually the loudest. Several of them are what I call Snape fetishists. Of course, among the general population of Potterdom, Slytherins predominate."

"Why do you think that is?" Terp asked.

"Well, most of them -of *us*- are Millennials and Generation Xers. And members of these age cohorts are smart enough to see that the political and economic systems are rigged against them. Cynicism abounds. And many of them naturally gravitate to Slytherin-like ethical practices, protecting themselves any way they can," Emma explained.

"But that doesn't hold in your congregation," Cloud noted.

"No, because spirituality and idealistic ethics are foremost in the Harry Potter church," Emma said. "That's why Gryffindors prevail in the congregation."

"Getting back to the subject of Snape, it's not the main reason we've asked you here," Cloud said. "But I was quite taken with your Snape sermon, and if you don't mind, I'd like to explore it with you. And for the record, Terp and I think of ourselves as Gryffindors."

"Well, then, go for it," said Emma.

"To start with," he said, "you clearly have strong feelings about this particular character."

"Strong *thoughts*," Emma responded.

"I would say both," Terp said.

"I've noticed on the Internet, especially on Facebook, and at fantasy conventions, and elsewhere in the vast *Harry Potter* community there seems to be a growing cult of adoration of Severus Snape," Emma explained. "Snape was a hero, they proclaim. He was so brave. Snape the redeemer! I just don't get it. Snape was not brave. Yes, he had courage, but it was the courage of the sociopath. That's not the same thing as bravery, which stands against evil for its own sake.

"Consistently throughout the novels, Severus Snape is portrayed as a sadistic bully, not just with regard to Harry but with many other students. He is driven by an infantile obsession with Lily Evans, with whom he has very little in common. The only thing he and Lily share is growing up in the same town. That's not much on which to base a healthy relationship, when in every significant measure of personhood, they are polar opposites. His great flaw was not being able to let go of this obsession with possessing Lily."

"True," said Cloud. "Yet he agreed to protect Harry at Dumbledore's request, and he served as a double agent for the Order of the Phoenix, at great personal risk."

"Yeah, but he was motivated by revenge, not by an honest commitment to the good," Emma responded. "T. S. Eliot described it well in ***Murder in the Cathedral***. 'The last act is the greatest treason. To do the right thing for the wrong reason.' Ultimately, Snape did the right thing but as ***always*** it was for the wrong reason.

"Inevitably the Snape adorers will pull out their trump card and say Dumbledore ***trusted*** Snape. Dumbledore believed that he was truly reformed."

"Why do you think he did?" Cloud asked.

"Well, as I said in my reflection, there are several ways of looking at the relationship between Dumbledore and Snape," Emma recited. "One is that the headmaster was co-dependent with the potions master. Another is that Dumbledore was, perhaps cynically, using Snape's dysfunction for his own ends. Well, we already know that Dumbledore was a manipulator - usually for beneficial ends. So, I'm on the side of Dumbledore using Snape as a pawn in a terrible game of wizard chess against Voldemort."

"Would you agree that there are other reasonable motives that could be inferred from the narrative?" Terp asked.

"Certainly," Emma responded, "but along with this veneration of Snape comes a fascination with Slytherin. A huge number of ***Harry Potter*** fans fancy themselves as Slytherins. This I also don't get. My guess is that many generally good people recognize, consciously or unconsciously, the Slytherin elements in their own shadows. Even the best of us have things we consider unacceptable, and these pile up in a part of our mind that Carl Jung called the shadow.

"I think those who outwardly acknowledge the content of their shadows are free to align themselves with any house that fits, while those who hide their shadow elements also laughingly hide under the umbrella of Salazar Slytherin."

"That's really interesting. I should run that theory by some of my psychologist friends," said Terp.

Emma paused, wondering if she had wandered too far beyond her area of expertise, and then extemporized, "The only other thing I can think of to explain the veneration of Snape is some sublime mental trick that conflates the immensely talented and charismatic Alan Rickman with the dark role he plays in the *Harry Potter* films. It's fine to enjoy Snape as a complex and very interesting character, like my brother Jared does, but let's not bandy him about as a brave and good guy, because as far as I'm concerned he was neither."

"Was Harry wrong to give his younger son the middle name Severus?" asked Cloud.

"Apart from the character, it is a beautiful and elegant name," said Emma, evading a direct answer.

"You make a cogent argument about Snape," said Terp. "But remember you're doing it through an idealistic Gryffindor lens. Gryffindors see things as they should be and are troubled when others are not similarly motivated."

"Is that a bad thing?" Emma responded.

"Not at all," said Terp, "but it is a minority view."

"This has been a great discussion," said Cloud, "but now it's time for the real reason we asked you here, Emma."

"You see, we believe it is important that the Alchemical Church succeed," said Terp. "We've taken quite an interest in it, and we want to help. Zara raves about the congregation and especially your reflections. But from all we've been able to discover, its financial foundation is precarious."

"Well, I don't want to be greedy, but if you could lower the rent a little, that would help a lot," said Emma.

"We could negotiate that if needed," Cloud said. "However, we have something else that should make that unnecessary."

"As you know, the NCC is deeply involved with the interfaith community," Terp said. "And we have come to look upon your congregation as an important element in that community. We have made inquiries about a grant from the board of the Interfaith Ministry Endowment, and one is available for your congregation if you will accept it."

"How much is it?" Emma asked.

"Enough to provide a full time salary for you for the next two years," said Cloud. "This congregation was subsidized by our denomination for that period of time, until we became self-sufficient. Our ecumenical and interfaith partners want to provide you with the same opportunity to succeed."

"That's wonderful," Emma stammered. "I'm overwhelmed. Thank you, so much. Do I know anybody on this board?"

"You know Cloud and me," Terp said.

"I want to send a letter of gratitude," Emma said. "As soon as I recover from being stunned."

Since the board was a fictional entity devised solely for the purpose of providing anonymous financial aid to the Holy Rowling congregation, Cloud and Terp did not want to divulge that various members of Emma's family, including her father and aunt, along with some well-connected friends had created this endowment. Cloud and Terp had made a generous contribution. He replied, "You can send a letter care of the Sedona NCC."

"This is still mysterious," Emma said. "It's a life line for sure." An intuitive insight told her not to ask more questions but to reside in the mystery for the present.

Emma was thrilled by the endowment and interpreted it as a sign that she was on the right track. Her first phone call was to her parents. In the course of that conversation, she told her dad that she was now able to make it on her own, so he should discontinue the monthly checks from her settlement. David took this in stride and did not reveal his major support for the endowment. He genuinely wanted her to succeed.

Cloud and Terp took a deeper personal interest in Emma. Now that their own children were grown and on their own, they treated Emma as another daughter as well as a protégé. To this latter end, they offered to tutor Emma in pastoral care, institutional dynamics, conflict management, and how to think theologically. They also taught her how to do ecclesiastical functions, such as weddings and memorial services, and they set aside one evening a week to spend with her, imparting whatever wisdom seemed apt at the time.

One evening, Emma asked, "Why are you so interested in my congregation?"

Cloud replied, "Selfishly, when I retire, I won't be able to attend the church Terp and I founded. And that's just as well, because I would find it hard to refrain from comparing how I did it to the less than perfect way my successor approaches things. I'm smart enough not to say anything about that, but just fallible enough that I might accidentally let something slip. At any rate, I will need someplace to go, and the Holy Rowling congregation is at the top of my list. I think I could find a spiritual home there, and be assured of a worthy sermon –or reflection as you call it- at every service."

"The same goes for me," said Terp. "Although, since Cloud is an older man, he is likely to retire long before I get around to it." She playfully poked her husband in his side and then addressed him. "But I take issue with you unfavorably comparing your successor to yourself. That's not who you are. And there is a 100% chance that the one who follows you will be someone you already know and respect."

"As I know personally every clergyperson in our denomination, that's a fair assessment," Cloud said.

Terp turned toward Emma. "The truth is, he just doesn't want to admit that his appetite for **Harry Potter** is insatiable. There is no other congregation on his list, only yours, Emma."

"Curses, nailed again," said Cloud.

Emma decided that Cloud was an Albus Dumbledore figure and Terp a Minerva McGonagall. Jared had called them Clomo and Termo. Emma now created her own affectionate combined nickname, AlbuMin. She liked the pun, because albumin was a protein in blood plasma, and they were protean in their abilities to accomplish many and diverse things.

For one of her tutoring sessions, Emma's homework assignment was to take notes on the church-related services described in the **Harry Potter** series.

"There aren't very many of them," she reported to Cloud.

"What did you find?" he asked.

"Well, on the grieving side there are the informal graveside services for Dobby and Aragog the acromantula and the full-blown funeral service for Dumbledore," Emma said. "On the celebratory side, there is the wedding service for Bill and Fleur. Both the funeral and wedding services are done in generic civil manner rather than as formal church services, and neither takes place in a church. The same wizard leads both, so it is possible that the Wizarding world has people set aside to function as clergy. But there are no ordinary services for worshipping God, not even for Christmas and Easter."

"Which bolsters your argument for a humanist Harry Potter church," Cloud responded. "What else did you notice?"

"In **Half-Blood Prince**, the presiding wizard wears a plain black robe. No scripture is read and no hymns sung, although there are music and white smoke. In **Deathly Hallows**, the service is traditional, with processional music and Fleur escorted down the aisle by her father. The presiding wizard says, 'We are gathered here today to celebrate the union of two faithful souls…' The word marriage is not used but rather union. After Bill and Fleur exchange vows, the presiding wizard then declares them 'bonded for life,'" Emma recited.

"And what do you deduce from all this?" Cloud asked.

"That the rituals, liturgies, and services in **Harry Potter** are not anchored in religious doctrine, church tradition, or systematic theology but in psychology, mystery, and social needs," Emma said.

"More ammunition supporting your humanist approach to congregational life," Cloud said. "Well done, Emma. Full marks on your homework assignment!"

In addition to her tutoring sessions, Emma became a frequent dinner guest at Angel Nest. Thinking that Emily Hale would enjoy the repartee around the table, Emma invited her to come along once in a while, but the answer was always a polite no.

"The place is clothing optional," Emma assured her. "You would be under no obligation to disrobe. And Cloud and Terp would like to meet you. Wakhan has told them what a delightful person you are."

Nevertheless, Emily Hale continued to decline the invitations.

On some occasions only a few people gathered for dinner, but other times many.

On one visit, Emma sat next to K. P. and Zara. The long oak table was laden with food, which Emma reacted to by saying, "This reminds me of a feast in the Great Hall at Hogwarts."

"But much healthier," said Terp.

"That's one of the things that bothers me about Hogwarts," said Zara. "The presence of so much unhealthy food could have a negative affect on efforts to counter the explosion of childhood obesity."

"I think it's just a fun part of the fantasy," Emma responded. "Wizards can consume tons of calorie rich food and not gain weight, but Muggles can't."

"Some Muggles can," said Cloud. "When I was sixteen, I could eat four full meals a day, including milk shakes and fries, and not gain an ounce."

"But that didn't last long, did it?" Terp noted.

"No it didn't," Cloud said with a chuckle. "By the time I was in the Army, I was putting on the pounds unless I was careful about my diet. Then again, three months in the Mekong Delta had a diuretic effect, and I lost a lot of weight then."

"Nevertheless, Muggles would do well to avoid the dietary excesses of witches and wizards on trains and at school," Zara said.

"Muggles shouldn't eat meat. It's not good for them," said K. P. "Merven don't."

"Who's Merven?" Emma asked.

"Vegetarian friends of ours," said Zara. "You may meet them someday."

"Are they naturists?" Emma asked.

"Yes, and distinctively so, as they are intersexual. Key is a librarian and lives in Australia. Sojourner and Pilgrim live in Northern Arizona," Zara said.

"I'm named for Key. My whole name is Key Person Morgan," said K. P.

"And they all have the last name Merven?" Emma said.

"In a way," said Zara.

"I look forward to meeting them," said Emma.

Emma now scanned the loaded food platters and bowls on the table. "I don't see any beef, pork, or fowl, but plenty of dairy and fish. Is that significant?"

"Yes," said Terp. "We're not vegans and not even true vegetarians, because we serve dairy and fish, but we agree with K. P. Meat is not good for Muggles."

"My aunt Sheba calls herself a piscatarian," Emma said. "She follows the same dietary practices as you."

"Cutting down on meat consumption also helps in the fight against global warming," said Cloud.

"Wow! From the unhealthy food at Hogwarts to global warming in one brief exchange," said Zara.

"I think all the candy and puddings in **Harry Potter** are intended as humor," said K. P. "A really funny joke, actually, when you consider that Hermione's parents are dentists. From a kid's point of view, it represents sticking out your tongue at your parents when they say you can't have dessert until you've cleaned your plate."

"I am amazed at you," said Zara to her son.

"Yes, that is an amazing insight for someone so young," Emma said.

"No, it's not that," Zara explained. "K. P. is always coming up with precocious notions." She turned to K. P. and continued, "We've never treated you that way. No one around this table has ever told you no dessert unless you eat your vegetables. You *like* vegetables."

"I wasn't speaking from personal experience," the boy said. "But the scenario about cleaning your plate and threats of no dessert is a cliché of American culture. Given all the food related humor in **Harry Potter**, I suspect this is true in the UK, as well."

"On that note, let's eat," said Terp.

Though she did not reveal this to her lodger, after the dinner when Emma, Willow, Camelot, and Wakhan had disrobed, Emily Hale began puttering about her home naked when Emma was away. She found the experience deliciously sensual.

One day, Emma came home earlier than expected, and as she paused to remove her key from the lock, her peripheral vision caught sight of Emily Hale hastily tying a knot in the sash holding her robe closed. A look of embarrassment covered the older woman's face. An intuitive flash told her that her landlady had been undressed when she heard Emma unlocking the front door and had quickly donned her well-worn robe.

"Are you OK?" Emma asked.

"Why of course, dear," Emily Hale said.

"Good," said Emma. "I just had a momentary sense that something was amiss."

"Quite the contrary," said Emily Hale, suppressing a smile.

Emma looked at the widow quizzically. "Is there something you want to tell me, Emily Hale? Anything at all?" she asked.

"No, dear," Emily Hale said.

"Are you sure?" Emma pressed.

"Well, there is one thing," Emily Hale said. "It's my turn to fix dinner, and I don't feel up to it. Let me take you out to dinner."

"OK," said Emma. "But I need to get gas first."

"Oh don't bother," said Emily Hale. "We'll take my car. I need to drive it more to keep the battery from dying. Let me get dressed, and then we can go."

Twenty minutes later, Emma eased herself into the passenger side of Emily Hale's Crown Victoria. Emily Hale carefully backed out of the garage and slowly entered the residential street. When she reached the outlet to the main road, she turned right, accelerating with sufficient speed to make the tires squeal. Thereafter, she maintained at least ten miles over the posted speed limit until nearing the shopping district, where the volume of traffic made speeding impossible.

They settled on a trendy vegetarian restaurant, where Emma ordered a fake-bacon, lettuce and tomato sandwich with sweet potato fries, and Emily Hale selected black bean soup with a green salad.

"It may be rude of me to bring this up," Emma said, "but you were driving a little fast. I expect young guys to do that, but it's surprising in a senior citizen."

"I hate that term," Emily Hale said. "I'm not a senior. I'm old. Deal with it."

"OK. I'm surprised to see an old lady speeding," Emma said.

"It's a bad habit," Emily Hale confessed. "I've had a few tickets in my day, but usually police take pity on me and let me off with a warning. Tom used to sing that song to me when he was riding shotgun, and I was a little too heavy on the gas pedal."

"What song?" Emma asked.

"It was before your time," Emily Hale said. "Jan and Dean recorded a novelty number in the sixties called 'The Little Old Lady from

Pasadena.' It was about a granny with a lead foot. But I always told him that I was not little and not from Pasadena. That was one of our private jokes."

"There's a lot to learn about you," Emma said.

"Indeed," said Emily Hale.

CHAPTER EIGHTEEN
SORCERY AND MUGGLETONIANS

Judas Crucible, a prominent resident of Cornville, known for his crusading spirit, was sick at heart because the daughter of a neighbor was attending Emma Round's church. Not one to let things be, he wrote a letter to the Verde Valley Intelligencer exposing the evil doings of the Alchemical Church of Harry Potter Prophecy.

Duffy Davar, religion editor of the Intelligencer and father of church member Sol, was initially inclined to recommend rejecting Crucible's letter, but after mulling it over decided that if published, it might generate publicity favorable to the Holy Rowlings. He approved it for the editorial page while also sending a copy to his son, who in turn, showed it to Emma.

Here is what Judas Crucible wrote:

"Insidious forces are practicing bizarre rituals of witchcraft and worshiping evil witches and warlocks and demons right here in Central Arizona. A so-called church that commits blasphemy by substituting the Harry Potter books for the Holy Bible is operating in the bosom of that deranged nudist church in Sedona. Central Arizona is already infested with too many weird New Age religions, sexual debauchery, and other sinful heresies, but this Harry Potter church is the worst. It must be stopped, before these hyenas of witchcraft devour our children."

As a result of this letter, Crucible was interviewed on a conservative talk show on KNUT radio. In the course of the conversation, Crucible cited a book that he said proved that J. K. Rowling was demonic. "A White House speechwriter for George W. Bush named Matt Latimer published a book in 2009 called *Speechless: Tales of a White House Survivor*," Crucible noted. "In it he revealed that J. K. Rowling had been considered for a Presidential Medal of Freedom but White House officials objected to the notorious socialist author getting a medal, because the Harry Potter books encouraged witchcraft. And the White House would know these things. You can bet your bottom dollar that the CIA briefed the president on the extent of Rowling's wickedness."

"You don't say," the radio host responded. "That sounds pretty official to me. Do you think Rowling's involved in the left wing plot to undermine American Christian youth?"

"Not just American, but the whole world," Crucible said.

"So what are you going to do about this disgusting Harry Potty cult in Sedona?"

"The first thing we need to do is form a posse of demon busters to hold vigil outside the church and pray away the witches," Crucible said.

"Nothing violent," the host added.

"Not physical violence," Crucible said. "Only the godly violence of focused prayer."

"Good luck with your efforts, Judas. Thanks for calling in and keep in touch," the host said.

On Saturday afternoon, Crucible and five of his friends stood outside the NCC compound and repeatedly chanted, "Pray away the witches, pray away the demons, pray away the devils."

Sol greeted Emma when she walked into the chapel. "I suppose you saw those nutcases outside."

"Yeah," she said. "I'm not worried unless they start talking about the Second Amendment. But their slogan isn't very catchy. They'd be further ahead if they changed it to pray away the fey."

Sol laughed. "Good one, Emma!"

Emma responded with her own letter to the Intelligencer, refuting Crucible's claims and inviting him to attend worship and see for himself how undemonic it actually was.

Crucible did not respond in writing, nor did he return to his chanting spot the next Saturday. Instead, he called into the KNUT talk show and said, "We made our point, now it's up to God to smite this nest of evil."

As a result of this publicity, a dozen curious people who had not previously heard about the Holy Rowlings began attending services.

The Crucible caper, as Emma came to think about it, led her to offer a reflection about book banning. "With regard to the utter stupidity of banning books that mention witches, I offer one title that has been required reading in high schools throughout this country for generations: *Macbeth*. Also, I can't help but wonder about the millions of young Americans who have been sucked into the wicked world of witchcraft by watching such TV series as Bewitched and Sabrina the Teenage Witch, or the Broadway play and 1958 film *Bell, Book and Candle* that inspired both TV shows. James Stewart starred in the movie version, and we all know how many red-blooded Americans have been snared into his demonic ways."

Hearing no response from the congregation when she was expecting at least a few chuckles, Emma said, "Oh well, so much for my feeble attempt at sarcasm. So, instead, I'll offer a serious quote from Ralph Waldo Emerson: 'Every banned book enlightens the world.' And the first enlightenment from a banned book comes from examining why someone or some institution wants it banned. What are they afraid of?

"I want to thank James W. Thomas, a professor at Pepperdine University and author of *Repotting Harry Potter*, for a brilliant insight into this subject. Professor Thomas speculated that Arthur A. Levine, the editor for the American *Harry Potter* editions may be responsible for the strong negative reaction from the Christian right. Levine is the one who changed the name of the first book from *Philosopher's Stone* to *Sorcerer's Stone*. Thomas suspects the word sorcerer is what set off the fundamentalists. If the title had been left Philosopher, conservative religious critics might *not* have noticed and thus not attacked the book, at least not so quickly. The word sorcery can be simply a synonym for magic, but it's usually associated with invoking evil spirits, which Harry Potter most certainly is not about. Religious fundamentalists, not known for their subtlety, may not appreciate philosophy and may even disparage it, but they *fear* sorcery. And fear tends to produce irrational over-reactions."

Emma created a Facebook page for the Holy Rowlings and used alchemy related images that she found on the Internet as background and profile photos. The background photo showed two nudes, male and female, as the quarreling couple. The profile picture was an etching of Nicholas Flamel. Starting with asking her friends to like the page, and then asking them to ask their friends, the page soon attracted more than 500 likes.

<><><>

It was Malcolm Drumheller's obsession with Emma Watson that led him, out of curiosity, to check out a Holy Rowling service. He quickly became a regular attendee, however, because of Emma Round. Malcolm had lived in Sedona most of his 25 years and knew about the naturist church there but had never visited. In the realm of Harry Potter activities, Malcolm was a Draco cosplayer, who championed Draco and Hermione shipping, which in his mind meant himself and Emma Watson.

His fixation transferred to Emma Round when he learned she was a naturist. For the first few months, the tall and blond Malcolm was circumspect in worship, mentioning to no one that he had personal feelings for the Hallowed Philosopher. He was polite in interactions with Emma. By December, however, fantasy images of Emma being intimate with him had taken over his mind.

After church one day, Malcolm took Emma's hand as if to shake it but did not let go. "You know I'm a Draco cosplayer," he said.

"I'd heard that," Emma responded. She tried to disengage but he grasped her hand more tightly.

"And I heard that you are a Hermione cosplayer," he said.

"I used to be, before college," she replied. "Please let go of my hand."

"Oh, I'm sorry. I didn't realize we were still holding hands," he said, releasing his grip. "I just wanted to confess, as a penitent to a priest, that I am also a Draco-Hermione shipper. And you are the closest real woman to Hermione I've ever met. Let me take you to dinner tonight."

"I've got a commitment tonight, Malcolm," she said, and then added, "And I make it a general rule never to date parishioners."

"But I'm not a member here, just a visitor. I'll try again. You can't hide from me for long."

The next Saturday, Malcolm maintained a strategic distance from Emma during fellowship time, not near enough to talk with her but sufficiently close that she could hear him speaking in a raised voice. He selected Alexis for a provocative conversation. "My assertion is that Mundungus Fletcher is the smartest character in the entire series. The man lives by his wits and is usually a step ahead of everyone else. He probably quit school early but has street smarts and is intelligent enough not to be foolishly brave. I'll bet he would have been a Ravenclaw if he'd been sorted."

"I seriously doubt that," Alexis said calmly. "Mundungus is definitely Slytherin material."

Emma heard the exchange and guessed that it was addressed to her, but she found it difficult to discern whether Malcolm was serious or simply being deliberately shocking. In the end, she decided that the two were not mutually exclusive.

The next week, Malcolm came to church dressed as Draco and addressed Emma as Hermione. She put up with this good naturedly, but when he did the same thing a week later, she publicly addressed him as the ferret. And he responded in a voice that carried throughout the room, "That was mean and uncalled for, you bitch!" He spun dramatically and stormed out.

"I hope he never comes back," Frieda said.

Emma remained silent.

Malcolm did not return to the church as time passed, but he would not remain fully absent from Emma's life.

Emma invited Uncle Henry to a service to deliver a guest reflection on literary and mythological allusions, and he enjoyed the congregation so much that whenever possible, he returned on Saturdays to sit in a pew and listen to his niece preach about the Boy Who Lived. Sometimes he brought Sarah, Thomas, and Meiyin with him. Beatrix was busy with parish responsibilities on Saturdays, but occasionally she carved out time to join her husband and children when they attended Emma's services.

The second time he was guest reflector, Emma left the service when he began to speak, and from a vacant office, she floated out of her body and returned to the sanctuary, floating into the body spaces of parishioners, many of whom reacted like they'd been goosed when she did so. When she floated into Sol, he smiled broadly and felt as if a long-expected blessing had filled the cells of his body. Everyone had sensed her presence in a positive way, to varying degrees but none more than the music director.

She returned to the chapel before Henry had finished speaking, and he and Emma winked at each other. She never told the congregation what she had done, but afterward, the place was abuzz about the physical reactions to Henry's words. Sol, however, kept his experience to himself.

Henry spoke about Muggles while Emma was floating in and out of his audience. "An obscure American writer named Nancy K. Stouffer claimed to have invented Muggles, alleging in 1999 that J. K. Rowling had infringed her copyright on a book that included characters called Muggles that had been published by a vanity press in 1984. Stouffer filed suit, including a similar claim regarding her character from another book, Larry Potter, contending that the first printings of each of these books had been 100,000 copies and they had sold out in a week. The case was dismissed with prejudice, and in addition to legal costs, Stouffer was fined $50,000 for submitting altered documents to the court. In case you are interested, I checked out Stouffer's books on Amazon, and the reviews are dreadful. So, scratch that possible source.

"Given J. K. Rowling's extensive research, a more promising origin for the term Muggle is a Christian sect called Muggletonians. Developed in the middle of the 17th century, it was named after a London tailor named Lodowicke Muggleton. Lodowicke and a colleague proclaimed themselves to be the two witnesses with authority to prophesy that are mentioned in Revelation 11:3.

"Muggletonians believed that God pays no attention to what goes on in everyday life and will not intervene in human affairs until the time has come to end the world. Except for a half dozen brief doctrinal statements, they relied on the individual conscience for guidance. They believed in a material deity, namely that God is no more than the glorified body of Jesus Christ, who, incidentally, stands somewhere between five and six feet tall. Muggletonians did not believe in Satan and considered angels the embodiment of Pure Reason. Heaven, they averred was just beyond the stars six miles up from the surface of the earth. They also assumed the authority to damn or bless whomever they wished in full accord with the will of God. People who spoke ill of them were targets for their curses, among whom was the novelist Sir Walter Scott. Despite their proclivity to invoke damnation on critics, Muggletonians were pacifists who were nevertheless bitter rivals of the pacifist Quaker sect.

"Most significant for our purposes, Muggletonians believed that the soul does not continue to exist at death but dies with the body, although both soul and body would be subject to resurrection whenever God decided it was time to put an end to earth.

"Muggletonians avoided worship, preaching, and evangelizing and met solely for socializing and discussion. In 1979, Philip Noakes, the last of the Muggletonians, left the accumulated archive of Muggletonian papers, correspondence, and publications to the British Library, the news of which brought the sect to the attention of the general public. Rowling could have heard the name in the news. Or maybe it just popped into her head.

"Given the importance of the fate of the human soul in the *Harry Potter* narratives, using a variation on the name of a religious sect that denied the immortality of the soul might be tempting to a writer as clever as J. K. Rowling.

"I am continually amazed to discover just how much careful detail she paid to names. Take for example Harry's snowy owl Hedwig. St. Hedwig cares for and educates orphan children. It is consistent with the role of St. Hedwig that Hedwig the owl died just as Harry was on the cusp of turning 17, the age of adulthood for wizards, and was leaving home for good. At that point Harry was no longer a child and thus beyond Hedwig's saintly oversight."

Greeting parishioners after the service, Henry shook hands with Alexis, who solemnly said, "How did they find out heaven is six miles above the earth?"

Gazing intently into her eyes, Henry said, "They didn't say."

"But there weren't any astronauts back then," Alexis continued. "It's amazing, isn't it?"

Sol's artistry was with the notes of the musical scale and from his hands sculpting beautiful pieces, but not with words. Thus, he was not having much success adapting folk songs for congregational singing. He experimented with the old union song "Solidarity Forever," replacing all mentions of union with Order (as in of the Phoenix) and changing "worker's blood" to Phoenix wand. But after leading the congregation through it once, multiple people expressed dislike for it, vowing to boycott worship if they had to sing it again.

"We're pro-union," Frieda explained, "but that's where the song belongs, with the union folks."

"Or in a Pete Seeger concert," added Dwight.

"Anyway, it's not a Potter song. And if we're going to sing something to the tune of 'The Battle Hymn of the Republic,' we'd rather sing the original words," Frieda continued.

In frustration but also in agreement with the response to his efforts, Sol gathered a delegation of members to discuss the situation with Emma.

"The congregation wants to sing hymns but not orthodox Christian ones or those of any other religions," he explained.

"And those hymns don't yet exist," said Emma. "So what solution do you propose?"

"That you write Harry Potter hymn texts to familiar tunes," said Rob.

"Me?" she said, surprised at the suggestion.

"You did such a great job with the benediction," Sol said. "You are the one who is good with words."

So Emma set about writing texts to fit existing hymn tunes. She felt a creative burst of energy, in part from the support of Cloud and Terp and others, as well as the growth of the congregation. She showed the texts to Sol, seeking his evaluation as director of the music program, and he said he was impressed. Emma thought she saw in his eyes a glimmer of interest in her beyond the professional relationship, but he said nothing to indicate anything more than simple friendship. Then she remembered she had put off Malcolm Drumheller by saying she did not get involved with parishioners, so she put the idea of Sol as a beau out of her mind.

The first hymn she and Sol provided for the congregation to sing was "Guide Me, O Thou Great Patronus" set to the tune Cwm Rhondda following the pattern of "Guide Me O Thou Great Jehovah"

> Guide me, O thou great Patronus,
>
> Courage of my inner mind.
>
> Give me strength to face tormentors,
>
> For the sake of wizardkind.
>
> Incantations, incantations,
>
> I will ever cast for thee,
>
> I will ever cast for thee.

When the response to this was enthusiastic, they introduced the congregation to "Dear Dumbledore of Wizard Fame" set to the tune Rest following the pattern of "Dear Lord and Father of Mankind"

Dear Dumbledore of wizard fame,
We rest our trust in you.
Protect us from the lake and cave
And save us from the Riddles' grave
Let Fawkes and sword sail through.

Next came "Hark! The Witch Hermione" set to the tune Mendelssohn following the pattern of "Hark! The Herald Angels Sing"

Hark! The witch Hermione,
Muggle-born to set us free.
Even Muggles do agree,
Brightest witch in history.
Joyful now her praise we sing.
Let the bells of Hogwarts ring.
Hark! The witch Hermione,
Brightest witch in history.
Hark! The witch Hermione,
Brightest witch in history.

This was followed by "Harry, Harry, Harry" set to the tune: Nicaea following the pattern of "Holy, Holy, Holy"

Harry, Harry, Harry, Dark Lord is vanquished.
Early in the morning his wand obeyed your call.
Harry, Harry, Harry, merciful and mighty,
All wizardkind rejoices in his fall.

The congregation's favorite proved to be the Harry Potter hymn that soon came to be sung at the start of every service. "Prophet and Chosen One" was set to the tune America, following the pattern of "My Country 'Tis of Thee"

Prophet and Chosen One,
Who makes Death Eaters run,
Of thee we sing.
Auror of destiny,
From whom Dementors flee,
Our hearts abide in thee,
O brave Harry.

CHAPTER NINETEEN
STAR VISITOR

Henry called Emma on a bright spring day in 2013. "Are you free for lunch? I'm on campus for a creative writing class this morning, but I've come across some interesting HP trivia that I'd like to pass on to you."

"Sure, Henry. What's the subject of the trivia?" she asked.

"Foreign translations," he replied.

They arranged to meet at a newly opened vegetarian restaurant close to the college. Once they had ordered black bean tamales, Henry said, "I came across a comment about the difficulty of translating anagrams, which set me to thinking about the famous anagram in *Harry Potter*."

"Rearranging Tom Marvolo Riddle into I am Lord Voldemort," Emma said.

"Exactly," Henry replied. "But it doesn't work in other languages. I pulled out my Latin edition of *Chamber of Secrets* and found the Dark Lord's name rendered Tom Musvox Ruddle and rearranged into the Latin phrase '*Sum Dux* Voldemort.'"

"Musvox, how funny," Emma said with a laugh.

"At any rate, that got me to thinking what the name would be like in other languages to make the anagram work," Henry continued.

"I can't wait to hear what you've found," Emma said.

"In German, the translator settled for an English paraphrase, 'Is Lord Voldemort' for 'I am Lord Voldemort.' His name is Tom Vorlost Riddle, which becomes '*Ist* Lord Voldemort.' The French translator came up with a memorable middle name. The one who became the Dark Lord is Tom Elvis Jedusor, which becomes '*Je suis* Voldemort.' In Norwegian, it's Tom Dredolo Venster, turned into 'Voldemort **den store**,' which means Voldemort the Great. And in Spanish, Tom Sorvolo Ryddle becomes '**Soy** Lord Voldemort.' It seems all the translators I could find kept the name Tom but they all changed the middle name and most fiddled with his last name as well. There are dozens more, but I don't remember them all."

"I know that translations often have different names for Voldemort and other characters," said Emma. "Someday, someone ought to make a directory of all of them."

"But there are many different alphabets and characters involved," said Henry. Arabic, Chinese, Cyrillic, and so on."

"Not only that, but the books have been translated into more than 70 languages, including Faroese, Greenlandic, and Tibetan," Emma added. "And also, of course, Americanese."

"Apparently, many unauthorized translations have been released as pirated editions," Henry said. "There were even fake novels released in China before Rowling had completed the series. Some poor Chinese fans were snookered into buying **Harry Potter and the Porcelain Doll** and **Harry Potter and the Golden Turtle** among other bogus books attributed to Ms. Rowling."

Emma's phone sounded, and she reached into her purse. "Pardon me. It might be a parishioner." She stared at the number with a puzzled expression.

"Something wrong?" Henry asked.

"It looks like a number from the UK," she replied.

"Better take it then," Henry said. "It might be J. K. Rowling."

It was not Emma's favorite author, nor anyone she knew, but it proved to be an important call. The woman at the other end identified herself as a personal assistant to Emma Watson. She said that the actress was on holiday and would be in Sedona on Saturday. Would it be alright if Ms. Watson attended the Holy Rowling service that day?

Emma thought this could be a prank, but her intuition said it was real. "Absolutely wonderful," she replied. They spent a few minutes talking about not publicizing the matter and the low-key security that would be involved.

"You look ecstatic," Henry said when she ended the call.

She explained. "I won't believe it's true until it actually happens," she added.

Attendance was higher than usual that Saturday. Emma had not spoken publicly about the expected visitor, honoring her agreement with the personal assistant, but also because she would be terribly embarrassed if the actress did not appear. However, she had told her family. Thus the ranks were slightly swelled by the presence of her brother Cameron as well as Uncle Henry and Aunt Beatrix. Their children, Sarah, about to graduate from Anasazi College, Thomas a sophomore at the school, and eight year-old Meiyin were also excited to be there. Henry carried a replica of Professor Dumbledore's elder wand that Sarah and Thomas had given him for his birthday.

An excited buzz pulsed through the chapel when people became aware that Emma Watson had quietly slipped into the side of the room. The Holy Rowlings would have received any cast member from the **Harry Potter** films as royalty, but Emma Watson was unquestionably queen among them.

Members of the congregation unanimously expressed a preference for the books over the movies, but images of the actors who portrayed various characters in the films were nevertheless imprinted in their brains. When re-reading the books, they saw the face and heard the voice of Emma Watson as Hermione and the same for Daniel Radcliffe as Harry. A small number of diehards rejected Rupert Grint as Ron, because he wasn't tall and thin enough, but most now associated him with the character he played. The great majority saw Richard Harris in their minds as Dumbledore, though he played the part in only two films.

Only four actors were broadly rejected as images for the book characters. Jim Broadbent was not nearly fat enough to portray Professor Slughorn, and Emelda Staunton, though acting the part well, was too tall and too attractive to play Professor Umbridge. The other two deemed to be miscast were Geraldine Somerville and Adrian Rawlins, who played Harry's parents. Lily and James Potter were both 21 when they died, but they are played by a woman in her thirties and a man in his forties.

Jordan expressed the prevailing view among Holy Rowlings. "They should have cast much younger actors for those parts. Otherwise, they're trying to sell the sorry notion that after they're dead people actually continue to show the effects of aging. Get real!"

As it happened, Emma Watson and Emma Round shared more than a first name and a birthday. The congregation well knew that both women had been born April 15, 1990. In addition, each one possessed Hermione level intellects and the courageous instincts of Gryffindor.

Having learned that members of the church occasionally came to services dressed as Harry Potter characters, the actress attended wearing the robe and hat of the transfiguration professor, Minerva McGonagall, to the especial delight of the pastor.

Emma, the Hallowed Philosopher, wore her usual white alb and a red stole with the Hogwarts crest emblazoned on both ends. A Deathly Hallows pendant necklace dangled from her neck. In her reflection that afternoon, the pastor said, "Last week we examined the theme of free will in the **Potter** series and its congruence with the biblical view of that concept. Today I will focus on ways in which **Harry Potter** theology is different from traditional Christian doctrine. Markedly different. First, there is no virgin birth, and second, no sacrifice to wash away sins. Sacrifice yes, but not substitutionary sacrifice. Rowling seems to be among the growing chorus of Christians who question the logic of blood atonement to explain Jesus' crucifixion. Indeed, in **Half Blood Prince**, when Harry and Dumbledore are at the cave where Voldemort has hidden a Horcrux, the Headmaster discovers that he must offer a blood sacrifice in order to get in, and he calls that crude. I suspect this is Rowling herself commenting on the crudeness of blood of the Lamb theology.

"That's not to say that the novels are bloodless. Plenty of blood is shed by many characters, especially Harry. Still, blood is more important as a positive symbol. It is critically important in Rowling's work in a protective rather than atoning sense. The blood of loved ones flowing in his veins acts as a shield.

"Harry is a human savior, who sacrifices his life for the sake of people he loves, but not to save them from their iniquity. His is a personal not a universal sacrifice, made to put an end to their suffering, not atone for their sins. His motivation for giving his life is not theological but like that of a soldier who falls on a grenade to spare his buddies.

"Like Jesus, Harry struggled with the burden placed upon him, but unlike the gospel accounts of Jesus, Harry was not born to be the savior of anybody. Certainly God did not choose him to carry out God's plans. To the extent that he is a Messiah, Harry is more Jewish than Christian.

"If Harry had been born to save the world, there would be no need in the story for Neville Longbottom. Other people proclaimed Harry the

Chosen One, but only after Voldemort picked Harry over Neville as his enemy. In *Order of the Phoenix*, Hermione tells Harry he has a 'saving-people-thing,' but that's a statement about his character not his divinity. He is not an all-wise healer like Jesus but an Everyman making his way through difficult trials with alternating awkwardness and determination.

"And to the extent Harry does save people, he does not do so single-handedly but greatly relies on help from friends and mentors. He would have failed utterly without the aid of Hermione." She glanced at Emma Watson, and the actress smiled. "In some ways, Hermione is also a Christ figure. She is the only one who can turn, well not water, but vinegar into wine. The allusion to Jesus at the wedding in Cana seems clear to me. She abandons her parents for the sake of the mission. She directs the saving of innocent lives for Sirius Black and Buckbeak, which Harry could not have done without her. She heals Harry and Ron on multiple occasions.

"But back to the Chosen One," the preacher continued. "After experiencing resurrection, Harry does not ascend to heaven or become divine but leads a consuetudinary life including marriage and children. If anything is salvific here it is knowledge. Not in the Gnostic sense of secrets of special revelation benefiting an inner circle but in how knowledge is useful for human progress and personal growth. Even so, Professor Dumbledore, the closest we get to an omniscient presence in the saga, didn't tell Harry everything he needed to know but made Harry find out for himself.

"Harry is a natural Seeker, an apt metaphor for someone searching for illumination rather than revelation. In the spirituality of *Harry Potter* we find no external scriptural revelation of God's infallible truth. The answers are not zapped down to us from heaven but are found within the minds and through the deeds of the characters. We find no orthodox allegory such as we read in Tolkien's *Lord of the Rings*. Instead, we encounter Harry and friends seeking wisdom to save the beloved community from destruction. This is humanistic Christianity. This is Christianity for our century, not a hangover from the fourth or seventeenth centuries.

"Indeed, the spirituality and theology of the *Harry Potter* series transcends any one parochial faith and shows the way to a transcendent humanism for all humankind."

Following the service, Emma Watson thanked the pastor for the edifying service and added, "Dan Radcliffe is a non-theist who, I think, would really appreciate your sermon. I'll tell him about it next time I see him."

"I'll give you a copy you can pass on to him, if you wish," Emma Round said.

"Thank you. That would be lovely," the actress responded. "Incidentally, I've heard that the church your congregation nests with practices nude worship. Is that true?"

"Most certainly," said the pastor. "All my family are members of the naturist church. I grew up with naturism. Would you like to visit? I can arrange a private tour. It's clothing optional, so you wouldn't have to disrobe."

"If my schedule permitted, I would be tempted to take your private tour and even attend a service. Unfortunately, I have to be on a plane in a few hours," Emma the actress said. "But if I were to visit, I wouldn't hide behind a robe. When in Rome and all that. That's assuming that photography is prohibited."

"It is; no cameras allowed in the sanctuary and no cell phones either, since they have cameras in them," said the pastor.

"One can't be too careful," said the actress. "I wouldn't want anything leaked on the Internet. I've been told that there are thousands of fake nude photos of me on the Internet, photoshopped, of course. And many other actresses as well. I shudder to think what kind of poses my face has been attached to. My sense is that if I looked at any of them, I would be angry enough to sue, but if I did, and managed to get one web site closed down, the pictures would show up on some other site almost immediately. That's the cursed side of the Internet."

"You wouldn't have to worry about that at the naturist church," said Emma Round. "These are people with a profound ethic of respecting privacy and anonymity."

"I believe that," said Emma Watson. "And ironically, if an actual nude photo of me should somehow appear on the net, everyone would assume it was fake."

"I saw an interview about four years ago where you said you might do a nude scene in a movie," Emma Round said.

The actress laughed. "I said that in a couple of interviews, but I also said I wasn't getting my kit off for just anyone or any time soon. As I recall, I used a Bernardo Bertolucci film as an example. If nudity were organic and necessary to the integrity of the film and consistent with the role, and assuming I trusted and respected the director, yes I would," Emma Watson replied. "There's nothing wrong with nudity in art, including film. Dan appeared nude on stage in *Equus* because the play required it. In similar circumstances I would as well."

"That would take care of the actual nude photo scenario," said the pastor.

"Too true," the actress responded.

"Actually, I loved your bathtub scene in *Ballet Shoes*," Emma Round said. "That was a nude scene of sorts."

"Well, I wasn't really nude," Emma Watson explained.

"But everyone imagined you were," said the Hallowed Philosopher.

The actress laughed again. "It's perfectly fine as long as it stays in the imagination. That's where the allure is."

Emma Watson lingered for the refreshment time after the service, answering questions and signing autographs. Most of the congregation circled giddily around her, but Henry made a beeline for his niece, hugging the pastor and telling Emma how enthralled he was of her reflection.

Frieda Waring, assuming her self-appointed role as designated adult, shook hands with the actress and said, "On behalf of your American fans, I want to say it's an outrage that none of the *Harry Potter* films won an Academy Award."

"I think they received a dozen nominations," said Emma. "That's quite an honor."

"But they were all in technical categories, like Visual Effects, Makeup, Costume Design, and Art Direction," Frieda responded. "And they didn't even win in those categories. It's a crying shame."

"Oh, I think there were nominations for Cinematography and Original Score, too," said the actress. "And all those you mentioned are critically important to a film."

"But none for acting," Frieda continued. "At the very least, Alan Rickman…"

Frieda was cut off by Dwight Cooke, who took her arm and gently steered her away, while whispering, "Time to let someone else have a turn, Frieda."

Frieda turned her head as she departed and added a postscript. "And snubbed by the Golden Globes, too. There's no justice in the world."

Next in line to speak to the actress was Alexis Whidge, who said, "I read that you are related to a real witch."

"Apparently so," Emma Watson replied. "Zealous researchers have traced my family back 14 generations to Joan Playle, who was convicted of witchcraft during the Elizabethan Age, the reign of the first Queen Elizabeth, that is."

"Was she executed?" Alexis asked.

"The evidence is that she was excommunicated from the Church of England but for some reason not burned at the stake or anything like that," Emma said.

"Maybe like real witches, the fire just tickled her and she pretended to be in pain," Alexis said. "That's a sign that you have actual magic blood. Maybe that's why you got the part of Hermione. You're a real witch. But more likely it was your natural talent."

Emma smiled but did not respond.

"Do you usually bring a witch's robe and hat when you travel?" Alexis continued.

"I didn't bring them," said the actress. "I bought them in a shop here in Sedona. And I really don't want to lug them home." Emma removed the hat and robe and handed them to Alexis. "We're about the same size, so you can keep them if you like."

Alexis was thrilled and said, "Oh thank you. You're so kind and generous. Of course, we Aries people are like that." Alexis winked and produced a stifled giggle.

The Saturday following Emma Watson's visit, Emma Round offered a reflection about the books that made up the biblical canon of the Holy Rowling church. During the fellowship time afterward, Alexis Whidge, bobbling a plate of carrot and celery sticks, approached Emma and said, "You've never mentioned the movies in your reflections. What place do they have in the HP canon?"

"I've thought about that," Emma responded. "Given our recent visitor, I know how deeply the movies are imbedded into the consciousness of our members. But I don't think of them as part of the canon. I see them as *pia fraus* -pious frauds."

"That's a pretty harsh judgment," Alexis said.

"Not really," Emma said. "Not in ecclesiastical circles. Lots of worthy literature falls into the pious fraud category, because it's not scripture. Even some of the books in the Christian Bible are technically pious frauds, because they were written by someone other than their ascribed authors. In the context of films, think of all those biblical epics by Cecil B. DeMille or even Mel Gibson. All the Hollywood hype in the world won't make them authentic. Still, they are useful in promoting healthy piety as well as entertaining. Well, maybe not that ghastly Mel Gibson thing, *The Passion of the Christ*."

Jordan Inge had slipped in to listen to the conversation, and now said. "I'm not sure how pious the movies are, but I don't see them as frauds. Just different."

"But should those differences be included in the canon?" Alexis said. "That would make the canon self-contradictory."

"The Bible is full of contradictions," Jordan said.

"Yeah, but the nice thing about the Holy Rowlings is that we have a religion without inherent contradictions," Alexis responded.

"But lots of gray areas," Jordan said.

"Gray areas indeed," Emma said. "This seems to be a sensitive subject."

"Oh, I think pretty much everyone here would place the books above the movies," Jordan said.

"Yeah, but what frosts my butt are the people who have only seen the movies and never read the books," said Alexis. "I mean, how could anyone see the movies and not want to read the books?"

"Exactly!" said Jordan. "It's OK to have a thing for the actors, but at some point, a *normal* person would pick up the books to find out what *really* happens."

"I think this congregation illustrates a healthy integration of the book and film communities," Emma said.

"That's because we've done both," said Alexis. "But I have no use for the filmies who have never opened a single *Harry Potter* book."

"Me neither," said Jordan. "As a group, they're pretty lame."

Three weeks after Emma Watson's visit, Emma Round received a thick packet of forms with instructions from the actress's charitable trust on how to apply for a grant to benefit the ACHPP. A handwritten note signed with the initials ECDW encouraged her to do so and added: "I have posted your sermon to our mutual friend DR."

Early in 2013, Willow had successfully completed work on a Master of Forestry degree and almost immediately accepted an entry-level management position with the US Forest Service. She carried responsibility for promoting healthy forest activities in the Coconino National Forest and was based in Flagstaff.

Emma's cousin Jeff left his position in Salt Lake City to join a small law firm in Flagstaff. His remuneration would be less than in the large office in Utah, but he would still be dealing with environmental issues. And there were other factors that more than compensated for his lower income.

Willow and Jeff were joined in marriage in a naturist service at the Sedona NCC, where both were members. Willow asked Jeff's twin sister Annagreta to serve as her matron of honor, and Jeff asked Annagreta's husband Whit Morgan, Cloud and Terp's son to be best man. But they asked a clergyperson from a different denomination to officiate. Emma had the honor of joining them in matrimony. Wishing to demonstrate complete equality between the sexes, Willow asked Henry to escort her down the aisle to join Jeff, who had been escorted to the same place by her mother, Kiee.

After the service, Jared said to Emma, "Did they do the double trips down the aisle for some sort of incest symbolism?"

"You cannot be serious," Emma said.

"Well, Uncle Henry is Jeff's father, walking Willow to the altar, and Kiee is Willow's mother doing the same. It seems kind of kinky to me."

Emma stared at her brother with incredulity showing on her face, and then he began to laugh. "Gotcha again!" he said.

"Honestly!" she said as she swatted him playfully on the shoulder.

Following their honeymoon, Willow and Jeff began attending the Holy Rowling church on Saturdays, while continuing to worship at the naturist church on Sunday mornings. Willow was now a member of three churches, as she had never resigned from the Native American Church in Prescott, although she rarely attended.

Emma had devised a survey to help prospective members in the sorting process. Though it was not required, many people found it helpful in confirming what they already suspected about themselves. Willow and Jeff were among the early users of this quiz, which revealed that both belonged in Gryffindor.

"No surprise there," said Emma.

CHAPTER TWENTY
THE REAL WORLD

After its July 13, 2013 publication, Emma bought a copy of J. K. Rowling's first non-*Harry Potter* book, ***The Casual Vacancy***. The first time through, she found it troubling to read because she wasn't used to the explicit profanity Rowling used in telling the story. It seemed inelegant to Emma, after the euphemistically theatrical idioms she was so familiar with while inhabiting Rowling's fictional worlds. Among her peers she had often heard and read these words, but that seemed different to Emma. She expected it in her real world.

Maybe that was the problem, she decided. She had been expecting an enchanted land and was disappointed to find herself deep in a world close to her own. The story line was depressing and not romantic. She knew people like the ones portrayed in ***Casual Vacancy***. After reading it again, Emma came to see this new novel as Rowling's attempt to be a 21st century Jane Austen, complete with the coarser idioms of the new era. But as for use in church, any reflections she derived from it, she thought, would be cautionary tales about how not to live and what not to do.

Jiminy Farwing, a young man who lived in a trailer on the outskirts of Cottonwood, appeared at a service one afternoon. During the fellowship time afterward, he sidled up to Emma, and while looking away from her face mumbled, "I have a Horcrux in my head."

Emma was not certain she had heard him correctly. "I'm sorry. Could you say that again?"

This time he spoke more clearly and increased his volume so that the people around them could also hear. "I have a Horcrux in my head. The

Sorting Hat rejected me. I kept telling it not Hufflepuff, and it said I was in Horcrux House."

Emma sensed that he was not joking, so she responded in a calm fashion. "When did this happen?"

Jiminy looked around at the people who had now turned their attentions to him and Emma. "They're after me! Please help me. The Death Eaters are here."

At this, the members began to form a circle around Jiminy, and he screamed for help and threw himself into Emma's arms.

"Everybody stop and back away," Emma instructed. "Dwight, please call 911."

They did as she said.

Looking directly at the young man clinging to her, she said, "Tell me your name."

"Thank you for saving me," he replied.

"Please tell me who you are," Emma said

"Jiminy Farwing. I live in Cottonwood. But the Death Eaters found out about my Horcrux, and they're trying to get it from me."

"You're safe here," Emma said. "It's safe for you to let go now."

Jiminy released his grip on Emma's shoulders but remained in place.

Taking his hand, she led him to a chair and offered him something to drink.

"No thanks. I'm not thirsty," he said.

"Stay here. I'll be right back," she instructed. Motioning for Karl to keep Jiminy under surveillance, Emma ducked out of the room and returned a minute later with a bar of dark chocolate. His eyes widened with pleased recognition as she put it in his hands.

An ambulance crew arrived, and Dwight efficiently told them what had happened. When the EMT saw Jiminy munching on the chocolate, he looked at Emma, standing beside the troubled youth, and made a thumbs up gesture. Jiminy made no protest at being escorted to the ambulance, as Emma walked with him saying that they were taking him to St. Mungo's Hospital.

<><><>

An Air Force pilot relaxing in Sedona on leave came to a service one Saturday. Chatting with Emma before the service, she told Emma that she flew a C-17 Globemaster III.

"Do you still name your planes like they did in World War II?" Emma asked.

"I do," the officer replied. "Mine is named Hedwig."

"Cool!" Emma said.

As usual, Dwight was hovering near the Hallowed Philosopher, and he entered the conversation. "When I was in Viet Nam, I had a jeep officially designated MP-34, but I called her Natasha."

"After a girlfriend at the time?" the pilot asked.

"A fictional one," Dwight said. "I was really into the **Rocky and Bullwinkle** cartoons when I was a kid, and I especially liked the fake Russian spy Natasha Fatale."

"Never heard of her," Emma and the Air Force pilot said in unison.

Frieda Waring received a visit from an Army Chaplain, informing her that Rick had been killed in a suicide bomb attack in Kabul. The first call that Frieda made after the chaplain left was to Emma, asking her to preside over a memorial service. Saddened by the news, Emma immediately agreed, but as soon as the phone call ended, she felt a streak of panic slice through her brain, because this would be her first such service as Hallowed Philosopher. Cloud and Terp had tutored her on the subject in general, but she had no Potter-related liturgy for the occasion.

Be calm and think, she told herself. Searching through her memory, she remembered the service that Kwan-yin had done for Sylvia. Somewhere amidst her pile of files, she still had the bulletin for that service. It took half an hour to locate it, but once she had it in hand, she felt relief. This was, at least, a starting point. It was an order of worship from a different religion, an explicitly Christian rite, but she could modify that to fit the linguistic peculiarities of the Holy Rowlings.

Since it would be a memorial service, there would be no body present, or even ashes as with Sylvia. This simplified the choreography, as there would be no pallbearers or questions about open or closed coffin.

Emma's first call was to Terp, for guidance about doing funerals and to ask for permission to use the chapel on a Saturday morning as well as the usual Saturday afternoon. Terp checked the calendar and found no prior reservation for the morning and wrote in the calendar "ACHPP mem svc" for the time requested.

Following up on advice from Terp, Emma made a visit to Frieda's home to be a pastoral presence and to ask if Frieda had a favorite passage from the canon that she would like Emma to read at the service. Frieda sat in silent meditation for a moment before looking up at Emma and saying, "the next great adventure."

The chapel was full for the Rick Waring memorial, including many people who had known the fallen soldier in other contexts. Most of the Holy Rowlings were present, but they formed the minority.

Frieda had invited her ex-husband to attend, but he declined. Wink Waring was certain that Frieda's church was a satanic cult that should be shunned at all costs. Instead, he arranged for his pastor, Nick Winger, to lead a memorial for Rick at his Fundamentalist Perfection Church congregation. Even though Wink was a member, his son had not been, so he was obliged to pay a $500 honorarium to Rev. Winger for the service. Winger readily accepted a small fraction of that amount for doing funerals of non-members at mortuaries, but in Nick's mind, Wink could well afford it and as a member was captive to the demands of the pastor anyway.

Emma used a format and language familiar to those who had attended Christian funerals but adapted to the conventions of her church. After reading the requested passage from *Philosopher's Stone*, Emma began her meditation for Rick Waring:

"When Albus Dumbledore faces off against Voldemort in *Order of the Phoenix*, Voldemort says that there is nothing worse than death, and Dumbledore responds that he is quite wrong and that Voldemort's failure to recognize that there are things worse than death has been the chief Death Eater's greatest weakness. But Voldemort is unable to grasp fully the concepts of life after life and the heroic nature of the death of the physical body.

"J. K. Rowling has repeatedly said in interviews that her mother's death had an impact on her writing. From the moment of her mother's passing, death became a central theme of the series. Through her characters, she explored how people react to death. Characters' attitudes toward death, ranging from fear to respect, reveal who they are.

"Dumbledore, unlike Voldemort, does not fear death, as Rowling has illustrated over and again as the narrative unfolds through seven novels."

Emma looked out over the assembled people and said, "You all know this line. You all have it memorized. Say it with me now. 'To the well-organized mind, death is but the next great adventure.'"

The assembled group, including most of the non-Holy Rowlings, responded in unison with Emma.

"It is reasonable to infer from this that Dumbledore has faith that there is more to come after the death of the body. What the exact nature of that is, no one this side of the grave knows. But we always have grounds for hope. It is cliché to say that Rick is in a better place, or that he is at peace, or any of the dozens of similar phrases designed to comfort and reassure those of us who grieve his passing. I have no quarrel with any of these sentiments, but as one who has experienced the sudden and violent death of a dear friend, I have found the greatest comfort in the words of Albus Dumbledore. And knowing Frieda as I do, and since she chose these specific words for this memorial for her son, I am confident that she also finds them reassuring and full of meaning and truth.

"Farewell, Rick Waring, as you now venture on to this next great adventure."

Emma closed the service by adapting language that Kwan-yin had used at Sylvia's service. Kwan-yin had said, "All of us are made of dust beautifully spun into patterns of bodily form. Sylvia, you began as dust and to dust you have returned." Emma reached for her wand on the lectern and said, "Like all humans, Rick was formed from clouds of stardust and to stardust he has now returned." Raising the wand straight up in the air, she continued, "Enjoy your adventure among the stars, Rick."

In the weeks that followed, Dwight tried to comfort Frieda, but found it difficult to give too much to this effort, because he did not want it to become an invitation for a romantic relationship. Keeping a grieving mother at an emotional distance to discourage her from ascribing deeper intentions was the most difficult eye of a needle that he had ever threaded. Frieda, of course, recognized what she deemed his two-faced behavior for what it was and came to resent him for it. In the end, she decided that she had been foolish to try to kindle a relationship with such a cold fish as Dwight.

Feeling restless on a sleety Saturday morning, Emma decided to make a run up to Flagstaff to see if Bookmans Entertainment Exchange had any new Harry Potter related treasures in stock. As she turned right off Milton Road into the strip mall parking lot, she noted icy patches on the asphalt that had not yet been cleared. Berms of old hard snow created barriers here and there, limiting parking options. Emma navigated into a space with no vehicles on either side, and as she exited her car, another car pulled into the space one over to the right. It seemed vaguely familiar, but she couldn't see the driver, so she made her way into Bookmans, careful to avoid patches of ice.

Her instinct for Harry Potter merchandise had been on target, as she found five jigsaw puzzles, ranging from 500 to 1500 pieces, each with a different Potter inspired picture.

Laden with a bag full of puzzles in one arm and her purse in the other, she stopped beside her car and put the shopping bag on the hood so she could fish the keys from her purse. As she did this, the door of the vaguely familiar car one space over opened, and Malcolm Drumheller emerged.

Peripherally perceiving that someone was approaching her, Emma turned and saw Malcolm striding toward her. Glancing quickly to his right and left and seeing that no one was in view, he said, "You can't escape me forever, Hermione."

"Get lost, ferret!" Emma spat out.

"Temper, temper, Granger," Malcolm chided. "Time for a cease-fire. Let's bury the hatchet and smoke a peace pipe. We should be intimate friends."

"What are you doing here?" she said, her tone betraying a quarter note of fear.

"I followed you. I've done it before, but the time wasn't right to act. Now it is. We were made for each other, Hermione, and I can't live without your sweet love."

"I think you should go," Emma said, her voice now steadier.

"I think you should show me some respect," Malcolm responded as he stepped directly in front of her.

Rather than look for an escape route, Emma held her ground and stared into her pursuer's eyes.

Again glancing right and left and seeing no other people, Malcolm clasped his hands firmly on her shoulders and with his mouth open and his tongue out swept his head down to kiss her. Acting with trained intention, Emma raised her right leg and rammed her knee smartly into Malcolm's groin.

He screamed in pain and yelled, "You bitch! I'm going to have you arrested for assault."

An unfamiliar male voice said, "Not with me as a witness. I saw what you did to her."

Malcolm looked up and saw a tall, muscular man standing on the other side of Emma's car. The Draco cosplayer turned and ran the short distance to his own car, but slipped on the ice and inelegantly fell on his rump. Scrambling to regain an upright posture, he pulled open the door, jumped in, started the ignition, and recklessly backed up into a snow bank. His car spun around and fishtailed as Malcolm sought the exit.

"He's gonna have a mighty bruise on his butt," the stranger said. "Serves him right, though."

Emma looked at the stranger and saw that he had neatly trimmed black hair with a crisp part on the left and deep-set brown eyes. "Thank you," she said.

"That's pretty impressive leg work. Where did you learn self-defense?" he said.

"I was on the fencing team in high school and college, but my older brother taught me that particular technique," Emma answered.

"Is he in the military?" he asked.

"No. He has friends who have been targeted by bullies, and he made it a point to learn how to protect himself and thought I should know how too," Emma said.

"As any big brother should rightly do. Why did that creep call you Hermione?" the stranger asked. "Is that your name?"

"No, she's a character in *Harry Potter*. He pretends that I'm that Hermione."

"Ah, I thought so," he said. "It's such an unusual name that I guessed he was referring to that Hermione. I take it you're a fan."

"You might say that," Emma said. "By the way, I'm Emma Round."

He walked haltingly around the front of Emma's car and extended his hand. "I'm Tom Corazon, and I'm a fan too. And you don't have to answer if you don't want to, but I'm still curious about why that guy called you Hermione."

Feeling at ease now, she laughed and said, "He thinks he's Draco and is a Draco-Hermione shipper. Are you familiar with shipping?"

"I know what it is, but I'm not into it," Tom said. "I figure the author knew what she was doing, so why should I second guess her."

"Now it's my turn to ask a question. How did you happen to be next to my car? I didn't see or hear anybody as I was walking here," Emma said.

"Well, the parking lot is icy in spots, and I'm not confident of my new prosthesis, so I stopped near your car and bent down to check that the shoelace was properly tied. I thought about going back to my car to get my cane, before venturing on to Bookman's, and in the time that took, that Draco character accosted you. You know the rest."

"I have a cane in my car that you can borrow," Emma said. "I keep it there for emergencies."

"I'd like to hear more about why we both have canes, but it's freezing in this parking lot. Would you be open to getting a cup of coffee?" Tom said.

"Let me just stow this stuff in my car," Emma said. She lifted the bag of puzzles from the hood, held it up and said, "Harry Potter jigsaw puzzles."

"Put them in the back. That's more secure," Tom said.

She did so, and the two carefully made their way to a small restaurant at the end of the mall. Over coffee, Emma told Tom about the drunk driver who had killed Sylvia and broken her left leg years earlier. "I keep the cane around because the leg occasionally aches, especially in cold weather."

"I guess you could say that I lost the lower half of my left leg in a vehicular incident, too," Tom said. "But the other guy wasn't drunk, and it wasn't another car that collided with me, and it was a long way from Arizona."

"You're a veteran, aren't you?" Emma said.

"Yep," Tom said. "I lost my leg in Kandahar, Afghanistan, thanks to an IED that exploded in the middle of my convoy, inconveniently right in front of the vehicle I was riding in."

"I'm so sorry," Emma said. And then searching for something to add, said, "Thank you for your service."

"You're welcome," Tom said. "And I know you mean it, so I'm not being critical, but that phrase, 'thank you for your service' has become a convenient cliché for politicians to show they support the vets while screwing us behind their hypocritical asses."

"Well then, let's change the subject," Emma said. "How long have you been a fan?"

"When I was in Walter Reed for rehab and fitting for my first prosthesis, I had lots of time on my hands. One of the nurses suggested I read the ***Harry Potter*** books, and I got hooked. I was depressed at the time and feeling sorry for myself. I was also grieving over my driver, who was killed by that IED. But reading Harry's saga was as therapeutic as the physical therapy I was getting."

"I know," Emma said with enthusiasm. "I was already a big fan when I ended up in the hospital and rehab, but I re-read all the books then, and it really helped me get through the loss of my best friend."

In the course of the conversation, Emma learned that Tom's full name was Tomas León Corazon, and he lived in Cottonwood. He had driven to Flagstaff specifically because he loved searching for treasures at Bookmans, especially atlases and maps, of which he had a large collection. Tom had graduated from ASU, where he completed the ROTC program. In the Army he had been a first lieutenant at the time he was wounded. "I was on track to make captain, but my career was cut short, so to speak, by that IED," he said with a chuckle.

"You seem pretty cool about it, enough to joke about it, I mean," Emma said.

"It took me a while to get here, to acceptance and a positive outlook," Tom said with a shrug. "I went through a time of heavy alcohol abuse, but I credit Harry Potter for my sobriety."

"Even with all the fire whiskey that wizards consume?" Emma said.

"Reading those books was all that kept me from going over the edge," Tom said. "About the third time through them, I realized that being drunk was like living with a Horcrux, having part of my soul damaged. Harry's courage motivated me to quit."

Tom, in turn, learned about the Holy Rowlings. "I founded an HP related church," Emma said.

"Hewlett-Packard has a church?" Tom responded with a note of surprise.

"Not that HP," Emma said. "What heroic boy have we been talking about?"

"Oh right, Harry Potter," Tom replied. "I think of him in terms of magic and all that hocus pocus, but I suppose HP has connections with religion and a lot of other things besides."

"Give me an example," Emma said.

"Oh, I don't know…high priest." He said.

"Or high priestess," Emma added. "And as it happens, my title is Hallowed Philosopher."

"Higher Power," Tom said. "Anyone who's been to an AA meeting knows that HP stands for Higher Power."

"That definitely passes the religious test, and highly personal I'll bet," said Emma. "What else do you have?"

"There's Holy Paladin, if you're into World of Warcraft," Tom said.

"Thanks, but Harry Potter role-playing is enough for me without getting sucked into online games. But that's an inspired HP," Emma said.

"HP could also mean high priced, hot potato, or huge payoff," Tom said. "Or Highway Patrol."

"Those are hardly pertinent. How pathetic," Emma said with a chuckle in her voice. "But there's a scholar named John Granger who's written books about **Harry Potter** who calls himself the Hogwarts Professor, and Luna has a hare Patronus. And if you want to talk about people, there are Broadway musical producer-director Hal Prince, British dramatist Harold Pinter, and German writer Heinrich Pudor."

"Heinrich who?" Tom said.

"Oh he's an obscure German advocate of naturism," Emma explained.

"In other words, someone we *hoi polloi* would never have heard of," Tom said. "How about the highly political Huffington Post?"

"Do you read that?" Emma responded. "I check it every day. I like their high powered articles about high profile people."

"But they can be highly partisan," Tom retorted and tentatively added, "Happy Passover?"

"More likely hurried Passover," Emma said.

"Help please, I'm all out of HPs for the moment," said Tom.

"OK, here's an obscure one," she said. "Hermione Puckle."

"Who?" Tom asked.

"That's the original name for Hermione Granger that J. K. Rowling was going to use. But it didn't seem to suit the character, and by switching to Granger, she made a pun on the chemical symbol for mercury."

"And if she hadn't changed it, Hermione and Harry would have the same initials," Tom said.

"You're really good at this," Emma responded. "Were you an English major?"

"No, geography. When I was a kid I wanted to be a mapmaker," he replied.

"Hence the collection of atlases," Emma said.

"Yeah, but I've spent a lot of time watching reruns of shows like Match Game on the Game Show Network. I like word play," he said.

"Match Game? Never heard of it," Emma replied.

"With Gene Rayburn?" he said.

"Nope," Emma said.

"Then I guess we're even for Heinrich whoever," Tom said. "But I'm curious about why you would worship Harry Potter. I know he's a Christ figure in the books, but do you actually pray to him like Jesus?"

"We don't worship him as a god," Emma explained. "And we don't pray to him or anything like that. But the books are loaded with wisdom, and ethical models, and affirmations about the nature of God and human souls. It's a metaphorical religion."

"You wouldn't mind if I showed up at one of your church services, would you?" Tom said.

"Not at all! It would be great if you did," she replied. "Which reminds me, I've got a service to get ready for this afternoon. I need to get on the road. Any chance you could drop by today?"

"I just might," Tom said with a grin.

He did, and came back the following Saturday. The third week of his attendance, he sorted himself into Hufflepuff, announcing as he did so, with a wink at Emma, "I'm going to be a Hufflepuff Prefect!"

After the service, Frieda told him, "Welcome to Hufflepuff. It's good to have someone like you to bolster our ranks. But you're a war hero, Tom. Shouldn't you be in Gryffindor?"

"Hufflepuff has its heroes too," Tom said.

Frieda slapped her forehead. "Doh! How could I forget Cedric Diggory? Shame on me." And then she remembered her son Rick and began to weep. Tom wrapped a strong arm around her shoulders.

Soon thereafter, the Sedona ACHPP received an invitation to participate with other non-traditional churches in the Sedona Alternative Ministerium. The Sedona Natural Christian Church, in whose chapel the Harry Potter Church met, was a founding member of SAM, although the idea to include Emma's congregation came initially from other members and was then enthusiastically endorsed by the Sedona NCC.

"Now that we're recognized as a genuine church not only by the IRS but more importantly in the community," Emma told the congregation, "we should celebrate our transition from an experiment in fantasy worship to ministry in the real world."

At the end of the service that day, Tom offered to help tidy up the chapel.

"Won't all the bending put a strain on your leg?" Emma said.

"Not this piddly effort," Tom said. As he moved around the room, picking up abandoned bulletins and coffee cups, he watched for a chance to speak privately to Emma. When he saw her walking in his direction, he took his chance. "Say, Emma, I was wondering if you would like to go out to dinner with me."

This startled Emma. "On a date, you mean?"

"Yes, on a date," Tom replied.

"Well, uh, I, uh, have a policy not to date parishioners," she said following a brief pause.

"But we met before I was a parishioner," he countered. "So that should count as an exception to your policy."

"You've got a point there," she said. "But even so, I have to say no."

"It's because of my missing limb, isn't it?" Tom said.

"Heavens no!" Emma replied.

"Then I can think of only two reasons why you won't go out with me," he said. "Either it's sexual orientation or there's somebody else."

"If it were the former," Emma said, "everyone would know about it, because I would claim it with pride."

"Then there is somebody else," Tom said.

"In a way," Emma answered, not looking at him.

"That sounds pretty vague," he said.

Now she looked directly at him. "The truth is, I'm holding out for someone."

"And he hasn't made a move yet. So make the first move yourself," Tom said.

"It's complicated," Emma responded.

"Another parishioner?" Tom asked.

"I'm not going to answer that," Emma said.

"Fair enough, but let me offer a compromise," Tom said. "If you want to motivate a guy to get off his butt, maybe a little competition might do the trick. Go out with me and see what happens."

Emma thought about it for a moment and said, "OK, where shall we go?"

"A new fish and chips pub just opened in Flag, that I've been wanting to check out," he said.

Over dinner on their first date, Emma said, "Since I was born here, I call myself an Arizona native, but some people confuse that with Arizona Native American, which I'm clearly not. But my Arizona ancestry goes back to Territorial days, which I'm rather proud of. Where were you born, Tom?"

Tom laughed genially. "You want to know if I'm legal?"

"Of course not," she replied. "I wouldn't care if you were undocumented, but that's not what I meant at all."

"Well, I was born here too," he said. "And my ancestors have lived in Arizona back before Territorial days when it was part of Mexico, and before that when it was claimed by Spain. Some of my people go back even further when the land was owned by no one but was cherished and protected by all the people who lived upon it."

"I bow humbly to your heritage," said Emma.

And so Emma and Tom entered upon a series of social engagements, sampling international cuisines throughout Central and Northern Arizona. She did not advertise this fact but news of her dating Tom nevertheless spread quickly through the congregation. Sol, in particular, took note of it, and rather than feel jealousy or competitiveness, concluded that Emma had no interest in him.

When Jordan heard the news, however, she recognized an opportunity. The members of Merlin's Board had recently been assigned responsibility for various aspects of church operations. Jordan was now liaison to the music program. In this capacity, she invited Sol to dinner at her apartment.

"I have something to run by you about music," she told him.

"Shouldn't you discuss this with Emma?" he responded.

"In time," Jordan said. "But we haven't reached that stage yet."

"I've got a few minutes right now. Let's talk here," Sol said.

"If I'm going to be the music liaison, I need to get to know the director in a less stressful setting," she replied. "And I have a specific proposal that will need to be fleshed out. I don't want anyone here to catch a word of it until I know it's a go."

Sol realized that she would find a way to force the meeting to happen at her place, so he accepted the dinner invitation.

As he entered Jordan's apartment, he noticed a white linen tablecloth over the dining room table bearing two elegant place settings complete with wine glasses and accompanying candelabras.

"Looks like you've gone to a lot of trouble for a business meeting," Sol said.

"No trouble at all," Jordan said. "I enjoy fine things."

She wore a deep red cocktail dress that clung to her figure and revealed a significant proportion of her breasts. Spinning slowly to show it off, she said, "I'm wearing Gryffindor colors just for you, Sol."

"That's quite a concession for a Slytherin," he said.

"Well, I have a proposal for you, and I want you to accept, so I'm a Gryffindor for tonight," she said.

"A business proposal, I hope," he said.

"To be sure," she purred. "What other kind is there?"

Soon he was sitting at the table, and Jordan carried in a tray of oysters. "I hope you have a big appetite. These are my specialty," she said.

"Sorry to disappoint you," he replied. "I do have a big appetite, but I'm allergic to shellfish."

Her countenance fell momentarily, before she recovered and said, "That is a pity. Before I bring out anything else, you may as well tell me if you're allergic to anything else."

"Grapes," he said.

"No problem, we're not dining Mediterranean tonight," she said. "Are you ready for wine?"

"What is it made from?" Sol asked.

"Oh crap, grapes," she said. "I used to have a bottle of dandelion wine, but it's all gone."

"A beer will do," he said. "Or just plain water."

As the meal progressed, Jordan consumed most of the oysters and wine, while Sol drank water with his salmon steak.

"So, what is this business proposition?" he asked.

"I've been thinking about the hymns we sing, and they're all good, but they're based on Christian tunes. I think it's time we had some original melodies to set Potter related words to."

"That's a good idea. Where are you going to get them?" he said.

"From you," she said with a smile. "I want you to compose some music for the congregation. You could copyright them and keep any royalties from outside sales, but grant permission for the church to use them free."

"I'm a pretty good player, but no composer," Sol responded.

"You're a great artist. I've seen some of your sculptures. If you can do that, you can create a few tunes," Jordan said.

"I'll mull it over," he replied.

"That's all I could ask for," she said. "But I have another question, not related to music."

"Oh?" he said.

"I'm curious about the Natural Christian Church you belong to," she said.

"You're welcome to attend a service any time you like," he said.

"Several Holy Rowlings have added NCC attendance to their weekend schedules."

"I'd feel funny going by myself. I'd go if you would accompany me," she said. "That way I'd feel safe."

Sol was skeptical about Jordan needing anyone with her to feel safe but did not challenge the assertion. "Let me know when you'd like to try it, and I'll introduce you to some of the pastors. They have a large staff."

Jordan's mind immediately turned to wonder about the size of Sol's staff. "I need to work on getting an all-over tan before showing up naked in church," she said. "Maybe you could help me find a place to do that and we could sunbathe nude together."

"Services at the NCC are inside, and not everyone has a complete tan," Sol said.

"But I'm curious if you do," she said. "Care to show me? I'll show you my tan lines." She stood, reached around to the back of her dress, unzipped it, and began wriggling to loosen its hold on her body. As the garment fell to the floor, Sol saw that she wore bra and panties of matching emerald green.

"See, I'm still Slytherin underneath," she said.

"Gryffindor colors for the dress but Slytherin where it counts," he said.

"Maybe I dyed the dress in Polyjuice Potion," she said sassily.

Sol bent over to pick up the red dress and pretended to examine it closely, running his fingers across the fabric. "It's been more than an hour, and it's still red. Nope, it's not dyed."

"Time for you to see proof that I've never dyed my hair either," she said as she unsnapped her bra and then slipped out of her panties. "See! A perfect match above and below. Now come on, get out of those clothes and let's be nudists for the rest of the evening."

"Obviously I have no problem with nudity around the home or anywhere else, and I'm quite comfortable in my own skin," Sol said. "But context is everything."

"You think I'm trying to seduce you, don't you?" she said.

"The thought crossed my mind," he said.

"Surely you're not a virgin, or are you?" Jordan said.

"No, I'm a Gemini," Sol responded.

She playfully pinched his cheek. "Well, I'm a Virgo but not a virgin, and that's not an answer."

"The answer would be the same regardless," he said.

"No, you're not?" she queried.

He nodded. "Yes. But I was under the impression that this was a business meeting."

"Meetings can have more than one item on the agenda," she replied. "And I am genuinely interested in your naturist church. Come on, show me what it's like to talk spirituality in the buff. Don't be such a prude."

Sol stood and undressed. "The first lesson about naturist spirituality is don't touch another person's body without permission."

"No hugging?" she asked.

"If someone signals an invitation to hug or shake hands, that's easily recognized. And it's perfectly OK to hug someone in those circumstances," he said.

She spread her arms apart and said, "Please give me hug."

When he stepped forward to comply, she pressed her lips against his and pushed in with her tongue.

This caused Sol to laugh, which caused Jordan to move her head back far enough to look at his face. "Are you laughing at me or because you think you're about to get laid?" she asked.

"A little of both," he replied.

"You're not allergic to sex are you?" she whispered in his ear.

"No," he answered.

CHAPTER TWENTY~ONE
UNFORGIVABLE CURSES

Over dinner at Angel Nest, the conversation turned to private for-profit prisons and capital punishment. Cloud and Terp were opposed to both and had said so in many sermons.

Cloud looked across the table at Emma and said, "What would Harry do? What insights do you think we can glean from *Harry Potter?*"

"The first thing to keep in mind is that the Ministry of Magic doesn't practice capital punishment, at least not on human beings," Emma said.

"Wouldn't sucking out souls count as tantamount to capital punishment?" Terp asked.

"I see it as spiritual punishment, which is far worse," Emma responded. "At a minimum, imprisonment at Azkaban involves driving people mad and in its ultimate form, destroying the soul. By definition, capital punishment pertains only to the body and is indifferent to what may or may not happen to the soul. The common belief is that when a person's physical body dies by any means, including execution, the soul survives. But in the world of *Harry Potter*, if a Dementor's kiss kills the soul, the physical body remains but is an empty shell, with no sense of self and no memory. The theological claim to be drawn from this, according to J. K. Rowling, is that a human body can exist without a soul."

"The reality of this portrait," said Terp, "is that a benign government, the Ministry of Magic, uses malignant means to discipline its prisoners. The good guys are not good in this respect."

"On the surface, the result of a Dementor's kiss sounds similar to a person who is brain dead and kept alive by the functioning autonomous system or a person whose brain has been fried by electric shock," said

Emma. "But it has deeper implications. With the Dementor's kiss, Rowling is describing the death of that part of a person that provides sentience and identity, and that, according to many religious beliefs, is what lives on after death, that is, the immortal soul. But if a Dementor can destroy the soul, then it is not immortal but is vulnerable to destruction by an evil force.

"Voldemort has shown that souls may be gravely damaged, and Dementors can completely destroy them. We have to assume that there are other means of killing souls in the wizarding world. This makes human life imbued with both body and soul more vulnerable."

"It also raises the specter of dualism in Rowling's work," said Cloud. "If body and soul are separate entities, each capable of life without the other, that's dualism."

"Yes," said Emma, "but that's the dystopian dimension to the vision. That's the part where the essential unity of creation goes awry. Even then, the soul that's split into a Horcrux requires the protective presence of a physical object to survive. And when the soul is split, the body is diminished, becoming less human. For Rowling, the ideal is clearly when the body and soul are unified."

"You haven't said anything about private prisons," said Terp. "I suppose this is because there are none in the wizarding world."

"Correct," said Emma.

"But what do you think Harry would do about the spiritual punishment allowed by the Ministry of magic?" Cloud said.

"It's clear that Harry is not a murderer," said Emma. "And he isn't too fond of the Dementors, either. My sense is that when Harry and also Hermione are in positions of leadership, they will both work hard to reform the penal system to make it more humane."

"My thoughts exactly," said Cloud.

A flush of pain coupled with embarrassment coursed through Emma's body when she saw Jordan sitting next to Sol at an NCC service. She told herself that she was seeing Tom, and Sol had never shown interest in her anyway, so she had no reason to feel bad if Sol developed a relationship with Jordan. But her feelings did not respond to reason.

During the fellowship time after worship, she walked up to Jordan while Sol was in search of cookies and said jauntily, "So, Sol talked you into trying the naturist church, I see. I hope it's not too Christian for you."

"I've evolved on that matter," Jordan said.

"Should I read anything more into your presence here with Sol?" Emma asked, with an attempt at a twinkle in her voice.

"We're dating, that's all," said Jordan. "Nothing too serious, just keeping it light and breezy."

Sol returned with a plate of brownies. "No chocolate chips today; hope these will do," he said. "Hi Emma. Want a brownie?"

"No thanks," she said. "I've already had my daily dose of medicinal chocolate. Good to see you're recruiting for the NCC." Emma looked directly at Jordan and said, "Maybe Sol will go with you to Burning Man."

"I hope so," Jordan said. She thought but did not say aloud that going to Burning Man would be preferable to the NCC, because she had not, in fact, evolved toward comfort with the Christian ethos of the naturist church. But she was willing to sit through the services to make Sol happy.

Responding to Jordan's suggestion about writing service music, Sol worked out a processional anthem on the piano in the chapel when no one else was around. He felt good about what he had created, but did not play piano well enough to demonstrate it for Emma much less play it during a service.

During the coordination and walk around time prior to worship the following Saturday, Sol showed the piece to Emma.

"I can't sight read," she told Sol. "Can you play it for me?"

"I'd ruin it if I did," he said. "The thing is, that piano has been in this room the whole time we've been meeting here, and it never occurred to me to ask if anyone in the congregation can play it." He surveyed the chapel and in a loud announcement voice said, "Does anybody here play the piano?"

"I do," said Alexis. "Are we going to use the piano now in church? I've been wondering why we haven't been using it all along."

"Didn't it occur to you to volunteer?" Sol asked.

"I was waiting to be asked," she said.

"Well, I am asking you now, please and thank you, Alexis," said Sol. "See if you can play this." He handed her his handwritten sheets.

Alexis scanned the pages several times and without a word placed them on the piano. Sitting on the bench, she lifted the lid covering the keys and began to play the processional at a stately cadence. When she had finished, she said, "This is beautiful."

"Thank you," said Sol. "Would you mind playing it again, just the way you did it the first time."

"Only if you tell me the name of it," Alexis said.

Sol looked around the room and saw that everyone was watching Alexis and him, and Emma and Jordan had drawn next to the piano. "It's called 'The Hallowed Philosopher Enters the Great Hall.' I thought we needed something with a little pomp to open the service."

Emma and Jordan blushed but for different reasons.

Thereafter, Alexis played Sol's composition at the beginning of each service as Emma entered the sanctuary and walked solemnly to sit in her designated chair beside the lectern.

A young man wearing a sleeveless shirt revealing both arms covered with elaborate tattoos and sporting gold earrings in both lobes sauntered in to a Holy Rowling service one Saturday. Chip Shoverly commented to the greeter that he had come out of morbid curiosity.

After completing one year of community college, Chip had jumped from job to job, working as an appointment clerk in a doctor's office, a data entry clerk, a fast food cook, a pizza delivery driver, and as a clerk in a Kinkos store. He had tried to get on as a driver at FedEx through his Kinkos job, but had a bad driving record arising from his short stint delivering pizza. The only thing in his life that Chip took any positive pride in was his collection of coprolites.

Chip had seen two of the **Harry Potter** movies, **Chamber of Secrets** and **Order of the Phoenix** but had not read any of the books. As a child, he had been emotionally wounded by an archconservative church and as a result had grown hostile to Christianity specifically and organized religion in general. The day he arrived at the Harry Potter church, he assumed it was a vehicle for mocking religion, which was motivation enough for him to check it out. The reception he received that first Saturday was warm, and no one quizzed him about his knowledge of HP subjects, but he was disappointed to find that the members and the pastor were sincere about what they were doing. This was not a joke.

Still, something about the experience led him to return. The second time he attended, Emma offered a reflection on social justice and authority.

"Among other things, the **Harry Potter** series functions as social and political criticism. From the outset, Rowling is satirizing how corporations and governments function. The Ministry of Magic is clearly portrayed as dysfunctional.

"It is also a plea for social justice. Hermione's Society for the Promotion of Elfish Welfare is an example of a social justice theme. But a larger politically contemporary theme emerges in **Goblet of Fire** and continues through the rest of the books.

"In this pivotal book, Sirius Black offered Harry, Ron, and Hermione a history lesson about the Ministry of Magic and Barty Crouch, Sr. responding to Voldemort's first reign of terror. Taking off from Dickens' best of times and worst of times, he applied that to the ways people behave in dangerous times. He spoke of Barty Crouch's meteoric rise to power in the Ministry and the harsh measures he took against Voldemort's supporters. Aurors were granted enhanced authority, for example they were given the power to kill rather than capture suspects. He told the trio that he wasn't the only suspect who was handed over to the Dementors without trial. Crouch's strategy was to fight violence with violence, and he went so far as to authorize the use of the Unforgivable Curses against suspects. In this sense, the Ministry of Magic became as ruthless and cruel as supporters of Voldemort. And many folks opposed to the Deatheaters thought Crouch was doing it the right way.

"If this makes you think of the Patriot Act and the authorization of torture to interrogate **Al Qaeda** and Iraqi prisoners in response to 9/11 and our invasion of Iraq, then Rowling may have been eerily prescient, because **Goblet of Fire** was published in 2000. Although the dynamic she described here did become a model for the Bush Administration a year later, Rowling couldn't have known this would happen. The phrase **enhanced interrogation techniques** had not yet burst onto the scene. But having worked for Amnesty International, she did know how authoritarian and repressive regimes worked in Latin America, Africa, the Middle East, and Asia. The Bush Administration reacted to 9/11 in patterns already well established in world history.

"Rowling had already developed the theme of repressive governments using external threats as excuses to centralize power and gain further control through bureaucratic violence before 9/11. As it happened, however, three of the seven **Harry Potter** books representing more than half of the total narrative were written after that date, two of them after the pre-emptive invasion of Iraq. So it should be no surprise that Rowling would expand the prominence of these themes critical of repressive government violence.

"She makes seemingly prescient points about political leadership and the role that fear plays in motivating reactionary groups in **Goblet of Fire**, when Dumbledore tells Fudge to get rid of the Dementors because they will defect to Voldemort. Fudge responds negatively, noting that he would be ousted from office for even raising the suggestion. He added that half the community felt safe in their beds only because of their faith that Dementors were guarding Azkaban.

"Dumbledore then suggests that Fudge establish diplomatic relations with the giants. Fudge is incredulous at such a preposterous idea, asserting that if the wizarding community learned that he had contacted the giants it would end his career.

"Dumbledore's response is one that unfortunately describes far too many political leaders in this country and the world over. He tells Fudge that his love of the particular office he has attained is blinding him to the truth.

"Dumbledore then lays out a plan of action for Fudge, which if followed would result in his being remembered as one of the greatest and bravest Ministers for Magic in history. Failing to act would cement Fudge's place in history as the man who stood by and gave Voldemort a second chance to destroy the wizarding world.

"Substitute the name Hitler for Voldemort in that sentence, and a clear World War II allusion is seen. Dumbledore offers Fudge the choice to be Neville Chamberlain, who appeased Hitler, or Winston Churchill, who courageously did not.

"In the first post 9/11 **Harry Potter** novel, **Order of the Phoenix**, Rowling seems to take aim at governmental over-reaction and perhaps the Patriot Act in an exchange between Dumbledore and Fudge. The Headmaster accuses the Minister for Magic of inadvertently overlooking a number of inconvenient laws in his zeal to uphold the laws that fit his intentions.

"Fudge savagely reacts by asserting that laws could be changed. Agreeing that this is so, Dumbledore points out the many changes the Ministry had already made, in particular the practice of holding a criminal trial before the whole Wizengamot for a trivial case of underage magic. This, of course, is a jab about Harry's trial for casting a Patronus charm.

"Late in *Order of the Phoenix*, Umbridge justifies the use of torture to interrogate Harry by claiming that it's a matter of Ministry security. During the time Rowling was writing this book, the Bush Administration approved the use of so-called enhanced interrogation techniques such as water boarding and justified it as a matter of national security. *Order of Phoenix* was published before the 2004 revelations of the torture practices used at *Abu Ghraib* prison in Baghdad, so one can only speculate what words Rowling might have put in Umbridge's mouth had she known about Abu Ghraib.

Judith Rauhofer, a research fellow at the University of Central Lancashire, said that after 9/11, the *Harry Potter* books evolved into 'a social commentary on current events. I think there are certain parallels in the way in which the Ministry of Magic deals with the Voldemort threat and the way the British government deals with the terrorist threat…I'm not saying she has done this deliberately to show up the Government, but I think the books could be interpreted as a subtle social commentary on contemporary British society'

"By this time, of course, Rowling had participated in many book tours in the U. S. and had endured harsh criticism from the political and religious right in this country, so I would add that commentary on *American* society and not only British were part of Rowling's aims.

"Certainly the arrest and imprisonment without trial of Stan Shunpike in *Half-Blood Prince* is a reference to actions of the Bush Administration. Harry confronted Scrimgeour about it twice with the same frustrating kind of non-response that the Bush Administration gave for holding people without due process. U. S. Forces detained men who were not terrorists and kept them in Guantanamo Prison in Cuba for years, which had the effect, when they were finally released, of turning them into terrorists to revenge their unjustified incarcerations. Stan Shunpike's experience in Azkaban parallels this phenomenon of creating terrorists -Death Eaters- through clumsy attempts to give the appearance of doing something about security.

"Parenthetically, I read a report that Guantanamo has a fairly large library for use by prisoners there. The top seven requested titles by prisoners are the seven **Harry Potter** novels. That provides a fascinating insight into the minds of those held in unlimited detention. Next on the book request list, after J. K. Rowling, is **Don Quixote** by Miguel Cervantes, and next after that is **Dreams from My Father** by Barack Obama.

"In 2004, the British government issued pamphlets to the public titled 'Preparing for an Emergency.' The Ministry of Magic did the same thing in **Half-Blood Prince**, and they were made fun of by magic folk just as the British Government was on the receiving end of jokes about its pamphlet. Harry tells Dumbledore that he received a leaflet from the Ministry of Magic describing security measures to be taken against Death Eaters. Noting that he also received one, Dumbledore asks if Harry found it useful, to which Harry responds with an indifferent no.

"Subsequent scenes involving Molly and Arthur Weasley and their security questions add humor to this theme. The humorous treatment of governmental security techniques continues in **Half-Blood Prince** with Filch's Secrecy Sensor searches of students going in and out of Hogwarts, reminiscent of airport security wands, and in book seven, the Gringotts Probity Probes, which are said to have been used in un-named body cavities.

"The first chapter of **Half-Blood Prince**, 'The Other Minister,' where Fudge and Scrimgeour meet with the British Prime Minister, is a brilliant but surprisingly gentle social commentary on the dysfunctional dynamics of contemporary politics and how inept political leaders behave in times of crisis.

"The books function on many levels. One is satire. The **Harry Potter** series is a humorous social commentary in the tradition of **Gulliver's Travels** and **Alice in Wonderland**. Each of these books satirized some aspect of contemporary society, with some subjects becoming running gags. The prime example of this is Rowling's satirizing life in British suburbia through the fictional but realistic Little Whinging.

"Among other objects of Rowling's barbed pen are: incompetent teachers (Binns, Lockhart, Trelawney, Umbridge, even Snape), corporate business (Vernon Dursley and his drills), racists and bigots (the Malfoys, Mrs. Black, and the Death Eaters), New Age types (Trelawney, Xenophilius Lovegood, and perhaps the Centaurs), and Tory Prime

Minister Margaret Thatcher (Aunt Marge). Parenthetically, Rowling supports the Labour Party in Britain and has campaigned for Labour in recent elections. In any event, Aunt Marge may be taken as a symbol of the British Conservative Party.

"Also satirized are journalists and the media (Rita Skeeter, The Daily Prophet, the Quibbler, Witch Weekly), professional sports (Ludo Bagman, inept professional Quidditch teams), government bureaucracy and politicians (Barty Crouch, Percy Weasley, Cornelius Fudge, Rufus Scrimgeour, the Ministry of Magic), and the War on Terror (Inane government instructions on how to protect oneself from Voldemort –ala duct tape and color coded alerts). And I suspect that J. K. Rowling may have had some rather unpleasant encounters with press photographers, because the one who accompanies Rita Skeeter in *Goblet of Fire*, though only mentioned once, is named Bozo. Or this could be a comment about the paparazzi who hound celebrities, sometimes even to death."

A murmuring chorus of "Princess Diana" filled the room.

Emma continued, "The parallels between Death Eaters and Hitler's Germany are intentional, but have broader relevance to contemporary totalitarian and terrorist states. Rowling has acknowledged that she modeled Cornelius Fudge on Neville Chamberlain, the British Prime Minister who caved in to Hitler's demands in the late 1930s. In an October 2007 interview at an event sponsored by Scholastic at Carnegie Hall, Rowling said, 'You should question authority and you should not assume that the establishment or the press tells you all of the truth.'

"In this sense, the series provides a literary model for social activism. Incidentally, this was also the well-publicized occasion when she told the audience that Dumbledore is gay. She had previously revealed this to David Yates, who directed the *Half-Blood Prince* film. When she reviewed the screenplay for the film, there was a scene where Dumbledore reminisced about a woman he had been attracted to in his younger days. Rowling crossed it out and wrote, 'Dumbledore is gay' on the script.

"With regard to social activism, the books inspired the creation of the non-profit Harry Potter Alliance, which uses the books to educate and mobilize people around issues of genocide, torture, and the rights of workers. Founder of the Harry Potter Alliance, Andrew Slack, calls himself a Harry Potter rabbi and uses examples from the books as a rabbi might use scripture. Slack sheds light on social issues by relating them to themes in Harry Potter. In a Los Angeles Times interview in July

2009, he said of the Alliance, 'We always connect everything back to the books. It's very Talmudic.' One of the Alliance's major campaigns has been against the genocide in the Darfur region of Sudan.

"In 2007, J. K. Rowling endorsed the Harry Potter Alliance by selecting its website as the fan site of the month on her own web site and leaving it there since then. Rowling said, 'What did my books preach against throughout? Bigotry, violence, struggles for power, no matter what. All of these things are happening in Darfur. So they couldn't have chosen a better cause.'"

This reflection was electric in the congregation, and members surrounded Emma with enthusiastic support. Chip Shoverly was disquieted. Emma did not make fun of the institutional church or Christianity, as he had hoped, but did identify governmental behaviors that he distrusted. He liked what she had to say but was scared that these people were serious about worshiping Harry Potter and J. K. Rowling.

His dissatisfaction and simultaneous attraction to the church led him to read the first book and thus become hooked and move on to the others. He continued to attend the services, but held back from fuller participation or joining. Eventually he made the affirmation and sorted into Slytherin. Chip's antagonism to religion in general mellowed but he retained his resentments toward hyper-conservative Christianity.

The effect on the two combat veterans in the congregation was different, however. Both Dwight and Tom were troubled by elements of what Emma said, and jointly, they sought a meeting with her to discuss the matter.

"What you said was fine as far as it went," Dwight acknowledged, in order to open the discussion. "But you left out something equally as important."

Tom added, "Dwight and I experienced the same reaction."

"What did I miss?" Emma said. She did not feel defensive in the presence of these former soldiers and was genuinely interested in what they took away from her reflection.

"The effect of war on the good guys," Dwight explained. "You mentioned World War II. The 20th century saw the rise of increasingly cruel techniques of warfare, things like gas and other chemicals designed to inflict pain and death on the enemy. We like to think that only the bad guys did stuff like that, but the truth is more complicated. Certainly by World War II, the Allies were using flamethrowers and indiscriminate saturation bombing of civilians in search of military victory."

"And who first used nuclear weapons?" Tom said. "The United States. Set aside for a moment that ending the war sooner rather than later was a noble goal. What about the means?"

"Think about napalm and agent orange and burning down villages to save the residents in Viet Nam," Dwight said.

"What does this have to do with Harry Potter?" Emma asked.

"Only that J. K. Rowling was honest in her portrayal of the good guys, the ones who fought Voldemort and the Death Eaters," Dwight said. "You hinted at it with your comments about the behavior of the Ministry, but I was hungry for that to be fleshed out. But you don't have the life experience to do it."

"Does this have anything to do with unforgivable curses?" Emma asked.

"It has everything to do with them," Tom said. "Near the end of **Order of the Phoenix**, Harry is chasing Bellatrix Lestrange, and he used the cruciatus curse on her. She dismissed his paltry effort, because, she said, you need to mean it with those kinds of curses. Harry was essentially too kind to really mean to inflict pain."

"But by the end of **Deathly Hallows**," Dwight continued, "Harry and other Order of the Phoenix members were routinely using unforgivable curses and they really meant them. Imperio at Gringotts, and cruciatus in the Ravenclaw common room, for example."

"OK, but they were justified; it was self defense," said Emma. "Even officials at the Ministry of Magic approved of those curses in extreme situations. And they never used the big one, avada kadavra."

"Never?" Tom said. "What about at the Battle of Hogwarts?"

"Harry didn't use that. Voldemort did and it bounced back on himself," Emma said.

"What about the duel between Molly Weasley and Bellatrix Lestrange?" Dwight said. "The text says the two women were fighting to **kill**. Granted, the text does not reveal exactly what spell Molly used on Bellatrix, but it specifies that it was a curse, and its affect on Bellatrix was consistent with other descriptions of people killed by avada kadavra. I think Order of the Phoenix members and allies ended up using all of the unforgivable curses in order to win the war."

"And I agree with Dwight," Tom said. "That's just what happens in war. Even the good guys are corrupted. The good end is used to justify the bad means."

Emma was silent and numb.

"And Rowling got it right. Voldemort lost the war but won the argument over the means of fighting it," Dwight said.

"That's depressing," Emma said.

"It certainly is," said Tom. "I hope that gives you an insight into PTSD."

"It traumatizes the soul when soldiers in battle kill other people they don't know simply because those other people are trying to kill them. At the time, they just do it, because it's kill or be killed. The traumatic stress will show up later, and even then, there are ways to justify what they've done," Dwight said.

"They aren't killers at heart, most of them," Tom said. "They are brave people doing their duty for their country or their side. And if they suffer depression as a result, that can be treated and healed."

"But there's a special kind of sadness that comes as a result of war, that I think J. K. Rowling recognized," Dwight said. "The worst let down, the profoundest depression comes from recognizing that warriors from your own side have taken up the worst tactics of the enemy. No pain is deeper to the soul than seeing your own good guys committing cruel and savage acts. I know that from first hand experience."

"As a lover of all things Potter," said Tom, "I am saddened to see Harry and his allies use unforgivable curses. But on the other hand, I know that this is the way it is in real life."

"Now I'm thoroughly depressed," Emma said.

"So use that as a way of deepening your ministry," Dwight said. "You can rise above it, disillusioned but stronger, and be a better Hallowed Philosopher."

"Not that you're not a great one already," Tom added.

"Thanks, Dwight. Thanks, Tom. I feel older and wiser already," Emma said.

"And more compassionate?" Dwight asked.

"That too," she said.

Returning to the fish and chips pub that had been the scene of their first date, Tom told Emma that he had something important to talk over with her. Fearing that he wanted to move the relationship to a deeper level, Emma tensed. At that moment, a text message chimed on her phone.

"Excuse me," she said, as she opened the message. After reading it, she responded and then looked up at Tom. "OK, what were you going to say?"

"Sometimes I think of you as Hermione with a smartphone," he said.

"Funny," she replied. "My old high school friend Susan called me Hermione with a BlackBerry. I wonder what ever happened to her?"

He looked at her wondering if she would tell him who had texted her but did not ask the question.

"Sorry for the interruption," Emma said. "That was Sol. He wanted to know if the hymn 'Hark! The Witch Hermione' was a compatible choice to fit with my reflection theme for the service on Saturday."

"That's a pretty long text," Tom said.

"He used abbreviations and acronyms, but I understood him. He's very efficient with words," Emma responded.

"Seems like an odd thing to text about," Tom said with a tinge of irritation in his voice.

"Not at all," said Emma. "We strive to make our services thematically consistent. If my reflection focused on Harry, for example, we would need a different hymn."

"And what did you text back to Sol?" Tom asked.

"Perfect!" she said. "But you wanted to tell me something, and we were interrupted. I apologize for that."

"You know how frustrated I've been living with my parents," he said. "And that's pertinent to what I have to say. But first I have a question."

Emma's mental antennae quivered, suspecting that he was about to propose that they live together. Warily, she said, "And what's that?"

"I take it that going out with me has not elicited any response from the mysterious Mr. X," he said. "Am I right about that?"

"Yes," she confessed honestly, while still fearful of how to deal with a proposal that would involve deeper commitment with Tom.

"Well I'm sorry about that. I truly am," he said. "The thing is, I feel a lot of affection for you, and under different circumstances, I could easily fall in love with you. But our relationship feels more like brother and sister than anything else."

This caught her by surprise, and after thinking about it for a second, she felt hurt also. "Complete with incestuous snogging along the way," she said waspishly.

"I'm sorry. That didn't come out right," he said. "Maybe like second cousins or someone from the old neighborhood."

Emma sighed deeply. With an opening like that, she realized that he was not going to suggest moving in together, but that did not assuage the perceived insult to her feminine appeal.

"Don't give me that second cousin crap. We've shared significant intimacy, Tom. I've seen you without your prosthesis. I've even rubbed ointment on your stump," she said.

"I'm not handling this very well," he said. "The thing is, I sense you're holding back. There's not as much passion as there should be if…"

"So I'm a cold fish?" she responded.

"No, no, please, let me try to explain," he said.

"There's no need to explain," Emma said. "I understand what you're saying and to be completely honest, I know it's true. There is a lot to love about you, Tom, but…"

"Stop," he said. "Don't say any more. I need to confess something. I've been getting by with part time work and community volunteering, but as we've talked about many times, I've been very dissatisfied with the lack of a real career."

"I know you've said it makes you feel inadequate, but you're not, Tom. You are a gem of a person," Emma said.

"Thank you," he said. "But there's been a development. I've been offered a job as director of a veterans outreach program in Phoenix. It's a big opportunity. Full time professional work."

"Then you should accept," Emma said firmly.

"It doesn't necessarily mean the end of our relationship, whatever it may be," he said. "But in practical terms, it means leaving the Holy Rowlings behind."

"I suspect you may miss the church more than you miss me," Emma said.

"Not a chance of that," Tom answered. "But I'll need to find a new support system in Phoenix. Luckily, the vets organization can provide that, although not on a spiritual level."

"I could recommend the naturist church in Phoenix that I used to belong to," Emma said.

"Yeah, but as we've discussed, I'm not ready for that," he replied.

"Nobody will look twice at your prosthesis," Emma said.

"Yes they would," he retorted, "but that's not the issue for me. I'm just not comfortable with nudity. Too much residual guilt from my pious mother, I suppose. Public nudity in mixed company feels sinful at some level."

"Then why date a naturist?" Emma asked more from curiosity than animus.

"I don't know. I thought you'd grow out of it," he offered with a shrug.

"Well…I'm sure you'll find something to meet your spiritual needs," Emma said with an inflection of doubt. "Phoenix is a big place and filled with all sorts of transcendent venues. And one of these days maybe that guilty voice of your mother in your head will grow dim, and you can do what you truly feel called to do."

The Saturday when Tom announced to the congregation that he was moving to Phoenix and that this would be his last day at the church produced a memorable outburst. Frieda gasped audibly and began to weep. Everyone turned to look at her and then quickly looked away. Emma told Tom that the congregation was sending their good wishes along with him and thanked him for all the blessings he had contributed to the Holy Rowlings. She tapped his left shoulder with her wand and said, "*Pax vobiscum.*"

After the service, as various people gathered around Tom to say goodbye, Frieda kept her distance. Instead, she sought out Dwight and said to him, "Tom never told me he was leaving. Of all people, he should have warned me in advance. This was thoughtless of him."

"Why you in particular?" Dwight asked.

"Because he's practically a second son, the one who returned from the war," she said.

"Oh Frieda, I'm sorry he has taken on that place in your mind," Dwight said.

"He's a special young man," Frieda said. "How could I not love him?"

"He's only going to Phoenix," Dwight said. "And his parents live in Cottonwood, so he'll probably drop in to the congregation for a visit from time to time."

"You think I'm over-reacting?" Frieda said.

"Unfortunately, I do," said Dwight.

"That's because you don't know anything about women," she responded.

"Guilty as charged," he said. "Glad we got that cleared up."

Building on its recognition as a legitimate religious institution, in 2014, Emma's congregation officially endorsed the social justice work of the Harry Potter Alliance and pledged regular financial support to the Alliance as a mission project of the church. In late 2014, the Alliance won a notable victory in its campaign against child slavery when Warner Brothers agreed to sell only certified Fair Trade USA chocolate through its Harry Potter franchises. The Alliance also joined with other groups in the successful campaign to maintain net neutrality on the Internet. Members of the Alchemical Church of Harry Potter Prophecy participated enthusiastically in the work of the Harry Potter Alliance.

The congregation also endorsed Emma Watson's gender equality movement, He for She, and in a series of reflections, the Hallowed Philosopher made liberal use of quotes from the speech that Emma Watson gave to the United Nations in September 2014. A line from that speech was reproduced on a large sign that was prominently displayed in the sanctuary: "It is time that we all see gender as a spectrum instead of two sets of opposing ideals."

"Emma Watson is truly a grown up Hermione," Emma Round averred.

Things were going so well for the Holy Rowlings, that Emma entertained the notion that something bad was bound to happen. In the event, it was a good development that caused Emma to lament. Zara received an invitation to join the faculty of a seminary in Lahaina, Maui and left Sedona for her new post for the fall term. Now in a short span of time the congregation had lost three vital members, Tom Corazon, Zara Morgan, and her son K. P. Emma prayed that this was not a harbinger of things to come.

III
STRANGE BLESSINGS

Strange blessings never in Paradise
Fall from these beclouded skies.
Edwin Muir

The desolation only missed
While Rapture changed its Dress
And stood amazed before the Change
In ravished Holiness
Emily Dickinson

CHAPTER TWENTY~TWO
BRIAN PERCIVAL AND EMILY HALE

Zara had told Emma about her intersex friends, Sojourner, Pilgrim, and Key. However, she had not told Emma that these three were Merven, beings of another species related to but distinct from Homo sapiens. Emma was delightedly surprised one evening to meet Pilgrim in person at a dinner at Angel Nest.

"I am so glad to meet you at last, Emma," said Pilgrim. "I greatly admire the **Harry Potter** books and have been most curious about your congregation."

"You didn't know that you were famous beyond Central Arizona, did you, Emma?" Cloud said.

"Famous, not likely," Emma responded.

"To the contrary," said Pilgrim, "your work with the Holy Rowlings is known far and wide, in circles you never dreamed of. Merven the world over know about what you are doing in Sedona. And I assure you, my interest in your congregation is most serious."

"The world over?" Emma said with a note of skepticism.

"Yes, my species exists in every continent except, at present, Antarctica," Pilgrim replied. "And, of course, the writings of J. K. Rowling are known to Merven everywhere. What you are doing here with a Harry Potter church has attracted wide attention among Merven."

"Well then, Pilgrim, please accept my invitation to attend a service any time it suits your schedule. Dress is casual. Not naturist casual, but people often come in costumes of their favorite HP characters," Emma said.

"I do enjoy costumes," Pilgrim said.

245

"Who would you come as?" Emma asked.

"Oh that should be a surprise," Pilgrim said. "But I have not found any intersex characters in the series, so my choices are limited in that regard."

"But you could dress as any other character male or female," said Emma.

"Indeed," said Pilgrim.

"As far as I know, you're only the second intersex person I've met. The other is my second cousin Kelly," Emma continued.

"People used to say that about LGBTQ folks," Pilgrim said. "But as was inevitably true, they actually knew far more such people than they were aware of. It is safe to say you know more intersex people than you think you do. And you may be surprised to learn that I know your cousin Kelly Fife. A wonderful person."

"That does surprise me," Emma confessed.

As the meal progressed, the conversation turned to language. "Do Merven speak the human language of whatever country they live in?" Emma asked.

"We do when engaged with humans," Pilgrim explained. "But we have our own language when we're among our own."

"Just one language across the entire world?" Emma asked.

"There are minor differences with accents," Pilgrim said. "But yes, one language for our entire species that we all understand."

"That's quite an accomplishment," Emma said. "Humans speak thousands of different languages."

"And some, such as English speakers, have so many distinct dialects that speakers in one country or region cannot understand the English spoken elsewhere," Cloud said.

Pilgrim laughed knowingly.

"So, how have the Merven with all that geographic isolation managed to maintain one mutually understandable language?" Emma asked.

"We never built a Tower of Babel," Pilgrim said in a jocular manner.

"That's a myth to explain the existence of so many different tongues," Emma said. "It didn't really happen."

"I know," said Pilgrim. "The answer, I think, lies in anatomy. Given the intersex nature of our bodies, we are naturally inclusive rather than exclusive with social relations. Mutual intelligibility is exceedingly important to us. Whereas humans tend toward tribalism and us versus them social constructions, Merven intentionally keep everyone involved regardless of where we live. Tribalism leads to linguistic shifts that distinguish one group from another. Merven work to keep everyone in the linguistic loop."

"But your language has evolved over time, hasn't it?" Terp asked.

"Of course, but when neologisms and novelties of speech are added, we quickly spread the new words, so everyone knows them. Being able to communicate telepathically provides a distinct advantage for us to do so."

When dinner was over, Terp explained to Emma the long friendship that she and Cloud had enjoyed with Pilgrim and other Merven, and also how the Merven species was related to Homo sapiens through a common ancestor.

"To make a Harry Potter analogy," said Emma, "Humans are Muggles and Merven are wizards."

"Something like that," said Terp. "But this is a family matter, not to be spoken of outside the Angel Nest community."

"Do not worry about accidentally divulging a secret, Emma," Pilgrim said. "It is a matter of tradition and not security that prevails here. And most people would not believe you anyway if you should mention our existence."

"But when you visit my church, I'll pretend you're human," Emma said.

"Dressed the way I plan, I think no one will wonder about my particular place on the hominid tree," Pilgrim said.

The next Saturday afternoon, Pilgrim visited the ACHPP convincingly dressed as Albus Dumbledore. Pilgrim's tall frame, long white, hair and piercing violet eyes lent credibility to the role, as did the verbal performance that tracked the pacing and speech of Richard Harris. Pilgrim claimed the alias of Brian Percival, but everyone knew these were among Professor Dumbledore's middle names. Still, Pilgrim made such a hit as Dumbledore that no one challenged the assumed name.

The room buzzed after Pilgrim left.

"There's just something compelling about Brian," Alexis said.

"Like he is a real wizard," said Frieda.

"Yes, but more than that," Alexis continued. "There's something gender fluid about Brian. I can't say exactly what, but my intuition says Brian does not fit any stereotypes of maleness. Definitely non-binary."

Emma smiled knowingly but said nothing.

"I sensed a genuine Dumbledore," Rob said.

"Yeah, but those eyes –bright violet- must be colored contact lenses," said Jordan. "Nobody has eyes like that in real life."

"As it happens, I've seen Brian without the Dumbledore costume, and those eyes really are that color," Emma said.

"Wow!" said Alexis. "I hope he comes back."

"I do too," said Emma.

For several years, Emma labored at a project of love, dividing the entire *Harry Potter* canon into chapters and verses after the structure of the Bible. She followed Rowling's chapters but devised verses for use in her church. Many verses were entire paragraphs, some were divided paragraphs, and some were several paragraphs linked together. She used the last word in each canonical title to identify the book (except Fantastic Beasts, which she called Beasts). *Them* didn't sound right as a book identifier. Thus, for example, she might announce that she was reading from Stone 1:1-7, Secrets 2:2, Azkaban 7:7, Fire 19:52, Phoenix 5:27, Prince 10:27-29, Hallows 19:43, Beasts 6:6, Ages 2:2-4, or Bard 5:1-5. *Fantastic Beasts* was the most difficult to divide, because it was not arranged in easily identified chapters and because it included textual glosses purportedly written by Harry himself. These latter she integrated into the text and counted them as separate verses.

Next, she recruited a task force to compile a *Harry Potter* concordance, listing every word and number appearing in the Bloomsbury editions of the Harry Potter books, except *a, an, and, but, for, of, or, the* and *to*. Each word was identified by chapter and verse and shown in context by a few words around it in the text.

When completed, the resulting concordance was to be privately printed as *An Exhaustive Concordance to the Harry Potter Canon.* As years passed, however, it often seemed that the task would never be completed.

Emma herself devoted countless hours to the effort, but volunteer assistants seemed to burn out quickly, and recruiting new ones became increasingly difficult. Emma grew frustrated at the slow progress, especially when the most active members of the church, who had assisted in the early days of the project told her she was being obsessive about something that was likely to benefit only one person, namely the Hallowed Philosopher. A concordance would make it easier for Emma to locate specific passages for writing her reflections.

Emma maintained that many people would find such a tool helpful for study of the literature, but no one else seemed more than mildly interested in it.

Nevertheless, a team of volunteers did complete the other laborious task of writing the chapter and verse notations by hand into the paperback pew copies of the ten books. In this project, they likened themselves to medieval monks copying manuscripts in a monastery. For ethical reasons, Merlin's Board decided they would not photocopy the pages of Rowling's book but notated only books they had purchased. Emma also developed a three-year cycle of lectionary lessons for weekly readings from various books of the canon.

At a meeting of Merlin's Board, Emma explained, "Magical folk observe the Christian holidays of Christmas and Easter. The celebration of Christmas is generally secular, with trees and exchanging gifts, but includes singing Christmas carols. Twelve trees are placed in the Great Hall at Christmas, which may be symbolic of the twelve days of Christmas, but in the secular world, that is associated with a song about gifts. Dumbledore, Sirius Black and others sing carols, including 'O Come All Ye Faithful' and 'God Rest Ye Merry Gentlemen,' with Hippogriffs substituted for gentlemen. Christmas and Easter are important markers in the Hogwarts school year calendar and are mentioned in every book in the series."

"Are you leading up to adding Christmas and Easter as Holy Rowling celebrations?" Dwight asked.

"Not specifically," she replied. "But it gave me the idea to create our own church calendar of red letter days." Emma distributed copies of a list that she had drawn up. "This is what I propose for special days for our church calendar, one in each month of the year. Some of these would be observed on the Saturday closest to the actual date and others could be assigned arbitrary Saturdays."

The five board members studied Emma's list, which read as follows:

January: Erised Day (reflect on individual desires for the new year)
February: Valentines Day
March: Silver Doe Day
April: Magical Creatures Day
May: Voldemort's Demise (5-2)
June: Time Turner Day (the Longest Day, 6-6)
July: HP & JKR Birthdays (7-31)
August: Wizengamot Day
September: Sorting Day (9-1)
October: Halloween
November: Pensieve Day (remember the past and give thanks for those who are gone)
December: Godric's Hollow Day (Xmas Eve)

"Well? What do you think?" Emma asked nervously after no one had spoken for several minutes.

"I like it," said Karl. "But I wonder about including Halloween. It fits as a motif in the novels, but it was also the day Harry's parents were murdered. Wouldn't All Saints Day be better? It's one day later, but that shifts into November."

"I thought of that," Emma replied. "That's the day in 1981 that Hagrid delivered baby Harry to the Dursleys' doorstep. It is a day worthy of commemoration, but it's also problematic."

"How so?" Alexis asked.

"The opening chapter of the first book, functioning as a prolog, begins on November 1, 1981."

"And that is problematic how?" said Jordan.

"Jo Rowling identified that date as a Tuesday," Emma replied. "It was actually a Sunday, but Vernon Dursley wouldn't be going to work on a Sunday, and it was important to the tale that Vernon be at his office and also that the previous night's activities occur on Halloween. When asked about this discrepancy, Jo confessed she wasn't very good with numbers. That's likely, because later on she puts Harry's eleventh birthday on a Tuesday when it was actually a Wednesday. Anyway, if we added it to our liturgical calendar, we would be commemorating an author's error."

"I read somewhere that J. K. Rowling was born about ten miles south of the town of Dursley," Alexis said. "It makes me wonder what she had against that town to name such mean characters after it."

No one responded to this.

"Emma, I think you may be over-thinking this," Karl said. "The importance of All Saints Day outweighs a tiny error that only a handful of people on the planet would even be aware of. After all, the story begins on All Saints Day, the day after Voldemort killed Harry's parents and tried to kill him. At midnight that day, at the cusp between All Saints Day and All Souls Day, Hagrid delivers fifteen-month-old Harry to Dumbledore, who is waiting in front of the Dursley house. The tension between saintliness and soulfulness symbolized by this particular convergence of the church calendar will persist throughout the entire series."

"I think Karl is right," said Alexis. "Let's add All Souls day to the calendar. We can keep Halloween in there too. No reason we can't have both or even celebrate them on the same Saturday if need be."

"So should we delete Pensive Day from the November calendar?" Emma asked the group.

"Why would we do that?" Dwight said.

"Because if we don't we'll have 13 red-letter days," Emma responded.

"Tripe, Sybill?" Jordan said.

"OK, you're right. We'll add one more day and keep all the rest," Emma agreed.

"I have a hard time keeping all these dates and chronologies straight in my head," Jordan confessed. "Numbers are for nerds, anyway."

"All the more reason for having a church calendar," Dwight said. "It will serve as a reminder of when stuff happened."

"And how old people were at the time," added Alexis. "But I'll bet you have all that memorized, don't you, Emma?"

"Most of it, I think," Emma said. "It's my job to know these things."

"So do your job and tell us," Jordan said. "When did what happen?"

Emma took a deep breath and began to speak. "Mostly you just need to remember the 90s, summer 1991 to spring 1998. Those were Harry's Hogwarts years, from meeting Hagrid on the island to dueling Voldemort in the Great Hall. Harry's year in school tracks with the last digit in the year in the decade, first year ninety-one, second year ninety-two, and so on.

"Remembrances and scenes from the Pensieve depict action back to the 1920s, 1930s, and 1940s relating to Tom Riddle, Hagrid, and Dumbledore and to the 1960s and 1970s relating to Lily Evans, James Potter, Sirius Black, and Severus Snape. Recollections and a biography of Dumbledore describe actions concerning him in the 1890s. The time of the famous Nineteen Years Later epilog will soon be upon us in 2017.

"Hogwarts was founded in the Scottish Highlands in the late 10th century, at a time when Scots were struggling to oust Viking invaders. We don't know exactly when, but about 990 CE is generally accepted. The first Quidditch match was played in the middle of the 11th century, about 1050 CE.

"Harry James Potter's birthday is July 31, 1980, which was the fifteenth birthday of Joanne Rowling. In generational theory, this makes both Jo and Harry members of the Generation X. Hermione Jean Granger was born September 19, 1979, and Ronald Bilius Weasley was born March 1, 1980.

"Tom Marvolo Riddle, also known as Lord Voldemort, was born in London on December 31, 1926 and died at Hogwarts on May 2, 1998. Albus Dumbledore was born in Mold-on-the-Wold about July 1881, became Headmaster of Hogwarts in 1955, and died in June 1997 at the age of 115. Would you like me to go on, Jordan?"

"No, I think that's enough for the moment," Jordan said.

"Your mention of Dumbledore makes me think we should have a day to remember him, too," said Dwight.

"Yeah, and if we did that, we'd have 14 holidays, which would solve Emma's problem with the number 13," said Jordan.

"I don't have a problem with 13," Emma said with a defensive tone to her voice, "but I do like the idea of a Dumbledore Day. We don't know his exact birthday, so we could add it anywhere. Any suggestions?"

Dwight scanned the sheet Emma had distributed and said, "Let's make it mid to late January," he said. "And while we're at it, why don't you write a new hymn text to celebrate it."

"Actually, I've been playing around with another Dumbledore hymn," Emma replied. "I was thinking of introducing it around Christmas, but it's better to save it for an actual Dumbledore Day."

"How does it go?" asked Frieda.

Emma ruffled through her briefcase and pulled out a manila folder, from which she extracted a sheet of notebook paper with a draft written in pencil complete with lined out words and editorial changes. "It's set to the tune St. Louis, better known to you as 'O Little Town of Bethlehem.' I'm not done with it yet and have only one verse. But here it is so far:

"How great the wizard Dumbledore whose struggle was nobly borne;

Who sought the best in everyone; whose death we deeply mourn.

Yet still his wise eyes shineth: an everlasting light

To show a path for all of us and guide us through the night."

"Wonderful," said Karl. "Keep working on more verses. It'll be perfect for our first Dumbledore Day worship."

After the meeting adjourned, Emma spoke to Jordan. "I haven't seen you at the NCC lately."

Jordan replied, "No. I gave it a try, but it just isn't my thing."

Emma's heart leapt. She wanted to ask about Sol but hesitated, because she thought that would be too revealing of her inner life. "Good that you at least tried it," she said and then added, "Any plans for Burning Man this coming summer?"

"Nothing definite. I haven't convinced anyone to go with me yet," Jordan said. "And since the Hallowed Philosopher should have an interest in what's going on in the lives of her flock, you might be interested to know that Sol isn't my thing either."

Feeling an unexpected burst of affection for her Slytherin board member, Emma said, "Are you OK? Was the break up amicable?"

"Everything's fine," said Jordan. "We just mutually recognized that our temperaments don't match. And he's allergic to things I love. Sol really needs someone more like you."

Emma blushed deeply and Jordan noticed.

Emerging from her morning shower, Emma toweled off and left the bathroom on the way to her room. Emily Hale, wearing her robe, intercepted Emma and said, "Do you have a few minutes?"

"Certainly," Emma replied. "All I have on my agenda for today is work on my reflection, and that's almost finished."

"I have tea made in the kitchen," Emily Hale said.

Seated across from Emily Hale at the kitchen table, a mug of strong tea cradled in her hands, Emma said, "What's up?"

"I have been struggling with whether to tell you something, but I keep losing courage every time I decide the time is right," Emily Hale said. "This morning I have the courage and the opportunity, so I'm determined to get this off my chest."

Emma reached out and put a hand on Emily Hale's folded hands.

"Don't interrupt or I might not be able to do this," Emily Hale said.

Emma removed her hand and pressed a finger to her lips.

"Not another living soul knows this," Emily Hale said. "It's probably moldering in some ancient medical files somewhere, but all the people directly involved are gone. You've probably noticed that I never wear sleeveless blouses or dresses. It's not that unusual for women my age, to hide sagging skin and such, but that's not the reason for me. The fact is, I never shave my armpits. Tom, bless his departed soul, preferred it that way. He wanted me to be as natural as possible, under the circumstances. He loved my hairiness. Given the fashions of the day, I prefer not to advertise my personal custom."

A dozen questions popped into Emma's mind but she restrained herself from speaking.

"When I was an adolescent, I learned something terrible that happened to me in infancy," Emily Hale continued. "I was late starting my period and when I did it was extremely painful. So I graduated from the care of the pediatrician who had attended me from birth to a gynecologist whose honesty would change my outlook on life forever.

"This gynecologist thought that I needed to know the truth in order to manage my life wisely. My parents were furious that he told me what had happened, but he did the right thing. I saw pictures of my body taken at birth and a few months later. The report said that I was born with 'ambiguous genitalia.' From my teenage perspective, they didn't look ambiguous at all but complete.

"The pediatrician recommended to my parents that I have sexual assignment surgery, as he phrased it, 'before the age of memory.' And that's what happened. I was born intersexual but was subjected to a 'feminizing procedure' before I was old enough to express a preference.

"Needless to say, when I found out, I was livid. Circumcision is a violation of a child's bodily integrity, but what happened to me is much worse. It was nothing less than a sadistic travesty born out of fear and…and an overwhelming compulsion that I be seen as normal, whatever the hell that is."

Emily Hale grew red in the face and her voice faltered. Emma remained silent.

"They removed my entire penis and testicles, without my permission!" Now she began to sob quietly. For an uncounted interval of time, she did not speak.

"I wish I had been able to read something like **Harry Potter** when I was young," she resumed. "Then I would have known, been reassured that it is alright to be different. That it's a blessing to be different. More to the point, I wish my parents and all those smarter-than-thou physicians back then would have learned that lesson somewhere along the way.

"My response as a teenager, apart from the anger, was shame. I spent too many years living in secret shame. For all outward appearances, I was a girl and then a woman. A tomboy to be sure, but clearly female. Except that I wasn't. Not really. I was both, but the opportunity to experience that to the fullest had been ripped away from me with scalpels.

"And then Tom came along and fell in love with this tomboy. Tom was an Ace. Do you know what that is?"

"An asexual," Emma replied softly.

"Yes," Emily Hale said. "I never met anyone more capable of deep love and affection, but his body chemistry produced only the barest sexual response. Tom loved me and wept for my loss and encouraged me to be as natural a person as was left for me to be. He is the only person I ever told my secret to. He was the only person I ever needed to tell. Oh, my parents and a pack of medical people knew, but from my lips there has been no one but Tom until this moment."

Emma was now in tears, and all she could do was nod and reach across the table to caress Emily Hale's cheek.

"You have given me courage I never knew I had," Emily Hale continued. "You and your young naturist friends. I have a flat chest that should have been covered with hair like my father's was. I rather like hairy chests, because they exemplify maleness. But that pubertal development was stolen from me. As an adult, I have never shown my body to anyone but Tom. He cherished my maimed frame because he loved me. But you can see now why I am averse to being naked in a group."

Emma nodded again.

"You may have guessed that of late I have been running around the house naked when I'm alone," Emily Hale said.

"I suspected that," said Emma.

"Well, I'm enjoying that more than an old lady has any right to," she said.

"I would take issue with that statement,' Emma replied.

"Yes, I do have a right to bodily pleasure," Emily Hale said. "But I'm still not ready to be in the buff in your presence."

"Not a problem," said Emma. "In fact, I think that from now on, I should phone you when I'm on the way home, so you can cover up. I'd offer to text you, but you don't have a cell."

"And not likely to get one any time soon," Emily Hale replied.

On the inaugural observance of Voldemort's Demise Day, Emma reflected on Donatism. "There was an obscure but important development in Christian Church history in the 4th century that has some bearing on our canon. In *Half-Blood Prince*, Bellatrix presses Snape to explain his behavior after Voldemort disappeared when the curse aimed at Harry Potter backfired. She piously claims to have remained faithful to the Dark Lord even after the apparent fall of her Master. Snape tells Bellatrix he believed Voldemort was finished, but that now the Dark Lord has forgiven those who lost faith during the time when Death Eaters were being rounded up and imprisoned.

"Snape's explanation to Bellatrix has something in common with the tribulation caused by Emperor Diocletian in the 4th century, when Christians were rounded up, tortured, and imprisoned by the Roman government. It's another one of those ironic reversals Rowling is so good at. During the time of persecution, many Christians, including some priests, recanted their faith in Christ under torture. When the persecution ended, those who had not died for the faith but had renounced it, came back to their congregations seeking forgiveness and reinstatement.

"Those who had escaped capture or torture or who had relatives who had died at the hands of the Romans were not all in favor of letting bygones be bygones. A conflict arose in the church about what to do with those returning with blemished records. A group called the Donatists decided that purity was a necessary dimension to the Christian life, and thus those who had recanted the faith, even under torture, were no longer pure and could not be forgiven and received back into the fold.

"Cooler heads ultimately prevailed and the Donatist position was declared heresy. It was determined that purity was not an essential to church membership or leadership. This led to the clarifying doctrine that the good effect or validity of a sacrament, like baptism or communion, does not depend on the goodness or purity of the priest or elder who officiates. The good that redounds to a person from taking communion, for example, does not depend on the goodness of the minister pronouncing the words of institution. Thank God!

"When he returned to power, Voldemort, it seems, decided to forgive those who had recanted of their devotion to him, much like the Christian Church did for those who had done the same during the Diocletian persecution. But it was a practical, not a doctrinal matter for Voldemort, for he wouldn't have many Death Eaters left if he did not forgive them. And he did mete out punishment in the form of torture before granting that forgiveness. Another irony is that Voldemort and the Death Eaters are obsessed with purity of blood while completely ignoring purity of spirit or soul.

"A continuing theme in all the books is social inclusion. Hogwarts is a multiracial, multifaith, multicultural, and coeducational institution. The Death Eaters are the ones obsessed with genetic purity, as were the Nazis, along with purity of devotion to their master. Dumbledore's pet phoenix recognized those who exhibited faithfulness to the Headmaster, but that faithfulness or the lack of it was never mandatory or cause for punishment if deficient.

"Love is inclusive, while purity is exclusive. If a society puts purity above inclusion, it will wither and die. The theme of degeneration of the pureblood Slytherin line is significant here.

"Many conservative Christians today work vigorously to uphold the supposed purity of the Church, but the Church has never been pure.

Rowling seems to connect purity with bigotry. The characters who are most concerned with genealogical purity are also the most bigoted.

For the first Time Turner Day, Emma announced that since the day they were commemorating had three extra hours, she would deliver a reflection that was three hours long. The congregation groaned.

Then she said, "I'm Sirius. No, I'm not; I'm Lupin." She waited for laughter, but none came.

"Maybe you're Dementoid," Jordan shouted.

"Oh for heaven's sake," Emma said. "Why is everyone in such a bad mood?"

"Because we all know you are capable of speaking for three hours without repeating yourself," said Alexis, "but we can't sit that long."

"Well then, let's stand and sing the Harry Potter hymn," Emma announced. "Maybe that will cheer you up."

With a clatter and shuffling of chairs, the congregation rose. Sol strummed a chord on his guitar and the congregation joined in spiritedly singing, "Prophet and Chosen One, Who makes Death Eaters run, Of thee we sing."

CHAPTER TWENTY~THREE
THE SEEKER

Emma called Emily Hale one afternoon to say she was on her way home in case she needed to cover up. Emily Hale thanked her for the warning. When she entered the house, however, Emma saw Emily Hale standing in the center of the living room completely nude.

"I decided to show off a bit," Emily Hale said. She pirouetted and then raised her arms in the air to form a vee. "This is who I am, for your eyes only."

Thereafter, both women strolled about the house without clothing whenever they felt like it, but Emma never told anyone else about Emily Hale's secret.

Fantasies about being wooed by tall and tan Solomon Davar, danced in Emma's brain, but she also harbored lingering concerns because of the clergy ethics training she had received from Cloud and Terp. They maintained that it was a boundary violation for pastors to become involved romantically with parishioners. And she had already breached that boundary once by going out with Tom Corazon. Sol was a charter member of her congregation, and as director of the music program, he was practically a colleague, which carried another level of ethical boundary issues.

On the other hand, his family had been members of the Sedona Natural Christian Church for years, so he and Emma had the practice of naturism in common. And they had known each other in college, long before the Holy Rowling church was formed. Sol had graduated from Anasazi College a year ahead of Emma, and they had been part of the same circle of friends on campus. For years, however, she had assumed that he had no romantic interest in her, because he never showed anything but modest congeniality toward her.

As a senior in college, Sol had been Seeker on the Anasazi Quidditch team, the year the Vortex Whompers won the state championship and placed second to Middlebury College in the national tournament. Though she had declined his invitation for her to try out for the team, Emma had been a huge fan of the Whompers, not least the Seeker, who had achieved extensive mastery of the canon of **Harry Potter** literature, as well as athletic skill on the Quidditch pitch. But as a fan/athlete relationship, it was not reciprocal. And after graduation, Sol left the area for San Francisco to pursue a career as a sculptor and New Age musician, playing guitar, mandolin, and dulcimer.

Now that he was music director for her congregation, Emma had many occasions to meet with Sol, and he had never even hinted at any personal interest in her. And then one day at a meeting to discuss the music for next Saturday's service, with no preliminary verbiage, he said, "My parents have season tickets to the Broadway productions at Gammage but they can't go this week. Would you fancy a drive down to Tempe next Thursday to see **Wicked** with me?"

"I saw it with my aunt. It's a great show. I'd love to see it again," Emma said.

"Can I take that as a yes?" Sol said.

She paused to think about it, and then without thinking at all said, "Yes!"

Emma ran straight to Terp for advice on how to handle Sol's apparent shift from friend and parishioner to wooer. Terp was inclined to see this particular boundary as already porous and advised Emma not to fret but let things evolve naturally.

While they were talking, Cloud came into the room, asking if he were interrupting something private, and Emma said no. After briefly explaining her situation, Emma asked Cloud how he and Terp had met. Together they unfolded for Emma the story of how Cloud had become the floating boy and Terp had been told to look for that boy.

"Wow! That would make a great transrealist novel," Emma said,

"Are you a fan of transrealism?" Cloud asked.

"Sure," she replied. "I'm fond of paranormal antics in realistic settings. It's the story of my life."

Cloud laughed in delight. "How about that, Terp? Emma just characterized our love story as paranormal antics."

"That's the best description I've heard in a long time," Terp said. "Emma, do you see **Harry Potter** as transrealism?"

"I see **Harry Potter** as full blown fantasy, although partly set in a historic place. Floating and prescient dreams are well documented in reality, but the magic in HP goes well beyond the things that happened in your lives."

"Well, as to your predicament," Cloud said, "I don't see it."

"What don't you see?" Emma responded.

"I don't see any ethical impediment. If you have a romantic inclination toward Sol, and he has the same toward you, then by all means pursue the relationship," he said.

"On the other hand," Terp added, "if you don't feel comfortable dating Sol, then use clergy ethics as a convenient way of letting him down. In any case, be gentle with him, because he is such a dear young man."

After a lonely year in the Bay area, Sol decided he could follow his artistic bliss as easily from Sedona as from San Francisco and so came home. At first, he lived with his parents, as so many of his friends were doing, but this conflicted with his sense of being an artist. In his mind, artists simply did not live with mom and dad. Though nearly broke and carrying $40,000 in student loan debt, he cashed in a life insurance policy that his parents had bought for him at birth and rented a garage in the back of the Angel Nest property to use for a studio. To save money, he also fixed up a loft for sleeping and frequently took showers using the garden hose attached to a spigot at the side of the garage. The instant community of artist colleagues at Angel Nest provided him the critiques and encouragement he needed for his sculptures. And in time, Darshan Pratyaksha's gallery in town provided a sales outlet for his creative work. He fed himself by playing gigs at various New Age venues around the Sedona area, including street concerts and piping to lure customers into retail stores in Sedona's commercial district, though he was a mediocre piper.

When Emma incorporated the Alchemical Church of Harry Potter Prophecy in 2012, Sol joined as a charter member and in the early days provided music for the services. Since he had no money to contribute, music was his offering. And then Emma asked him to become more involved in congregational leadership as music director.

At first, he assumed that his feelings for Emma arose from respect and awe at her intellect and initiative in establishing the church, as well as brotherly affection from a long friendship. It took him a long time to recognize that he was in love with the Hallowed Philosopher who so ably led the congregation. But he hesitated to pursue a relationship because of his financial instability. When she started dating Tom Corazon, he abandoned the improbable notion that she might harbor an interest in him.

Much later, after Tom had left the congregation and Sol had withdrawn from an ill-suited relationship with Jordan Inge, he needed only to solve his monetary problems in order to feel sufficiently worthy to pursue a relationship with Emma. Much sooner than he had expected, he gained a commission for a large bronze sculpture of a phoenix that would net him more than ten thousand dollars. Now he felt confident enough to let his feelings for her be known, and he made up his mind to seek after Emma's affections with the same skill with which he had chased the Snitch in Quidditch. His first move was to ask Emma to the theater.

It was late when the play ended and they finally left the Gammage parking lot. Once on I-17, two more hours of driving were ahead of them. Sol suggested they stop at a coffee shop for caffeine fortification for the road ahead. Seated in the booth across from Emma, he thought of proposing that they play it safe and rent a motel for the night, so they could return to Sedona fresh in the morning. But he held his tongue.

Emma was thinking the same thing but hesitated to say it out loud. With coffee in their systems, they returned to the road. Sol drove and Emma kept watch for errant semis and other road hazards.

The fact that Emma was dating Sol quickly became public knowledge, and it was impossible for either of them to pretend otherwise. Both walked around with smitten looks on their faces. At first, Emma worried that there would be negative feedback from members of the congregation, but none came.

Frieda expressed the general sentiment when she told Emma, "You and Sol look so good together. You're right for each other. Everybody says so."

Even Jordan gave Sol and Emma a broad grin and a thumbs up when she saw them conferring about music for the service.

During the course of their courtship, Sol suggested exchanging security questions that they alone would know, as had Molly and Arthur in book six and Order members after the seven Potters episode in book seven.

Emma's secret was that she counted by sevens, especially when doing exercises. This prompted Sol to recite, "How do I love thee? Let me count the reps."

Emma responded, "Making a pun from an Elizabeth Barrett Browning sonnet will get you a long way in the romance department. But before we pursue any of that, I need to know your secret."

Sol said, "My family has always been concerned about water conservation. To be good stewards of water, we often say 'Don't flush' after someone pees."

"This cancels what I said about quoting sonnets," Emma said.

Feeling vulnerable but knowing she had to do it if the relationship were to develop in a healthy way, Emma told Sol about Sylvia's death. It had been easy to talk about it with Tom, because he had suffered in a similar way. But he was out of the picture, and she now had no one to talk with about her friend. "None of my current friends or colleagues knew Sylvia. I feel like Vera Brittain years after the deaths of her fiancé and brother in World War I when she wrote, 'I have grown accustomed to revisiting that past alone.'"

"Though I never knew Sylvia," Sol responded, "I would like to get to know her through your eyes and voice. Let her become real to me as an extension of your mind, your remembrances."

"Oh Sol," Emma said, "I couldn't ask for anything more."

"Tell me a favorite memory of her," Sol continued. "Just talk; I'll listen."

Emma paused to think and then said, "One time Sylvia and I dressed up as both Hermione and Harry, with Hermione wigs and wands and Harry's scar and glasses and trainers. It was a spur of the moment lark. She was such a spontaneous soul. We could do things like that on the fly. Anyway, we went to Sheba's bookstore and hung around, and there was this Hufflepuff guy there who was really freaked out about our cross-character-dressing. I suppose we were a little mean to him, but he needed to lighten up.

"It was so much fun that we went to the Old Spaghetti Factory on Central Avenue for lunch dressed that way, curious about what reactions we might get. Our server thought the outfits were cute. A couple at the next table stared at us but were trying not to be caught at it. The guy asked the girl if she knew who we were trying to be, and she said 'Harry Potter and Hermione Granger. I think the books are great. They are obviously big fans.'

"And the guy made a scoffing noise and said, 'I read some of the first one, but the part about Harry living under the stairs was preposterous, so I quit.' He made a dismissive gesture with his hands.

"The girl didn't say anything, but just stared at him incredulously. Sylvia whispered to me, 'I bet she never goes out with him again.'"

"Wicked story," Sol said. "Any time you want to reminisce about Sylvia, I'll be there to listen."

As their courtship rapidly progressed to the serious stage, Uncle Henry invited Emma to bring Sol to his place for dinner. There, the conversation led to a discussion of floating. Beatrix suggested a floating party, but Sol did not know how, although he had heard about it from a conversation with Cloud and his dad, Duffy. Henry offered to teach Sol, who accepted.

As an aside, Henry told Emma that this was a test to see if Sol was right for her. "If he can float, he's OK. If not…"

"Don't say that too loud, he might feel pressured," Emma responded.

But Sol had heard Henry's remark. Still, he had handled much more pressure as a Quidditch seeker, and Sol succeeded in leaving his body after several tries.

One evening, when Emma visited Sol in his studio, they made love. In the afterglow, she told him about her floating into the physical space of church members at a time when Henry was giving the reflection.

"I remember that vividly," he said. "I felt blessed in every pore of my body. It was so extraordinary and uplifting, but also strange because I couldn't connect the feeling with Henry's words. And I felt especially close to you, Emma, but that didn't make any sense because you were not in the room."

"Now you know that I was," Emma said.

"I didn't want to reveal that experience to anyone. I didn't think anyone could possibly understand what I felt," he said.

"No one but me," Emma said. "And I love you, Sol Davar, even more now than I have secretly loved you for years."

A few weeks later, they returned to the mansion for another floating party, and over dinner, they all discussed the fantasy literature roots of J. K. Rowling.

Henry opened the conversation. "We couldn't do justice to studying the **Harry Potter** series without looking at its place within the genre of fantasy literature, particularly that part of the genre written for children. Because of her use of Christian symbols and themes, it is inevitable that Rowling would be compared with J. R. R. Tolkien and C. S. Lewis."

"That's a well-covered path," Emma responded.

"But there is a bigger picture," Henry said. "Before Tolkien, fantasy works were not considered serious literature. They were lumped in with popular and children's books and dismissed as schlock and fairy tales. Tolkien took issue with that. In a 1947 essay 'On Fairy Tales' he called fantasy a 'higher form of Art' that demanded special skill and an 'elvish craft.' When done well, fantasy literature is the most potent form of story-telling, he argued."

"That's good to know," Emma responded.

"And have you encountered the gap theory?" Henry asked.

"Gap theory?" Emma said. "Tell me more."

"Michael D. C. Drout, a professor of English at Wheaton College in Norton, Massachusetts, identified a three-decade long gap in the writing of quality children's fantasy literature between Lewis and Tolkien in mid-20th century and Rowling in the late 20th century," Henry explained. "Madeleine L'Engle published her wonderful children's fantasy in the 1960s, but there wasn't much in the way of quality children's fantasy from then until J. K. Rowling and Philip Pullman came along in the 1990s.

"Professor Drout noted that the earlier children's fantasy shows evil as fully formed and without complexity, nuance or development. The greatness of J. K. Rowling is that she shows the evolution of evil, particularly in Riddle/Voldemort. I would add that she also shows the failings of the good guys."

"I agree about the dearth of solid material for young people during much of the late 20th century," said Beatrix. "J. K. Rowling was a refreshing wind."

"Do you think she was trying to walk in the footsteps of Lewis and Tolkien?" Sol asked.

"I think it's clear she was not trying to emulate the work of either Tolkien or Lewis," Emma said. "She started reading but never finished *The Lord of the Rings* and hasn't read all of Lewis' *Narnia* novels. In a Time Magazine article in July 2005, Rowling commented on C. S. Lewis' attitude toward children in the Narnia novels. She said, 'There comes a point where Susan, who was the older girl, is lost to Narnia because she becomes interested in lipstick. She's become irreligious basically because she found sex. I have a big problem with that.' So Rowling was not buying Lewis's theology at all."

"Not theology, I agree," said Beatrix. "But Rowling did borrow some names from Tolkien."

"Such as?" Emma asked.

"Both authors used Dark Lord and Chosen One," Beatrix responded.

"Those are generic terms," Emma said.

"Yes, they are," said Beatrix. "But consider these: Tolkien named an innkeeper and barman Butterbur, while Rowling named a pub beverage butter beer. Bagshot Row is where Sam Gamgee lived in Middle Earth, and Rowling named her historian of magic Bathilda Bagshot. Tolkien invented Longbottom, a place where pipeweed was grown, while Rowling gave that name to a significant wizard family. Wormtongue is a character in Tolkien's fantasy. Rowling opted for a lower part of the anatomy with Wormtail."

"Cool!" said Emma.

Henry rose from the table and trotted upstairs to his office, returning a minute later with a thick file folder. "You reminded me of an article I clipped years ago. I was going through the folder in anticipation of your visit and found this." He removed a glossy page and said, "Listen to this. Lev Grossman, a book critic for Time interviewed Rowling for the July 2005 Time issue. He wrote, 'It is precisely Rowling's lack of sentimentality, her earthy, salty realness, her refusal to buy into the basic clichés of fantasy that make her such a great fantasy writer. The genre tends to be deeply conservative -politically, culturally, psychologically. It looks backward to an idealized, romanticized, pseudofeudal world...Rowling's books aren't like that. They take place in the 1990s - not in some never-never Narnia but in modern-day Mugglish England, with cars, telephones and Playstations. Rowling adapts an inherently conservative genre for her own progressive purposes. Her Hogwarts is secular and sexual and multicultural and multiracial.' What do you think?"

"Brilliant," said Emma.

"Something that Rowling and Lewis do have in common," said Sol, "is ignorant villains. Lack of knowledge is something that Voldemort shares with C. S. Lewis's White Witch in *The Lion, the Witch and the Wardrobe*. Both baddies lack the deepest kinds of knowledge and the downfalls of each come about because of what they do not know."

"True," said Henry. "And if pressed, I could find any number of similarities simply because of the genres."

"With regard to Lewis and also Tolkien," Beatrix said, "I find it peculiar that these two mid-20th century writers should be so attractive to American conservative evangelical Protestants. Most U. S. evangelicals come from low-church backgrounds. I mean that in the liturgical sense. They tend to be from independent and congregational churches, democratically organized. The worlds created by Lewis and Tolkien are Medieval, monarchical, and hierarchical; worlds in which people are born into their places in society and destinies.

"Rowling's world is democratic and non-deterministic. Only the bad guys are hierarchical, aristocratic, and obsessed by the innate restraints of birth circumstances. For all its failures, the Ministry of Magic is essentially democratic.

"Free will is important in the Harry Potter world but not in Narnia or Middle Earth. Their worldviews are traditionally Catholic rather than Protestant. They are also pre-industrial and pre-technological worlds. Indeed, in *Lord of the Rings*, industrialism is portrayed as evil. Contrast that with Arthur Weasley's fascination with Muggle inventions and technology.

"Free will and a preference for non-hierarchical society is also something Rowling shares with her contemporary Philip Pullman. Near the end of *The Amber Spyglass*, the third of the *Dark Materials* trilogy, Pullman has John Parry's ghost tell Will and Lyra, 'we have to build the *Republic* of Heaven where we are.' I love that. The Republic of Heaven. No Kingdom for Pullman."

"How Protestant of him," Emma said.

"Yes perhaps," Beatrix continued. "And this may be counterintuitive, but among Christians, conservative evangelicals have enthusiastically embraced new technology, bringing audio and video equipment into the sanctuary. On the other hand, theologically progressive Christians tend toward traditional liturgies and services with human interaction rather than high-tech production values. So it is no surprise that liberal Christians would be attracted to J. K. Rowling's literary world, but it's odd that conservative Protestants would celebrate authors like Tolkien and Lewis who create mechanically primitive, low-tech worlds."

"Perhaps evangelical Protestants who are enamored of Middle Earth and Narnia are revealing the Catholic desires hidden in their shadows," Emma responded. "What would they see in the Mirror of Erised? Lewis and Tolkien are also Neo-Platonists, who avoid dealing with the sexual nature of the world, so this may explain some of the comfort that evangelicals feel with these authors.

"It's easy to find elements of the *Harry Potter* books that traditionally orthodox Christians would find troubling, not because they involve witchcraft but because they point to a non-traditional, progressive form of Christianity. A new expression of Christianity is emerging now in the 21st century that does not rely on firm doctrines or ancient creeds but on symbolism and metaphor. It is more centered on relationships than holiness or morality. Transcendent experience is embraced but not the view of God as judge and punisher. The theology of the Harry Potter books contributes a share of light for those who are seeking to discern the nature of emerging Christianity."

"And yet, the church is not portrayed negatively in *Harry Potter*," Emma said. "Compare Rowling's depiction of the church with Philip Pullman's *His Dark Materials* in which the Church specifically is the enemy. Its institutional power is fearful. In HP, Christian holidays are observed at Hogwarts, although not with services of worship. Christmas carols are sung at Hogwarts and by witches and wizards.

"Church buildings are used as landmarks in the narrative. When Dumbledore takes Harry to recruit Slughorn in **Half-Blood Prince**, they arrive and depart close to a church. This detail is entirely unnecessary to the narrative, unless it is there deliberately. The Church in **Deathly Hallows** is a symbol of a safe haven. This contrasts with the place of the Church in Philip Pullman's **His Dark Materials** trilogy, the first book of which was made into the film **The Golden Compass**. Pullman's work is contemporary with Rowling's and features hero and heroine in their pre-adolescent and young teenage years. Like Rowling, adults may enjoy his books, perhaps more than children. Where they differ is that the Church is the enemy in Pullman's books, while though it is present only marginally in Rowling's work, it is described in positive terms."

"Before we leave the subject of C. S. Lewis, here's another item," said Henry. "William Manchester called his massive biography of Winston Churchill **The Last Lion**. Churchill had a staff member who practiced Wicca and liked to do her personal devotions in the nude. The Prime Minister walked in on her while she was praying one evening, much to her consternation. The incident became known as the Lion, the Witch and the lack of wardrobe."

Emma, Sol, and Beatrix groaned in unison.

"It's not true, but I couldn't resist," said Henry. "Sorry."

"You should be," Emma said. "Do you have any Harry Potter puns?"

"Not off the top of my head," Henry replied. "But I can say that anagrams for Hogwarts include ghost war, straw hog, worst hag, throw gas, short wag, and grow hats.

"Good to know," said Sol with less than sincere inflection.

CHAPTER TWENTY~FOUR
A TIME FOR EVERY MATTER

Vacation had not been a part of Emma's vocabulary since her ordination. Occasional middle-of-the-week trips to the family home in Scottsdale and retreats at Henry's place provided respite, but she was always present for Saturday services. Now her perfect attendance record was in jeopardy.

Seeking to take the relationship to the next level, and guessing that she could convince Emily Hale to concur with the arrangement, Emma spoke to Sol about the possibility of his moving in with her. He immediately countered with a marriage proposal, which she promptly accepted. Now that wedding plans were on the agenda, the subject of a honeymoon inevitably arose.

"Surely you can miss one or two Saturdays," Sol said.

"I need a break, that's true," she admitted. "And the idea of a leisurely sojourn with just the two of us to do whatever we want seems heavenly. But I don't know who I can ask to cover while we're away."

"Henry or Beatrix would probably do it for you," Sol suggested. "Why don't you run it by the board and see what they think?"

The response from Merlin's Board surprised Emma.

"Do not fret for a minute," Dwight said. "We can handle a couple of weeks."

"I'd be happy to do a reflection," said Karl. "I have a few thoughts on therapy and healing in the canon, and knowing I had to offer a reflection would motivate me to put them together in a coherent narrative."

"And I would love to do a reflection," said Jordan.

Emma was entirely comfortable with Karl in the pulpit, but Jordan gave her pause.

"See, everything is taken care of," said Alexis. "Just go on your honeymoon and have a great time. It's all settled."

"No argument now," said Dwight. "We'll take care of your flock. Your baby is in safe hands."

"And we won't forget to change the diapers," Jordan added.

Emma and Sol married in a naturist ceremony in June 2014, with Wakhan Begay Wickham officiating at the Sedona NCC. Sol's younger sister, Windy, who was living in Phoenix and working on a Master's degree in journalism at the Walter Cronkite School of Journalism and Mass Communications at ASU, came for the wedding. Prior to this, Emma had only seen Windy in passing when she visited home and came to the NCC on Sundays. At the wedding, Emma came to enjoy Windy's sharp wit. Like her older brother, Windy was a Harry Potter fan.

Also attending, though fully clothed, were Professor Magda Lena Zwingvin and Emily Hale Norton. Emily Hale, in particular, grieved the marriage, but only because it meant Emma moving out of her home. Emma had made Sol promise that Emily Hale would receive regular invitations to dinner at their new home, at least until her surrogate grandmother had adjusted to living alone again.

The wedding gift from Emma's family was a trip to the U. K. Now Emma could show her husband the many special places she had visited with Sheba and Cameron. The excursion was restorative, erotic, indulgent, fun, and full of Potter-related adventures.

The first Saturday she was gone from church, Karl acquitted himself well as substitute Hallowed Philosopher. He began by saying, "Emma has described for us the ways in which Harry and Hermione function as Christ figures. But J. K. Rowling was not satisfied with only two such characters. In a sense, the roster of characters in the series is replete with beings who emulate Jesus in one way or another. Dobbie certainly comes to mind. But I want to focus on the one I believe is the most significant Christ figure in the canon, Albus Dumbledore.

"The bird in his office is a phoenix, whose tears bring healing and who is clearly a symbol of resurrection. But Dumbledore is a complex and worldly-wise Christ, who stands in need of healing himself as much as he offers it to others.

"The telling scene, however, can be found in **Half Blood Prince**. Dumbledore offers a blood offering to enter the cave, and in a sense, both he and Harry can be said to have descended into hell there, surrounded as they are by the dead lurking in the lake. But it is with his agonized drinking from the cup that the biblical imagery comes most to bear.

"According to Luke 22:42, Jesus visits the Mount of Olives and goes apart from his disciples and prays that the cup of death facing him be taken away. Yet he yields to a higher call and accepts what is to come. Dumbledore does not want to drink Voldemort's cup but does so in preparation for his own sacrifice and to save Harry and others. After drinking the cup, Dumbledore thirsts. On the cross, Jesus also thirsts.

"When Jesus was arrested, Peter drew a sword but Jesus told him to put it away, noting that he must drink the cup God had given him. Likewise, on the Astronomy Tower, when he was caught by Draco, Dumbledore immobilized Harry to prevent him from drawing his wand to keep him from interfering with what must take place. And Dumbledore willingly surrendered his life.

"Of course, in keeping with a humanist form of Christianity, Dumbledore wasn't resurrected in the same manner as Jesus, but his ultimate appearance to Harry in the ethereal King's Cross fulfilled the purpose of his sacrifice."

Following the service, Alexis approached Karl with congratulations for a job well done and added, "The scene on the Astronomy Tower always reminds me of *The Sound of Music*."

"How so?" Karl said.

"In the graveyard, Captain Von Trapp walks up to Rolf, who has been drawn in by the Nazis, and says 'you're not one of them, come away with us' and he disarms Rolf. On the Astronomy Tower, Dumbledore tells Draco he's not a killer and offers him and his family protection from the Deatheaters. The difference is that the young man Draco disarms Dumbledore, while the young Rolf is disarmed by the old captain in *Sound of Music*. But otherwise, they are very similar."

Karl said, "Interesting."

A week later it was Jordan's turn. She stood behind the lectern wearing a black robe with a deep green stole draped over her shoulders.

"I'd like to share with you the gospel according to Salazar Slytherin. A non-Slytherin once summed it up for me with: Do unto others before they do it unto you. I'm not offended by this quip, but it misses the subtlety of the true Slytherin spirit. Another non-Slytherin once told me that a Slytherin's response to Jesus' admonition to turn the other cheek would be to moon someone. This is just lame.

"It is patently evident from the narrative arc of the novels that J. K. Rowling includes Slytherin House and its members among the contributors to the ultimate common good. And any fair-minded Potterhead ought to acknowledge this fact.

"You've heard the adage that it's not pretty watching how sausage and legislation are made. Well, Slytherins are the ones who can do both. We do not shy away from tasks simply because they are unpleasant or not nice. Slytherin politicians are the ones who can scheme and manipulate behind the scenes to get important legislation passed. Somebody's gotta do it.

"If they had been wizards, I venture to say that presidents Franklin D. Roosevelt, Lyndon Johnson, and Richard Nixon would have been sorted into Slytherin. Say what you want about their many flaws, all three accomplished great things for the good of the nation. So, I would say that the gospel according to Salazar Slytherin is to do the right thing with whatever means necessary, but don't be stupid about it, and don't get squeamish if getting it done is not pretty. The simple truth, friends, is that Slytherins are necessary for the functioning of a free society."

"You made a strong argument," Dwight told Jordan after the service. "But you got one thing wrong. FDR would not have been a Slytherin. For all his political maneuvering, the courage he showed in overcoming the pain and debilitating effects of polio show him to be a true Gryffindor. Remember that Gryffindor champion Albus Dumbledore was a shrewd manipulator too. Johnson and Nixon you got right, though."

"If that's the worst response I get, I'll count it as a victory," Jordan said.

"I would look forward to you giving the reflection again when Emma's away," Dwight continued. "You have an engaging alternative point of view. But you're still wrong about FDR."

"I'll concede the point if you can name another Slytherin president," Jordan said.

"Reagan, maybe?" Dwight said, not at all confident of his answer.

"Nope. Definitely Hufflepuff," said Jordan.

"Then I'd have to go all the way back to Ulysses S. Grant," Dwight said.

"I'll take Grant and give you back Roosevelt," Jordan replied.

Though the newlyweds planned to delay having a family, they were not particularly careful about birth control, and in December Emma became pregnant. Each admitted to the other that they were secretly glad.

Sol was feeling more secure about family finances, as he had gained two more large commissions for statues from a buyer who wanted him to produce 21st century images following the styles of the Art Deco era of the 1920s and 1930s. The sculptor had been enchanted with Art Deco for many years and was thrilled to oblige. His smaller pieces placed on consignment with Darshan Pratyaksha's shop in town were also selling well.

Pre-natal development progressed normally for Emma, and an ultrasound revealed that she was carrying a girl. As her due date approached, her obstetrician recommended a pediatrician to examine the child when delivered, but Emma already had another one in mind. Dr. Helene Finn was a member of the Sedona naturist church and her practice included many children from that congregation.

During fellowship time after the service one Sunday, Emma approached Dr. Finn and asked her to attend her baby.

Helene said, "Of course, Emma. But I need to tell you that if he's a boy, I do not countenance circumcision."

"Well, she's a girl, so that's not an issue," said Emma. "But if it were otherwise, we're on the same wavelength. Both of my brothers are intact. My Dad was circumcised, and when he grew up and learned about the puritanical history of the custom, he went through a stage of intense anger and swore no son of his would ever be mutilated and know that kind of indignity."

"I've heard so many similar personal stories," Helene said. "By the way, I've also heard very positive things about the Holy Rowlings. How is that enterprise getting along?"

"Very well, thanks," Emma said. "We've carved a niche as a therapeutic humanist church."

"Tell me more about the therapeutic dimension," Helene said.

Emma told the physician about members using the *Harry Potter* narratives to help them through difficulties and traumas.

"Wow! I've been tempted to read *Harry Potter* but have never gotten around to it," Helene said. "When I was a girl, most of the young adult fiction was sappy. But many of my current patients are heavy Potter readers. You've given me the impetus I needed to find out what my patients are up to."

The following Sunday, Helene sought out Emma to say that she had read the first three novels and looked forward to beginning number four that afternoon.

On September 19, 2015, Emma gave birth to a daughter, whom they named Hermione Round Davar. At Sol's suggestion, they also visited the animal shelter and adopted two kittens, a male they named Stag and a female they named Otter.

Windy Davar received a master's degree from ASU in May and moved in with her parents temporarily as she searched for a job with a newspaper. Duffy found her a part-time position with the Intelligencer, and she became active in Emma's congregation, sorting herself into Ravenclaw. She also wrote blogs for Huffington Post and began work on a non-fiction book exploring the history of legal issues and cases dealing with nakedness in North America. Windy made herself especially useful to her brother and sister-in-law as a babysitter for Hermione and often hung out at their place for the companionship and conversation.

One day, Windy came over with a bag of DVDs. "We're having a Daniel Radcliffe movie marathon," she announced.

"I'm not in the mood for the *Harry Potter* movies," Sol said.

"Not to worry," his sister replied, reaching into the bag. "See what I have? *December Boys*, where he plays an Australian orphan. Then there's *My Boy Jack*, where Daniel is the son of Rudyard Kipling, who was killed in World War I. And here's *Kill Your Darlings*, where he plays Allen Ginsberg, who was gay by the way. Should be interesting to see how Dan does in a film about the Beat generation, although it's set in the forties, before the rise of Beat poetry, beatniks, and bongo drums. The word is that this is not a groovy movie, but dark and serious. And finally, the romcom *What If*, set in Canada. I've seen it already but it's definitely worth a rerun. Dan has great chemistry with Zoe Kazan. After the dark and tragic *Jack* and *Darlings*, we definitely need to watch this one last."

And so they watched Daniel Radcliffe movies.

Another day, Windy brought over Emma Watson DVDs for a movie marathon. They watched *Ballet Shoes*, *My Week with Marilyn*, *The Perks of Being a Wallflower*, and *Noah*. Then it was Rupert Grint day, when they saw *Driving Lessons*, *CBGB*, and *Into the White*.

Though their evaluations of the various films varied greatly, they all agreed that the three major child actors from the *Harry Potter* films had grown into first-rate adult performers, and by consensus deemed that Emma Watson had the greatest range with Daniel Radcliffe a close second.

After a meeting of the Sedona Alternative Ministerium, Terp invited Emma to lunch at Angel Nest. Over vegetarian enchiladas they discussed the nature of prophecy.

"The prophecy that led Voldemort to try to kill Harry is central to *Order of the Phoenix*," Terp said. "But in a technical sense it does not function the way biblical prophecy works, but rather the way biblical prophecy is commonly misunderstood."

"Well, Jo Rowling is not clergy, so she wouldn't think in technical theological categories," Emma responded. "But I'm clergy of sorts, so tell me more."

"You're not clergy of sorts, you're bona fide clergy," Terp chided. "Stop selling yourself short."

"Yes, Mother," Emma responded as if addressing a Mother Superior in a convent. "But please say more about misunderstood prophecy."

"Many people equate prophecy with predictions of the future," Terp continued. "Tonks does this in *Order of the Phoenix* with her supposition to Harry, concerning his vision of Arthur Weasley being attacked by Nagini, that it was not actually prophecy that he was producing, because he was not seeing the future, but rather the present. The prophets whose words and deeds are recorded in the Bible were not, as Tonks put it, seeing or predicting the future but critiquing their present situations. When they pronounced some particular gloom and doom scenario, what they were doing was calling for a change in behavior right then, in other words immediate repentance. If the change did not happen, thus and so would be the result. Biblical prophecy is akin to the efforts of modern day prophets of global warming. They identify the present dangerous situation and project what will happen unless we change soon. This is very different from the common misunderstanding of biblical prophecy as something predestined to happen regardless of what people do."

"Yeah, I see," said Emma. "Voldemort understands the prophecy about vanquishing him as a prediction of literal fact. He is a narrow-minded literalist as opposed to someone who understands metaphor. Not only that, but the prophecy could apply to either Harry Potter or Neville Longbottom, but Voldemort, who has only learned the first part of the words spoken by Sybill Trelawney, decides that it must be Harry, and thus unknowingly fulfills one phrase of the prophecy."

"That's the part about Voldemort marking the July baby as his equal," Terp said. "And old Voldy accomplished that by his failed curse and resultant scar on Harry's forehead."

"And the part about the marked one having power the Dark Lord is ignorant of, clearly refers to love, particularly sacrificial love, as Dumbledore explains to Harry," Emma continued. "But the part I have trouble with is the business about 'either must die at the hand of the other for neither can live while the other survives.' The first part is grim but internally coherent. But the second part is logically incoherent, because it's perfectly possible for both of them to live at the same time, which they do for years."

"It is puzzling," said Terp. "When he learns what's in the prophecy, Harry, of course, makes the same mistake that many Christians make about biblical prophecy, assuming that it is a prediction of something which must come to pass. Dumbledore, though, warns Harry not to place too much credibility in prophecy and then tells him not to believe that all the prophecies in the Hall of Prophecy have been fulfilled.

"This statement can also be applied to prophecy in the Bible. Biblical prophets played limited roles, speaking of the consequences or implications of the behavior they were addressing or railing against. And even when their prophetic words came to pass, they did not do so in exactly literal ways. Neither Jews nor Christians of the first century understood scriptural prophecy as literally true in its particulars, or even logically so, but as thematically true."

"But what about the internal contradiction in Trelawney's prophecy?" Emma asked.

"What about it? For literary purposes, Rowling can make prophecy mean whatever she wants it to mean," Terp continued. "And she warns the reader not to be too literal about it, through Dumbledore expressing doubts about the validity of Trelawney's words as well as confirming that not all prophecies in possession of the Ministry come to pass. My point is only that prophecy in *Harry Potter* is not akin to biblical prophecy."

Cloud had remained quiet during this exchange but now entered the conversation. "This talk about prophecy reminds me of the rescue mission to the Ministry in *Phoenix* and all those shelves full of prophecies, which leads me in a roundabout way to a thought about equality. Rowling is amazing at providing balance and parity among her characters."

"Be more specific," said Emma.

"Six students participated in that mission," Cloud said. "Three females and three males. Gender balance. They also divide nicely into three matching pairs. First is the pair of possible subjects of the prophecy Voldemort wanted to hear, Harry and Neville. Second, there are the siblings, Ron and Ginny Weasley. Third are the two intellectually confident and strong-willed females, Hermione and Luna. All perfectly balanced."

"I don't know about the last pair," said Emma. "Luna is smart but spacey and not the equal of Hermione."

"But she is equal in her confidence in what she believes to be true. And she is no intellectual slouch," Cloud responded.

Emma nodded in general agreement but squinted her eyes in a gesture that indicated she wanted to think about this a little more. After a pause, she added, "Another set of three pairs is possible here. The potential romantic partners: Harry and Ginny, Hermione and Ron, and Luna and Neville."

"But Luna and Neville don't end up together," said Cloud.

"No, but loads of fans expected them to," Emma replied. "And maybe they picked up that idea from this episode. Readers absorbed the symmetry of three pairs, consciously or not, and played that out in their minds."

"I'll buy that," Cloud said.

"There is another way the three primary characters are balanced," said Terp. "Harry, Hermione, and Ron all have one, and only one, prior romantic relationship before settling in with their life partners. So they each bring that kind of experience to their marriages."

"That's true. I've thought about that," said Emma. "And there are dozens of other examples of the way Rowling shows balance, parity, and reciprocity with characters and plot structure."

"I'll have to look for them the next time I read the series," said Cloud.

Emma arranged a surprise for Emily Hale to celebrate her 75th birthday in 2015. After making arrangements to visit her former landlady, she and Sol, along with Wakhan and Camelot, and Willow and Jeff, descended upon Emily Hale's home on the special day.

When Emily Hale saw how many people Emma had brought with her, she said, "I hope you're not counting on dinner. I was anticipating perhaps two guests for tea."

"We won't be staying long," Emma said. "We have a gift that requires all of us to provide."

"Now you have me fully intrigued," Emily Hale responded.

When they had gotten the birthday celebrant settled into her favorite chair in the study, Wakhan said, "Now just relax and sit quietly. Close your eyes if you want to, although that's not necessary. We're going to slip into Emma's old room for a minute or so."

"You're all going to get naked, aren't you?" Emily Hale said with a hopeful glint in her eyes.

"In a manner of speaking, but not the way you think," Willow replied.

"Now I am truly puzzled," Emily Hale said.

The six entered the bedroom and each found a place on the bed or rug to lie back and begin the breathing process that led to floating from their bodies. When all had achieved that non-corporal state, they made their way invisibly into the study, where they floated into the space occupied by Emily Hale's body.

Emma and Sol nestled in the area of her brain, Wakhan and Camelot in her heart, and Willow and Jeff stretched out across her lungs.

Emily Hale gasped audibly. The six bodiless souls concentrated on expressing affection for this woman they had come to love and admire, and Emily Hale quivered with tactile pleasure as tears poured forth from her eyes.

Continuing their outpouring of loving energy, the couples rotated among her organs -brain, heart, lungs- until they perceived that Emily Hale was physically and emotionally sated, and then they withdrew.

Back in Emma's old room and into their physical bodies, they decided to undress. Eager to hear the seventy-five-year-old woman's reaction to their gift, they trooped into the study, each with a bright smile.

"We thought we'd add to the gift by getting naked," Sol explained.

"What just happened?" Emily Hale asked.

"Did you like it?" Willow said.

"It was extraordinary," she replied. "I've never experienced anything remotely close to it. How did you manipulate that? It felt like magic, but I don't believe in magic."

"Do you believe in astral projection?" Jeff asked.

"I've read scholarly studies on that," Emily Hale said. "There are documented accounts of that phenomenon. British scientist Robert Crookall did a great deal of research on the subject. Is that how you did whatever it was you did to me?"

"The short answer is yes," said Emma. "We'll say more, but first we want to know whether we need to apologize or not."

"Apologize?" said Emily Hale. "Most certainly not. I've never had anything so intensely precious. I'll remember this for the rest of my life."

"So, you wouldn't mind if we came back and did it again for your next birthday?" Camelot said.

"That's more than I deserve or have any right to expect," Emily Hale said.

"Well then, put it on your calendar for next year," Emma said.

The six sat on the rug in a semicircle before Emily Hale's chair while Emma explained floating and described how they had occupied her body.

"If you've read Crookall," Emma said, "then you know he deemed it a 'serious mistake to endeavor deliberately to obtain out-of-the-body experiences.' He thought floating was just fine as long as it came unbidden. But he had no convincing arguments for not inducing OBEs at will."

"And obviously, we don't agree with his view, because we leave our bodies whenever we want to," added Jeff.

The widow insisted they stay for tea, after which the sextet dressed and departed.

Emma telephoned Emily Hale the next day and offered to teach her how to float. She assumed that Emily Hale would be reluctant and was prepared with all sorts of arguments to persuade her to give it a try.

To Emma's surprise, Emily Hale immediately said, "Crookall was a great researcher, but not very adventuresome, I'm afraid. You young people have won me over. Let's give it a try."

When Emma arrived at Emily Hale's house for the lesson, her former landlady was naked.

"You don't have to be naked to do this," Emma said.

"I didn't think so," Emily Hale said, "but I just felt like being nude."

Emily Hale was an apt student, strongly motivated by the prospect of bursting free from her physical frame, and within an hour she had achieved an out-of-body state.

Emma left her body and connected telepathically with her student. "Where would you like to go?"

"First into your body," Emily Hale said. "I want to tell you how much I love you in the most intimate way I can think of."

Emily Hale wafted inside Emma's skull and concentrated all the love she could muster into that space. Emma emitted a loud hoot. When she had exited Emma's brain, Emily Hale said, "Now let's go visit that nudist church. I am naked, after all."

And so they did.

Sol looked up from his phone and said, "J. K. Rowling just tweeted that people have been mispronouncing Voldemort's name all along. The t on the end is silent. But she wrote that she's probably the only one who pronounces the name that way."

"That's old news," Emma responded. "And she's not the only person who says Voldemore. Jim Dale uses the silent t in his audio recordings for Scholastic. But Stephen Fry pronounces the t in the British audio books. In fact, the first time he mentions the Dark Lord's name, he says it with clear added stress on the t, like he wants to make a point about how it's pronounced."

"Why do you think that is?" Sol asked.

"Well, both recordings of the first book were made in 1999. I wish I knew who went first," Emma said. "But since Jo studied French while at Exeter and even spent a college year abroad in Paris, she is certainly comfortable with French pronunciation, and no doubt she prefers it for certain words. On the other hand, Brits in general are notoriously averse to French pronunciations, especially the silent t. I suspect most of them haven't gotten over the Norman Invasion in 1066. Americans, however, look back to Lafayette as a role model and love a bit of French flavor in our language. Jim Dale recorded for the American audience and Stephen Fry for the British."

When Emma learned that Alan Rickman had died on January 14, 2016, she knew that members of her congregation would expect her to acknowledge, during the service two days hence, the man who had inhabited the role of Severus Snape on screen. Asking worshipers to raise their wands or hands skyward during a moment of silence seemed the appropriate way to do this.

As she reflected on this development, however, her mind took her back to the death of Richard Harris in 2002. He, too, had inhabited the role of Albus Dumbledore, at least in Emma's view. And, she thought, it had not been all that long ago that Richard Griffiths, who portrayed Vernon Dursley in the films, had died. Emma googled him and was surprised to find that it had been nearly three years since the death of Griffiths. And the following year, Roger Lloyd-Pack also had died. He had acted in only one film, *Goblet of Fire*, playing Barty Crouch, Sr. Still, he had made an impact on Emma in that role, and she remembered him fondly from her mom's DVDs of the Dawn French British comedy *The Vicar of Dibley*, which Emma had begun watching because French had also played the Fat Lady in the portrait.

Therefore, she set aside time in the service to remember these four actors whose visages and voices were fixed in the psyches of Potterheads everywhere. Each one was given a moment of individual silence and the raising of wands. The response was universally positive.

The script for the play, *Harry Potter and the Cursed Child*, was released in book form at the end of July 2016. J. K. Rowling worked in a team with two others to produce the newest Harry Potter fantasy, director John Tiffany and playwright Jack Thorne. Barnes and Noble and Amazon reported the largest number of pre-orders for this work since 2007, when the seventh Harry Potter volume had taken that honor. Bookstores all over the country, once again, hosted midnight release parties, but those days were long in the past for Emma, so she pre-ordered the play and waited patiently for it to be delivered a few days after release.

She wasted no time in reading it, however. That night, she fell into a deep sleep but was roused into semi-consciousness by a nightmare induced by an element in the play. In the dream, she snuck into the Ministry of Magic and stole a Time-Turner in order to go back in time to rescue Sylvia from death at the hands of a drunk driver. Desperately she tried to set the instrument to the correct time, but it took her to unhappy places and distressing times she did not want to visit. Unable to get to that fatal intersection before the crash would happen, she broke into tears and woke up.

"What's the matter?" Sol asked. Her thrashing about the bed had awakened him moments before.

"Nothing," she sobbed. "Just a nightmare. Something in **Cursed Child** brought back a memory of Sylvia, that's all."

The next day, Emma brooded about the dream. "I've never before had a nightmare brought on by a **Harry Potter** book," she told her husband over breakfast. "Just the opposite, actually. They've helped me get through rough times."

"Don't worry about it, Em," Sol said. "But since I haven't read it yet, is it darker and more violent than the previous books?"

"No," she said. "It's just that a particular notion that had never occurred to me took hold in my mind. I can't tell you about my nightmare because that would be a spoiler for your enjoyment of the book. I'll tell you everything when you've finished."

That night, the nightmare returned but unfolded differently. This time, she found herself sitting at the intersection of Tatum and Shea at the correct time to create a diversion, that caused the Emma driving her car to pause when the light turned green, allowing the drunk driver to pass through the intersection without colliding with her car.

Her flush of success was quickly washed away, however, as she saw a ghostly Sylvia approach her, furious that she had been called back from a place where she had been at peace.

"But I wanted to fix my mistake," the dreaming Emma said to Sylvia.

"Get over it," said Sylvia and evaporated.

Emma awoke refreshed.

Sol had finished reading the play before turning in the previous night, and at breakfast said, "Before you tell me about your nightmare, let me take a guess at what triggered it."

"OK," Emma replied.

"The Time-Turner bit reminded you about Sylvia, and you felt compelled subconsciously to bring her back from the dead," he said.

Emma grinned. "I'm so glad I married you," she said. "You know me so well."

"You seem much more cheerful today," he said. "Apparently the nightmare did not recur."

"You're wrong about that," she said. "It did come back but evolved in a therapeutic way. I am at more peace about Sylvia's death than I have ever been since it happened." She described each of the dreams.

"Well then, the **Cursed Child** caused you nightmares that proved to be a huge blessing," Sol said.

"That's true," Emma replied.

"What do you make of this thing between Scorpius and Rose?" Sol asked.

"Oh, I think that's just Jo giving a sop to all the Draco-Hermione shippers out there. A little next generation thing to make them happy."

"And how does that make you feel?" Sol said.

"I'm OK with it," she said. "If it makes certain people happy, well, they need something to be cheerful about."

"I was disappointed with it in some ways," Sol said. "It's not up to the level of literary quality of the ones written solely by J. K. Rowling."

"I know what you mean," Emma said. "Parts of it reminded me of fan fiction that I read years ago. It's like fanfic with Rowling's name attached. I'd love to read the story she wrote that Jack Thorne turned into a play."

"Me too," said Sol. "By the way, I assume you've already googled St. Jerome and St. Oswald to see if there is any spiritual significance to the names of the church in Godric's Hollow and the old folks home for wizards."

"Of course I have," Emma said with a grin. "More fodder for future reflections."

"And?" he said.

"St. Jerome is the patron saint of translators, librarians, and encyclopedists," Emma said. "In other words, just the kind of people Jo Rowling would admire. St. Oswald is the patron saint of soldiers, and I would interpret that to include veterans of the wizarding wars."

"I like the way the play reinforces your view that the Ministry of Magic does not practice capital punishment," Sol said.

"I was tickled to see that," Emma replied. "There was a clear statement against it, even for murder."

"On the other hand, Ginny referred to Harry's sacrifice in the forest as his doing it for the whole world," Sol said. "Your humanist interpretation is that Harry sacrificed himself for his friends."

"Well, that's just Ginny making her husband out to be bigger than life," Emma responded. "*Deathly Hallows* makes it clear what Harry's motivation was, and it was not to save the world. Besides, the same thing happened to Jesus. As time went on and the stories about him grew, the scope of his sacrifice kept getting bigger and bigger."

"Slytherins came out looking a lot better in the play," said Sol. "Young Scorpius said he was ready to die to stop the return of Voldemort. And one of Harry's sons is sorted into Slytherin."

"That's a healthy development, I think," Emma said. "But I'm having a hard time accepting the new more noble Snape."

At the next meeting of Merlin's Board, Alexis said, "So, is *Cursed Child* part of the canon? Do we have eleven books now?"

This caught Emma by surprise, because that idea had not yet occurred to her. "I suppose we need to consider that," she said. "Any thoughts, anybody?"

"Do we have any other categories where we could put it?" asked Dwight.

"Why do you say that?" Emma asked.

"Well, to begin with, it's not Jo Rowling's exclusive work," he said. "It's been tinkered with by two other writers, and not for the better, as far as I'm concerned."

"Dwight has a point," Karl responded. "We have never considered any of the movie screenplays as canon. The essence of Rowling may be distilled from the play, but it's full of theatricality that feels forced or designed to dazzle. It seems somebody, probably the director, wanted to provide against-type star turns for some of the actors."

"I think there are enough narrative details about the main characters that ring true that it qualifies for canon status," Frieda said. "I certainly like the evolution of Draco."

"What you like about it is irrelevant," said Jordan. "There are things in the actual canon that I don't like, but too bad for me. The words are the words."

Frieda shot Jordan a dirty look.

"The thing that bothers me," said Dwight, "is that some details in the narrative are problematic. The big one is Bellatrix being pregnant at the time that the trio were captured and brought to Malfoy Manor. Given the elapsed time between then and the Battle of Hogwarts, she must have been quite far along. It would be noticeable to anyone in the family, including Draco. That means he would have evidence to refute the claim that Scorpius was Voldemort's child."

"Tish!" said Jordan. "She could have used a concealment charm so no one would see she was preggers."

"But when she grabbed Hermione and threatened to cut her throat, Hermione would have felt Bellatrix's enlarged belly," Dwight said. "I'm sure that Jo Rowling could provide some kind of pat answer to cover the shaky chronology problem, but it doesn't ring true to me."

"All it says in the play is that Delphi was born before the Battle of Hogwarts, but it doesn't say how long before," Jordan countered. "Bellatrix could have delivered her daughter while Draco was away at school."

"And before the seven Potters episode?" Dwight responded. "Give me a break!"

Alexis extended her arms in a calming gesture. "So, apart from criticizing the plot, what are we going to do about expanding the canon?"

"As far as I'm concerned, the canon is open to additions, as long as J. K. Rowling is alive and I'd even include posthumously published works written by her. But I'm inclined to agree with Dwight, that only things produced solely by her should be canon. So, I would suggest a new category that's used in the Christian Bible to account for disputed books. We can call it deuterocanonical. Second canon. That way, it has special status, but not on the exact same level as the ten canonical books."

"Separate but equal?" Jordan deadpanned.

"Not at all," said Emma. "Just occupying a different category because of its multiple authorship."

The board voted unanimously to adopt Emma's proposal.

CHAPTER TWENTY~FIVE
DEPARTURES AND ARRIVALS

Emma and Sol drove to Scottsdale to show her parents how well Hermione could walk, and to let Hannah dote on her first grandchild. Emma was pregnant again and due at the end of October. While Grandma babysat one afternoon, Emma and Sol went to a movie matinee. Sol had read a review of an animated feature by a French screenwriter and filmmaker named Alain Gagnol, and he was intrigued enough by its premise to insist they see it. Emma, who had not read the review, was initially skeptical about spending a precious afternoon out watching what she described as a French cartoon, but **The Phantom Boy** quickly took hold of her attention.

"Why didn't you tell me it was about out-of-body experiences?" she said to Sol as the credits were whizzing past.

"The element of surprise," he responded.

"I'll have to tell Terp and Cloud about this," Emma said. "Some of the things that boy did while floating were like what we do."

"But we've never experienced a fading for being out too long," Sol said. "That added tension to the plot, but it's not true to life."

Emma kissed Sol tenderly. "Thank you for the element of surprise."

"We're in a dark theater. Wanna make out?" Sol responded.

Emma playfully pushed him away. "I think the kid waiting to clean up would prefer that we didn't."

"Well then, let's head back to see how your mom and Hermione are getting along," he said.

Later that summer, Emma and Sol were pleased to receive an invitation to the retirement party for a group of Sedona NCC pastors. Four pastors who had served that church from its first year, would retire all at once.

Terp and Cloud Morgan, beloved by Emma since they preached sermons about Harry Potter when she was a teenager, were stepping down, along with Malama Kohana Cumming and Tallis Bede Glee.

The hall would be packed with well-wishers, Emma knew. So many lives had been influenced for the better by this particular set of pastors. Emma wondered how this leadership transition would affect her congregation of Holy Rowlings. Would the NCC church continue to provide space for them at a nominal cost? Membership was on a downward course, and the little congregation could not afford an increase in rent. She wasn't overly worried about higher rent, but was eager to know for certain what the financial reality would be. And would Terp and Cloud follow through on their intimation that they would join the Holy Rowlings on Saturdays?

Then a week after the invitation, news arrived about the pastoral succession. Emma cried out in joy to learn that the new pastor of the naturist congregation would be Wakhan Begay Wickham, the person who had officiated at her wedding to Sol, baptized her daughter and had promised to baptize the boy due in the fall. The Holy Rowlings had no worries now, Emma was sure, because Wakhan not only approved of the Harry Potter congregation, but came to services from time to time.

But Wakhan wouldn't have much time to do that now, thought Emma. She will have her hands full building a new staff of pastors to carry out the extensive ministry among the naturists of Central Arizona.

At the retirement event, Cloud took Emma aside and said, "I want you to know that Terp and I plan to take part in your congregation, but we'll be traveling for a few months, so we won't be around much until the fall."

"That counts as very good news all around," Emma said. "You need time for well deserved travel, but knowing that eventually I'll be seeing you in worship on Saturday afternoons brightens my outlook. Your presence will also help boost the attendance numbers."

"Sol told me worship attendance was slipping," Cloud said. "It's probably only a temporary blip."

"I truly hope so," Emma replied.

That same month, Den Tran and his wife Sarai, co-pastors of the NCC congregation in Lake Havasu City they had begun serving together a quarter century earlier, were out for a stroll along a grassy area near the

London Bridge. Holding hands contentedly as they ambled in the heat of the evening, a beefy white man, apparently in his forties but who had aged badly, accosted them.

"How'd a slope like you end up with a white girl?" he spat out.

Sarai looked at him intently. Over the years of their marriage, she and Den had rarely received racist remarks directly, although she was sure that they had been directed behind their backs. "Well, you know what they say about Asians. They're very smart. Smart is very sexy, but I guess you wouldn't have the faintest idea about sexy or smart."

The man glared back at Sarai and said, "At least he's not a coon."

Den turned to his wife and said, "What do you think, dear? I would guess this one's IQ is about 40."

"Oh no," Sarai said. "Not that high. You give him too much credit."

At that moment, the bigot charged at Den, and Den casually swung his left leg into the side of his attacker's leading leg, sending the man sprawling face down into the grass. The co-pastors continued their walk, although their pace quickened.

"That guy seems too young to use those particular slurs," Sarai said.

"He probably picked them up from his parents," Den said. He turned around to see if the man had followed them and noted that he was scrambling in the opposite direction.

"This event feels like a sort of catalyst for us," Sarai said. "Not that anyone like that could drive us away, but I have a sense that it's time for a move, a new challenge."

"I've been thinking along the same lines," said Den. "Let's call Cathy Blake in the morning to find out what the opportunities are for a new pastorate."

Before they could place that call the next day, the antiquated landline phone in Den's office rang and a melodic voice responded to his hello. "Hi Den. This is Wakhan. Is Sarai in the office?"

"In the kitchen," he said. "Hold on, I'll get her."

"Then put the phone on speaker," Wakhan instructed.

A minute later, Sarai and Den were seated across from one another listening to Wakhan talk.

"You know, of course, about the mass retirements at the Sedona NCC," Wakhan said.

"We were invited to the party but had a commitment here and so we missed it," Sarai said. "But we haven't heard anything about successors."

"That's why I'm calling," Wakhan explained. "I've been asked to serve as pastor."

"Congratulations! Well deserved," said Den.

"Thank you, but four pastors retired, and I can't possibly do this job alone," Wakhan continued. "But given the support staff still here, I'm confident we can do it with three."

Den and Sarai looked at each other sharing a sense of synchronicity but did not speak, waiting for Wakhan to do so.

"I know how difficult it is for pastors to give up congregations they gave birth to," Wakhan said. "But I really need you to think seriously about joining me here as co-pastors. The Board has authorized me to see if you'd be interested." Before they could respond, she added, "In case you're worried about leaving LHC in the lurch, we have a couple of seminarians from Las Vegas ready to be ordained who would be perfect to succeed you."

Sarai and Den remained silent, staring at one another as if in a dream.

"Den? Sarai? Are you still there?" Wakhan said.

"As it happens," Sarai said with more steadiness in her voice than she felt in her body, "Yesterday evening we were talking about looking for a new call, a new challenge."

"We don't need time to think it over," said Den. "If you want us with you, we'll be there as soon as we can."

Following their retirement, Terp and Cloud attended a Holy Rowling service once before departing on a trip to Southeast Asia. By this time, word had spread that in addition to Wakhan, their successors would include a married couple currently serving a naturist congregation in Lake Havasu City, but Emma did not know anything about them.

Members of the congregation warmly greeted the retired pastors, one after another expressing hope that they would come back and worship with the Holy Rowlings, but eventually Emma managed to get them aside for conversation.

"What can you tell me about the new NCC pastors?" she asked Terp. "I suppose you know them."

"We know every one of the pastors in the NCC world-wide," Cloud said. "But these two joining Wakhan as your new pastors are especially dear to us."

"We are thrilled at this development," Terp said. "Den was one of the boat people who fled Viet Nam, and we sponsored him as a refugee. He lived with us for years until he married and was ordained. For all practical purposes, he is a son to us."

"And Sarai is the daughter of the pastors of the New River NCC that I attended when I was in high school. We watched her grow up, and she too lived at Angel Nest for a time," said Cloud.

Emma was a Bernie Sanders supporter in the 2016 primary election, having decided while in college that she was intellectually aligned with European style democratic socialism. She was, however, content with the nomination of Hillary Clinton, telling diehard Berniecrats that three quarters of a loaf was better than having the loaf you already have taken away. By Election Day, she and Sol had become enthusiastic about Hillary.

David Round was a liberal Republican, very liberal on social issues but pro Wall Street on economic ones. "It's wrong to be completely greedy on taxes and oppose sensible regulations, but the so-called progressives go too far," he told Emma in a rare conversation about politics. Like his idol, Michael Bloomberg, David staunchly supported stricter gun regulation. In 2016, however, he was appalled by Donald Trump and decided to vote for Hillary Clinton. "At least she knows how to entertain Wall Street folks with her speeches," he said.

When Michael Bloomberg endorsed Clinton, David felt vindicated that he had made that same decision even earlier. On the 7th of October, when the ***Access Hollywood*** tape of Trump making predatory and misogynist comments about women reached the public, David said, "Now even some of that basket of deplorables surrounding the Donald must be ashamed of supporting him."

"Perhaps," said Hannah, "but I suspect what they're really ashamed of it that he has out-deplorabled them."

This election marked the first time that the Round family was unanimous on a presidential candidate.

Karl came to church with an article he had printed from the Internet.

"Have you seen this, Emma? I found it on Daily Kos." He handed her the pages.

"Hmmm. 'How 2016 presidential players fit in Harry Potter world,'" she read from the headline. "By Sher Watts Spooner."

"Spooner links political leaders with their HP equivalents," Karl said.

Emma glanced at the article. "First on the list, Hillary Clinton is Hermione. OK, I can see that. Let's see. Oh, Donald Trump is Gilderoy Lockhart. Yep, nailed it. Where's Bernie? Oh here he is. Bernie Sanders is Xenophilius Lovegood. I'll have to think about that one for a while. Bernie is much more grounded that Xenophilius."

"Check out the next page," Karl said. "You'll find Harry there."

Emma shuffled to the next page and scanned down the text. "Aha! Barack Obama is Harry Potter! Yeah, I'll buy that! Thanks, Karl. Now I'll have something to chuckle about all day. Trump is not man enough to be Voldemort. Trump is the narcissistic bumbling Lockhart, and Hillary is the whip smart Hermione. And that reminds me of an article I read last month about reading *Harry Potter* and Donald Trump."

"There's a connection?" Karl asked.

"A political science professor at Penn, Diana C. Mutz, has been studying the political attitudes of HP readers for years. This year she polled over a thousand people to see how they felt about Trump. It turns out that American HP readers are about equally divided among Democrats, Republicans, and Independents, but the more *Harry Potter* books people have read, the lower they rate the Donald," Emma said.

"That tracks. I've seen pieces in the educational literature about increased social tolerance among young people raised on *Harry Potter*," Karl said. "The books are having a profound effect on political attitudes in this country."

"That's a blessing," said Emma.

Jared's best acting skill was a voice full of sarcasm. A media consultant for a conservative Super PAC took note of this when he appeared in an episode of *The Mindy Project*. The consultant called Jared and invited him to audition for a voice-over political ad attacking Hillary Clinton.

At the time, Jared was nearly broke and facing the humiliating prospect of asking his father to bail him out so he could pay the rent on his studio apartment. He went to the audition and read the script.

The director said, "You've got a great snide. Read it again and see if you can add a tinge of ominous to it."

Jared tried but could not muster the necessary menace. "I'm sorry, but I just can't do it."

"Sure you can. You've got a great voice," the director said.

"It's not that," Jared said. "I can't say this because none of it is true."

"So what?" the director said. "You're an actor, right? Ever played a villain? It's the same difference. And it's only your voice. Nobody will see your face. Let's hear you run through it again."

"It's not the same thing," Jared said. "I'm sorry, because I need the work, but I just can't do it."

Back at his apartment, Jared steeled himself to call David and ask for money, but he couldn't muster the energy to follow through on the task. He put it off that day and the next. When his rent was due in three days, he called Emma instead, prefacing his request for a loan with an account of his turning down a well-paying job.

"No prob, Jar," she said. "I'll go to my bank and transfer money to your account today. But I have to say, I thought you were a Slytherin. You're acting like a Gryffindor."

"I am a Slytherin," Jared responded. "Even Slytherins can do the right thing every now and then."

By this time, word had circulated through the industry about his refusal to do the anti-Clinton ad. As a result, Jared received a call from a producer for an ad arguing for the overturn of the Citizens United v. Federal Election Commission Supreme Court decision. He brought his best snide voice to this advertisement instead, which quickly led to work doing ads for other progressive causes and candidates.

Jared promptly repaid Emma as 2016 was shaping up to be his most successful year as an actor. But something better was yet to come. A casting director for Pixar Animation Studios heard Jared's voice in an ad for a senatorial candidate and tracked him down. Soon Jared had plenty of opportunity to use his snide voice in animated shorts and feature films.

A Japanese family vacationing in Sedona saw a poster for the ACHPP in a shop window and decided to visit the church on a Saturday in the fall.

The teenagers particularly enjoyed the service, but their parents found it agreeable also.

During the fellowship time afterward, Dwight warmly greeted them and said that he had found Japan a delightful place when he took his wartime R and R there. "I was at Camp Zama, and managed to get in a couple of rounds of golf on the wonderful course, but I was also able to travel a little."

"What did you like best of what you saw?" the father asked.

"Well, Mt. Fuji is spectacular," Dwight replied. "But I also found Kyoto to be enchanting and beautiful."

"You have good taste," the mother said. "We live in Kobe, not too far from Kyoto."

Emma joined the conversation. "What is the Harry Potter phenomenon like in Japan?" she asked.

"It is huge," said the boy. "A year ago a Wizarding World of Harry Potter opened in Osaka as part of Universal Studios Japan. We are fortunate that we live close to it."

"Harry Potter is so popular in Japan that the world premiere of the *Order of the Phoenix* movie was held in Tokyo. Not London, not New York, but Tokyo," said the girl.

"*Harry Potter* has even become part of international relations," said the father. "In 2014 in London, the Chinese ambassador to the UK defamed the famous Yasukuni Shrine in Tokyo that has honored our war dead since the 19th century. He called it a Horcrux of the darkest part of the Japanese soul. In response, our ambassador said that China is Voldemort."

"Wow!" said Emma and Dwight in unison.

On October 31, 2016 Emma gave birth to a son Albus Round Davar. She made it clear to anyone who asked and some who did not that the name was in honor of the professor and not Harry's son. Members asked why the boy was not named Harry, to which Emma replied, "Too many people know I was once a Harry-Hermione shipper, and I didn't want to hear any shipping jokes that might lead to speculation about reverse Oedipus complexes."

<><><>

The results of the presidential election stunned Emma and Sol. On Wednesday, the Sedona NCC office sent out notices by email and on Facebook and Twitter that the entire church staff would be available in the sanctuary all afternoon and evening for people who needed to grieve, vent, be comforted, or process the news. Emma thought that was a good idea and sent out similar communications to her congregation. After lunch she went to the chapel to await visits from Holy Rowlings. They came in a steady stream. The first to arrive was Dwight, and without premeditation, Emma greeted him with the words, "The Ministry has fallen. We must organize to resist in every way we can."

Thereafter, she said that to everyone who came in that day.

Hannah called to check in on Emma. In the course of the conversation, she said, "Your father tried to jolly me up by saying that at least the stock market was going up. There was some good news. But he confessed that it was because of oil, coal, and private prison stocks, and in the long run, that would be devastating for the planet and the economy."

"I give Dad credit for being honest about that stuff," Emma responded.

"But he left out the most important part," Hannah said. "I told him that it was mostly because they could smell the repeal of the Dodd-Frank Act, and he gave me a shame-faced look and said, 'Yeah, that too.'"

"So much for protecting the public from predatory Wall Street," said Emma.

Then came the Great Unfriending. Emma and Sol both had hundreds of friends on Facebook, more than a thousand between them, not counting their mutual friends. In her mind, Emma put them into three overlapping categories. There were family and friends she had known personally for years, plus two worldwide networks of friends she had met only via Facebook. The networks were Harry Potter fans and naturists.

The day after the election and continuing for a week, people began adding denigrating, threatening, and racist posts to Sol's and Emma's respective News Feeds. Some gloated over the Trump victory and others put various targeted groups of people on notice. The word libtard was frequently used to describe progressives. There were only a few dozen such posts on Emma's page, representing a tiny fraction of her friends, but she determined that she would not quietly accept the abuse. After acerbically chastising the offenders in the comments section, she unfriended them. Sol did the same.

What surprised them was who these abusive posters were. Some came from the family and old friends group, all of whom were high school classmates.

"I had no idea that some of my peers in high school were secretly racist," Emma said.

"Me neither," said Sol "But they're not secret about it anymore."

The other unfriendings came about because of postings from naturists, although none from any naturist church members. Not a single Harry Potter friend posted ugly things.

"Well, that tells us something important," Sol said.

In the days and weeks that followed the election, Emma often felt demoralized and sapped of energy, but she found hope in casting the situation in the context of the *Harry Potter* saga. She drew strength from the Rowling canon, because she knew the guiding metaphors had been drawn from the real world and actual history. Emma also decided to avoid saying Trump's name, not in fear but in defiance, referring to him only as Gilderoy. Among members of her congregation, this became common practice.

Following the xenophobic Brexit vote in the UK to leave the European Union, a campaign of solidarity with immigrants and refugees began there. People began wearing safety pins to show support for people threatened by extreme nationalists and racists. A similar campaign began in the United States after the election of Trump, and Emma took to wearing a safety pin whenever she went out in public. She put a basket of pins in the rear of the chapel and encouraged her church members to do likewise.

"All you have to say if asked about wearing a safety pin is that you stand with all the people threatened by the politics of hate," she told them. "Oh, and carry a few extra in your pocket to give to allies."

Members of the Sedona NCC also took up the safety pin campaign, when they were dressed. Many, while nude, wore them attached to chains around their necks.

Members of Emma's congregation, including Slytherins, followed her example with safety pins and came closer together as they genuinely felt themselves part of a dangerous struggle. Repeatedly, they sought her encouragement for the trials ahead, and she came to believe that the forces of good would eventually prevail. Thus she gained a renewed sense of purpose as 2016 lumbered to an end with daily reports of pernicious activity from the emerging Trump kakistocracy.

When the news broke that the CIA knew that the Russian government hackers had intervened electronically to influence the American election, and there was evidence that the Trump campaign had been complicit in it, Emma felt doubly violated.

"Do you still think Trump is Gilderoy Lockhart?" Sol asked her during a commercial while they were watching The Rachel Maddow Show.

"More than ever," Emma replied. "The truly scary part is that Vladimir Putin is Voldemort, and the vain and stupid Lockhart doesn't have a chance dealing with the mad dictator of Russia."

"What about Trump as Pius Thicknesse?" Sol continued.

"You have a point," Emma replied. "Putin has Trump under the Imperius curse and thus controls his behavior. But overall, I think the narcissistic Lockhart better describes Trump."

The one bright spot that fall was the release of the film and screenplay of ***Fantastic Beasts and Where to Find Them***. Since J. K. Rowling had written the screenplay, there was no question in anyone's mind that this was canon. Emma noticed when Newt Scamander opened his suitcase for the customs inspector there was a Hufflepuff scarf in it. So, she thought, another Hufflepuff hero. Frieda will be thrilled.

What thrilled Emma was the thunderbird that Newt rescued in Egypt that he was taking back to its home in the Arizona desert. She resonated with Newt's work of nurturing and protecting animals and educating others about these fantastic beasts. She also resonated with Eddie Redmayne's portrayal of Newt Scamander and Katherine Waterston's role of the American auror Tina Goldstein. Emma was surprised to discover that Katherine was British, but played an American convincingly. The screenplay was published on the day the film premiered in the United States, and Emma bought it before seeing the film but did not read it until afterward.

The news that this was the first in a series of five films tickled Emma and gave her something Potter-related to look forward to. A younger Dumbledore would be featured, and the chronology would span from 1926 in this first movie to 1945 in the last one. Emma wasted no time pointing out to people that 1945 was the year that Dumbledore bested Grindelwald in a duel and won the Elder Wand. But, she acknowledged, it would be a long wait to see that on the screen.

Emma and Sol were invited to the Angel Nest family reunion at the end of 2016 and found themselves in conversation with Sojourner.

Sol said, "This presidential election reminds me of something Philip Pullman wrote near the end of the last book in **His Dark Materials** trilogy. The witch Serafina Pekkala tells the scientist Mary Malone, 'all the history of human life has been a struggle between wisdom and stupidity.' For the moment, stupidity has won out."

"It would seem so," Sojourner responded.

"Well, I was completely blindsided by the election results," Emma said. "Do Merven follow human politics?"

"Indeed yes," said Sojourner. "And *we* were not blindsided. We were not expecting the particular results, but were also not surprised."

"Why is that?" Sol asked.

"Are you familiar with the term psychohistory?" Sojourner said.

Emma said no, while Sol said yes.

"The term was invented during World War II by science fiction writer Isaac Asimov," Sojourner explained. "It is a method of plotting out future developments as they apply to large groups. It's not fortune telling but searching out historical probabilities. Merven social scientists have been using a form of this for several centuries, and when Asimov coined the term in English, Merven adopted it as an apt name."

"And the current political darkness can be explained by psychohistory?" Emma said.

"Two decades ago, Merven scholars perceived the strong possibility of another era of violence, ignorance, xenophobia, and repression world-wide. The terrorist attacks in 2001 and the subsequent reactionary responses fit our psychohistoric model, and the consensus was that these dynamics would continue to play out for decades. The election of President Obama seemed to portend otherwise, but our social scientists insisted this was a temporary blip. A larger backlash was welling up from the shadowed interior of this and other Western nations."

"So what do we do now?" Emma asked.

"The Angel Nest community is strong enough to endure what is to come," Sojourner said. "And I consider you two and the Holy Rowling church as extensions of this community."

"So all we have to do is wait for all this to pass?" Sol said.

"Be patient and plan for recovery," Sojourner said. "Things will get much worse before they get better, but taking the long view helps one get through the devastation."

"It's always darkest just before dawn and all that trite blather," said Emma.

"Not quite," said Sojourner. "I do not wish to make light of the situation, and solving the massive global problems created by human behavior will take a long time, but rather than sitting in the dark and grieving the reality, it would be more productive to lay the groundwork for the next renaissance. Along the way, strengthen your bonds among the healthy communities you are part of. Gain sustenance and courage from the people of Angel Nest, the Natural Christian Church, the Sedona Alternative Ministerium, and the Holy Rowlings."

"That gives me hope," said Emma.

CHAPTER TWENTY~SIX
SURVIVAL OF THE FITTEST

Deep in a nocturnal dream, Emma found herself wandering aimlessly through the Sinai Desert until she saw an arrow pointing to a steep hill marked Mount Sinai. She knew that she must climb that mountain, which she did with frustrating difficulty. The staff she was carrying offered little assistance.

All at once she found herself atop the mountain and in the presence of God. She heard God say to her, "Listen Emma, there are only seven commandments, not ten. And they are actually goals, not absolute."

"What am I supposed to do with them?" Emma asked.

"Write them down and show them to your flock," God replied.

Somehow her laptop appeared in her hands as if by magic.

"Number one," God intoned, "Be kind to one another. Number two, treat people with respect."

"Wait a minute," Emma interrupted the Deity. "What about no other gods and being a jealous God and all that stuff?"

"No, no, no," God replied. "These are not about me; they're about humans. I can look after myself, thank you very much. I do not need humans to bolster my already healthy ego by bowing and scraping or worshiping me. I don't like forced compliments, anyway. Loving me or being in awe of me are your choice. I'd just like you earthlings to behave better towards each other."

"OK," said Emma.

"Now, on to number three," God said. "Take responsibility for your own excrement. Number four, be discerning rather than judgmental.

Number five, think for yourself, and number six is like unto it: Don't for a minute think you know everything."

"Please give me a second to get all this," Emma requested. A moment later she said, "OK, I'm ready for number seven."

"The most important one of all," said God. "Try not to be a jerk."

Emma chuckled at this. "My peers would say, 'Try not to be an asshole.'"

"Well, I don't approve of that language," said God.

"Yeah, it's pretty gross," Emma responded.

"That's not what I mean," God said. "I created the anus, or as your friends so commonly call it, the asshole. I consider it to be quite useful. It is an elegant organ with a vital function. Using it as a derogatory term offends my sense of the essential beauty of the anus among all the other beautiful body parts."

"I see what you mean," Emma said.

"I am glad that you do," said God. "And when you wake up, I want you to share my seven goals with your congregation."

The mood in the congregation was unsettled. People seemed to want reassurances that things would be alright, and though the traditions in the Harry Potter church were only a few years old, they seemed to hold the authority of long standing doctrines. The world was changing enough that novelty in church was not appreciated.

After Emma had presented these seven goals in a reflection, along with the story of her dream, the reaction was mixed.

Frieda said, "Slow down, Emma. You're going beyond the conventions of the canon or even the Harry Potter universe in general."

Jordan told several other people, but not Emma directly, that the Hallowed Philosopher seemed to be branching out into her own revealed religion. Nevertheless, the comment reached Emma within minutes of Jordan saying it.

Karl was more tactful, but suggested to Emma that her reflection would have been improved if she had made a connection with the body of Potter lore.

All these felt like accusations to Emma, and she went home angry, defensive, and hurt.

At dinner, she said to Sol, "Help me find a Potter connection with my dream. There must be something I missed."

"The only thing that leaps to mind is the number seven. Seven books or seven Horcruxes," he said. "According to numerology or astrology or whatever source, seven is supposed to be a magical number, isn't it?"

"Six intended Horcruxes," Emma responded automatically. "That skewers the whole numeric scheme."

"Unintentional or not, there were seven of them," Sol said in his defense.

"Thanks, but that's no help," she said. "Do you think I've strayed from the canon by introducing personal experience?"

"No, I don't," Sol said bravely. "And too strict adherence to canon leads in the direction of fundamentalism, which is antithetical to the Holy Rowling ethos."

"Maybe I should say that next week," Emma said.

"I'd wait a while before tackling fundamentalist urges within your flock of metaphor believers," Sol advised. "It would be smarter to thank the congregation for their sensitivity in not discerning a Potter connection in your last reflection, and say that in response, you have studied the experience and found one."

"If only I could find one," Emma said.

"Work on it, you'll discern something. You always do," said Sol.

That night, she had another dream in which she was in detention in Dumbledore's office. Harry came into the room and said, "Headmaster, I've been out in the countryside chasing Horcruxes, not very successfully, and I'm struggling with whether I can trust you anymore. I need to believe in you, but I have my doubts."

Emma woke up in a sweat, and realized that she too was struggling with what to believe. Her doubts were with the sufficiency rather than the content of the canon. Shall we be exclusively restricted to this body of work, or can we incorporate the larger world of literature, science, and experience into the ACHPP? This is like religions searching their scriptures in vain for answers to modern problems that were not mentioned or even conceived of when the scriptures were first codified, she thought. They could either look elsewhere for wisdom or force inauthentic answers from texts like some churches do in feeble attempts to cope with scientific discoveries that contradict their scriptures. Except, in this case, there were no threatened theological doctrines and the canon was contemporary with their world.

In the morning, she began work on a reflection that described J. K. Rowling venturing beyond **Harry Potter** to write other novels completely unrelated to her fantasy masterpiece, mentioning the murder mysteries **The Cuckoo's Calling, The Silkworm**, and **Career of Evil** written under the pseudonym Robert Galbraith. Rowling had also written speeches and editorials, and engaged in political action. If Rowling has the courage to explore beyond canonical themes, the Holy Rowlings should take heart from that and do likewise, Emma decided. And her job as Hallowed Philosopher was to lead and assist the congregation venturing into the wilderness beyond the canon. This was the needed connection with what she now called her Moses dream.

Her reflection the following Saturday was well received and settled any lingering concerns from members. However, this wilderness revelation came at a time when the congregation was continuing to dwindle, which had the effect of increasing anxiety among the faithful remnant. The only new members joining in recent months had been Cloud and Terp, who brought a great deal of energy and mature stewardship giving to the congregation. But they were out of town much of the year, so their attendance was sporadic.

That particular Saturday, Sarai and Den came to the Holy Rowling service in the chapel, both listening intently and resonating with Emma's words. Since arriving, they had been visiting all the activities, sponsored events, and organizations using NCC space, in order to get to know people and what they were doing.

Den praised Emma's reflection and said, "We want to be as supportive as possible to this congregation and see no conflict of interest between your NCC membership and your ACHPP leadership. If we can help in any way, please let us know."

"We know that Cloud and Terp are worshiping here now," said Sarai. "And they are the best possible ambassadors between the two churches."

"Well, a few of our members are also members of the NCC. It would be really great if you would suggest to a few more of them that they add Saturday afternoon worship to their weekends," Emma said in a joking tone of voice.

"That's not a bad idea," said Den. "I won't tell people to do it, but a little bit more publicity for the Holy Rowlings wouldn't hurt."

"I think more would attend if they could do it without clothes," Sarai said.

Emma laughed.

The year 2017 did not start off well for the Holy Rowlings. Emma remained distraught that Gilderoy Lockhart was inaugurated as the 45th president of the United States on the 20th of January, followed five days later by the death of John Hurt, the silver screen embodiment of Mr. Ollivander. Her grief at this loss was as great as that of Alan Rickman a year earlier. Both of these new events seemed like ill omens to Emma.

The only piece of good news came in February when the Fantastic Beasts film won an Oscar for Costume Design. This was a first for the Harry Potter movie franchise, and Emma enjoyed a moment of elation.

Otherwise, each morning, she woke up with the same question running through her mind. What has Gilderoy done overnight to embarrass or endanger the country? This was followed immediately with clenched teeth at the thought of what he might do this day.

Often at breakfast she asked Sol, "Any news on his impeachment yet?"

"Vegas bookmakers have it at 3 to 1 in favor, and British bookies have it at 50/50," Sol said one morning.

"Well, that's the silver lining I need," Emma responded. "American bookies are more optimistic than the Brits."

One morning in March, Sol said, "Have you seen the Emma Watson flap? She did a photo shoot for Vanity Fair, and one of the shots reveals quite a bit of her right breast, though not the nipple."

"You know I don't read Vanity Fair," Emma said.

"But it's all over the Internet," Sol explained. "Apparently there's been a backlash from some feminists calling her a hypocrite for posing that way."

"That's just stupid," Emma said.

"Yeah, well Emma Watson responded to the criticism," Sol continued. "She told the media, 'Feminism is not a stick with which to beat other women. It's about freedom; it's about liberation; it's about equality. I really don't know what my tits have to do with it.'"

Good for her!" Emma exclaimed.

Sol handed his iPhone to Emma. ""Here's the photo in question, and follow the link below to a Reuters interview."

After viewing and perusing the subject, Emma said, "I remember our conversation about nudity when she visited here. I think I'll write her a letter of support. I much prefer Emma Watson's feminism to the puritanical version."

"A little action to cheer you up. Go for it!" said Sol.

She also felt a brief boost that month with the release of an expanded version of the 2001 *Fantastic Beasts and Where to Find Them* that included more beasts and a foreword by Newt Scamander. Here was another book to add to the canon. And she was momentarily elated in early May when the MTV Movie and TV Awards initiated a gender-neutral category for acting, and in a mixed-gender field, Emma Watson won best actor for her role as Belle in Beauty and the Beast. She called Emily Hale to tell her that MTV had eliminated categorizing by sex and that the first award for acting went to the woman who created the He For She campaign for human rights.

Yet Emma remained on the brink of depression, as closing the congregation became a serious item for consideration. Month by month, membership losses continued. Average worship attendance dwindled to a dozen members.

"I wish I knew what to do," Emma said to Dwight and Frieda. They were older than most Holy Rowlings and prominent among the faithful remnant.

"It's a miracle that all the Merlin's Board members are still here, even Jordan," said Frieda. "But it is a problem that over half of the regulars left are Gryffindors. That includes you and Sol."

"It's not your fault," said Dwight. "Some of the youngsters have simply grown out of their HP infatuation. They've moved on to other narratives for entertainment. Ironically, some of those who have moved on are the most supportive of exploring beyond the Potterverse. They need to be connected with something that's cool, and Harry Potter is becoming shelf worn."

"That's just natural attrition," Frieda added. "Nothing you can do about that. It happens in all kind of churches. Drifting away is normal, especially for teens and twenty-somethings. My ex's church has had a huge exodus of that demographic."

"And some are just getting on with their lives by taking jobs in other towns or moving out of state," Dwight said. "And, of course, two of our families are leaving the country because of the election. Vancouver Island, British Columbia and Wellington, New Zealand will be the richer for our loss."

Emma produced a shrug of resignation. "Yeah, intellectually I know all that, but I'm discouraged and depressed anyway. And what's the deal with Portland? Half a dozen of our members have moved there."

"Well, it's on the list of cool cities for Millennials," Dwight explained. "It's progressive and environmentally minded, and its number one attraction is a bookstore. What's not to like about that?"

"A bookstore?" Emma exclaimed. "That sounds too good to be true."

"But it is true," Dwight said. "I've been there. It's called Powell's City of Books, and it occupies an entire city block with three floors of stuff. New and used, every category you could think of."

"Harry Potter?" Emma proposed.

"They have a huge selection of Harry Potter related material -books in multiple languages, recordings, films, games, coloring books, toys. You name it," Dwight said.

"Sounds like I need to fly to Oregon," Emma said.

"Or go to www.powells.com," Dwight said. "I've ordered stuff from them on-line that I couldn't find anywhere else, even Amazon. Browsing their inventory would be a great way to take you away from your woes."

"A moment of cheer amid the drear," Emma said and smiled.

Dwight and Frieda put hands on her shoulders and nodded encouragingly.

"If it were only Slytherins who were leaving, I suppose I could live with it," Emma continued. "On the other hand, most of our self-sorted Slytherins are more into acknowledging their own shadows than taking advantage of other people. They like to think of themselves as fascinated with the dark arts, but they wouldn't survive a day against truly evil folks."

"Well, young people think it's cool to be Slytherins," said Frieda. "They laugh about it and claim that Jo Rowling affirmed them as superior in the epilog to book seven, and even more so in *Cursed Child*, with Harry's own son Albus sorted into Slytherin."

"Yeah, but I think our Slytherins use it as an excuse for being cynical," Emma said. "But Slytherins are not the problem with the congregation. Our losses are from all the houses equally."

"Except Gryffindor," said Frieda. "They seem to cling more than others."

"They do not cling," Emma retorted. "They're simply loyal."

"Welcome to the world of disillusionment," said Dwight. "As I've probably told you too many times, mine came when I was younger than you, in Viet Nam. War is guaranteed to bring a belief-shattering crisis."

"This isn't war," said Frieda. "That's not a helpful metaphor for Emma, Dwight."

"It's what I know," he said. "Do you have something more apt?"

"Well, this is certainly more profound than discovering that Santa Claus is not real," Frieda responded.

"It feels like a betrayal," said Emma. "Like people are not reliable, not trustworthy. They have no vision or staying power."

"People *are* flaky," said Dwight. "But that doesn't mean you have to let go of *your* vision or your dream."

"But there's no point in continuing with church if nobody comes," Emma said.

"We'll come as long as you conduct services," said Frieda. "You know the verse; as long as two or three are gathered in his name, Harry Potter is in our midst."

Emma laughed despite an attempt to suppress it.

"Another irony," Dwight added. "Thanks to generous members like Rob, Willow, and Jeff, we're enjoying better financial health than we've ever had. The faithful remnant will see us through this crisis."

The next day, Emma received an anonymous letter:

Dear Hallowed Philosopher,

You can't really believe all this nonsense! You're just cashing in on the success of a famous author. You call it a church, but you're just hiding behind the Constitution and Bill of Rights to profit from J. K. Rowling's work. It's a scam. Your so-called church is all phony. Nobody really believes in Harry Potter, because he's not real like Jesus. It's all a game. Why don't you just quit and save us all a lot of abdominal pain. You've had a few years of good fun, but admit it, it was all a lark. Time to give up childish ways and get a life. Turn to Jesus before it's too late.

In His Name,

Someone who cares about your soul

When Sol read the letter, he said, "Forget it. Don't let it get you down."

"Thanks, Sol," she said. "This hurts but I can get over it pretty easily because all I have to do is consider the source. But this only highlights what really hurts. It's the continual disappointment from being let down by people who are friends and supporters not honoring their commitments. I guess that's the cost of being an idealist."

"Yeah, friends can hurt a person far worse than enemies," Sol responded.

"I don't really have any room to complain," Emma said. "I'm so blessed in the love department, with you and the kids, and so many dear mentors. I know I'm being greedy to lament about parishioners I've developed deep affection for only to see them fail at reciprocity."

"Speaking of mentors," Sol said, "I think it's time for you to have another chat with Terp."

Emma visited Angel Nest the next day and found Terp an encouraging listener to her tale of diminishing church membership and hate mail.

"I won't give you any nostrums about one door closing and another opening," Terp said. "You have every right to feel disappointed. But this is not the end of your life."

"Thanks," Emma said. "But I've been thinking about the survival of the fittest, and wondering if my vision is simply not fit enough to survive."

"The influence of the Social Darwinists is still with us, I'm afraid," said Terp. "But the Social Darwinists got it wrong. Likewise, their descendents in the Eugenics Movement were egregiously mistaken in their endorsement of genetic purity. According to Charles Darwin, survival of the fittest did not refer to the strongest, wealthiest, or most powerful, or even the most intelligent. The fittest are those most adaptable to change. And this notion is epitomized in the novels of J. K. Rowling.

"A prime example of survival of the fittest in the ***Harry Potter*** series is the Weasley family. They are economically marginal and clearly not a powerful clan, but they are open to change and adapt easily. Seeing the value of magic folk marrying Muggles is one instance. Survival of the species depends on it. The Malfoys, on the other hand, are on their way up an evolutionary blind alley with regard to intermarriage and genetic purity. In other respects, however, they also adapt to survive. It's an open question as to whether political adaptation will be enough to sustain the Malfoys in future generations.

"Hermione is academically brilliant and powerful at casting spells, which is important to the unfolding of the plot, but it is her ability to change her mind at critical times that leads to her survival and that of her companions.

"And Harry Potter himself is not the brightest wizard but he ruminates tenaciously, continually adapting to the realities of his changing circumstances. Despite the extraordinary means he uses to extend his life indefinitely, Voldemort can't adapt."

"In other words, you're telling me to adapt to the present reality," Emma said. "As that letter said, get a life."

"Stay alive," Terp said. "If the fledgling Christian movement had insisted on staying as pure and consistent as it was in the first century, it would have died out in the second. Between its practice of Christian communism and the Roman Empire, it didn't have a chance of survival without major adaptation."

"I guess it's time to figure out what the Alchemical Church of Harry Potter Prophecy can do to adapt and survive," Emma said.

"Either that, or figure out how Emma can survive without the church," Terp said. "Congregations have lifecycles. They age just as people do, and the children leave. It used to be that the children came back when they had children of their own, but no more. This happens in the NCC too, although the proportion of children who drop out after high school is lower for us than with evangelical and mainline churches."

"But the Holy Rowlings are not old," Emma countered. "It's too soon for lifecycle dynamics to kick in. My congregation is mostly younger people, Millennials and Generation Xers. It's much younger than the average Protestant congregation."

"That's true," said Terp. "But Millennials and Gen Xers change jobs and locations more than older generations. They are highly transient.

The unfortunate reality is that you would have a better chance of survival in Phoenix where there is a much larger population to draw from."

"You've given me a lot to think about. Thanks, Terp. I feel a sense of relief just from having you listen and understand," Emma said.

After a few days of pondering Terp's words, Emma reached the point where she could imagine the congregation folding without dooming her life to perpetual depression. Running through her mind like an earworm was the Disney movie *Frozen* and the song "Let It Go."

Part of the problem, she told herself, was that she was not the perfect pastor, but she decided to give up on trying to be perfect. What will be will be, even if that means the death of the heroic church. The death of a dream. She would just have to come up with a new dream.

On her way out the door one morning, she turned to Sol, who was fixing breakfast for Hermione and Albus, and said, "I think Charles Darwin would have enjoyed reading *Harry Potter*."

Sol looked up and said, "Huh?" But she had gone.

So many of the faithful remnant had plans to be away for significant parts of the summer that in May, Emma decided to suspend services from June through August. With the endorsement of Merlin's Board, the congregation would continue to make lease payments, in order to be ready to resume services after Labor Day. With no gatherings on Saturday afternoons, Emma visited the chapel alone to meditate. Sometimes, other members of the board also came by during the scheduled time, to chat and make plans for the fall.

During this period, Sol encouraged his wife to explore other careers, to look for a regular job. In return, she berated him for choosing to be an artist while telling his wife to get a regular job. He tried to explain this is not what he meant. For a reason she did not understand, her husband's encouragement to try something else made her more determined to sail on and, if necessary, go down with the ship.

Lamenting the fate of her congregation in a phone conversation with Cameron, Emma spoke about how hard she had worked and how little she had to show for it. "I feel guilty for all the money spent on a project that seems headed to failure. I wonder if the endowment from the ministerium should be paid back? I think I have a moral obligation to do that."

"If anyone should be paid back it's Dad," Cameron said. "But he would never take the money."

"Why would you say a thing like that?" Emma asked.

"Dad put up most of the money for the endowment," Cameron replied. "I assumed you knew that."

"No, I damn well did not know that," Emma fumed. "How the effing hell did you know?" Emma was furious that Cameron was aware of something this personal about her while she wasn't, but even more so that her father would do such a thing anonymously. She felt like a fool and a spoiled brat at the same time.

"I overheard him and Mom talking about it," Cameron said.

As soon as she got off the phone with her brother, Emma called her father. She did this before telling Sol what she had learned from Cameron, because she knew that Sol would get her to calm down and probably counsel her to let the matter go. When David answered her call, she launched into an angry tirade about his duplicity.

"I'm sorry you feel that way, Em," he said. "I did it out of love and a desire for you to succeed."

"Well, it didn't work," she spat back. "I'm a failure."

"The most successful people have all failed multiple times," David said.

Eventually, Emma did calm down, and as expected, her father refused her offer to pay him back. Her level of guilt increased, however, when he told her that he had not at any time tapped her insurance settlement, and in fact, it had increased in value considerably.

After confessing all this to Sol, Emma proposed that they use some of her settlement money to buy a house in West Sedona. That way at least they would have a place to live without rent or mortgage, which would make it easier to get by relying only on Sol's intermittent commissions. He thought it was a prudent step.

CHAPTER TWENTY~SEVEN
CHAMBER OF SECRETS

Merlin's Board convened at the end of August to make a decision about resuming services in September. All the members of the board expected that they would begin afresh and were therefore surprised at what Emma had to say.

With all the members present and gathered around the table, Emma began the meeting by saying, "I'm tired." She had not intended to say it. Her conscious thoughts had been focused on finding a way to carry on with limited resources, but the words slipped past her superego and filled the air with tension.

"How can you be tired?" Jordan asked. "You've had the whole effing summer off to rest."

"Not that kind of tired," Emma said. Mentally, she tried to formulate an explanation that would satisfy everyone, but in her current emotional state, she knew that it would be wiser simply to tell the truth. The inner sense of obligation that had urged her to keep going evaporated. Feeling trapped, she looked down at her lap for a few seconds and then raised her head, making eye contact one at a time with each person around the table. "I'm tired of working my ass off to get people interested in the congregation, when there's obviously no interest out there any more. Even among avid fans, the level of interest in the Holy Rowlings is tepid at best. I thought the biggest threat to our church would come from religious fundamentalists screaming heresy and blasphemy. Instead it turns out to be indifference from people who if pressed would agree with our philosophy. Church, even a Harry Potter church, is not all that attractive to most Potterheads. The Age of Harry Potter has passed. Now we're in the age of…I don't know what."

"The Age of Marvel super heroes," Dwight suggested.

"The Age of **Sherlock Holmes**," said Jordan.

"The Age of Aquarius," said Alexis.

"Yeah, whatever," Emma said. "And I just can't go there. I'm ready to close the church."

"Maybe a sabbatical would help," said Karl. "Why don't we just suspend activities until after Christmas? By then, you should be in a better place."

"That's only postponing the inevitable," said Emma. "I need to free all of you to pursue your lives in other ways. I don't want you to be in limbo wondering if I will come back or not. Let's just do it, close the doors for good."

"It wouldn't be for good in my book," said Alexis. "It would be a tragedy. And I don't have a problem with hanging out in limbo."

"This is freaking me out," said Frieda. "I can't imagine never coming to church here again. This has been a lifeline to me. Please, Emma, don't do it."

"I'm sorry, Frieda, I don't see any other way," said Emma. "I'm not happy about it, but it's time for all of us to move on."

"I think we need to hit the refresh button not close," said Jordan. "Start over with a different approach."

"What do you have in mind?" Emma asked without any real interest.

"We should try some razzle-dazzle to attract new people," Jordan explained. "You know, lasers and magic tricks, stuff like that."

"Do you like that kind of thing?" Emma asked.

"It turns me off, actually, but it attracts unattached males. They like special effects," Jordan said. "If we can get single men here, the women will follow."

"Does anyone else think we need to jazz up the service?" Emma asked.

No one spoke.

"I'm just trying to bring some creative thinking to the problem," said Jordan.

"And we appreciate that," said Dwight. "Do you have any more ideas?"

"We could combine elements of the naturist church that Emma goes to with the Holy Rowling service," Jordan replied.

"Liturgical elements?" Emma asked.

"No, a bit of nudity," said Jordan. "That would bring them in."

"Be more specific," said Emma.

"Well, like re-enacting the nude scenes from the **Potter** books," Jordan said. "You know, like Harry in the Prefects bathroom and in the heavenly King's Cross Station when he was naked and wished for a robe and it appeared."

"And how would we stage something like that?" Alexis asked. "We don't have anyone who could play Harry."

"I was thinking that Emma could do it," Jordan said. "A cross-gender re-enactment of sorts. We could make a little train station set in the corner, and before the service Emma could lie there naked. Then when the processional music starts, she could rise and put on a robe and walk to the lectern. Something like that would draw a crowd."

"Wouldn't that be syncretism?" Alexis asked.

"No, exhibitionism," said Emma.

"No, just no!" said Frieda.

Karl and Dwight agreed with Frieda.

"But I give you credit for creative thinking, Jordan," said Karl.

With great reluctance, the board agreed to suspend all church activities indefinitely and to let the lease lapse at the end of the year. Unanimously, however, they refused to vote on dissolving the church. "There are legal implications, including your status as an ordained person, and corporate filings, and who knows what other details we will have to tend to," said Karl. "Formal action on dissolution can wait until sometime next year."

"That's acceptable," said Emma in a hollow voice. "Meeting adjourned."

The next day, she drove to Emily Hale's house for tea and sympathy.

"I feel so terrible letting all those people down," she told Emily Hale. "I just need to confess my abject failure to someone safe. And you're the one who fills that bill."

"Abject failure is the last thing I would call you. Think about all the people whose lives you have touched in beneficial ways, including me. What you need is a good cry," Emily Hale said.

Upon hearing those words, a torrent of tears burst from Emma's eyes, and she began to sob. For some minutes, no one spoke.

Eventually, Emma said, "Sorry I lost control."

"I'm not," said Emily Hale. "Feel better now?"

Surprised at her answer, Emma said, "Funnily enough, I do."

"Then drink your tea, and I'll read the leaves for you," Emily Hale said.

"You haven't become a Trelawney fan, have you?" Emma asked.

"No, just seeing if I could get a response from you. Apparently you aren't completely dead yet," said Emily Hale.

Emma laughed.

Emma found her days filled with childcare, which she enjoyed, and sending out her resume throughout cyberspace, which she did not. No interviews developed as a result of her position inquiries. Though not happy, Emma became resigned to giving up the dream of Holy Rowlings as her true calling in life. She told herself that it had been a lark for a few years, but the magic was gone. Apart from the busyness, however, Emma knew she was drifting and suffering from intermittent bouts of depression.

One night as Emma and Sol were snuggling in bed after making love, Sol said, "If your true vocation in life is that of pastor, which I think it is, why don't you look into ordination in the NCC? You have a lifetime of experience as a member and have hung out with NCC clergy for years."

The idea slapped her from contented ease to full attention. "That had never occurred to me," she said, "but it makes sense. The only thing is, it would probably mean moving to another location for a call. We'd have to sell our house and find you a new studio."

"Maybe," said Sol. "But if it provides you with the sense of authenticity you need, we can find a way to make it work."

"I love you, Solomon Davar!" she shouted.

"Shhh, don't wake the kids," he whispered.

"You really know how to turn me on, Sol," Emma said. "Let's make love again."

They did.

The next morning, Emma called Terp and asked about the NCC ordination process.

"I think that's a wonderful idea," Terp said. "You would definitely qualify for the fast track. I'll set up an interview with the care committee in Phoenix for some time after the first of the year. Keep in mind, however, that your service to the Holy Rowlings may not be over yet. Until that's certain, you should not fully commit to NCC ordination."

"I'm confident that my days of being Hallowed Philosopher are numbered," Emma replied. "It may not be official yet, but it won't be long."

In December, Emma received a call from an old flame. "Hi Emma, it's Duncan Cooper. Cameron gave me your cell number. I hope you don't mind."

Surprised, Emma said, "Hi Duncan. How are you?"

"I'm doing just fine," he said. "I'm married now. Just thought I'd get that out of the way in case you suspected anything."

"That never occurred to me," Emma replied. "I'm married now, too."

"Yeah, I know. Cameron told me," he said. "Do you remember Charlotte Callum from our geeks' tour? She's my wife. But the reason I called is I need your help."

"If I can," Emma said tentatively.

"Here's the deal," Duncan said. "How can I get a Holy Rowling congregation going here in Tempe? I've got a dozen friends who want to replicate what you've done in Sedona. One of them, in fact, moved here from Sedona, which is how I found out about what you have going there."

Emma was stunned into silence, and then remembrance of a comment Terp had made about the congregation having a better chance of survival in a large population center like Phoenix came to her. An image of selling up and moving to Phoenix flowed through her mind.

"Hello? Are you still there?" Duncan said.

"What? Oh yes, I'm here," Emma stuttered. "I'm just trying to process what you said."

"Let me be more specific," Duncan said. "Is there any training for Hallowed Philosophers? Any manual of operations or service guides? Where can I go to learn the ropes?"

"*You* want to become a Hallowed Philosopher?" she responded. Now she was conflicted. This wasn't a call for her to move and start over, which was a relief, but it involved someone else taking over her work, which hurt. Of course, he doesn't know we're closing down, she reminded herself, so he isn't thinking of replacing me.

"Yes," Duncan said. "Very much so."

"Let me get back to you on that," Emma said. "My training was piecemeal, with tutoring from pastors in other denominations and my own directed study."

They exchanged email addresses, and Emma promised she would respond in detail within a few days. She chose not to tell Duncan that the church was not functioning and its services were suspended indefinitely. Gathering together resources she had used over the years proved an engaging task that took her mind away from thoughts about changing denominations.

Two days later, Susan Sinew called Emma.

"Wow, you're the second old friend I've heard from this week," Emma said.

"I ran into your brother Cameron at the mall," Susan explained, "and he brought me up to date on what you're doing. This Holy Rowling church sounds like it was made for me."

"Since you know everything about me, tell me what's happened in your life," Emma said.

"I don't know everything about you," Susan replied. "Cameron only talked about the Harry Potter church. That's what interests me most. But to bring you up to date, I left home after high school and lived with my lesbian cousin for a while. I put myself through ASU by working as a cashier in a grocery store. Now I'm engaged to a wonderful woman who is also an HP nerd."

"I'm so glad you're at a happy place," Emma said.

"What would make me even happier is knowing where the nearest Holy Rowling congregation is," Susan said.

"I have good news and bad news," Emma said. "There are no congregations in the Phoenix area. That's the bad part. But my former boyfriend Duncan Cooper wants to charter a congregation in Tempe. He has a list of people interested in joining. It may be a while, though, before he can get the training to do it."

"How long does the training take?" Susan asked.

"I don't know. We've never done it before," Emma confessed. "I'm working on a packet of resources to send him. What I can do is give you his email address, and you can contact him to say you'd like to be on his potential members list."

"That's a start," Susan said.

Emma conferred with Cloud, Terp, Wakhan, and Magda Zwingvin about developing an educational enterprise for prospective Hallowed Philosophers.

Terp said, "I am pleased to say that I told you your days as Hallowed Philosopher might not be over. It's nice to be right every once in a while."

"Yes, but that doesn't solve the problem of closing the Sedona Holy Rowlings. This would be an entirely different endeavor. And by the way, I wasn't looking at the NCC as a consolation prize," Emma said.

"Of course not," said Terp. "And that still remains an option for the future, but now I think you need to give your full attention to training other HPs."

Susan called back to say that she had corresponded with Duncan, but he lived in the East Valley in South Tempe and she was in Litchfield Park on the opposite side of the Valley. "After thinking it through," she said, "I got excited about the possibilities of getting whatever education is available so that I could start a Holy Rowling congregation in the West Valley. The idea of being a Hallowed Philosopher holds great appeal."

"Fabulous!" Emma exclaimed. "I'm almost done with a packet of information to send to Duncan. I'll make a copy for you too."

"Better make a bunch of copies," Susan said. "Just in case. You never know who might pop up next wanting to be trained."

"That sounds so optimistic," said Emma. "It's good to hear an optimistic voice. By the way, are you still estranged from your parents?"

"Oh yes," Susan said. "My sister Zane keeps me informed on them from time to time. She's moved out too, but they accept her in the house because she's straight. One thing I like about the idea of pastoring a **Harry Potter** church is that it would further nettle my parents when Zane told them about it. And she couldn't resist telling them just to see their horrified reactions. Their church bought an industrial grade shredder so members of the youth group could bring Harry Potter books for shredding parties."

"Hmmm. An interesting form of biblioclasm," said Emma. "In the old days, they just threw books into bonfires."

"They've caught up with the technology to more efficiently destroy words and ideas they're afraid of," Susan said.

"But it won't work," said Emma.

"No, they're only hurting themselves and their children," Susan replied. "But I wish I could be there to see my parents' faces when Zane tells them there is a Harry Potter *church*. Maybe I'll ask Zane to secretly record the conversation. That way at least I'd be able to hear their gasps."

Emma mailed thick packets of resource material to Duncan and Susan, including DVDs of several services.

At Christmas, Emma, Sol, and their children visited her parents in Scottsdale and were pleased that Jared had come home also. Jared took that opportunity to ask his sister about developments in the ACHPP.

"Are you still going to officially pull the plug when the lease expires?" he asked.

"Actually, there's been a change on that front. We're going to hold on to our lease so we can use the chapel for training. The board is hopeful of resuming regular services some time next year," she said. "Of course the congregation would be quite a bit smaller than it was at the high point. At one time we were attracting 70 people on a Saturday afternoon. Then it went downhill fast. But the big news is that we have two people ready for the training program who want to create new congregations in the Phoenix metro area."

"Funny you should mention that," Jared said. "I've been doing a lot of thinking about the direction of my life, and your church keeps popping up in my meditations."

"You're doing so well as an actor," Emma said.

"Yeah, I get more calls than I can handle for voice acting roles," he said. "And I still get calls for minor roles in sitcoms, soaps, and commercials. In fact, my income is so flush that last week I was finally able to get out of my tiny pad and lease what in adspeak they call a luxury apartment. It's not luxury the way this house is, but I have a lot more room.

"Even so, the thought of opening a Holy Rowling church in Los Angeles has taken hold in my mind. I just know it would be a successful enterprise. So, when you get your first training class together, I'd like to be in it."

"Fascinating," said Emma. "You're the third person to express interest in Holy Rowling ordination. A straight male, a lesbian, and a gay man."

"You got a problem wid dat?" Jared said with his mock gangster voice.

"You know damn well that I don't," she said. "But I'd love to see even greater diversity in prospective Hallowed Philosophers."

Taking advantage of everyone being in the Phoenix area at the same time, Emma arranged a meeting with Duncan, Susan, and Jared at a mutually convenient location, which turned out to be Sheba's house in Central Phoenix. There the Hallowed Philosopher and her protégés discussed plans for their studies and got to know one another.

Wondering if Tom Corazon's cell phone number had changed, Emma called the one in her contact list. Her number was still among his contacts, and he answered right away. "Hi Emma. This is a pleasant blast from the past. To what do I owe the honor of your call?"

"I was wondering if you had found a place for your spiritual needs to be met?" she replied.

"I still haven't visited that nudist church, if that's what you mean," he said. "And no other church either."

"Next question. What part of the Valley do you live in?" she continued.

"Chandler. Why?"

"Because friends of mine will be starting Holy Rowling congregations in Tempe and Litchfield Park, and I wanted to know which one to recommend for you," she explained.

"I'm only six blocks from the Tempe boundary," Tom said.

Emma gave Duncan's contact information to Tom, who was genuinely pleased at the development. They chatted for another quarter hour, from which Emma learned that Tom thoroughly enjoyed his work and he had a lady friend.

Emma established a Potterological seminary on the grounds of the Sedona Natural Christian Church. For classroom space, she used an available kiva and a room in a tower accessed through a tunnel and hidden staircase. Emma had been delighted to learn from Cloud that when the church was built, the architect added tunnels and secret passages at his request. Sol likened the underground kiva and tunnels to the Catacombs, where Christians gathered for nurture and protection from the depredations of the Roman Empire. Emma thought the kiva should be called the Chamber of Secrets and the tower the Astronomy Tower, to distinguish it from Trelawney's classroom. She called her seminary the Hallowed Philosopher Academy.

Along with traditional pastoral subjects and Harry Potter lore, at Jared's suggestion, seminarians were taught to float. He, of course, already knew how. Emma became the primary professor, but Cloud, Terp, and Magda offered course leadership *pro bono*.

She gathered core members from the original congregation in the chapel for demonstration services, which quickly led to the renewal of regular worship on Saturday afternoons. Within a few months, the resurrected congregation grew even larger than before. The members especially loved nurturing seminary students when they offered reflections to fulfill class assignments.

The first class of seminarians, who would be ordained to start new congregations, consisted of Duncan Cooper (Ravenclaw), Susan Sinew (Gryffindor), and Jared Round (Slytherin). They were required to spend a weekend together with Emma and then individually spend a week in residence in the kiva and another week in the tower, plus participate in worship leadership at least three times. Cloud, Terp, Wakhan, and Magda also provided instruction during the intensive residential weeks. From their homes, the students wrote papers and did assigned reading.

As part of their week together, the students took Emma's sorting survey. The responses from Susan and Duncan clearly confirmed their houses of Gryffindor and Ravenclaw respectively. Jared's results showed a conflict. Out of 49 questions, Jared preferred his self-sorted choice of

Slytherin on 18 but also scored 18 for Ravenclaw. His score for Gryffindor was 8 and Hufflepuff 5.

"I always wondered if you were a true Slytherin, Jar," Emma said.

"What do I do now? I can't be in two houses at once?" he asked.

"You know what to do. You choose," said Emma.

"OK. I'll stay Slytherin," he replied.

"What's your rationale?" Emma asked.

"Are you questioning my judgment?" he replied.

"Not at all. But if you are going to be a Hallowed Philosopher, you will need to be clear about who you are and be able to discuss such decisions with others," she said.

"I see remaining Slytherin as a way of honoring Severus Snape," Jared said.

"Still faithful to Snape after all these years?" Emma said.

"Always," said Jared. "I think that if Severus had survived the Battle of Hogwarts, his outward demeanor would have changed and he would start treating Harry and his friends with respect and kindness. With Harry knowing the truth about his double agent work, I think they would have become friends."

"If Snape had survived, Harry would not have gotten his memories for the Pensieve," Emma said.

"I have that figured out," said Jared. "Voldemort relents and allows Severus to bring him the boy. Snape is to escort Harry to the forest. He finds Harry and tells him the truth, even putting memories in the Pensieve so Harry can verify what he's told him. According to plan, Severus accompanies Harry to the Acromantula grove, where Voldemort is pleased that Severus has succeeded in bringing in the Chosen One. The rest unfolds pretty much according to the canon, except that Severus kills Nagini."

"Full marks for imagination," Emma said.

While fulfilling his first residence requirement in Sedona, Jared reconnected with Rob Luke, and before the week was out, their romance from college days had been rekindled. In the weeks following Jared's return to Los Angeles, they talked by phone every day. Ultimately, Rob decided to leave his job with the college and live with Jared in his new and spacious apartment.

Optimistic about his prospects, Rob emailed his resume to dozens of potential employers, learning in the process that all of them required a level of computer literacy that he had not attained. His spirits remained high, however, because he was so happy simply being with Jared.

One evening, Jared received a phone call from Anna Magic, his dear friend from acting school days. Anna's career was ascending rapidly now after her breakout performance in a film about sex trafficking, for which she received a supporting role Oscar nomination. She didn't get the Academy Award, but she was now inundated with screenplays and calls from casting directors.

"I need help," she told Jared. "I've never been a good administrator, but now I'm on the ropes with all the offers of parts, and the time devoted to the ones I've accepted, that I can't cope with everyday life. I have an agent, and an accountant, and a clipping service, but I need someone to help me manage the rest of my life."

"Like a personal manager?" Jared asked.

"Something like that. I don't know what to call the position, but I know what the job entails," Anna said. "It's handling the paperwork, overseeing the clipping service, seeing that repairs and maintenance on the house are taken care of, screening visitors and running interference when I'm on the town, acting as my spokesperson, sorting through fan mail looking for the few I should answer personally and giving the rest to my service for responding with an autographed photo, making sure groceries are in the house, and dozens of other things I can't think of right now."

"You didn't mention butler," said Jared.

"That, too," said Anna. "Do you know anyone who could fit that bill?"

"As a matter of fact, I do," said Jared. "My partner just left a position running a college alumni association in Arizona to join me in L. A. He is an excellent administrator. He lives to administrate, and he's almost as good at cooking as I am."

"How exciting," Anna said. "You deserve some love in your life, Jared. When can I meet him?"

"How's your calendar for this evening?" Jared asked.

"Open," she said. "I've got a script to read, but that can wait till tomorrow. This is more important."

"Come to my place at seven, and I promise a gourmet meal and an introduction to Rob Luke," he said.

By the end of the evening, Anna and Rob had settled on a compensation package, a start date, and the position title of Personal Administrator. Privately between the two of them, she referred to Rob as "my butler," and he called her "milady."

To accommodate Rob's mother, who hated flying and disliked travel in general, as well as making things much easier for Jared's family, they arranged for their wedding to be done at the NCC church in Phoenix, with Emma officiating as Hallowed Philosopher.

Because Rob's family and many other guests were not naturists, the participants and guests were fully clothed. However, to maintain family tradition, Emma conducted a private naturist ceremony for the two men after the rehearsal the night before. The marriage license signing took place following the textile event. As the Holy Rowling service drew to an end, Emma said, "Jared Auden Round and Robert Lewis Luke, I now declare you bonded for life." Then Jared and Rob walked hand-in-hand under an arch of wands that Emma had supplied for family and special guests to use. Among the wand wielders were Kathleen Ford, Rob's former pastor at Celebrating Creation Church in Mesa, and her Potter geek husband, Alan.

The reception was held at the church. Among the guests attending were Jared's former governess Xandra MacUmberland and her husband, and Rob's employer Anna Magic. After they had cut the wedding cake, and Jared danced with Rob's mom while Rob danced with Hannah, many of the guests began to drift away. When all of the presumed textiles had made their exits, Emma suggested they continue the celebration in naturist fashion. And this they did, including Anna Magic.

Anna was clearly enjoying her nude socializing, prompting Emma to say, "Might you have an interest in checking out the NCC, Anna? We have several congregations in the Los Angeles area."

"No thank you," Anna replied. "I've decided to be Jared's first recruit when he starts his L. A. branch of the Holy Rowlings. My presence there will ensure a lot of interest and help fill the pews. I'm not bragging; that's just how it is with celebrities. I may as well use it for something good."

"We had a good turnout when Emma Watson visited us in Sedona, even without any publicity," Emma said.

"Let me know when the other Emma visits," Anna said. "Emma Thompson. I absolutely adored her as P. L. Travers in *Saving Mr. Banks*. I wish I had been able to meet her when she was in L. A. working on the film."

"I loved her in that role too," said Emma. "Travers preceded Jo Rowling among the women writers who were shamed into using initials to hide being female. My prayer is that Rowling is the last of that cohort, that she has shattered forever that misogynistic practice."

"Amen!" said Anna. "By the by, I doubt that he's ever told you this, Emma, but Rob is in awe of your brains and talent. He told me that you perfectly embody the position of Hallowed Philosopher."

Emma blushed.

Having overheard Anna's remark, Rob joined the two women. "I could have told her that myself," he said to Anna, "but I didn't want it to go to her head."

"Yeah, right," said Anna.

"Actually, that's one of the things I'm in awe of her for," said Rob. "She is the antithesis of the narcissistic clergyperson."

"May her kind blossom and grow," said Anna. "And for all his snide veneer, Jared is like Emma in that regard. He will also make an outstanding Hallowed Philosopher."

"I heard that," Jared said, joining his sister, husband, and friend. "Please don't blow my cover."

"Too late for that," Emma said. "At least three people here know what's in your heart, and we won't let you forget it."

As a result of gathering material for the first class of Hallowed Philosopher seminarians, Emma produced a textbook for future students to use. She told people that writing **Hallowed Philosophy** was an act of optimism, because no one else had come forward seeking the training.

Within a week of its publication, a woman identifying herself as a Hufflepuff called Emma from Zelienople, Pennsylvania. "I'm interested in the Hallowed Philosopher training and was wondering if it is only for Gryffindors or would a Hufflepuff be allowed?"

"Hufflepuffs are certainly eligible," Emma assured her.

"I have a friend in Mars who also wants trained, but she's a Slytherin, so I guess that's a no go," the woman continued.

"My brother is a Slytherin, and he was in our first class of seminarians," Emma responded. "We require that our students be sorted, but it doesn't matter which house they are in. I'd be happy to send you both application forms. If you're qualified, you'll be invited to participate."

More calls came to Emma from Denver, Portland, Seattle, San Francisco, Honolulu, and Albuquerque inquiring about forming Holy Rowling congregations. There was interest from the East Coast, as well, as Emma heard from Kissimmee, Florida and Boston and Salem, Massachusetts. More North American calls came from Calgary, Edmonton, Saskatoon, Vancouver, and Winnipeg in Canada, as well as Mexico City. Because of this, Emma was not surprised at the inquiries from the United Kingdom, but the calls from Aix les Bains and Calais in France were entirely unexpected. New congregations with new leaders began to sprout first in Arizona, then in California, then nationwide, continentwide, and worldwide.

With this growth, the Sedona Alchemical Church of Harry Potter Prophecy became the mother congregation and in time was dubbed the Hallowed Home Church.

AFTERWORD

Factors established in two previous novels required, for the sake of continuity, that action in this novel be extended into 2018, a year beyond the publication date. Thus it is possible that in the interval J. K. Rowling may have published material that characters in this tale certainly would have talked about. This applies also to political developments in these turbulent times, which certain characters would be prone to mention. The author therefore begs indulgence for any such lapses that may become evident to observant readers.

An encyclopedic companion volume encompassing all seven books in the *Heretics in Occupied Eden* series is in process, including additional narratives, backstories, and character information. Any significant developments pertinent to the timeline of this novel will be addressed in *The Heretics Appendix*.

About the Author

Kenneth Alan Moe was born in Phoenix, where from an early age he experienced mystical events. At age ten he began writing poetry. His working life has included service in the U. S. Army as a prisoner of war interrogator, in the corporate world as an insurance investigator, and as a mainline Protestant minister.

Consistently underscoring it all, for more than half a century he has practiced the vocation of writer, evolving through pencil, pen, manual and electric typewriter, and computer to produce reams of fiction, non-fiction, and poetry. Moe's novels reflect his staunch advocacy for feminist and gay rights issues.

About Strange Angel Press

Strange Angel Press is a consortium of writers who act as editors, advisors, and cheerleaders for one another. We pool our collective experiences and talents to help participating writers with the art, craft, and discipline of fully telling the stories that have inspired us to put words to paper.

Visit our websites:
strangeangelpress.com
facebook.com/StrangeAngelPress
facebook.com/HereticsInOccupiedEden